THE GOOD GOODBYE

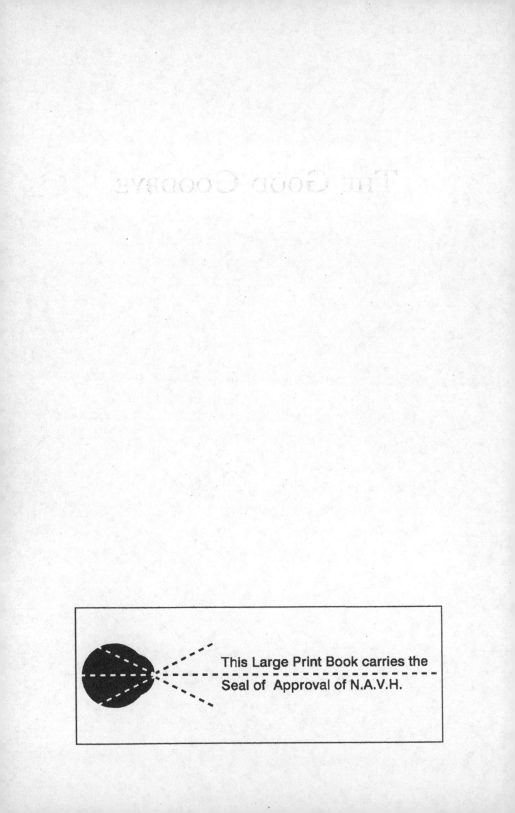

This Large Print Book carries the
Seal of Approval of N.A.V.H.

THE GOOD GOODBYE

CARLA BUCKLEY

THORNDIKE PRESS
A part of Gale, Cengage Learning

GALE
CENGAGE Learning

Farmington Hills, Mich • San Francisco • New York • Waterville, Maine
Meriden, Conn • Mason, Ohio • Chicago

GALE
CENGAGE Learning®

LIBRARY OF CONGRESS CATALOGING-IN-PUBLICATION DATA

Names: Buckley, Carla (Carla S.) author.
Title: The good goodbye / by Carla Buckley.
Description: Large print edition. | Waterville, Maine : Thorndike Press, 2016. | ©2016 | Series: Thorndike Press large print peer picks
Identifiers: LCCN 2015048365| ISBN 9781410488749 (hardcover) | ISBN 1410488748 (hardcover)
Subjects: LCSH: Burns and scalds—Patients—Fiction. | Family secrets—Fiction. | Large type books. | Domestic fiction.
Classification: LCC PS3602.U2645 G66 2016 | DDC 813/.6—dc23
LC record available at http://lccn.loc.gov/2015048365

Published in 2016 by arrangement with Ballantine Books, an imprint of Random House, a division of Penguin Random House LLC

Printed in Mexico
1 2 3 4 5 6 7 20 19 18 17 16

For my brother, Harley, with all my love

The first thing you should know is that everyone lies. The second thing is that it matters.

NATALIE

I keep a list of Arden's first words. *Banky, mimi, 'ghetti, Dada.* I treasure this list, keep it folded in my wallet. *Banky, mimi, 'ghetti, Dada, Mama, 'nana, rainbow, juice.* All the important things in Arden's life — her threadbare pink blanket, her favorite foods, Theo and me. I miss her. I miss hearing her voice. That first night after she left for college, I lay on top of her tousled sheets, breathing in the blended scents of her coconut shampoo and pear soap.

"So how do you want to celebrate?" my husband asks.

I thought Theo had forgotten. Maybe, if I'm to be completely honest with myself, I'd hoped he had. He squares off in front of the bathroom mirror to give himself his usual morning pep-talk look, his eyes half closed and his chin raised. Maybe, shocker, he'd remembered on his own.

"I don't know." I turn off the water and

drop my toothbrush in the cup. There's nothing I feel less like doing than dressing up and spending money on our anniversary. Just thinking about it makes me want to crawl under the covers and yank them over my head.

"Anything you want," he promises. "Sky's the limit."

Ha. We both know the sky is very much not the limit.

"I have that big party coming in tonight," I remind him. Eleven homecoming couples, a giggling pack of kids, uncertain in their finery. The tips would be meager, half the food would go uneaten or end up on the tablecloth, and the restrooms would be a disaster. But any port in a storm. And these past six months had been so stormy they'd ripped the shingles right off the roof.

"They'll be gone by nine, right? We can do something then."

"You know I can't close early."

There's always the chance an after-theater crowd could wander by and decide to come in — though that's been happening less and less frequently. Why? Too many seafood options, not enough vegetarian? A food trend I haven't picked up on? We used to have a line snaking down the sidewalk. Now whenever I glimpse people pausing outside to

10

read the menu posted by the window, I find myself catching my breath.

"Let Vince cover for you. You've done it often enough for him."

"Right. You want to ask him, or shall I?" I shut the medicine cabinet a little too hard, rattling the bottles inside.

"Look. We should do something, Nat. I don't know what. But I do know nineteenth wedding anniversaries only come around once."

I tug my hair back into its usual ponytail. "If it's so important, why didn't we plan something ahead?" Theo has no answer for that one.

Downstairs, the boys are waiting in the front hall. They'd rejected the bright, small backpacks in the back-to-school section, and like a team of matched ponies marched straight to where the adult-sized backpacks hung, the very same display from which we'd chosen Arden's. *Are you sure you don't want a Batman one?* I'd coaxed. *Or the Hulk?* Oliver had glanced tentatively at his brother, but Henry crossed his arms and pushed out his lower lip, and Oliver instantly followed suit. So here they stand, six-year-old boys huddled beneath enormous black carapaces each containing a slim folder of math homework and a single sharpened pencil.

Vince would applaud the twins' show of solidarity, but I can't tell Theo this. There are so many things I can't tell Theo.

"Did you brush your teeth?" Theo asks the boys, and both solemnly nod.

I'd heard them counting in their bathroom, mumbled shouts filled with toothpaste and spit . . . *eight, nine, ten*! Henry's the one who keeps the count, who makes sure Oliver brushes his tongue, too. *It tickles!* he protests. The differences between my sons are much vaster than the four minutes that separate their births. Henry had howled as the doctor held him up so I could see him over the draped fabric; Oliver had been terrifyingly silent. I hadn't even been allowed to see or hold him until the next day, Theo pushing my wheelchair up to the incubator where Oliver lay, surreally tiny inside, his arms and legs extended and taped down, his chest motionless. Fear clamped down hard. Then Oliver had turned his head and, slowly, blinked at me.

This morning, Oliver grips his ant farm between two hands, a plastic frame holding a half-inch of sandy dirt sandwiched between two rectangles of glass and crisscrossed by tunnels. Our dachshund sits by Oliver's feet with his long nose lifted, sniffing. *Friday's Sharing Day,* Oliver had told

Arden on Skype. *But I don't know what I'm supposed to take.* I'd stopped cramming things into my bag to listen. *What did Caleb bring?* I heard Arden ask. *A baseball,* he'd answered, dolefully. *You can do way better than that,* she scoffed. *How about one of your science projects?*

Like my ant farm? Oliver had suggested, his voice swelling with hope. Arden had led him there and now it was his idea. I'd walked over to where my laptop sat on the kitchen table and leaned over to smile at my daughter with her serious green eyes and long blond hair tucked behind her ears. *Sorry, honey,* I'd told her. *I have to leave for the restaurant. Can we talk later?* D.C. traffic was unforgiving. I was already cutting it close. Used to be Gabrielle would run over to watch the boys until Theo got home, but those days are gone. Arden had paused, then nodded. *I'll call you tomorrow,* she'd said. Which was yesterday. The whole day had come and gone, and she hadn't called. A million reasons why — she'd been out with her new friends, she'd been studying and lost track of time, she'd forgotten until it was too late to phone. But still, that hesitation — had there been something there?

13

I crouch to pat the dog bed. Percy trots over. "You be good," I tell him, rumpling his soft ears. "Keep an eye on the squirrels." During the day, he lets himself in and out of the pet door, and often I'll come home to find him sprawled outside in a patch of sunlight, just the thump of his tail welcoming me. He circles the cushion and lies down with a sigh.

"Want me to take that?" Theo asks Oliver, and I know he's thinking about ants crawling around the car. Oliver shakes his head, then pushes past his brother to run down the path to where our Volvo rusts in the driveway alongside our sputtering fourth-hand Honda.

"Remember when Arden stole your diaphragm?" Theo whispers, leaning close.

I laugh. At the time, though, I'd been mortified when the teacher called to let me know what Arden had smuggled in for Sharing Day. Theo had shaken his head and looked thoughtful. *We'd better keep an eye on that one,* he'd said, meaning Arden.

I have, haven't I?

Theo slides his arms around me. "You're right, sweetheart. I should have put some thought into it. I just assumed you wouldn't want to make a big deal out of it."

"We can't afford to make a big deal out of it."

"We can afford to make a little deal out of it."

I sigh, lean in to the circle of his arms. "Like what?"

"How about a movie? There are some good ones opening today."

We haven't seen a movie out in ages. The ticket prices, the time. I tell myself I want this, and all of a sudden, I do. I want to sit in a quiet, dark theater beside my husband, our arms touching, a bucket of salty buttery popcorn nestled in my lap. No worrying about my failing restaurant and bills piling up, my little girl grown up and gone. I smile at him. "I'll see if Mom can babysit."

Theo kisses my lips, soft, but it tingles all the way through. He scoops up his briefcase. "Arden will call," he says. "Try not to worry."

I watch him walk away. Nineteen years.

Vince has left me a note on the desk we share at the restaurant. He'd gone home before me the night before and his car isn't in the lot now, so I have no idea how he'd managed this impossible feat. Too bad his magic didn't extend to the stock market.

I frown at the bold ink strokes, as familiar

as my own handwriting. All those hours poring over cookbooks, calling across the kitchen, teasing and laughing and working in happy synchronicity side by side have come to this.

Nat — We need to talk.

I'm done talking. I've heard the excuses and explanations, the countless reasons why he couldn't have seen it coming. None of it changes the fact that he took a risk and lost, snaring all of us in the rushing downward spiral. That's Vince for you, always grabbing at the shiny brass ring, never stopping to look below. I uncap a Sharpie and slash a heavy line through his words.

I pick up the waiting sheaf of invoices. The top one is stamped in red — our meat purveyor. I'm surprised he'd agreed to extend us credit in the first place. It must have been Liz's doing. What would I do without Liz? I had to let two more servers go last week. Vince and I haven't drawn a salary since March, and we're down from thirty-seven employees to eight. We can light the place with candles and cook over charcoal briquettes if we have to, but the one thing we can't run a restaurant without is food.

16

Vince shows up around noon. I'm mixing pasta dough at the steel table. The one part of the day when I feel truly myself, my hands measuring and kneading, feeding the thin sheets of pasta through the pasta machine, letting my mind wander. I hear the back door open and know without looking up, recognizing his footsteps going down the back hall. A minute later he joins me, tying on his apron.

The first thing Vince and I had done when we'd taken over the building five years ago was knock down the wall between the kitchen and the dining room. We'd been absurdly happy, our dream realized at last. One big open space — no barrier between customer and chef. Who knew it would be the barrier between the chefs that would bring it all down?

He rolls up his sleeves. "You got my note, I see."

"Does it have anything to do with twenty-two teenagers who are going to be showing up in just a few hours?"

"No. I guess it can wait."

I sprinkle buckwheat flour on the mound of beige-gray dough and cover it with cheesecloth. "I need you to close tonight."

"No problem. Boys okay?"

"They're fine." The twins love their uncle

Vince. They ask after him and Gabrielle all the time. *How come she doesn't watch us anymore?* Henry had wondered just the other day, and I'd replied, *She's busy.* He'd scrunched his eyes at me. *Busy doing* what, *exactly?* he'd demanded.

"Hey, that's right." Vince brings out the double boiler and sets it on the stove. "Today's your anniversary. Congratulations. You and Theo have big plans?"

Last year, on their nineteenth wedding anniversary, Vince and Gabrielle had toured Napa Valley, a lavish six-day trip he later wrote off as a tax deduction. It should have been a clue.

"We're going out." I hear how curt my voice sounds. He nods, and heads toward the dry-goods section. "Apple strudel," I tell him, and he stops.

"Not raspberry mousse?"

Raspberries are six dollars a pint. "Not unless you've won the lottery." I turn away so I don't have to see his expression.

By seven-twenty, the homecoming couples still haven't shown. I bend a wafer-thin slice of pickle into a curl and nestle it alongside the piece of grilled cobia. Wiping my hands on the towel tied into my apron strings, I slide the plate beneath the heat lamp. I'd

18

called that afternoon to confirm the reservation. *What?* the teenage girl had said. I'd had to repeat myself. *Oh, yeah,* she'd said. *The restaurant. We'll be there.*

The restaurant. Not *Double.* I glance toward the front door and Vince says, "They'll be here."

Friday night and we've had only five tables, a total of sixteen covers.

"What if they're not?" I'd ordered a supply of shrimp and filets — the two proteins teenagers most like to order, as well as the most expensive. I should've stuck with chicken.

"Then we'll run a surf-and-turf special tomorrow."

"For the crowds thronging the door?" Everyone in town offers filet. Shrimp turns in a day. Vince knows this as well as I do, but he's always happiest with the easy solution, even if it makes no sense. He loops lines of puréed basil across the piece of flounder, a magical composition of confidence and artistry, but right now it looks all wrong. Too bright. Too hopeful. Just like Vince.

"Nat," he says. "We really do have to talk."

"About what, another wonderful investment opportunity?"

"Are you ever going to forgive me?"

19

Just then, the door opens into a swirl of laughter and gold lamé, yards of black tulle and a windstorm of Axe and perfume. For a moment, I see what they see: eclectic chairs painted purple, green, orange; red and yellow gerbera daisies in their glass bowls; flickering candles and white linens stiff with starch but looking cloud-soft. *Come in,* it all beckons. Arden had helped choose the colors, her hands on her hips, frowning at the selection.

Vince hands me the plate to finish and, grinning, goes over to greet and escort them to their tables. They tilt their faces to him and giggle, take their seats, and pick up their menus.

This is the Vince I loved. But this is the Vince who betrayed me.

Theo arrives as the homecoming couples are leaving. There's chaos by the door as kids push past in a happy clamor, and then Theo steps through. "Hey," he says. He looks tired, but he's taken the trouble to put on a jacket and tie and slide cuff links through the cuffs of his shirt. "You look nice."

"My Spanx's cutting me in half," I confess, and he laughs. I'm covered chin to knee in heavy bleached cotton, my feet are encased in dumpy clogs, and I must reek of grease and garlic and onions. But Theo's smiling at me and I feel the heat of his affection. "Ready?" he asks. He doesn't look around for Vince.

I go back to the office to get my bag and drop my apron into the laundry bin. I tell Liz I'm leaving. "I'll let Vince know," she promises.

The night air's breezy with an impending storm. The weather forecasters have been warning us all week. *Gonna have a wet weekend, folks. Better move those cookouts indoors.* I shrug out of my chef's jacket and fold it over my arm. "How was soccer?" I ask Theo.

"Fine. Henry still likes the coach."

T-ball had been a bust, Oliver ducking every time the bat swung; chlorine made Henry break out in a rash. But the boys had insisted on finding something they could both do, and so we were giving soccer a try. "What about Oliver?" He tended to look confused every time the ball headed his way.

"He fell and scraped his knee. He refused to go back onto the field."

"Shoot."

"Don't worry, sweetheart. It's all part of learning to play a sport. He'll be fine tomorrow."

I glance up at the clouds massing over-

21

head. "What if we're rained out tomorrow?"
"It might blow through quickly. Even —"
My phone's ringing inside my bag. "Hold
on," I interrupt. "It must be Mom." Or
maybe — at last — Arden? I pull out the
phone and don't recognize the phone number. "Hello?"

"I'm looking for the parents of Arden
Falcone." A man's voice, a stranger.

Trouble. Arden's in trouble. I know it
instantly. "This is her mother," I say. "Is she
okay?" I've stopped walking. "What's going
on?" Theo says, and I shake my head. I press
the phone hard against my ear.

"Your daughter's been in an accident,"
the stranger says, and everything slides away.

ARDEN

Someone's shouting in my ear. "What do we have?"

"Eighteen-year-old victim found unconscious."

I'm jostled up and down.

"Where are the lines?"

"We got two. Eighteen-gauge line in her right arm running saline . . ."

"Which room?"

"CAT scan."

A jolt. I open my eyes. Ceiling tiles swim past. A purple sleeve patterned with red hearts over my face. Above that, a hand gripping a metal pole. The light blinds me.

I am rolled, then lifted. A face leans close. A man. He needs to shave. "I'm Dr. Saunders. You're at Saint Luke's. You're going to be all right. Do you have any allergies?"

I can't remember.

"Does anything hurt?"

Panic rises in a huge wave.

23

"Is it possible you're pregnant?"

His face is gone. I feel cold air against my legs, my belly. The smell of something sweet and burned, then a pain so awful it carves a deep hole inside me. I hear moaning. It's me.

". . . need another line," the man says.

A new face, a woman's, hovering above mine, worried. "We're giving you some medicine that will make you feel better," she promises.

The whole white world telescopes to a dark dot and blinks into nothingness.

Buzzing. A fly, looking for a place to land. I try to lift my hand, but my arm won't move. *Why am I so sleepy?*

I'm in my bed. It's early and peaceful; the twins aren't up yet. I feel Percy on the covers by my feet. I try to move my foot to find him.

That fly won't stop whining. And there's something else, a soft whooshing. The ocean, rolling in waves to the shore. So I'm not in my bed at home. I'm at Rehoboth, with Mom and Dad, Oliver and Henry, and Percy.

The buzz is too loud to be a fly. *A bee?*

I can't open my eyes. I feel darkness press-

24

ing down on me. Something brushes my cheek.

". . . eight milligrams."

"When was her last morphine?"

Who are they? Why are they in my room? Fear. *I want my mom. I want my dad.*

". . . think she's awake."

"I'm Dr. Morris. I'm taking care of you. Are you in pain?"

Yes.

"You were in a fire. Do you remember?"

So hot I can't breathe. Flames and greasy, awful smoke. Rory twists away, her hair swinging out in a glowing circle, shrieking as Hunter flails around. I can't help him. I'm going to be sick. I gag, scrabble at the sheets. Something's stuck in my throat. I'm choking on it. My heart gallops, faster and faster. I'm screaming. *Why can't they hear me? Where's my mom?*

"It's okay. Don't worry. That's just a tube helping you breathe. You're going to be okay." Dr. Morris turns away. "Increase the drip."

Wait! A swoosh of heat. Flames leap across my bed, race up the walls. They claw at me. They hiss. Screaming so animal I feel my skin rip.

You were in a fire. Do you remember?

Why was I there? Why didn't I get out?
Why can't I remember?

RORY

The envelope arrives thick, crisp, and white. My mom practically dances, handing it to me at breakfast; she doesn't even do her usual up-and-down scan of what I'm wearing. It's all about the envelope. Mom must've bribed the mailman to come to our house first. That's just the kind of thing she'd do. My dad's already left for work — not a big deal, he's always at the restaurant, but I thought that today, of all days, he'd hold off going in. "Open it," Mom urges. Her red hair's combed back, her lipstick perfectly applied. She's got on her alligator pumps with the three-inch heels — she must have a breakfast meeting with someone really important.

She stood at the foot of the stairs calling up to me the whole time I was getting ready, but I'd taken my time, texturizing my hair and braiding it into a fishtail, trying on my Miu Miu sneakers to see if the ribbons were too much, switching them for Kate Spade flats — which looked great but told everyone I was trying — and ending up with blue Sperrys, then searching forever for my diamond studs. I'd dabbed concealer on the tiny scar on my forearm and spritzed on perfume. I sit at the kitchen table and pull my coffee cup toward me. "In a minute."

The phone rings — Aunt Nat, for sure — and Mom frowns but doesn't answer it. "Don't be like that, Rory. Open it, or I will."

"It's a felony to open somebody else's mail," I inform her, splashing in fat-free hazelnut creamer until my coffee turns a light brown. Her face sort of crumples.

"Whatever." I take the stupid envelope. I know what the letter says — I was online exactly at midnight and saw the results for myself — but I'm still nervous as I tear open the flap. What if it had been a mistake? But there it is, confirmed in black and white. I read the first word aloud, *Congratulations,* and my mom shrieks and throws her arms around me. You'd think she was the one who'd just gotten into Harvard.

At school, everyone's buzzing in the halls. There are some girls with their heads down, not looking at anyone as they shove books into their lockers. They'll be the ones stuck at the no-name schools clustered around Maryland and Virginia, where all you have to do to get in is breathe. Jessica got into Brown, and Beth is going to Cornell. Emilie got wait-listed for Dartmouth, but who cares, she says. She got into Smith, and Dartmouth can fuck itself. Mackenzie got into Princeton, but everyone knows her dad's BFFs with the dean. It would have been pathetic if she hadn't. I hug her anyway. "Congrats," I say. "You're going to do awesome."

"So? What about you?" she asks. I can tell she doesn't really want to know. She'd applied to Harvard, too, but it's obvious how that had turned out.

By now there's a crowd of girls standing around, listening. I shrug, but feel myself grinning.

Jessica jumps up and down, her breasts jiggling. "I knew it. I knew it I knew it I knew it."

Arden comes in, her arms filled with binders and books. We meet at our lockers, and she peels off her sweater. I've tried to help her fit in, but Arden always manages to do things just wrong enough. Like straightening her hair. There's always a section she misses, a wavy flag down the back of her head. Her green seersucker dress is wrinkled, her belt tied in a sloppy bow. I've told her a million times to do what I do and wear a leather belt instead of the lame fabric one that comes with the uniform. As soon as I graduate, I'm going to cut all my uniforms into ribbons. Not Arden. Uncle Theo's making her donate hers to the school bookstore for the scholarship girls. I'd rolled my eyes when she told me, made her swear she wouldn't tell anyone else.

"Hey, thanks for not texting me back," she says.

"Yeah. Sorry about that."

"I had to find out from my *mom.*" She jams her books into her locker.

"I meant to call . . ." My voice trails off. I should have called, but for some reason I hadn't wanted to. I hadn't slept at all.

"Whatever."

"My mom's out of control." I lean against my locker, but Arden won't look at me. My mom had been squealing on the phone with Aunt Nat when I left, and I'd bet anything she was still making phone calls. "Probably her manicurist knows now. Probably the president."

Arden's mouth quirks up at that one, but only for a second. She's really pissed.

"Definitely CNN," I continue. "And *Good Morning America.* Now she's trying to find out if NASA can relay a message around the world."

Arden sighs and her shoulders relax. She can never stay mad at me for long. She looks at me. Her green eyes are kind of sad. We have the same eyes. Her lips are chapped, her lashes pale, so much like the face I look at every morning in the mirror, before I color it in. "Congrats."

"Thanks." She's going to art school out in California. She applied early decision and heard back just before Christmas. For the first time in our lives, we'll be living thousands of miles apart. "We're still going to do it, you know."

She doesn't answer, but I know she heard me.

The bell rings and lockers start slamming. Arden reaches in for her binder and hands me back my copy of *Jude the Obscure.* She hooks her purse over her shoulder and looks at me again. Then she reaches out to give me a quick hug. "You totally deserve it, you know."

She turns and pushes through the chattering girls, in a rush to get to class before the teacher does. I don't know why she even cares. We're seniors, coasting on our last few weeks. I watch her make her way down the hall until she turns the corner and I

31

can't see her anymore.

My parents are waiting when I get home that night. A bunch of us had gone to Georgetown to celebrate, taking up three long tables in Mitchell's, my dad's biggest competitor, talking and laughing our heads off. When I'd ordered a bottle of Cristal, Mitchell raised his eyebrows. I remember when Aunt Nat was his sous chef. *Come on, I begged, we're celebrating!* I gave him a special smile and Mitchell caved, like I knew he would. Before I left, I slid the empty champagne glass into my bag. A memento.

I'm still kind of buzzing when I pull my car into the driveway and see Dad's SUV in the garage beside my mom's. Usually he doesn't get home until after midnight, but my mom probably nagged him into coming home early. Then again, maybe not. He'd been pretty quiet on the phone when I called the restaurant to tell him the good news. He'd gone into his office and closed the door so he could hear me.

I'm expecting crème brûlée set out on the dining room table, or a plate of basil and lavender macarons beside that gorgeously wrapped gold bracelet I know my mom got to surprise me, just in case. I expect my parents' faces to be proud and glowy, and prepare myself for all the hugging I'm going to have to endure. But when I step through the front door, they're in the living room, my mom on the couch with her hands knitted together and my dad standing by the fireplace and not looking at her at all. Something's happened. I calm myself. I tell myself: only four more months and I'll be out of here.

"What?" I say.

"You tell her." My mom's twisting her wedding rings around and around her finger. "It's your fault. You tell her."

They're getting a divorce. "Tell me what?" Am I upset? Relieved?

"Stop it, Gabrielle." My dad's still in his chef's jacket and he hasn't even taken off his clogs and lined them up in the garage by the back door, the way my mom likes us to do. She always makes him shower, too, no matter how late it is. She hates the smell of the restaurant clinging to his clothes, his hair. "That's not helping."

"It's too late to help, isn't it?" my mother snaps.

"Will you guys cut it out and tell me?"

My father's face is settled in heavy lines. "Are you sick?" I whisper. I look to my mom, her hair pulled back tightly, making her cheekbones look sharp. "Are you?"

33

She presses her lips together.

"We're fine," my dad says. "Here's the thing, honey. I made a bad investment." He says this fast, his face flushed. He and Mom have been going at it for a while, I can tell.

"So?" I say. Dad's always making bad investments and good ones. There's champagne and flowers and little gifts when he makes a killing, or silence when he doesn't. He stays up late, checking his computer; he has an app on his phone that's constantly chirping. Sometimes I think he loves the stock market more than he loves Double.

"Don't make it sound like it was just one of those things, Vincent." My mother stalks over to the dry sink and bends to unlatch the wooden door. I hold my breath. Will she notice the vodka bottle? She pulls out the big green bottle of gin and the glass with the grapes etched on the side. Okay, so she hasn't noticed.

"But it was. I pored over their financials. I talked to the right people." My dad rubs his face with the flats of his hands. "Everything was coming together. We all thought the patent would go through."

"But a million dollars?"

"It was the only way we could buy in."

"Don't make me part of this. This is all on you, Vincent."

I'm beginning to panic. "What million dollars?" I'm always sneaking looks at my parents' bank account statements. I've never seen numbers that large on anything.

"That's how much your father owes the brokerage company," my mother tells me. "He borrowed a million dollars to buy this sure-thing tech stock, and this morning it's worth nothing. Nothing!" She puts down her glass without taking a sip. "They don't care. They still want their money."

"Why can't we just declare bankruptcy?" Other kids' families do it all the time. It's like a joke at Bishop.

"We can't," my father says tersely.

"We'll lose everything that has your father's name on it. The restaurant, our house, my business. We'll have nothing left."

"We're going to have to liquidate what we can," my dad says. "We'll persuade the brokerage firm to let us keep the restaurant so we can make payments. And I'm sorry, Rory." He sucks in a breath, releases it. "But this means using your college fund."

I stare at him. He won't look at me. "Seriously?" I say, and hear my voice quiver.

"I've called Harvard," my mother says. "They've agreed to keep a place open for you for next year."

Next *year*? "But I'm not the one who

owes a million dollars!"

"*Je sais, ma cherie,*" my mother says, and I know this is real. My eyes burn and my palms are sweating.

"Call them again," I insist.

My mother's pacing, her heels clicking sharply against the wood. "It's no use. The scholarship money has been disbursed."

"Are you kidding me?" *Years.* I've spent *years,* my whole fucking life, trying to get into Harvard. Maybe my grades weren't perfect, but I had rocked the personal interview; I had scored the best teacher recommendations. All those AP classes, that horrible volunteer job at the nursing center, the lame cupcake business I started just because it would look good on my résumé, *everything.*

"It's just temporary," my dad says. "It's just one year. We'll set up a payment schedule; we'll get on our feet —"

"So that's it?" I refuse to cry. "I'm not going to Harvard?"

The look on my dad's face tells me it's true. I can't stand it. All my friends will leap ahead of me. I can see them pulling away. I'll never, ever catch up. What will I do for a whole year? My cell phone buzzes, a text coming in, and something occurs to me. "Wait. What about Arden?" Her mom and

36

my dad co-own the restaurant.

"Yes, what about her?" my mother spits, which tells me Arden isn't going to art school in California, either. She stops pacing and spins to face my father. "How can you live with yourself?"

"You're happy enough when I make money, Gabrielle! I don't hear any complaints then. You think I planned this? You think I wasn't careful? I was careful. This is just one of those things. One of those goddamn things!"

I back out of the room and they don't even notice me go. Upstairs, I close my bedroom door and their voices grow dull. I sit in the window seat, my knees drawn to my chest. On the other side of the Potomac, Arden's probably crying in her room. She's been texting, but I can't answer. My cell thrums in my pocket, another incoming text. Or maybe somebody's Facebook update: *MIT or Stanford?*

I hug my knees tight, so hard I can't breathe. A door slams below me, Mom retreating or Dad going out. On the other side of the window the garden is dark and ghostly, filled with grass and trees and bushes, the flowers my mother plants every spring. I feel it starting to sink in. A million dollars. I'm not going to Harvard. I hold my breath until specks dance before my eyes. I picture my dad's face, narrow with anger, shame, too. My breath explodes out of me.

I'm not going to Harvard.

A single feeling detaches itself from all the others churning inside me. It starts to grow, clear and sharp and strange.

Joy.

NATALIE

We have to get to the hospital. We have to get to Arden, but I can't move. People push past on the sidewalk. Rain taps my head and shoulders. *Keys. Where are my keys?* I fumble in my bag, clutch at the metal ring. Theo's talking, asking questions. His face is lit by orange neon. I watch his mouth move and try to answer. My words come out jumbled. I hear a loud whooshing, realize it's my blood pounding in my ears.

Theo grabs my arm. "I'll drive."

We inch through traffic lights. I press my foot against the floorboard as though I can force Theo's foot to punch the pedal harder. I'm trapped in this car and it's not going fast enough. "Take 295."

"New York's quicker."

"Not this time of night."

Rain smears the windshield. The dark road leaps from side to side. Oncoming headlights, the sailing blare of a car horn.

Theo glances over. "Your seat belt."

I fumble for it. He leans across and drags the belt over my lap. "Call your mom."

Yes, my mom. The boys. I pull my phone from my bag and stare at the display. I have to think before I press my own home number. "Mom?"

"Mm?"

I've woken her. "Arden's been in an accident. We're on our way to the hospital." Each word nails this down.

"What?" Now she's alert.

"She was in a fire. She jumped out her dorm window to escape it."

My mother gasps and I squeeze my eyes shut. Four stories high.

"Oh, my God. Is she —"

"She's in critical condition. She's . . . she's unconscious." *She's suffered trauma to multiple parts of her body. We are doing everything we can to stabilize her.* I'm having trouble breathing. I press my hand to my chest.

"What happened? Is she burned?"

"I don't know."

"What about smoke inhalation?"

"Mom, I don't *know!*"

Silence. "I'll call your father."

"Yes. Fine." I don't care.

A highway sign looms up out of the darkness. We're still so far away. *Hold on, Arden. Hold on, sweetheart. I'm coming.*

"What else can I do? Should I come to the hospital?"

"No. The boys." I struggle to latch on to something solid, routine. "Soccer. They have a game tomorrow."

"I can take them." She sounds relieved to have a task.

I press END, then redial. The hospital operator answers. "How may I direct your call?"

"Someone just phoned me about my daughter. She was in a fire . . ."

"Hold, please."

The rain comes harder, pounding the roof. Faraway lights blur in the wet.

"Anything?" Theo's focused on the road, his mouth set. The needle on the odometer nudges seventy-five, eighty.

"I'm still on hold."

"Try Rory."

Yes. She'll know something. But Rory doesn't answer. All I get is her merry voice telling me to *Go ahead and do it. You know you want to.* The beep sounds. I open my mouth to leave a message, but I'm suddenly flooded by all the things I want to say. Words clog my throat, choking. In the end, I hang up without saying any of them.

41

Theo puts his hand on my knee. "Hang on. We're almost there."

Your daughter has a tattoo? the man had asked.

Yes. A small green-and-purple butterfly.

In the distance, sirens shriek.

The emergency room's a blaze of light. The woman at the information desk says she'll get a doctor to talk to us; we just need to take a seat in the waiting room. Theo finds us chairs but I can't sit. I want to run down the hall, banging on doors until one opens to reveal Arden. People in lab coats walk down the hall toward us. I look at each of them in turn, searching their eyes. Are they going to take us to our daughter? But they walk past. "What's taking so long? Why don't they just tell us where she is?"

"Someone will be out soon." Theo's face is ashen.

"She *needs* us." The time Arden fell off her bike and split open her chin; the time she ran a fever so high she trembled, her eyes wide and fixed on mine. She must be so scared. Then I realize she's not scared. She's unconscious. I'm the one who's afraid, who needs to see her face, to hold her, to cry.

"I know, Nat. They'll tell us something soon."

People are everywhere, sitting, leaning against walls, looking weary, looking defeated. A little girl holds her arm to her chest, her red tights ripped. College-age kids huddle in a corner, blankets draped around their shoulders. "Where's Rory? She should be here somewhere." Arden and Rory are inseparable. The two of them on the boat, their laughter trailing across the lake. *Wait.* "Maybe she's with Arden?" Keeping her company until we got here.

"I bet she is. I bet that's exactly where she is."

Another man in a white lab coat strides past. He doesn't look over. The TV plays silent jumpy images. Outside the window, a police cruiser flashes red and blue lights.

"Mr. Falcone? Mrs. Falcone?"

A woman in green scrubs is holding a clipboard. "Hi," she says. "I'm Dr. Sisneros." She's young, plain-faced, and stocky, her brown hair scraped back from a square forehead. A green surgical mask hangs around her neck. "Let's talk in the family lounge."

What terrible thing does she have to tell us that she can't say out here? But she's already turned away, and so we follow her as she walks briskly down the hallway through a series of doors that swing open when she smacks the metal plate on the wall. The sounds from the emergency room fade and now it's quiet. We are crossing from one world to another. At last we step into a room. It's empty, a washed-out space.

"How's Arden?" I ask. "Where is she?"

She looks at me with an odd expression. "Your daughter's sustained several fractures and has second- and third-degree burns on her arms and torso. We haven't ruled out spinal involvement yet. We've put a tube into her airway to help her breathe, but right now we're mostly concerned with the swelling in her brain. We're about to take her into surgery."

Her spine, her brain. Arden's rushing away from us, in bits and pieces.

"For what?" Theo says. "No one said anything about surgery."

"We need to insert a drain into her skull, but we have to have your signed permission."

They want to drill a hole into my daughter's skull. I've cradled that head in my hands, seen the shadowy soft areas Theo and I'd been warned to protect lying between thin cranial plates of bone. The world tilts. I sit hard on a chair, grip the cold metal

44

arms. "Is it dangerous?" My voice comes from far away.

"Well, there are risks with any operation."

I force myself to look up at her. Her eyes are pale blue, as clear as water. "But is it *dangerous*?"

"It's more dangerous to let the fluid build up unchecked."

I let out my breath in a whoosh, then nod. She extends the clipboard to Theo. After a moment, he takes it and clicks the pen. "How long will this take?"

"Not long. It's a fairly quick procedure."

Theo hands the clipboard back and sits beside me. I reach for his hand and knit my fingers with his, familiar and comforting. "Can we see her?"

"I'm sorry, but we have to take her in right away. You can see her as soon as she's out of surgery."

"Is she going to be . . . all right?" *Is she going to die?*

"We're doing everything we can."

"Are you the surgeon?" Theo asks.

"I'm the resident." She's at the door, wanting to leave. "I was here when they admitted your daughters."

"Daughters?" I repeat.

The ICU's a circular spaceship with glass-

45

walled rooms radiating out. A large reception desk hovers in the center. Rory's room is dark, the curtain drawn across the glass wall facing the hallway, tiny red blinking lights on various machines casting an amber glow across the bed against the wall. Beside it, a ghost rises from a chair. Gabrielle, her slight form swaying. "Natalie, our girls . . ."

"I know. I know." I hug her close. Her head presses against my shoulder, her hair slippery against my cheek. She sobs, her shoulders shaking. The anger between us vanishes. This is what matters. "Oh, Gabrielle," I say. "I'm so sorry. I'm so, so sorry." She shudders, and I hold her closer. Over her shoulder I can see the bed, the shadowed figure lying there. *Rory?*

"My God," Theo says hoarsely.

She lies flat beneath a heavy web of looping plastic tubes. A thick helmet is fitted around her head; the white cast on her arm glows dully. All I can see of her face is the rise of puffy cheeks and eyelids behind the plastic straps of the helmet. Her lips, curved around a dangling plastic tube, are grotesquely swollen.

This isn't Rory. It can't be.

"Oh, Gabrielle," I say again, and she nods, pulls away. She snatches a tissue from the box on the nightstand and pats her eyes.

46

"They say it's the fluid they're pumping into her. They say it will go down in a few weeks. But I don't know."

Should we be talking like this in front of Rory? It'll only frighten her. She hasn't moved since we came in. She hasn't made a sound. "Hi, my darling," I whisper, leaning close. I can't see if her eyes are cracked open. "It's Aunt Nat and Uncle Theo."

"She can't hear you. She can't hear anything. She's . . . she's in a coma."

I'd better prepare myself. This is how Arden will be when she comes out of surgery. "What do the doctors say?"

"She broke her leg. It's quite . . . bad. They're going to operate in the morning."

Gabrielle's accent is thicker. She's stumbling over her words. I slide my arm around her shoulders and give her a reassuring squeeze.

"They're worried about her lungs," she says. "They say she breathed in hot air and did a lot of damage. They have her on a ventilator so her lungs can heal. I don't know. Is that how it works?"

I have no idea. But Christine might. She's a pediatric surgeon. "I'll call my sister," I say. "I'm sure she can explain a lot of this." Can Christine come? But she has that surgery coming up, a pair of conjoined twins flying all the way from Brazil. Christine's been preparing for months. Is it fair to ask her to compromise other people's lives? I don't know.

"Yes, that would be good."

Rory's so still. I can't see the rise and fall of her chest.

"Where's Vince?" Theo asks.

"He's on his way."

"We'll stay with you until he comes."

Gabrielle fidgets with the top button of her jacket. "How's Arden? Have you seen her yet?"

"No. She's still in surgery." What if we had gotten here thirty minutes sooner? Fifteen? Would that have made a difference? Only to me.

"I asked them to put her in the room next door."

"Yes. Good thinking." We'll all be together. We can help each other.

"What happened, Gabrielle?" Theo's looking down at Rory. His voice is confused. "All we know is there was a fire. And that the girls jumped from their window."

"That's all I know, too. But they told me the police are going to want to talk to us."

The police. They'll have answers. They'll tell us how this happened. "Were other students hurt?"

She looks at me. "You don't know?"

I shake my head. I have the feeling of something widening around us.

"The rescue workers found Hunter inside. He . . . didn't make it."

Hunter. I've never met him, but Arden's dropped casual comments for weeks about him. He's Rory's boyfriend. He's a sophomore. He plays baseball. Arden had blushed whenever she said his name. She hadn't wanted me to know what she felt for him, but how can you hide that at eighteen? I had seen it all the same. Sadness crests inside me. *Hunter's dead.*

Gabrielle wraps her arms around herself. "Rory's so afraid of fire. She must have been so panicked. And when she was . . . falling."

I go there. I go right to that narrow ledge so far from the ground you can't see it when you're standing below and looking up. Just a few inches wide, but Arden had crawled onto it. Had she looked down, or had she simply let go? Did she stretch out her arms, trying to grab hold of something to break her fall? Had she screamed, clenched her eyes shut? Did she lie there in terrible pain, wanting me? Needing me?

I'll call tomorrow, Mom. But she hadn't.

49

ARDEN

I take off all my clothes.

It's mid-afternoon and Rory's in class. The dorm is quiet all around me, but I lock the door because you never know, then crank up my iPod. I'm experimenting with jazz. Classical music puts me to sleep and alternative rock makes me only want to use dark colors. Hip-hop makes my hands shake. *Lame-o,* I can hear Rory say. *You are an embarrassment to your generation.*

I stand perfectly still in the middle of the room and close my eyes. Music swirls around me, the molten sound of the saxophone draping my body in warmth. I lift my arms, feel the muscles stretch along my rib cage. I sway, let the pictures come. A round, fat moon sagging low. An ear of corn, butter sliding slowly to a puddle on the plate. A sturdy little bee crawling down the throat of a flower. The gleam of Hunter's hair as he slides into home base. He didn't know I was standing by the bleachers, watching. It wasn't like I planned it. I was just on my way back from the pool when I heard his voice and went to see. He'd pushed himself up from the ground, smacking at his dusty knees, and high-fived another player as he jogged past. The low sun hitting the side of his face and making him squint into the distance. *That's the one.* I open my eyes and uncap the tube of cadmium yellow.

I love doing portraits. Last year, the seniors all lined up for me to draw them in charcoal. Even Mackenzie. I made her look prettier than she really is, straightening out her nose and making her eyes just a little rounder. She actually blushed when I handed the drawing to her and I had to bite back a laugh. I could so easily have pushed her eyes together a little too closely, made her forehead look like King Kong's. I could really have messed with her mind.

My art professor says we don't need a lot of different paint colors. We can mix every color of the rainbow and then some, just from the primary colors plus white and black. We're working on a color wheel in class, and then next week we're going to start self-portraits in oil. I've never worked in oil. I've never painted my own self.

I've got Hunter's face roughed out. The jazz is making me work fast and loose, so it's just the suggestion of cheeks and jaw and forehead. Hunter's eyes are slashes of blue, the way he looks at a person and lasers all the way inside. I'm bouncing on my toes and reaching for the tube of Alizarin crimson so I can start on his baseball uniform when I hear a loud banging on the door and someone yelling. "Hey!" *Bang bang bang.* "What's going on in there?"

"What do you think that is?" a guy asks me, pointing to the food behind the glass.

"The sign says lasagna."

"Looks more like roadkill, but I guess I'll take my chances." He nods to the lady behind the case and she dumps a spoonful of pasta on a plate and passes it to him. She looks at me and I shake my head. "Hey, don't I know you?" he asks.

I look at him now. He's a little taller than me, with scruffy blond curls and bright blue eyes, and a wide grin that makes me want to smile right back. His gray polo shirt is open at the neck. A prep — just like all the boys I'd gone to high school with — and somehow, not. "I don't think so."

"Seriously. That's not a line. Aren't you in my art history class?"

52

Now I know. "I think you mean my cousin, Rory."

"Rory." He says her name like it's delicious, filling him up. "I'm Hunter, by the way."

"Arden," I tell him, and shove my tray down the line. *Hunter.*

That afternoon, I tell Rory, "I met some guy you know." We're in our dorm room and she's lying on her bunk flipping the pages of a textbook with an irritated look. I know what she's thinking, what she wants from me, but that's over. I told her and she'd agreed. Still, I can't help the dread that fills my stomach. "Who?" She doesn't sound the least bit interested.

"Hunter. He thought I was you." This will annoy her. She hates it when people mix us up. She can't understand it. She's the thin one, but she never says this.

"I don't know a Hunter. What did he look like?" She turns another page.

"Blond hair, kind of wavy. Blue eyes."

"Sounds like half the guys on campus."

"I think he's in our art history class."

At this, she looks up. "Oh, right. He invited me to a party Friday night. Want to go?"

My mom's a list-maker. I make them, too. The one I made over the summer says *Stop*

53

biting nails. Also *Start swimming again.* Rory didn't even react at that one. At the very top of the list, the number one item: *Take chances.*

So I say, "Okay."

It's a frat party, crazy with people. Music thumping out the windows as loud as airplanes taking off. Everywhere I look people I don't know are holding red plastic cups, dancing and laughing. Hunter's a frat guy. He appears out of the crowd, that grin lighting up his face, and I suddenly feel warm all over, like he's smiling just at me. He comes toward us, but it's Rory's hand he takes. They dance, their bodies close but not touching. Rory has her arms up over her head as she swings her hips this way and that. It's obvious they're going to have sex that night. I hope it's not in our room.

"Come on," Rory calls to me. I dance with a dark-haired guy around my height with bloodshot eyes. "Try this," he says, holding out a tiny square of paper.

Take chances, right?

I let him place the paper under my tongue. Colors rain from the ceiling, bounce and break apart into confetti. I laugh and ribbons of pure gold spin all around me. He rubs his cheek stiff with bristles against mine. I pull away, but he grabs me back to kiss me.

My skin tingles in that pins-and-needles way. It burns and I realize I'm standing too close to the flames.

The bonfire leaps in the round fire pit. It's so pretty in the dark woods. It makes the tall trees look friendly. I hold my palms to the heat until my mom tells me to take a step back.

I share a cabin with five other Brownies. The plastic mattress squeaks when I kneel on it to spread out my sleeping bag. I don't care about the bugs and bears. They feel very far away. Later, we make s'mores when it gets too dark to see anything but our hobgoblin faces in the firelight. In the morning, we squish eggs in sealed plastic sandwich bags and drop them, one by one, into boiling water in the pot balanced on the metal grate. The whole time, Rory hides in the cabin. I bring her eggs, lifting the tail of the sleeping bag and passing her the soggy paper plate.

Fire makes me brave. It's the strong black line that separates me from Rory.

Am I awake? My throat hurts, but it's my head that's killing me. Dimly, I hear someone say, "Pulse one twelve."

"Blood pressure?"

Brisk hands on me, pulling the sheet taut, adjusting the thing in my mouth. It snakes down my throat. I try to spit it out, but my tongue won't move. My eyes are sealed shut. Tingling starts in my fingertips and down in my toes, angry bees buzzing in my veins, swarming up my wrists and calves, headed for my soft, helpless heart. They are determined. They climb over one another in their eagerness. I can't get away.

"One twenty-four over ninety. Maybe she's dehydrated."

"It's probably pain. Let's increase the drip, see how she does on it."

The bees slow down, fall asleep in gentle heaps.

RORY

I don't care what they say — cutting is for losers. I get all about how the sharp pain's supposed to be a relief, a distraction from what's really bothering you, but seriously? It's gross. It leaves scars. I tried it once in seventh grade. Everyone was doing it, so I locked myself in my bathroom and pressed the tip of a razor blade into my thigh. I felt nothing, not even pain. I wiped away the tiny drop of blood and tossed out the razor. My mother would have found out, eventually. You can wear long sleeves and pants for only so long.

I hate to admit it, it's such a cliché, but in eighth grade, I did the typical anorexia shuffle. It was clean and fairly easy. Hell, my mom even approved of how skinny I was getting. I felt powerful in a way I'd never felt before. But then Mackenzie told me Brice Hanover was calling me the Titless Wonder. After I bashed in the headlights of his Beamer with a brick, I ate one of my dad's banana cream pies with a spoon while it was still warm and decided there had to be another way.

There was. It had been there all along — at the Kangaroo gas station where they never asked for ID, Mackenzie's parties when her parents were out of town, even now on Arden's pontoon boat with the broken lock on the small refrigerator, the moon gleaming down as the lake bumps us gently against the dock. Three-thirty in the morning and my parents were finally asleep, having yelled at each other for hours while I sat huddled in my bedroom and waited them out. I reach inside for another cold can.

"My dad's going to know," Arden warns as I crack the top.

"No, he won't." I take a noisy sip. Uncle Theo sees what he wants to see.

"You better not drive home."

I ignore her. She's always saying stuff like that. I don't even know how we're related.

She's sitting on the bench opposite, with her knees to her chest, wearing pajamas, her feet bare, every toenail painted a different color. *No one does that anymore,* I told her, but she just capped the bottle of orange polish. *I do,* she said, and reached for the baby blue. But I saw her hesitate.

When we were littler and could fit, Arden and I would stretch out side by side on the springy Astroturf carpet and stare up at the sky as the water moved beneath us. *I don't get planking,* Arden would say. Or, *I got picked last again in lacrosse.* I wouldn't mean to, but I'd say, *I made myself throw up at school,* and I'd feel Arden's fingers curl around mine.

Percy's in my lap, the soft whiskers of his muzzle tickling my chin. "No kisses," I tell him, but still he swipes my cheek with his warm tongue. "Ick. Stop it, you dumb dog. Why'd you let him out?"

"You want him standing by the back door, barking? Just let him kiss you. I'm sure Blake won't mind."

"Don't be disgusting."

"Dogs' mouths have fewer bacteria than human mouths do."

"Dogs' mouths reek."

Above us, Arden's house is all glass on the side facing the lake. Stone steps wind down past spiky forsythia and tightly budded azaleas, rosebushes cut to stubby knots, empty wooden boxes filled with dirt that in a month will be mounded with green. Arden calligraphed the small signs that poke up out of the dirt: marigold, baby kale, purs-

59

lane, cutting celery, saltwort, hyssop, red-veined sorrel, oregano, mint, fennel, six kinds of basil, cilantro, rosemary. The only thing growing now this early in the year is the white lavender I'd given Aunt Nat years ago, a tiny sprig I'd won at Flower Mart that had taken root and taken over. Every winter she chops it down and every spring it springs up even bigger, bullying everything around it. *You should dig it up,* I told Aunt Nat, and she had rocked back on her heels and squinted at me in the bright sunshine, one gloved hand held up to shield her eyes. *Not in a billion years,* she said, and I felt her love bloom toward me.

"My dad says even if we did get reduced tuition, there's no way we could afford the airfare and housing," Arden says.

Airfare's only a couple hundred dollars. That's how much I spend on a shirt. I kick off my Toms and tuck my feet beneath me. Percy bounces a little in my lap, then tightens himself into a doughnut. I run my hand down his smooth head, dig my fingers into the thick fur of his neck. *I'm allergic to dogs,* my mother says every time I ask. *You could take medicine,* I say, but she ignores me.

"They're talking about EMU," Arden says. "Grandpa's on the board, remember?"

60

"EMU? Be serious."

"It's better than nothing."

"It's so much worse than nothing. Don't give up. Our parents will figure something out."

"How? They're not even talking to each other."

"They'll get over it." I mime looking at my wrist, at the imaginary watch. "Say, in about seven hours, when they serve lunch."

You had no right! Aunt Nat had stormed. The doorbell had rung and then I heard her and Uncle Theo come in and go into the living room, where their voices faded but still came up the stairs to where I stood behind my opened bedroom door. *I thought it was a sure thing,* my dad had argued. *I was going to use the money to expand the business. It wasn't about me.* The defensiveness in his voice made my skin prickle and I'd started to come out of my room to confront everyone and tell them it was just a stupid mistake when Uncle Theo said, *Who do you think you're kidding, Vince? It's always about you.* I'd been so shocked at the rage in his voice that I'd stepped back into my room to hide behind the door. My mother's voice had bladed through, piercing. *Everyone's talking about money, money, money. But don't you realize? We have lost*

61

so much more than that.

Arden's biting her thumbnail. "What if we have to sell our house? What if we have to sell the *boat*?"

"Don't be such a drama queen."

"I'm not. My parents are really freaking out."

Which doesn't mean we have to. "Listen. When you meet with Guidance, don't tell her why you're looking for a different school. Let her think you've decided you can't live so far away from home or something."

"That's what you're worried about, what people will think?"

"No offense, Arden, but you don't get it. You don't know what it's like."

The lake's a mirror, not a ripple showing. Trees stand dark and tall. My parents had argued about moving out here after Arden's family did. My dad wanted to live on the lake, too, but my mom had said she would never leave her beautiful old Tudor house and all her wonderful neighbors, who included a congressman, a grocery store magnate, the secretary of the treasury, and a former UN ambassador. We've lived there my whole life and my mother's never once talked to anyone but the mailman and the lady next door when she needed her to

62

move her car, but it's probably the only time I'm glad my mom won. I love living in D.C., right in the heart of everything. "Remember when you first moved here and we ate all those lizard eggs?"

"You told me they were Tic Tacs."

"I thought they *were* Tic Tacs." The tiny white oblongs littered the windowsills — what else could they have been?

"I can still remember how they tasted."

"Dry and crunchy. Yum."

"You were always getting me to eat stupid things. Remember the snail you told me was escargot?"

A plain gray garden snail I'd convinced her was a delicacy. "I couldn't believe you fell for that."

"I hate you."

"Remember when we tried to prick our thumbs?" Blood would make us closer than cousins. It would make us real sisters.

"What do you mean 'tried'? I *did* prick my thumb."

True. "No way was I going to do it after you screamed like that."

She snorts. "Typical."

An owl hoots, sounding close, and Percy lifts his head. "I'm sorry my dad screwed up," I say.

Arden, her face a pale smudge, her long

blond hair shining. "Not your fault."

I'll never tell her, never in a million years, but sometimes I love her more than anyone on this planet.

The cafeteria smells moist and sticky, like pasta and potato dumplings. Disgusting. I take an apple — Red Delicious, because the cooks have no fucking imagination — from the steel bowl at the end of the counter and scan the room. Jessica comes up beside me with her tray. Gravy swims across her plate, shiny with grease, and I look away. Jessica's a diver. She eats twice as much as the rest of us and wears short sleeves, even in the winter, baring her arms. "Over there."

I lead the way through the tables. "Oh, my God, you should see her picture," Mackenzie's saying. She's got three glasses of milk lined up on her tray, her latest diet. Three glasses of milk a day and a banana. I watched her eat a banana the day before as she cut it into tiny cubes that she placed one by one on her tongue and sucked. Next week she'll be on to something else. Mackenzie's diets never last more than a couple of weeks. Her long hair falls across her face as she frowns at her big-ass cell phone gripped between her hands. It cracks me up every time I see her pull it out. She inherited it from her geeky brother and was counting the days until she could get a new one. "She's so ugly."

"She can't be that bad," Abby says.

Mackenzie looks up as I pull out the chair beside her, bright blue eyeliner thick around her brown eyes, then back down again quickly. "She can seriously be that bad."

"What are we talking about?" I say.

"Roommates," Emilie says.

"She's a *voice* major," Mackenzie wails.

"Could be worse," Emilie says. "She could be into taxidermy."

"Or rugby," Abby says.

"I Facebooked a couple kids yesterday," Jessica says. "We're going for a quad."

"I got a single," Emilie says. "I told them I sleepwalked."

Abby laughs.

"I bet she's a virgin." Mackenzie sticks her phone in my face. "Doesn't she look like a virgin?"

A narrow face, long brown hair. Forgettable. I shrug. "Maybe."

Mackenzie groans. "Great. A virgin voice major."

"What about you, Rory?" Abby asks. "Who are you rooming with?"

"I haven't decided," I start to say, then notice how everyone's looking around the

65

room, everyone but Abby. A tremor goes through me.

Emilie shakes her head. "Idiot."

"What?" Abby looks at me, her eyes buggy. "What?"

They know. Somehow they all know.

Mackenzie tucks in the corner of her mouth, to make her dimple show. The fake sympathy on her face is sickening. "Sorry, Rory. We know how much you wanted to go to Harvard." She puts her icy fingers on mine and I snatch my hand away. In seventh grade, she spread horrible rumors about me, and that's when I knew she was the one I'd need to win over. More than win over — supplant.

"Yeah, you worked so hard," Jessica says. She'd put on too much blush. She looks like a clown.

"Will someone please tell me what's going on?" Abby begs.

"Later," Emilie hisses.

I stand and drop my half-eaten apple into the brown puddle of glop on Jessica's plate. She gasps and lurches back from the splash.

I push my way through the rising and falling voices, the clattering dishes, the laughter, and the clanging of metal spoons against serving dishes, digging out a tunnel for just me, all the noises trailing after and then closing up solid, sealing me out as though I'm a ghost. As though I never existed.

I drive straight home after school, turn off Connecticut and onto the quieter streets of my neighborhood, past the house with the broad brown stripes dug into the lawn from when Blake's Jeep accidentally jumped the curb, the fire hydrant Arden and I painted smiley faces on, the Israeli guard walking his German shepherds who doesn't even look at me, though I'm pretty sure he's the one who had to drag his gargantuan attack beasts off me when I had to walk home four years ago after a party my parents didn't know about.

Where r u? Mackenzie texted, adding a row of emoji: hearts cracked in half and bleeding bright red drops. She's at Zorba's with everyone else, smoking on the patio, hiking up the hems of their uniform dresses to get a little sun. They'll order pizza and leave it untouched on the table, crunch the ice in their diet sodas, and talk about boys, teachers, parties. Who's getting high in the bathroom; who's been pulled over for driving on the wrong side of the road. A couple of girls will rush in from tennis practice, with their short skirts and pale thighs, and drag chairs over from another table. Then the boys from Saint Anthony's will thunder in, freshly showered, their hair wet and their cheeks red, reeking of spicy cologne that always makes me sneeze. Then everyone will be sitting on everyone's lap, or pressed standing in small groups in the corners. At six-thirty, Mr. Zorba will shoo everyone out to make room for the Real Paying Customers, and everyone will spill onto the sidewalk, laughing and making plans.

My favorite time of day, usually.

My mom's car is in the driveway, her purse open on the passenger seat. The bill compartment is fat with bills. I have to be careful when I slide out a twenty, time it for when she's super-busy and might not notice. *Gabby,* my dad's always saying. *You have to be more careful.* It makes me crazy, too: I know lots of kids whose cars have been broken into. But my mom always thinks she's the exception. My dad would reach in to grab her bag and stow it in the trunk. *She's your mother,* he'd say to me, with a wink, and I'd toss back, *You married her.*

I hear her now in the sunroom, heels clicking on the terrazzo tiles. She's probably watering her orchids a drop at a time. She'll be in there for ages, talking to one important client after another on her cell phone. *Let me find you something more classic,* she'll say. Or, *Not many people can wear orange.* I set my book bag on the floor. If she asks why she hadn't heard me come in, I'll just tell her I'd called out. Sometimes that works.

I tiptoe up the stairs in my bare feet, go into my mom's dressing room, and haul her little stepstool over to the cubbies that line the wall, filled with shoes wrapped in tissue paper. Here's where she hides crisp hundred-dollar bills sleeved in bank envelopes, her Ativan, and chewy chocolate laxatives. I feel around behind the black silk rhinestone stilettos. Nothing. I stand high on my tiptoes to make sure. I check the one to the right. I check them all, but the robin's-egg-blue Tiffany box holding my beautiful gold bracelet isn't there anymore.

NATALIE

The hospital corridor's a winding tunnel of hard white surfaces reflecting noise and light. A headache starts, pushing its way between my eyes and settling in, a solid knot. My rain-damp clothes are dry, but my shoes squeak against the linoleum. After my first few circuits, the nurse at the nurses' station no longer glances up with a smile. She's checked and reassured me that Arden made it through surgery without complication, but she can't explain why Arden still hasn't been wheeled to her room, which is prepped and waiting — the equipment rolled in and positioned against the walls. The room is as dark as Rory's, intentionally so. The girls need to stay calm while they recuperate. I will have to get my nerves in check before Arden arrives. I will need to force down my jitters because surely she will sense it, but all I can think of is *I need a cigarette.*

I pat my pockets, reach into the bag hooked over my shoulder. Of course there's nothing there. I hide my pack in my desk at Double where Theo would never find it. I'd quit when I was pregnant with Arden. He doesn't know I've started up again.

Theo's in admissions, signing papers. Vince and Gabrielle are in with Rory, and I haven't seen any other family members. Nurses have been going in and out of the sliding glass doors leading in to patients' rooms. They talk quietly in the hall. One of them nibbles cheese crackers from a plastic bag as she stands beside a wheeled computer, pressing buttons. The smell is nauseating. It fights with the astringent odors of cleaning solutions.

I wonder where I can buy a pack of cigarettes — surely they don't sell them in the gift shop — when the metal doors behind me swish open to admit two nurses pushing a gurney. I run over. "Arden Falcone?"

The male nurse nods. "We'll get her settled and then you can visit."

I can visit? I clutch the railing of the stretcher and look down, but this girl has her head wrapped around with white gauze. Only her right eye, swollen shut, is visible, the small tip of her nose, a bump of chin.

71

Her mouth gapes open to admit a long plastic tube fixed in place by pieces of white medical tape. It makes her look dull, vacant. Arden has never been an openmouthed sleeper. A stubborn tuft of blond hair sticks out from amid the bandages. I walk alongside and reach to pat it into place, then catch myself from correcting this small rebellious act, this defiance that says *Here I am. I am here.*

"Arden," I say, despite myself. "Hello, my darling." She doesn't blink the one eye I can see. She doesn't part her lips and speak. I want to cry.

The head of the bed is elevated to let gravity help drain the fluid seeping into Arden's skull and dangerously pressing her brain against the bone. A tube protrudes through the mask of gauze above her temple and more tubes loop across her body, forming a heavy web of plastic. Both arms are bandaged. Very gingerly, I reach for her right hand and turn it fractionally toward me. A glimpse of a few inches of pale forearm stained with orange Betadine, and beneath it, a little purple-and-green butterfly, its hand-drawn imperfect outline, its not-quite-symmetrical wings looking bruised.

Then we're in her room, the nurses guiding the bed against the wall. I step back to allow them to move around Arden, hooking things up, plugging things in with the aid of small flashlights, eerie beams of light dashing around in focused concentration. So many machines clustered around the bed, more than there are in Rory's room. That's okay, isn't it? They are all different, tall, squat, rectangular, and square. Their screens vary. Yellow, pale blue striped with dark blue, a jagged trio of lines moving across a black screen. This last machine hangs from the wall in the corner, silent and foreboding, staring down. Another box hangs over the foot of her bed, and the nurse sees me looking. "She's got on compression boots," he explains, and lifts the sheet to allow me a quick glance, flashing the beam of his flashlight so I can see how Arden's legs are encased knee to ankle in thick white pads with Velcro straps. As I watch, they swell to double their size and then release, shrinking back down with a sigh.

"They'll help circulate her blood. We don't want a clot." He goes around the end of the bed and I follow to watch him shine his flashlight on the plastic bag of urine attached to the bottom of her bed tucked up and out of sight. It looks full, but I don't know what the normal rate is supposed to be. I don't know how long it's taken for her body to produce this. "Is that okay?" I whisper, and he says, "Looks fine." He speaks in a normal voice.

A tall metal rack stands sentinel, an array of hooks holding up dangling bags of fluid, plastic loops braiding and twisting and reaching across the top of Arden's bed to her. The sheet slides down her shoulders, her hospital gown untied and lying across her body. Here's another precious piece of real estate, a few inches of clavicle, the smooth skin stretched across her chest beneath thick pads of gauze covering her throat, from which an ugly worm of a tube pokes. The nurse shines the flashlight across my daughter's body to show me. "That's a drain. Don't worry. She can't feel it." Arrayed on each side are discs taped in place to sense the rise and fall of her heart, working away silently.

He pats my arm. "I'll be back in thirty minutes. Let me know if you need anything."

"Okay. Thank you."

He reaches up to slide the curtain across the glass wall and Arden and I are alone. All I can see of my daughter is the ghostly rounded shape of her bandaged head and the sheet covering her. I wait for the shadows to sort themselves out and carefully

74

reach again for the skin on the inside of her arm, just enough for the tips of my four fingers to line up, the fine hairs I know are palest blond, the soft rise of a narrow vein, the reassuring warmth of her skin. The small purple-and-green butterfly, wings open, seeking freedom. Fighting for it.

I should be worrying about the fire. I should be demanding to know how it happened, demanding to know how all the safeguards failed, leaving my daughter barely clinging to life, but all I can think of is *She's here.* She's in this room with me right this moment. I can see and touch her, and that's all that matters.

Rustling behind me. It's Theo, letting himself quietly into the room. "How is she?" he whispers.

"Talk to her." I'm so glad to see him. He brings warmth into the room, solidity. "She needs to know you're here."

"Hey, sweetheart. Hey, Arden Garden." His voice is forced and unnatural, and tears sting my eyes. "Daddy's here," I say to compensate, in a chirpy voice I instantly regret. We are all going to have to practice speaking normally. I inhale and try again. "Guess what today is. Our anniversary. Can you believe it?"

I tell her about the homecoming kids and

how the server had to break up a mashed-potato food fight. I pretend this is a regular conversation and that we are at home, in our kitchen, just the two of us. I tell her about the twins, and how Oliver took his ant farm to school and, miracle of all miracles, not one ant escaped. I tell her Rory's sleeping in the room next door, and that she'll be okay, too. What I don't tell her is that this might not be true, and that the doctors are all wearing grim expressions. I don't tell her I'm sick with fear.

Later, in the cafeteria, while the nurses are changing Arden's bandages and the Foley bag, I cry against Theo's shirt. "How did this happen?" I'm blubbering. I'm barely making sense. There had been fire alarms and smoke detectors, rules about appliances. No candles. Cooking in the kitchens. "How did this happen?" My hands are fists, gathering up the material of his shirt. Over and over, I see my daughter cartwheeling through the air, arms and legs outspread. The ground had been hard. It had been unforgiving as it rushed to meet her. "Why Arden? Why Rory?" *Why us?*

Theo rubs his hands up and down my back. "I don't know," he murmurs, and it only makes the images in my head spin faster. Arden on the ledge. Arden in the air.

Arden on the ground. I have to know that bad things don't just randomly happen. "I have to know," I insist, and the next day, I do.

"How is she?" my mother asks on the phone.

I'm in the ICU family lounge. The window offers a rain-smeared view of slanted utilitarian rooftops and concrete. The windowsill is wide and stacked with cardboard boxes of jigsaw puzzles in faded colors. A ruffled paperback of sudoku puzzles sits on the round table, a pen lying across its magenta cover. *I'll be right back,* the owner seems to have said, but it's been there for hours — overnight? A bulletin board offers celestial help, a suicide hotline, coupons for a local dry cleaner, and a missing poster for a dark-eyed girl staring unhappily at the camera.

"The same," I tell my mother. We've talked twice already during the course of the night — or has it been three times? I have nothing new to share. We're in a holding pattern; all we can do is wait to see if the extra fluid in Arden's skull starts to drain. She could make a complete recovery. I have made Dr. Morris admit this. *It's possible,* the doctor had said. *Anything is possible.*

Arden's surrounded by love. She's floating in it.

All night, I watched the machines in my
daughter's room pump and drip and measure and squeeze; I stared at the shadows of
the rise and fall of her body, and finally
when I couldn't stand it any longer, I
dragged my chair closer, lowered the
molded plastic railing, and laid my forehead
on the mattress beside her. This is as close
as I can get to actually holding her.

Liz had called first thing this morning. *I'm
so sorry. I know you're busy, but do you want
me to open the restaurant tonight?* I'd had to
stop and think. *What day is it?* Saturday,
our biggest night. But beyond scraping up
this basic fact, my mind wouldn't work. I
couldn't think. *I don't know,* I'd told her. *If
you think you can handle it, go ahead.* Her
answering hesitation had thrummed over
the line.

"I think you should move her to D.C.,"
my mom says. "The hospitals here are excellent."

"I talked to Christine." The prevalence of
twins in our family led my sister to focus on
what happens when twins don't separate in
utero. When I found out I was pregnant with
twins, Christine insisted I get an ultrasound.
We all held our breath until she'd read it

78

and confirmed the boys were okay. "She says it's too risky to move Arden right now." Christine had gotten on the phone with Dr. Morris and reported back that she was fucking awesome, and Arden and Rory were in excellent hands. If Arden's burns had been more extensive, had covered thirty percent of her body, Christine said she might have suggested otherwise. What's thirty percent? An arm and a leg? A torso? "She says to keep Arden here."

"All right. If Christine says so. When is she getting here?"

"She has that operation, remember?" I told Christine that there was no point in her coming now, and she made me promise to keep her in the loop. I told her I'd keep her so much in the loop she'd feel strangled, and she'd let out her breath. "I told her to wait until it was over. It's not like being here would change anything."

"She could give you moral support."

"She is. Plus I have you and Theo."

Mom sighs. "How's Rory? Is she any better?"

"She's about to go into surgery. They're fixing her leg."

"What about Vince and Gabrielle? How are they doing?" She stumbles over Gabrielle's name. Mom's never mastered the

French pronunciation. *Such a pretty girl,* she'd murmured, meeting Gabrielle at my wedding all those years ago. Mom had gotten tipsy, and her eyes were moist. She'd patted my cheek, whispered, *You picked the right brother.* As if there had been calculation on my part. Mom hadn't been certain I was doing the right thing marrying Theo. She'd worried I was only acting on rebound.

It's not as if Vince and I had broken up. We'd never even dated. But the night before he'd left for France twenty years ago, Vince had murmured in my ear, surprising me. *Come with me. We'll get married, master puff pastry together.* I'd leaned away and stared at him. *Just think about it,* he'd urged.

But he didn't repeat the offer when he sobered up. So I stayed home, and two weeks later, his older brother, Theo, walked into the restaurant where I was sous chef. After the initial shock of familiarity — Theo and Vince looked so much alike; their voices had the same timbre and resonance; they squared their shoulders the same way and tilted their heads to the right when they were thinking something through — I began to tease out the deeper and more meaningful differences between them.

Vince was restless, always looking for the next adrenaline rush. Theo was calm and purposeful. He looked at me; he listened. He made me laugh. With Vince I felt that I was always auditioning for his admiration, but with Theo I could just be the real, flawed me: impulsive, impatient, sometimes irritable. He carved out this warm, lovely space where I felt safe, where I felt found, where I felt treasured. And the first time Theo put his hand around my wrist to lead me across a crowded room, my entire body tingled with recognition. All I could think of at that moment was how much I wanted his hands to touch the rest of me.

"They're hanging in there," I evade, though Vince and I haven't spoken. Not really. While the doctors were talking to us the night before in the hallway outside our daughters' rooms, I had felt Vince watching me. But I couldn't look back. Even now, I can't jump the canyon between us. I can't pretend we're okay.

I hear the wind blow past the phone, muted shouts in the background. My mother's calling from the soccer field. "How's the game going?" I need to hear about the boys, and how their lives are staying on happy tracks.

Last night's storm breezed through D.C. but stalled along the Maryland shore, directly overhead. Earlier, I'd heard thunder booming. I hate rain — I always have — but I'm glad it's my mother and my boys getting a brief spate of sunshine now before the storm rolls back in. After the game, my mother will take them to lunch and then to Janey's birthday party, which I'd forgotten but was the first thing Henry reminded my mother about when he woke up. They will come home, happy and tired, to walk Percy and then sprawl on the floor of the family room playing with LEGO while my mom assembles dinner. A good day, and I'd been looking forward to it, but now I can't remember the woman I'd been just twenty-six hours before, scooping dog food into a bowl and eyeing the weather report on TV, worrying about a few inches of rain and pending soccer plans.

"I'm not sure," she says. "It's kind of hard to tell when someone's made a goal. And they talked me into ice cream for breakfast. I hope you don't mind. They were so upset about Arden. But I drew the line at sprinkles."

"That's right, Mom. You're the boss." Framed prints in hideous pastel colors hang on the hospital walls. Once Arden gets out of here we will bring her paintings over and hang them on all the walls. It will be a way of thanking the doctors and nurses for sav-

82

ing our child. It will be a way of supporting the other families who find themselves in the cheerless place where we are now.

"Dad called, by the way," I tell her. *What can I do, Princess?* he'd asked. He hasn't called me that in years. It makes me suspect everything.

"Are you letting him visit?"

I sigh. I have no energy to manage this, either. "No. And not Mary Beth, either." Which is really what she wants to know.

The door opens and people come in. Theo, Vince, Gabrielle, and a man I've never seen before in a dark suit, a tie folded crisply, round gold-framed glasses. Someone from the university, I decide. Someone with answers? "I have to go, Mom," I say, and we hang up. "How's Rory?" I ask Gabrielle, and she answers, "There was a delay. She should be going into surgery soon."

"This is my wife," Theo says. "Natalie Falcone. Natalie, this is Detective Gallagher."

A police officer. I'm instantly wary, though I've done nothing wrong. I stand and shake the officer's hand. "Who's with Arden?" I ask Theo. This is the first of the rules that I have made with myself. Someone always has to be here with Arden, and preferably in the chair beside her bed, until she comes home.

"She's okay," Theo replies, which only means *She's the same.*

"I just have a few questions, ma'am," Detective Gallagher says. "It won't take long." *Questions?* I thought he was here to give us answers. I must look worried, because he adds, "Talking to the family is standard procedure in a fatal fire."

A fatal fire. That's what this is, not merely one that blistered my daughter's skin, smacked her head against the wooden picnic bench beneath her window, broke her bones, and yanked her into a hushed space hovering between life and death. A violence that tightens my throat and makes it hard to breathe. My daughter will be okay — I tell myself this over and over — but Hunter will not. How will I tell her, when she wakes up?

Theo and I sit on the vinyl-covered couch against the wall. Vince and Gabrielle choose the one adjacent. Detective Gallagher picks up a chair and positions it to face us. There is a smooth economy to his movements that warns me to pay attention. Vince is on the other side of Theo, sitting safely back and out of view, but his knees protrude and I see he's wearing his khaki pants, the ones with the ghostly outline of his wallet worn into the hip pocket and the torn belt loop.

Don't you dare go out front in those, I'd chide, and he'd merely grin, go into the office, and reemerge fifteen minutes later, clean-shaven, dressed immaculately in fresh khakis and a crisp chef's jacket. I'd pat his cheek and wink.

"The fire marshal's released a preliminary report," Detective Gallagher begins. "We haven't released this to the media, and I'd like you to keep it to yourselves for now."

"Of course." Theo nods, finding my hand, as Gabrielle says, "What? What does he know?"

"He found traces of accelerant in your daughters' room. He's ruling this an arson, pending further investigation."

"*In* our daughters' room?" Theo says.

"The fire marshal believes it was the point of origin."

Point of origin. It sounds like a horror flick, not this. Not my life. Not Arden's. "Someone started a fire in their room?" *Were they asleep? How did they let it happen?*

"Is he sure it's arson?" Vince says. "I mean, kids keep all kinds of crap in their rooms. Nail-polish remover, hairspray, cigarette lighters."

"Rubbing alcohol." I'd packed the first-aid kit myself and stowed it under Arden's bunk bed.

"There's a difference between a flammable liquid," Detective Gallagher says, "and one that's used as an accelerant and is intended to spread a fire quickly. We found accelerant everywhere in your daughters' dorm room, the walls, the ceiling, the floor. The lab's analyzing samples now. We should know exactly what was used shortly."

"You're saying someone wanted to hurt our children?" It's crazy. It's impossible. "They're just *kids.*" Two eighteen-year-olds who spent this past summer watching *One Tree Hill* and eating gummy worms. Gabrielle has her fingertips against her mouth, her eyes blank and stunned. I look to Theo. I want him to agree, to argue that this is all an insane mistake, but his face registers nothing. He's processing, thinking. "How can we help?" he asks instead.

"Well, arson's an unusual way to hurt someone. Often, it's directed at property, but we don't think that's the case here. We believe this was a revenge fire, someone settling a grudge."

"Revenge for what?" Vince sounds bewildered. "These are good girls. What sort of grudge?"

"Did either of them mention any trouble on campus? Maybe some kids the girls have had run-ins with?"

"Rory doesn't have run-ins," Vince says. "She gets along with everyone."

It's true. Rory's always been surrounded by a laughing group of kids. They swarm to her. She's never been afraid to put herself out there and speak her mind. It makes her the unquestioned leader, but it has a price. Back when the girls were in seventh grade, Arden had told me how Rory was being picked on. *Don't you dare tell Aunt Gabrielle,* my daughter had ordered. *It'll only make things worse.* And then more recently, *Rory isn't who you think she is.* Her voice had been freighted with meaning and I'd stopped what I was doing to give her my full attention. *What does that mean?* I'd asked, but she'd just shrugged.

"It's a big campus," Detective Gallagher says.

"Rory would have told us if there'd been a problem," Vince insists.

Detective Gallagher looks to me, light reflecting off the lenses of his glasses.

I shake my head. "Arden never mentioned anything." But the fact is that Arden has confided so little in me since starting college. *The food here is disgusting. I have to memorize like fifty works of art. The girls in the room next door play Taylor Swift too loud.*

"Think. It could be something minor. An

argument."

I look to Theo, who says, "She didn't say anything to me, either."

"It's possible someone from town got into the building," Detective Gallagher says. "We're reviewing the student access-card records, but there's always the chance that someone let a nonstudent into the building. They're not supposed to, of course, but they still do it."

"Are you talking about drugs?" Vince asks, and I'm shocked at this, but of course he'd wonder. I should have thought of it, too. He'd just gotten there before me. "You think this is drug-related?"

"Did the girls experiment?"

It's a softball question lobbed gently. I wait for Vince to volunteer that I'd once caught the dishwasher selling Rory weed, but he remains silent. I rub my temples. I'm searching, scrabbling for meaning. I'm turning over all the rocks. None of this makes any sense.

"No," Theo says. "Arden didn't do drugs. Natalie and I would have known."

Theo's always saying that his biggest challenge isn't getting his students into the best schools, but making sure they stayed sober long enough to graduate. Drugs were rampant, despite his best efforts. He watched

88

Arden closely, and I know he worried about Rory. His conviction now is reassuring, but I am remembering the time I phoned Arden and she answered giggling. *Wait, who's this?* Arden always checks caller ID. She always composes herself before saying *Hello?* I push the pebble back into place: Rory isn't a drug user and neither is my daughter. Her grades are too important to her and she has her feet firmly on the ground. Arden doesn't take risks. My daughter's a careful child.

"What have you heard, Detective?" Vince says. "Do you know if our girls were in any kind of trouble?"

"We're just starting to track down the kids who lived in the dorm with Arden and Rory. You'd think they'd come forward and volunteer information, but teenagers have a weird code of conduct. They're at that age where they think the police are the bad guys. And, for some of them, we are." He taps the tip of his pen on his notebook, looks at me. "Do you know why your daughter wasn't at the pep rally?"

I didn't even know there had been a pep rally. I shake my head. "Why does it matter?"

"Homecoming's a big deal around here, and the pep rally's almost as big as the game itself. Everyone goes. So far as we can tell,

89

Hunter, Rory, and Arden were the only ones in the dorm last night."

Out of the hundreds of kids who lived there. It makes the hair on my arms rise. "But we saw kids in the emergency room when we first arrived."

"They went in to try and save their belongings. They didn't get far."

The flames must have been showing in all the windows, the smoke spiraling into the sky. And kids had still gone in, heedless. Only Hunter hadn't made it out. *Why?*

"Mrs. Falcone? Do you know why Rory wasn't at the rally?"

Gabrielle stirs herself. "I don't know. She told me she was planning to go. I don't know why she changed her mind."

Detective Gallagher jots a note. "Did either girl complain of illness recently? Any possibility they went to bed early? Maybe took some cold medication?"

Theo and Vince are silent. They aren't the lifelines to the girls. Gabrielle and I are, and because Gabrielle isn't saying anything, I do. I answer for us all. "Arden seemed fine when she called Wednesday afternoon. She didn't say anything about feeling sick. You think they were asleep when the fire broke out? But it wasn't that late."

"Maybe they'd been drinking," Vince says,

and I look at him. I don't want to, but I do, because this makes a little sense.

"Do you think that's what happened?" I ask. "A party that got out of control?"

"Accelerant," Theo says, and I frown. *Right.*

"All right. Well, I appreciate your time." Detective Gallagher closes his notebook.

"That's it?" Vince says.

"For now. I'll let you know if I have any other questions. In the meantime, if you think of anything at all that could be relevant, give me a call. You have my number."

"Do you think you're going to find this person, Detective?" Gabrielle asks.

"It's a priority for all of us. I'm going to be talking with Hunter's parents, too, when they arrive to pick up their son's body."

Not a body. Their *child.* They'd watched him grow up; they'd had dreams for him, hopes. How were they going to make it through this?

"Of course," he says, "the best thing would be for Arden and Rory to tell us what they remember when they wake up."

It's a soaring thought. *When they wake up.* I'm eager to get back to Arden. I've been in here too long. A million things could have happened in my absence, and the nurse might not have come to let us know. We've been in this hospital less than a day, and every single minute stretches to eternity. Still, I hesitate and look to Detective Gallagher. "Are you certain this wasn't some kind of prank?"

I'm not naïve. I know terrible things happen every day, but not to me. Not to my daughter. I don't want this to be a crime. I want this to be an error, an accident with a tragic outcome. "Kids can do the stupidest things." In culinary school, it had been the price of admission to a party that Vince and I desperately, for some reason, wanted to attend. All over campus, mailboxes had been pried free and dragged away. A federal offense, but none of us could possibly have cared less at the time.

"Kids don't typically set fires as a prank," Theo says. Of course he'd know this. He works with teenagers; his degree is in child psychology. He asks Detective Gallagher, "Do we know for certain our daughters jumped?"

I look at my husband with surprise. Where is this coming from?

"We don't," Detective Gallagher replies, and I feel surprise give way to horror.

"You can't really believe they were pushed," I say to Theo in a low voice. We're hurrying

92

down the hall and we're alone — Vince and Gabrielle having gone to the cafeteria for a sandwich — but there are still people around.

Theo holds open a door for me. "I don't want to, believe me, but you have to admit it's a possibility."

"It's horrible. Who would do that? How did they escape?"

"Who says they did?"

He means Hunter. We've reached Arden's room, but I stop and stare at him, shocked. "Jesus, Theo. What are you saying?"

"What do you know about him, anyway?"

"Nothing. He's just a boy. He was Arden's friend."

"You ever meet him?"

"You know I haven't." Now I'm angry. I feel helpless, riddled with doubt and regret. Why hadn't I met Hunter? Why had I waited for Arden to call me instead of calling her myself? But I know the answer. I didn't want to be one of those moms. I didn't want to be Gabrielle.

"Why don't you go lie down, Nat? You didn't sleep a minute last night. Try the family lounge. I'll come get you if anything happens."

I frown. Like any of this can be solved with a nap? "I'm fine." I grab the door handle to slide open the door to Arden's room but Theo puts his hand on my arm, stopping me.

"For now," he says, "but I know you. You'll push yourself too far. You're no good to Arden if you don't take care of yourself."

I shake free of his grasp. "Stop it, Theo. I know what I'm doing. If I need to sleep, I can sleep just as well in the chair in Arden's room as on that awful sofa down the hall." But I can't sleep. Every time I close my eyes, I see Arden falling. I hear her calling for me and I snap awake, stare wildly around me only to remember where I am, and why.

"Fine. Well, I guess you don't need me." His annoyance is plain. He looks behind me and I turn to see Vince and Gabrielle headed down the hallway toward us. "I'll go check on Rory. She should be out of surgery by now."

I let myself into Arden's room and slide the door closed behind me. It's a hushed and gloomy space, the curtains hanging open so the nurses can see in. I don't know what they can see from the hallway; it's so dark. I go over and look down at my sleeping daughter. Her mouth is slack. Her eye is closed. I glance to the heart-rate monitor, see the line zigzagging in exactly the same pattern. I look at the pressure monitor. The number holds steady. I look back to my child. "Who did this to you, baby? What happened?"

She doesn't move. Her eye doesn't open. The numbers don't flicker.

"You're going to get better, darling. Daddy and I are right here."

A clock ticks on the wall, its round face glowing like a moon, like a sun. The hour hand points to four. Morning or afternoon? I think about this, parse through the day to decide it's the afternoon. Of course it is.

I pull my chair close to Arden's bedside. I need a cookbook to page through, something to transport me to a happy place. Vince and I used to spend Sundays at my kitchen table paging through cookbooks, debating, arguing, laughing. We came up with some of our best menu ideas that way. Theo would sip coffee and lean against the counter, refereeing. Oliver would climb into my lap, and I'd rest my chin on the top of his head. *Beets?* he'd suggest, and Arden would groan. *You're just saying that to torture me.* Henry would tell us he wanted hot dogs for dinner, *please?*

Raised voices out in the hall. Theo. And Vince? Something's going on. Rory.

I push myself up. "I'll be right back,

95

honey," I murmur to Arden. Of course there's no answer. Still, I pause and reach to her cheek, my hand hovering there.

Theo and Vince stand outside Rory's door, Vince with his head lowered and Theo patting his arm. They're the same height, the same coloring. Our girls had taken after their fathers. "Let's not talk about this here," Theo's saying. He glances to me and I see the worry in his eyes.

Vince shakes his head. "I don't care who hears me. Let them hear me."

"What's going on?" I say, sliding the door closed behind me. "Is it Rory? Is she out of surgery?"

"She just got back to the room," Theo says.

"And?" I glance through the glass and into Rory's room, a mirror of Arden's with its dim shadows and blinking monitors. Gabrielle stands there beside her daughter's bed. "It went okay, didn't it?"

"Yeah, the surgery went fine." But Vince sounds so bleak.

I look to Theo, confused.

"When they went in," he says, "they found the bone had crushed a vein. She's been bleeding the whole time."

I'm stunned. "Since last night?"

"Yeah." Vince raises his head to look at

me. I see Rory in his features, fearful and troubled, asking for my help. A dart of sorrow. I had let her go, too. "They would have found it sooner," he says, "if they hadn't bumped her from the damn schedule, but they decided someone else was more important. It's not like Rory could say, *Daddy, I don't feel so good. Do you think you could check it out?* No. She's counting on me to take care of her, and I screwed up. I dropped the ball. I should have insisted. I should have told them, *Get my little girl in there.* But I didn't."

"Hey, come on, Vince," Theo says. "This isn't your fault."

"It's *somebody's* fault. Somebody has to *pay.*"

"But it's okay now," I say. "They got it under control."

"No," Vince says. "That's the thing. They can't stabilize her blood pressure. It's all over the place. And her heart's racing. It's too much for her. They say she can't handle it much longer."

"Of course she can," Theo says. "She's strong. She's healthy. Rory's a fighter."

"But she doesn't even know there's a fight going on!" Vince hasn't shaved, the dark bristles a startling contrast against his skin. "You send your kid to school; you expect

97

her to be safe. You don't expect something like this to happen."

"No," Theo says. "You don't."

"All I wanted was to make a better life for them," Vince says to me, pleading. "You get that, don't you? You understand."

"Of course." Theo looks at me.

I know he wants me to assure Vince that none of this is his fault. But is it true? If we unravel everything all the way back, doesn't it all start when he took that gamble and lost? Arden should be three thousand miles away. Rory should be in Boston. They shouldn't be here. This is the last place they should be.

"It's okay," I say again. "Our girls are going to be okay." This is as close as I can get to saying the words. "I'm going to check on Gabrielle. She shouldn't be alone." I don't look at Theo as I turn away.

ARDEN

This is how it happens.

A girl gives you a pill from her stash and you think, *Why not?* Nothing happens and you're disappointed. You say to yourself, *Can't you even get this right?* But then the leaves turn bright green, their edges so sharp they cut the sky into pieces. Facts and dates and words zoom out of the darkness, so fast you can barely keep up. The snarky comments sail with them, twisting and turning before disappearing into the ether without the slightest prickle. You are brave. You are magic. Then the sparkling sky dims and the leaves turn muddy-colored again. You ask the girl for another pill and she gives you a look. *What do you think they are — free?*

I think they're finally asleep, my dad says.

We drive through twirling snow dense as lace, our headlights carving a tunnel through

99

the darkness. The car radio's on, playing Christmas songs that fade in and out. Oliver and Henry sit on each side of me, asleep in their booster seats, their heads lolling. They smell of animal crackers and milk, their little hands curled like shells on their small chubby legs. Percy's curled up in my lap, softly snoring. My parents are talking about Grandma Lorraine and Grandpa Howard, who are now living in separate houses, and I'm listening to all the secret things they're saying. *It won't be the same,* my mother says and sighs, and my father reaches over and puts his hand on her thigh. She slides her hands over his, her strong battered hands that carry burbling pots from burner to burner, hoist me onto a stool so I can stir, too, tuck a long stray strand of hair behind my ear, tickle my ribs to make me giggle.

Henry's awake now, excited about Santa Claus coming. He kicks his legs and then Oliver does, too. Our tires crunch the crusted snow and we bump onto Grandma Lorraine's white wonderland driveway. My brothers blink at the glowing strings of colored lights twisted all around the trees and bushes. *We're here,* my mother says, and Henry starts to cry.

Snow falls into my shoes, icy and wet, and

I stomp them on Grandma's welcome mat. I am prepared for bad news — the unpleasant shock of strangeness — but her house smells exactly the same, of cinnamon candles on the hearth and sugar cookies on a plate. Pine floor cleaner and bleach. Things change, I see, but they can stay the same, too.

It's always the same routine at the playground: first Henry and Oliver want to swing on the swings, then go down the slide. Then the jungle gym — Henry hanging there and blocking Oliver until he can't hold on anymore — then the haunted house, which is really supposed to be a pirate's boat, but the big metal wheel fell off and sat there on the splintery wood until someone finally carted it away. But their favorite is the merry-go-round, which they always save for last.

They both climb on and Henry orders me to go, so I grab the rounded rusting bar of the merry-go-round and run, my shoes digging into the dusty mulch. Henry shrieks with joy, one arm lifting like he's riding a bucking bronco. Oliver sits in the middle of the platform, grimly wrapping his arms around his bent legs. But if I stop to let him off, he'll shake his head and refuse to move.

Sometimes I wonder about my little brother, about why he pushes himself to do the things he's afraid of. Then I think I should try to be more like him.

My mom says I used to beg to go to the playground, and that I could spend hours there and never want to go home. I don't know. An hour's way more than I can stand of the same mindless repetitive action, so after I've run around in so many circles my head pounds, I grab Oliver's hand and firmly say, "Time to go."

"One more time," Henry pleads.

But I'm already marching away, kicking up sodden piles of last year's leaves that no one got around to raking away. I feel bad for my brothers. They're the only kids who ever play in this lame park.

I wouldn't be here, either, except that my mom came out of the kitchen to ask me to take the boys to the park while she and Dad headed over to Uncle Vince and Aunt Gabrielle's. That was the third surprise, because she's never home this time of day and who's running Double if she and Uncle Vince both aren't there? I dropped my book bag on the floor, all ready to complain that I was beat and, besides, I hated that creepy playground, when the twins came charging down the hall, Percy running alongside them barking, his long ears flopping. The twins threw their arms around me, making me stumble. "Finally! We've been waiting FOREVER!" Henry was on my right side and Oliver was on my left, their two blond heads pressing against my waist. Percy was leaping to reach my face, trying to kiss me, and that was the second surprise. Because I said, "Fine."

The first surprise had come an hour and a half earlier, when I found out I had to take the bus home from school instead of getting a ride with Dad, something he didn't even think to mention this morning on our way in, leaving it to his assistant headmaster to come out of her office and tell me, her eyebrows crawling up her big forehead — Tyra Banks would call it a *fivehead* — that my dad had already left for the day. Seriously? Was he pissed because I spent too long in the art studio? No. That's not how my dad is. He doesn't try to teach me life lessons. Dad's whole thing is to let me figure things out for myself.

My mom didn't answer her cell phone. And neither did Dad. So I stood at the bus stop and waited with a bunch of strangers for the bus to appear over the rise of the hill. When it did, groaning to a stop a few feet away and making all of us shuffle to the door creaking open, I climbed up the steps and politely said hi to the driver as I dropped in my money, even though I knew she would pretend not to hear me. She always did. *Why do you even bother?* Rory hissed the one time she grabbed a ride home with me, before she got her license and her own car. *You're such a suck-up, Arden.* I'd shrugged. Anyone could see the woman hated her job.

Three surprises all in one afternoon, which was plenty if you ask me, but the fourth one was waiting for me when I got back from the playground with my brothers and found my mom and dad both home and wanting to talk to me.

"We know how much you wanted to go to USC." My mom reaches across the dining room table to slide her hand over mine. There are lines around her eyes. Tangles of hair have escaped her ponytail and hang loose around her face. She's upset and trying not to show it. "Sweetheart, I'm so sorry. Your dad and I have been around and around this."

Snap! I've gone from thinking everything was going to be okay to knowing it isn't. "But we already sent in the deposit." I'm desperate, snatching at anything.

"They've agreed to apply it to next year's

104

tuition," my dad says. "See? It's not forever. It's just this one year while we try and get ourselves back on our feet."

"What about Rory? Does she know?"

"Her parents are going to tell her when she gets home from school."

Good luck with that. Rory's out partying with her friends. She'd invited me to go with them, and now I wish I had. "What about this year? Do I just stay home?"

My mom glances at my father. "There are a lot of schools nearby we can try. Your grandfather says he'll talk to admissions at his college. He's on the board there. Maybe he can pull some strings."

"EMU?" That big jock school somewhere out in Maryland. It's a joke at Bishop. I've never been there. I don't know anyone who has.

"I know it's not what you've been wanting, what you've been working for."

"Will Rory have to go there, too?" Panic flutters in my rib cage. I try to keep my voice normal.

My mom looks down. I can see this thought hasn't occurred to her. I can see it's a thought she doesn't like. "Maybe. I don't know, honey. I don't know what her parents are going to do."

It's the merry-go-round at the playground.

I run so fast my feet barely touch the ground and when I sit with a thud onto the metal middle, I tip back my head and fly. But when I open my eyes, I see the same world spinning past. I tug my hand from my mom's hand and stand up. "I have a paper to write."

Upstairs in my room, I shake a pill into the palm of my hand. Does it really matter anymore? I could flunk all my classes, get 1's on my APs and not even fill out the application, and still get into EMU. I pinch it between thumb and forefinger. *Hello, little friend. What else are you good for?* I reach under my bed and pull out the bottle of vodka. Rory thinks she's the only one. I twist off the cap and swallow the pill in a rush of lukewarm alcohol. I wait for the happy tingling that tells me all the broken pieces are falling back in order. *We know how much you wanted to go to USC,* my mom had said, looking sad. I wanted to throw something. There are a million art schools. The only thing special about USC had been that it was three thousand miles away.

106

RORY

"I heard them talking," Arden whispers. It's our last shift at Double before we leave for college, and we're stuck scouring the prep table with prickly pads of steel wool — or at least Arden's scouring; I'm examining my fingernails and wondering if anyone can tell I'd done my own nails. Aunt Nat stands at the back door talking to the meat guy and my dad's at the bank.

"That's good."

"It was more like fighting."

"Alert the media." I'm sick of it, sick of the whole thing. All summer, my friends had hung out at the pool and worked on their tans, while I ghosted sale racks and babysat my dad and my aunt, making sure they didn't burn down the restaurant or cut off a finger by mistake. After those first few weeks where all they did was yell at each other, they'd gone silent, and now they were so focused on ignoring each other that they were missing everything else. Let them figure out there's cabbage wilting in the fridge or a big party's coming in that wants the front tables pushed together by the bay window. That Holly had had a monster fight with her boyfriend and will probably call in sick. That Gideon's hitting the weed too hard and the kitchen ninjas are all on the verge of killing one another.

"They're worried about paying workers' comp."

"Who gives a shit?"

"I do," Arden says. "You should, too."

What I care about, what I really care about, is the way things used to be: my dad high-fiving Aunt Nat over some soft-shell crabs he'd scored for cheap, my aunt turning from the huge kettle and holding out a spoon for him to taste the seafood stock. How they used to stand so close together, their heads almost touching, as they worked on the menu. All the stories they'd tell about their customers, opening them like presents, their voices bubbling over each other while we laughed and laughed; Thanksgiving at Arden's house, the long dining room table shining, Christmas at mine, my mom stringing pretty white lights and fir garlands all through the banisters and filling the house with the smell of the woods. Easter egg hunts and birthday parties, rainy days and sunny ones, always our two families braided together, sturdy.

But now my dad doesn't sing the *Superman* theme when he slides into his chef's jacket and Aunt Nat circles the dining room greeting customers without so much as looking my dad's way. Uncle Theo doesn't smile at my mom, holding up the bottle to offer her a refill. My mom doesn't lay her hands flat against his chest as she stands tall to kiss his cheek *bonjour.* My dad and uncle don't lean back against the sofa and argue over defense, then leap to their feet to cheer the Redskins on. They've all gotten pretty stellar at not seeing one another, and it scares me. It tells me nothing's unbreakable.

"Not my problem." I pick up my steel-wool pad because any second Aunt Nat's going to turn around and see. It's not like we make any money working at Double. They won't let us waitress, where the real money is, but Arden and I are expected to pitch in and help. It feels like punishment. I've complained to Arden that I should have talked Mr. Zorba into hiring me for the summer and she made a face. *His name isn't Zorba,* she'd said. *Yes, it is,* I'd insisted, but she'd shaken her head. *That's just the name* of his restaurant. *His name is Ed.*

"They're the ones who screwed things up," I say.

"What do you mean 'they'?"

Aunt Nat elbows the door shut, her arms filled with packages of meat wrapped in butcher paper, and we fall silent. She smiles at us a little curiously but doesn't say anything as she walks past. We wait until she's in the walk-in before I hiss, "Stop acting like your mom's the victim. She's as much to blame as my dad is."

"How can you say that?" Arden's eyes fill with tears and it infuriates me. She's always so quick to cry or blush or laugh too hard. It makes her seem desperate. I've warned her over and over again: *Stop being such a baby. You have to toughen up.* She only says, *I can't help it.*

"Aunt Nat should have seen this coming. She should have taken his name off the title."

"Why, because she's psychic?"

I give the table a vicious swipe. "Because your mom knows my dad better than anyone."

"Can't I just ride with Arden and her family?" I ask over breakfast, and my father looks thoughtful, but my mother shakes her

110

head. "There won't be room for all your things," she decides, and there's no getting around that. So I sit sandwiched between pillows and comforters, staring between my parents' heads at the bumper of Uncle Theo's dusty Volvo as sprawling fields of corn and soybean and whatever the hell else they grow out there stake their claim on both sides of me and real life grows smaller and smaller until it disappears behind me into a bobbing speck. A hundred and seventeen miles stretch between my house and East Maryland U and as each one passes, I know. This is a mistake. I shouldn't have agreed to it. I need to speak up and tell my parents before it's too late. My dad will be upset and my mom pissed at my sudden change of mind, but won't she be relieved, too? "Hey, guys," I say, just as my father changes lanes and my mom yells at him to slow down. "What is your big hurry?" she demands, and all of a sudden I can't wait to get there.

A sneaker's jammed under the door to prop it open as all the Dorks from Dorkville stream inside, carrying armloads of crap. I stand on the steps, suitcase leaning against my leg, arms crossed, while my dad and Uncle Theo creep the streets looking for

111

places to park and my mom and Aunt Nat try to keep them from running over each other.

Arden appears in the hallway, her little brothers trailing behind her, their blond heads bobbing. It always makes me smile to see the twins. Oliver runs right over and takes my hand. His palm is warm and damp, but I don't mind. "Elevator's broken," Arden tells me.

"Seriously?"

"There's no air-conditioning, either. I mean, like, they don't even have units."

That hadn't been in the college description. "Freaking fantastic," I mutter, and pick up my suitcase.

When our parents arrive, we all cram into the empty room and look around, my parents being careful not to look at her parents. Beige cinder-block walls with chipped paint, twin beds with thin mattresses that bow up at the ends, two scarred oak desks with chairs, one narrow window with battered aluminum blinds. The floor's covered in a sketchy yellow linoleum, and the mirror above the dresser is cloudy. Two closets with sliding doors with holes cut into the wood instead of doorknobs. No one says anything for a minute, and then Henry, crouched on the floor and peering beneath the bed, pipes up: "Is this going to be your new room, Arden?" When she says, "Yes," he claps his hands. "I *like* it!"

We take down the blinds and string up the curtains my mom and I found at an insane price in Georgetown. We shove planks of wood under the mattresses to keep them from sagging our butts to the floor and line the drawers with lavender-scented paper. We hang up clothes and tack posters to the walls, spread out the oval braided rug to cover the worst of the floor. We pile towels onto shelves, sort toiletries into rubber bath caddies. Aunt Nat rolls a long plastic bin packed with first-aid stuff and packages of soup and hot-chocolate mix under Arden's bed, and my mom loads the small refrigerator with coffee drinks and vitamin water. Uncle Theo hooks up the TV and my dad levers the printer onto my desk beside my laptop.

We work pretty much in silence. We keep the door open to let the air circulate, but sweat trickles down my spine. I yank my hair up into a ponytail and tug my thin cotton tank top away from my skin, but it doesn't help. Families walk past, laughing and calling out to one another. Music plays from down the hall. The girls in the room next door stop by to introduce themselves as D.D. and Whitney, and Oliver and Henry run up and down the hall, playing some sort of game they'd invented. *Just like you and Arden always did,* Aunt Nat would say. I could hear people stop to talk to them. My little cousins are so cute, the way they look up so earnestly through the blond hair that flops over their eyes. I used to hope for a little brother until I found my mom's birth control pills hidden inside a box of tampons, and then I stopped asking.

When my mom sets the big zippered bag with my bedbug-proof mattress cover on the bed beneath the window, Aunt Nat straightens. "Hold on a minute, Gabrielle," she says, and turns to us. "Girls, how do you want to figure who sleeps where?"

Arden and I play rock-paper-scissors. Two rocks, then two scissors. I stare at Arden. *Read my mind, read my mind, read my mind.* Third time, I do paper and she does scissors. I smile so only Arden can see. She gives me a slight nod. "I'll take the window," she says.

My mother frowns. "Then you should switch second semester. That is only fair."

"Sure," Arden agrees, but she and I both know that won't happen. She knows I have to sleep next to the exit. She knows I dream

114

about fire.

A guy knocks on the door, buzz cut, sleeves cut off leaving ragged armholes. That look is so yesterday, but he's okay-looking in a friendly sort of way. "Hey, welcome to D House. I'm Steven, the RA on this floor." He extends his hand, and though my dad and Uncle Theo and Aunt Nat all go over to shake it, my mother crosses her arms and stands back. *We are sending our daughter to an average school, filled with average kids doing average things,* she'd hissed to my father. *We can only expect her to meet an average boy.*

Like you did? my father said, and I'd been filled with shame.

"We're having a dorm meeting tonight to go over house rules," Steven tells Arden and me. "There'll be orientation activities all week. Don't worry," he says to our parents. "I'll keep an eye on your daughters."

I look at Arden and roll my eyes.

After greasy Chinese takeout no one eats — not even Oliver, who eats everything — and a round of hugs, my parents making sure not to accidentally bump into my aunt or uncle or even look in their general direction, our families leave and the room feels deflated. I look around at the stuff we still have to put away — the clothes and school supplies and kitchen crap my mom insisted I have so I wouldn't be infected by other people's germs — and wonder when it will start to feel like home.

Arden's kneeling on her bed, trying to pry open the jaws of the small fan so she can clip it to her headboard, and I go over to help her. "Thanks," she says, as the fan purrs to life and lifts my hair away from my face. I lean close and speak into the whirring blades so my voice comes out funny. "You'rrre welcommme."

She laughs. "We should go to that dorm meeting."

"You can if you want." I sink down onto her bed. "But I already know what they're going to say. No loud parties after midnight. Don't let strangers into the dorm. Don't leave your flatiron plugged in, and no smoking in bed. Blah, blah, blah." I've spent my life strung between rules. I'm in no hurry to be trapped by them again. I turn to the window, hoping for a stray breeze.

After a moment, Arden plops down beside me.

People's voices flit up from outside, and we look out the window through the trees to the path below, but all we can see is darkness and splashes of bright green where the spotlight hits the leaves. This could be

Anyplace, USA.

I've waited for this day my entire life. It's dangled in front of me ever since I can remember, a big, fat, glossy emerald. I knew that when it finally came I'd suck in my very first real breath ever. So today comes and I'm holding the emerald tight in my hand.

Don't forget, my mother warned me before she and my dad left. *You need to check in every day by six, okay?*

I open my palm to look at the emerald and see the dull sheen. It's not real. It's the cheap plastic of toy rings you get out of bubblegum machines. This day started out like any other, and that's the way it ends, too.

NATALIE

I glare at the coffeemaker. *Doesn't anything in this place work?* I'd done everything right: pour in the water, fit in the filter, push start. The green light had flashed; steam hissed. The aroma of brewed coffee rose into the air, tantalizing. I stood there, foam cup in hand, when coffee shot out in a scalding spray. I yank handfuls of paper towels from the dispenser to mop up the mess. I'll have to get my fix from the cafeteria. I used to cut myself off from caffeine around noon.

"I thought I'd take the boys for haircuts," my mom says. "There's a new place in my neighborhood we could try. They have cute little spaceships for chairs."

Another chore I'd been meaning to take care of. Just the other day, I'd contemplated taking nail scissors to their bangs. "Don't worry about it, Mom." Holding my cell phone to my ear, I press my shoulder against the family lounge door to push it open. I'm saving my energy for what matters. I glance to the window and see the sky's a uniform gray. It's Sunday morning. This weather front has lingered for two days. I can't see beyond it. "You've got enough going on."

I'm not certain how the boys would react to spaceship chairs. Three months before, they'd have clambered happily up, but first grade — more specifically, exposure to other first-graders — had begun to pressure them into rejecting anything that smacked of babyhood. Henry was having no problem adapting. Lately, he'd been refusing to sit in his car booster seat despite his small size and I'd taken to bribing and outright threatening him. It was Oliver who was hanging back, watchful. He still liked me to sing him a nighttime lullaby, while Henry lay stiff as a board, pressing a pillow against his ears.

We've had a miracle. Arden's condition hasn't improved, but sometime in the murky overnight hours, Rory's blood pressure finally stabilized and her heart rate thudded back into the normal range. We should all be weak with relief, but now something else has emerged: Rory has acute respiratory distress syndrome, ARDS for short. Her lungs have shut down. She has to rely on the ventilator to pump oxygen through her blood. She's at risk of complete organ failure, brain damage. She sleeps unaware, balanced on the impossibly slim knife's blade separating life from death.

People with ARDS can completely recover, I've reassured Gabrielle. I've talked to my sister and she's told me it's not a death sentence. But I'd heard the hesitation in her voice. I don't tell Gabrielle that. Gabrielle had closed her eyes and nodded. *Thank you.*

"Don't you worry about me," my mother says.

"I do worry about you. You're not getting any sleep, either. Maybe I should call a babysitter so you can go home and get some rest. I'll let you know if anything changes."

But Arden has shown no change. The hours have trudged past. Dr. Morris increased the medication and it's done nothing. I have stared at my daughter's face — the swollen eyelid, the rounded tip of her nose, her determined chin — trying to find her among the shadows. I can't place my palm to her forehead; I can't stroke her cheek or brush back her hair to soothe her. All I can touch are these few inches of warm skin on the inside of her right forearm and her socked feet protruding from the compression boots wrapped around her calves, which I cradle in my hands, gently tracing my thumb along one instep. She never even squirms, and Arden is so ticklish. I have leaned close and told her, *You can do it, sweetheart. You are stronger than you think.*

If Dr. Morris is worried, she hides it behind the snapping on and off of her gloves, her brisk march to the monitors, the quick glance with a flashlight beam. *Let's give the medication a few more hours,* she said, when she came in for morning rounds. She says everything in slow and careful language, as though she's handing us something fragile. She's warned us Arden might have sustained brain damage, but she says this only to prepare us for the worst case. She doesn't know. No one does. I cling to this narrow ribbon of hope. I hold it with both hands.

"Don't you dare," my mom chides. "I couldn't sleep even if I wanted to."

"Just close your eyes and count to one hundred." I hear her smile. This is what she used to tell me when I refused to nap.

"It helps to be with the twins."

How can I argue with this? "I'll talk to you later, Mom. Kiss the boys for me. Love you."

I let myself into Arden's dark room, and in that flash of hallway light I see it.

A new bag dangles from the metal stand

121

beside Arden's bed. This one is aluminum foil, small and dense. "What's that?" I ask Theo, going over to pick up the flashlight. The words printed on the label mean nothing.

"An antibiotic." He shuts his laptop. "The nurse says it's routine."

"It looks scary. Why is it in that bag?"

"I don't know. Maybe it's one of those new antibiotics that's light-sensitive."

"She doesn't have an infection, does she?"

"No. They're just being careful."

But is he sure about that? Has he asked?

A rap on the glass, and the door slides open. Then a hand reaches up to draw the curtain aside from the entrance, and Gabrielle steps through. She's wearing the camel-colored skirt and black knit top she'd worn all night, her auburn hair smoothly waved back, pearl earrings clipped to her earlobes. But there are magenta smudges beneath her eyes and her cheekbones rise sharply, newly hollowed. "Hello. I'm coming to check on you all. How's Arden? Has there been any change?" She looks to the thin flexible tube hanging from Arden's skull and snaking over to the thermometer-looking instrument on the wall. It makes me want to stand and protect it from view. I don't know why.

"Not yet," Theo says.

Gabrielle comes closer. "It's so terrible, isn't it? I keep waiting for Rory to wake up and tell us she wants the television on, or that her leg hurts. Anything."

"I know." It's okay to talk like this in front of Arden. It's neutral. She's asleep. She knows we're here, waiting for her.

"What does Dr. Morris say?" Gabrielle asks. "When does she think Arden will wake up?"

"That it's just a matter of time," Theo says with a forced cheerfulness aimed at Arden. He's not quite telling the truth. Dr. Morris hasn't said this. She's been far more circumspect. Her actual words had been *We should know more in a few days.* Every time we draw close to a deadline, she moves it forward. A few hours, a few more hours. Now it's been two days, edging into three. Christine has to keep assuring me that this is nothing to be worried about, that it really is a waiting game.

I pick up my purse. "I'm on my way down to the cafeteria, Gabrielle. Want to come?"

"Yes. All right."

"Want anything, Theo?"

"I'm okay."

The cafeteria's noisy and bright, tables filled with people in green scrubs and white

123

lab coats, and ordinary people like Gabrielle and me. My stomach rumbles, reminding me I'd missed breakfast. Lunch, too? We head for the trio of coffee urns.

Gabrielle tears open a packet of sweetener and sprinkles white powder over the surface of her tea. Her long nails are polished a demure apricot, impeccable. For my birthday one year, she gave me a gift certificate for a manicure and pedicure, a thoughtful gift I knew was her way of commenting on how short and plain I keep my nails. But a manicurist could have done nothing for the burns on the pads of my palms from gripping too many hot pots, the scars on my fingers from when the knife blade slipped, the ropy scars along the side of my right hand where the pasta machine had caught hold of my latex glove and pulled my fingers into its maw. I had given the certificate to Arden.

"I looked up Dr. Morris," Gabrielle says, crumpling the sweetener packet. "Did you know she's Harvard-trained?"

Harvard again. Gabrielle had confided once that Harvard was the only American school she'd heard about growing up. Rory had been destined to be a Harvard girl before she'd even been born.

Is your family coming over from France? I'd

124

asked Gabrielle, and she'd looked down at her hands and spread her fingers wide. She didn't know. There's been no sign of her family, not even now. She's mentioned a brother and a sister, but long ago, as though out of memory. Twenty years and they've made no appearance at all. I wonder if they even exist. *We're her family,* Vince once told me, and it's true. Gabrielle would watch Arden so I could work; I would ferry Rory to piano lessons so Gabrielle could meet with clients. The first time Gabrielle and I met — Theo and I going to the airport to pick up Vince and his new girlfriend from Paris — she had fastened her cinnamon-colored eyes on mine and extended a cool, slim hand. *You are Natalie,* she'd said, and I'd wondered how much she knew.

Gabrielle tosses the wooden stirrer into the trash. "Do you think he knows what he's doing? Detective Gallagher?"

"I think so."

"You haven't heard from him, have you?"

I shake my head.

"Neither have we. Not a word."

"He said he was going to talk to Hunter's parents. Maybe they'll be able to help him."

"Maybe."

"I feel so sad for them."

"Yes. We are the lucky ones."

Nothing about this feels lucky.

"Do you think he's telling us everything he knows?" she asks.

"I think so. Why wouldn't he?"

"I don't know. This is a homicide investigation, is it not? There are things he's going to keep to himself, certainly."

"Perhaps in the short term, but we'll have to know everything eventually. Our daughters are victims, too. We have a right to know."

"I suppose. But what if we never do?"

"We will," I say with a confidence I don't feel. "The girls will wake up and . . ."

"What if they don't? What if they never wake up?"

"Don't," I say, alarmed. I'm not a superstitious person. My feet are firmly planted but this feels dangerous. Saying this out loud lets in the monsters.

"Oh, Natalie." She looks at me. Even now, her makeup is smoothly applied and beautifully shaded to appear invisible. "We're both thinking it. Every time the doctor comes in, every time a nurse stops by, you say to yourself, *Are they going to tell me it's over?* Don't tell me you don't."

I set down my cup and take her small hand in mine. "Rory's going to be okay. You'll see. She's going to be just fine."

126

"Maybe," she replies, her eyes sliding away from mine.

We're walking past the information desk toward the elevator when someone calls out. "Mrs. Falcone?" We both turn.

A girl in denim cutoffs and a T-shirt darts toward us, her pixie hair dyed bright pink. I recognize her as the girl who'd introduced herself the day we'd moved Arden and Rory into the dorm. *She seems like fun,* I'd commented to Arden later, and Arden had merely grunted. She thought I was referring to the girl's wild hair, but it was more than that. It was her open friendliness, the way she had smiled at all of us. She's not alone today. She's got other kids with her, a little crowd of college students. I feel a surge of envy. They are still going about their lives while Arden's has been stopped.

"Hi," the girl says to Gabrielle. "I'm D.D. You probably don't remember me."

"Of course I do."

Gabrielle probably does. She keeps track of all the kids going in and out of Rory's life, and even Arden's. There have been times when Gabrielle will mention a Bishop classmate casually and the name will stump me. I'll have to think hard to figure out whether she's the short blond girl who sings or the brunette who plays lacrosse.

"You must be Arden's mom," D.D. tells me.

She's forgotten that we've already met. I'm just one of the many parents in and out of the dorm that first day, a busy blur to her, but I'd been alert to whether Arden would like her room, the kids on her hall, if she would find a way to fit in at a school that she had never wanted to attend.

"How are Rory and Arden?" D.D. asks.

"They've been very badly injured," Gabrielle says.

D.D. bites her lower lip and one of the boys slings his arm around her shoulders. "Can we see them?" he asks. "Just to say hello?"

"I'm sorry," Gabrielle says. "It's not possible. Only family is allowed."

"But they'll be happy to have visitors later," I say, "when they're up to it."

One of the girls nods. Her eyes are redrimmed and her cheeks blotchy. "It's just so awful. I can't believe . . ." She dabs her eyes with the edge of her sleeve.

"I had lunch with Hunter just the other day," another girl says.

"He was in my econ class," a boy says. "He sat right next to me."

"Are there counselors at school for you to talk to?" I ask gently, and he nods. Arden

128

would be horrified to hear me talk like this to her friends. *They're not babies, Mom,* she'd scold. My throat tightens. I take a sip of hot coffee. It burns going down. The pain chides me to get a grip.

"We saw it," D.D. says. "We were at the pep rally and people started standing in the bleachers and pointing. The sky looked like it was on fire. We all started running. But . . ."

But it was too late. There was nothing anyone could do. Gabrielle and I are alone waiting for the elevator when she says to me, "I don't trust that girl."

I've been thinking how nice it is to know that Arden has a close circle of friends who care about her, and now I turn to Gabrielle with surprise. She's watching the elevator numbers light up. "Who? D.D.?"

She nods. "Her posts on Facebook are quite odd. I don't understand half of them."

I'm astonished. "You check Rory's Facebook page?"

"Well, yes, now and then." A ding and the elevator doors slide open. We step inside. Gabrielle punches the button for the second floor. "Don't you check Arden's?"

Hunter's parents are tall. His mother's face is dusted with freckles and her curly brown hair hangs loose and long over her shoulders. She wears layers of drooping beige clothes — a knitted vest over a sweater and a collared blouse. She'd gone to the effort to apply lipstick at some point during the day, but now it's worn away, leaving behind a fuchsia echo on her wide, thin lips. Hunter had taken after his father; the shape of their chins is just the same, and their eyes the same aqua color. Hunter's photograph had been on the front page of the newspapers stacked in the machine in the cafeteria. The headlines ask if we know how safe our kids' college dorms are.

First Vince shakes Phil's hand and then Theo does. I'd been worried that Theo might be confrontational with Hunter's parents, given that he suspects their son of having set the fire, though why I would wonder this of my eternally circumspect husband, I'm not sure. I'm not sure of anything right now.

"I'm so sorry," I say to Janet, and hug her tight. Her body is bony beneath all those layers. She hugs me back and I realize I'll never have a chance to meet her son. They have come to the hospital to check on the girls who had been Hunter's friends, and I understand this is a small way of feeling close to the child they'd lost.

"How are the girls?" Phil asks.

"They're in critical condition," Gabrielle says, and I see Janet and Phil react to Gabrielle's accent, so flowing and lush.

"Could we see them?" Janet asks, and I'm surprised. My own mother hasn't been able to visit Arden, but how can I possibly deny this woman this request? The six of us go down the hall and into the ICU. We are a silent parade and we stop first in Arden's room, a brief pause where Hunter's parents stand in the doorway and peer through the darkness to Arden's bed. And then we move on to Rory's room, which is where Janet and Phil cross the threshold and go right up to Rory's bedside.

Arden's room is full of shadows. "They didn't even come in," I grumble to Theo after Janet and Phil have left. "I don't think they knew Arden's name."

"They just lost their son."

"I know. But he and Arden were such good friends. Isn't it strange they didn't seem to know anything about her?"

"Well, maybe they didn't. You're always saying you wished Arden would talk to you more."

Maybe I'm being too sensitive, a result of all those years Arden had been eclipsed by

131

her more confident cousin. I'd been worried, sending the two of them to college together. I'd suggested to Arden that she room with someone new, for a fresh start. But Gabrielle had wanted the girls together. *Don't make a big deal about it, Mom,* Arden had said. *Let Aunt Gabrielle be weird. Besides, Rory needs me.* And I'd thought sadly, *Oh, honey. You have it all backward.*

But my daughter had gotten a tattoo, without ever mentioning wanting one. She'd lost weight since she started college. I couldn't help but notice it when she'd visited the weekend before, the way her jawline started to emerge and her eyes glowed against her skin. She'd only picked at her dinner, excused herself early to go to bed.

"I'd better get going," Theo says. "You sure you'll be all right?"

He'll be gone only six or so hours, just long enough to see the twins and pack some clothes, but all of a sudden I'm not certain I will. "Drive safely. Don't break any speed limits."

"I could bring the boys back with me, you know. It wouldn't be such a big deal for them to skip a few days of school. We could get a couple hotel rooms. Your mom could help."

I'm tempted. I miss my sons. I've never

spent the night away from them and I'm about to do it for the third night in a row. But the ICU's no place for small boys, and I won't leave Arden. What if something happens while I'm gone? She could emerge from her coma terrified and in pain. More fluid could seep into her skull and another emergency procedure might need to be performed. The boys will have a million questions. They'll be frightened. "I don't think it's a good idea. Not now. They need their routine."

"They're old enough to understand more than we give them credit for. Better not let their imaginations have free rein."

He's the psych major and the one who works with kids, so maybe he's right. But these are my kids and my instinct tells me it's a bad idea. "Maybe in a few days. After things settle." After we get some good news. After Arden has opened her eyes and can turn her head to smile at her brothers.

"Bring *Is Your Mama a Llama*?" I say impulsively. "Bring all her favorite books." They're the worse for wear, having endured the twins and, before that, all those years of reading to Arden and Rory, one little girl cuddled in on each side of me: Arden with her stuffed bunny clutched in the crook of her arm and her head drooping as she

133

drowsed to the sound of my voice and Rory sitting fully alert with her legs sticking straight out and her thumb obstinately in her mouth. When kindergarten came around and Rory showed no signs of giving up her thumb, Gabrielle had resorted to all sorts of trickery, reasoning, prizes, noxious ointments, and outright threats. She'd been so afraid the other children would make fun of Rory. "The books are in the storage room."

Theo's standing by Arden's bedside, looking down at her.

"Hey," I say, softly. "It's going to be okay." I slide my arms around him, rest my head against his chest. His arms come up and I close my eyes, listen to his heart beat. "We've been here before. Remember? When Oliver was born, all the times Henry had croup? You said they should name the pediatric wing after him, we were there so much." I smile at the memory. "Arden's got great doctors. She's in a top-notch hospital. She's healthy and strong and she's going to come out of this just fine. Right?" He's silent. "Right?" He has to answer. I can't do this alone.

Finally, finally, he tightens his arms around me. "Right."

134

ARDEN

Time slides past like Dalí's melting clocks step into the painting, and I try to pick one up. I hear something. My mom's voice. I stop to listen. I'll paint her a picture — the fireworks over the lake, the water indigo and the sky an explosion of yellow and orange. I swirl the paintbrush in the can of water.

"Your friends came by to say hello. They'll come back as soon as you're feeling better."

Which friends is she talking about? Doesn't she know I lost all of them, one by one? Doesn't she know I never really had them to begin with? Mackenzie says she's Rory's best friend, but Rory never hears from her anymore. *Who are Rory's friends?* Aunt Gabrielle wanted to know. She leaned close, softening her face so I'd tell her. She thought she knew all the secrets. She thought she coaxed them out of me, one by one.

"Grandma and Grandpa will be by after

135

their trip."

Mom must mean Grandma Sugar and Grandpa George. She never talks about my other grandma and grandpa in the same sentence like that.

"I bet they'll bring you girls all sorts of crazy things. You'd better be prepared."

She's trying to make me smile. *Why can't I?* I lift the paintbrush and dab it in midair. The soft pink of her cheeks, the blue of her eyes, the messy brown waves that stick up on top of her head first thing in the morning before she's brushed her hair. After Uncle Vince lost our money, she'd come home from Double, tie on her apron, and start cooking. Whenever she's upset or worried, that's what she does — heads straight to the kitchen. Once it was beef vegetable soup, another time dim sum. This time it was croissants, and this phase lasted for weeks. She set out a dish of malt and flour and sugar to draw the yeast straight out of the air — magic! Layering and buttering, rolling with the heavy wooden pin, proofing in the big plastic bin. In the early-morning hours, I'd come downstairs and find her pulling another pan from the oven. We'd sit, just the two of us, with sweet butter and homemade apricot preserves, a jar of Nutella. *We'll figure it out,* she told me, over and over again.

All the things I want to tell her. She loves me, I know. But she's always moving; her mind is always somewhere else. She'll be looking at me and nodding, but then I'll see her eyes drift and I'll know she's suddenly remembered the linen order's got to be picked up, or she needs to call the VIP guests before they leave their offices. The twins need new shin guards, and why is the car making that weird noise?

I skim the very tip of my camel-hair paintbrush to make the finest line that winds all the way to where it started, a dandelion's fluff of nothing. One exhalation and it explodes and floats apart. I am left holding a limp stem, unaware.

Why can't I see you, Mom? Why can't I move at all?

"I hate Shakespeare," Rory complains as I steer the pontoon boat down the lake. She's lying on her back with her head hanging over the edge, her hair trailing in the water behind her. I don't tell her she looks like Ophelia. She's upset about the B she got on her paper. She slaved over it, I know, but it's a hard class.

"At least you can try to bring it up." Rory had talked the teacher into letting her rewrite it. No surprise there. Everyone says yes to Rory.

"I'll probably do worse." She props herself up on one elbow and frowns at me, sitting hunched in the captain's chair with my knees drawn to my chest. "Unless you write it."

"Ha, ha." I switch off the motor so we can float in the middle of the dark water. I close my eyes and rest my cheek on my bent knee. The sun beats down on the side of my face.

"I'm not kidding. What if you did?"

"This is why you ditched Mackenzie? So you could talk me into doing your paper for you?"

"No, of course not."

"Right." We both know she's lying.

"Please."

"No way."

"But this stuff is so easy for you."

"It's not easy for me. I work hard. It's just easier for me than it is for you."

A pause, and I wonder if I've gone too far.

"Whatever, Arden. I'm talking about one stupid paper."

"One stupid paper, a hundred stupid papers. It's all the same. If my dad finds out he'd suspend me." My dad has spies everywhere. People like him. They tell him things.

"No, he won't."

She's just saying that. My cheek's burning. I turn my head and expose the other cheek to the sun. I know Rory's really upset, not just acting to get her way. I feel bad for her. B's won't get her into Harvard, which is all she's ever wanted, ever since we were little kids, but getting suspended won't get me into art school and that's all *I've* ever wanted. Besides, I have my own homework — piles of it. "Ask Mackenzie," I suggest, a little meanly.

"Mackenzie's an idiot."

I lift my head and look at her. "I thought she was your BFF." Mackenzie gave Rory a BFF necklace and, swear to God, Rory's even wearing it.

Rory gives me a slitted look, then rolls over onto her tummy, dips her hand into the lake and lets the water sparkle through her fingers. She doesn't say another word.

That's how it is at school the next day, too, only it's not just Rory ignoring me. It's everybody, even my lab partner, who's supposed to be doing the experiment with me. She just sits there and doodles in her notebook, making it look as though she's taking notes. Gym's horrible, everyone either speeding up or slowing down so that I have to run the entire field alone. But

139

lunch is the worst. I set my tray down at my usual spot across from Rory, and everyone — even the loser girls — shove back their chairs and leave.

I sit there anyway and pretend not to care, moving the food around on my plate, knowing everyone's watching and laughing at the freak.

After that, I wait until I get home to eat in my room: cookies, crackers, peanut-butter sandwiches, and jars of pickles. "What's the matter?" Mom asks when I yell at the twins for making too much noise. I can't tell her. She'll only tell Dad and then he'll hold a special assembly about bullying.

A couple of days later, Kent Stegnor stops me in the hall to tell me he can't take me to the tea dance after all — something's come up. That's exactly what he says: *Something's come up,* which isn't how people talk. He's been practicing his exit line. "No problem." I hate the way my voice trembles.

That afternoon, Rory's at Double after school, goofing off with one of the dishwashers, when I show up. I thrust the pages at her. "I changed your topic sentence. It was totally lame."

Rory looks thinner, the bones of her face sharp and her eyes large. The effect of the tanning booth, I think, but later I find out I

140

was wrong. She's lost weight and I've gained it. All this in an instant. All the words we don't have to say.

The next day, I sit at lunch with Rory, surrounded by all her friends. "Hey, what's going on, Arden?" Mackenzie greets me with a big smile. Anyone looking would think I'm having a blast, talking and laughing with all my besties.

RORY

Chelsea Lee wears mirrored aviator sunglasses. When I call out, she glances toward me as I run up. "Hi," I say, breathlessly, looking straight into tiny twin reflections of my face. "I'm Rory Falcone. I'm in your Art History 101 class. Can I talk to you about something?"

"I have office hours tomorrow afternoon. I'd be happy to talk with you then." She starts walking. I fall into step beside her.

"I know. But I have econ."

"All right, then. Shoot."

"Your syllabus says there'll be a midterm paper and a final exam?"

"Yes."

"Well, it's just that the class description online never said anything about term papers."

"You have a problem with papers?"

"No." *Yes.* "I'm carrying a super-heavy course load paper-wise" — can she check

142

and see it's not true, and can she please stop walking so fast? — "and I'm wondering if you could let me take an extra test or something instead."

"It's not as though I have tests lying around."

"It's not fair to say a class is going to be one thing and then change." Chelsea Lee had stood there with her hands on her hips, surveying us. She wore a long black jacket with padded shoulders over a dark blue chiffon blouse and black leggings tucked into high-heeled boots. Her long black hair was parted in the middle and she had thick eyebrows that slanted up at her temples. I couldn't tell if they were real or if she'd drawn them in.

"None of my other students have complained."

"A, I'm not complaining, and B, I don't care what your other students do."

She stops then and turns to face me, pushing her sunglasses up onto her forehead. Her eyes are dark brown and serious. No eyeliner or mascara, just a hint of blush and nude lip gloss. I'm impressed, despite the fact that she's a super-bitch. It's a difficult look to pull off. She's eyeing me right back and I let her. I look good today, tough in my skinny jeans. "You said your name is Rory?"

"Rory Falcone."

"Let me think about it, Rory Falcone."

I watch her walk away.

"What do you think D.D. is short for?" I ask Arden.

She's crouched by her dresser drawer, pawing through her things. "I don't know. Ask her."

She's still upset about that stupid frat party. I teased her the next morning about disappearing off with one of the preppie guys and she flushed bright pink as she leaned over the sink to brush her teeth. She wiped her face on her hand towel and pushed past me without answering. I'd hit some kind of nerve.

"I did but she wouldn't tell me. It's got to be something awful. Dizzy Doolittle. Daffy Dishes. Double D's can't be it. She's a B cup, tops." This is a game we used to play, Arden and me, coming up with silly names for the strangers we spotted on the street or in Double. But Arden doesn't even look over.

I grab my pillow and hug it to my chest, roll over to stare up at the ceiling. "Art history was supposed to be an easy pass." I'd come into the auditorium and seen Arden all the way up front, rolled my eyes, and taken a seat near the back beside this guy with amazing blue eyes and day-old scruff. He'd grinned at me as he handed me the syllabus. I'd smiled back, taken the stapled sheaf of papers, stuffed it into my backpack — like I cared what it said — and crossed my legs. I was checking Facebook on my tablet when something the professor said caught my attention. "Does she really expect us to tell those lumpy stone sculptures apart? They all look exactly the same."

"They go in sequence, from primitive to more advanced," Arden says. "They show the whole development of depicting the human form. That fertility goddess . . ."

"Oh, God. I don't need to hear her lecture again. What a weirdo."

"I don't think she's weird."

Arden has no filter. "Well, she is. Trust me." I push myself off my bed and go to my closet. I flick through the hangers and stop at my green-and-white-striped Madewell tank top. I pull it out and pretend to consider it. "I don't know. I'm not sure I'm ever going to wear this. You want it?" I'd caught her eyeing it the day I pushed it over the counter at the store, credit card lying on top of the bundled fabric.

145

Arden eyes me suspiciously. "Why?"

"It's adorbs. It'll look great on you."

She folds her arms. "Uh-huh. What do you really want?"

"To give you a shirt?"

Arden looks around the room and then her gaze returns to my face, her green eyes flat. "No, thanks." She turns back to her dresser and pushes the drawer in as far as it will go. Arden's so messy. I hate offering her such a nice shirt, knowing it will only end up on the floor.

"You sure?" I dangle the shirt.

"No. No way. I told you. I'm not doing that anymore."

"I wouldn't have signed up for art history if I'd known. It wasn't on the class description. Come on. You know it's true."

"So drop the class."

"And take what, racquetball?" Arden knows I can't change my classes. My mom would ask questions. She'd call the school and demand to talk to someone. "Please, Arden. Just this one time." I hate the pleading note in my voice.

"No, Rory. I mean it. It's not like it was at Bishop. It won't work the way it used to. The tests are all computerized here."

"I'm not talking about tests. I'm talking about that stupid paper, the one that wasn't

146

even in the course description, the one she sprang on us during class." Arden knows this. She's just making me do the hard work of spelling it all out.

Focus, Rory, my mom said. *You know you can do it. You just have to try.* I'd leaned over the worksheet centered on the table before me, opened my eyes as wide as they would go as if that would make the difference. But the letters pushed together to make nonsense words. I couldn't unstring them fast enough. If only I could breathe a little, but my mother's face was so close to mine, the concern stamped into the lines of her forehead and dragging down her mouth. *You will never get into Harvard if you don't try,* cherie.

"It's hard enough coming up with one thesis, Rory. I can't do two."

"Of course you can. You're like a genius at this stuff."

"I'm not a genius. I'm just . . ."

"What?" She's not going there again, is she? It's not that I'm stupid. I'm not.

"Whatever."

"Come on. I'll do your econ homework."

"I'm not taking econ."

"Calculus, then. Come on. Please. It's just one paper. You can write it in your sleep."

She rocks back on her heels and looks at

me. "Rory, don't do this."

"I'm stuck, okay? I really don't get this stuff. I'm already jammed up with all my other coursework. You're the only one I trust."

"You could buy a paper online."

"Dude. People get caught doing that shit."

"You could find a really obscure one."

"You know that won't work. They have software that searches for this stuff."

She stands, crosses her arms, and shakes her head. "I can't. I can't compromise my grades anymore."

She's looking at me, begging me to understand, but I won't. It means nothing to her and everything to me. "Your grades are fine. Better than mine."

"I killed myself to get them."

Impatience jolts through me, hot and red. "Here's a plan. Help me with this one class so that I don't screw up my chances of transferring to Harvard and I'll leave you alone. I'll go to Boston and you'll go to California, and we'll be three thousand miles apart. Just what you wanted, right?"

"Wow. Three thousand miles. I'm surprised you know that. I didn't think you'd been paying any attention in geography."

She thinks she's so brave. "I wonder how Ignacio's doing," I say mildly.

Her face goes white; her eyes spark green. I spread the shirt out on the rumpled covers of her bed and leave, closing the door quietly behind me. I'm meeting D.D. for dinner and she's waiting in the dining hall, but I stop, lean against the wall, and collect my breath. *I need help,* I'd begged my mom, and she'd frowned. *We had you tested. You do not need help. You just need to be more disciplined.* She never sees how hard I work. She only sees what she wants to see. She never sees me at all.

When I get back to the dorm later that night, there's a note taped to the door, the familiar handwriting, dark and upright, an assault on the white paper, all the vowels with their tiny curls in the middle of their foreheads. I'd practiced forming my letters the same way until my second-grade teacher cupped her hand over mine, stopping me. *That's not the way Americans write,* she'd said.

I yank the note free. My mom's been here. I should have guessed a hundred and seventeen miles wouldn't be enough.

NATALIE

I wash up in a white-tiled bathroom with steel fixtures and signs posted everywhere, CALL DON'T FALL, quick with guilt at getting a little clean while my daughter lies defenseless. I've been on her Facebook account, all of it so innocent. I'd smiled at Arden's face, splotches of orange paint on her cheeks and chin. Who knows why? It could have been face paint from some college activity, or acrylic paint from her art class. Either way, she looks so happy. I held this happiness close, then signed out. Gabrielle had been wrong. There was nothing suspicious there.

I pull on the jeans and T-shirt Theo brought me. He'd forgotten to include a fresh bra, so I hook back on the lacy, black push-up I'd worn for our anniversary date Friday, two nights ago. It feels ridiculous beneath my cotton T-shirt, the swell of my breasts pushing out against the fabric. I comb back my damp hair with my fingers and step into the hall. The floor's sticky, sucking at the soles of my shoes. Why doesn't someone clean it? I hate dirty floors. I make sure we keep Double's floors spotless. Vince used to say that if we ran out of tables, we could always seat customers on the floor.

Tomorrow's Monday, a new start to the week. It's also the day they're going to begin debriding the girls' burns. Arden has some areas of concern along her left arm and torso, but Rory's the one with burns along the fronts of her legs, her chest, both shoulders. Treating her burns is a more extensive process, but it won't affect her prognosis. The nurse has told us it's a blessing the girls will be unconscious during the process.

Lately, whenever I asked Arden how Rory was doing, Arden would impatiently say *Fine,* and I'd let it go. It would have been easy enough to call Rory myself and see how college was going for her, but I'd let all the opportunities slip past. I loved my niece as much as I loved my own children, but I'd let this break with her father spill between us and push us apart. She'd taken her cue from me. She'd stopped pulling up a chair to nibble biscotti and watch me tackle a new sauce or entrée; she'd stopped texting me upbeat updates. She'd slip past at Double with just a breezy hello. I'd noticed and let it go, telling myself I need to focus on saving Double, but the truth was I'd welcomed the distance. I hadn't figured out how to manage keeping her in my life and not Vince. I'd failed Rory just as much as I'd failed Arden.

A man heads toward me, pushing a little girl in a stroller. They both look so happy, the little girl kicking her legs to make her skirt dance, and her father with a half-smile on his face. I was that complacent parent once. I want to grab his arm and say, *This can all change in an instant.*

The room across the hall is bright with light, revealing a woman leaning forward to spoon Jell-O into a patient's mouth. I'm seized by envy. This is what I want, suddenly and passionately — to be able to slide a quivering orange spoonful into my daughter's mouth. Surely the nurses have a refrigerator full of Jell-O and juices somewhere for requests such as these. Surely they have a spoon and will permit me to feed just one small bite to my child. But when I reach Arden's room and step inside, the flash of the hallway light briefly falling into the darkened room, I see her lying exactly as I left her, flat on her back with her mouth agape and filled with a thick rubbery tube. Theo glances up from where he sits in the corner. "Feel better?"

"A little more human." I drop the bag with my dirty clothes onto the chair inside the door.

This dark crowded space with its rickety padded chairs and rolling nightstand. A tall cupboard stands against the wall, intended for Arden's possessions, all of which were consumed in the fire. The clothes she wore into the hospital had been cut away and discarded, so we use these drawers to stash our things instead — tissues and notepads where we jot copious notes, Theo's laptop when he's not using it. He brought framed photographs from home, all the ones that stood in our den, swept up in one great armful, and placed them on top of the dresser: the boys peeking out from the tree house Theo and Vince built them the previous summer, Rory and Arden on graduation day with their arms around each other's waists, Sugar and George on the gangplank of their first cruise, my mother lifting an Easter egg from its cup of dye, me and Vince standing in front of Double the day it opened, the four of us at a restaurant table, our wineglasses raised in a toast I've long forgotten. It's too dark to make out any of our smiling faces. It's too dark to see even the general rectangular shapes of the frames, but their presence is enough — a reminder of the love that surrounds Arden as she sleeps.

Theo's got his laptop balanced on his knees, but I don't think he's really getting any work done. He nods to the arrangement with a bobbing balloon. "Liz sent flowers."

"That's nice." She'd volunteered to drive my car home from the alley behind Double and arrange for a ride back. My mom had invited Liz in when she arrived bearing pastry, and the two of them had visited briefly while Oliver and Henry played with Percy. *We were careful,* my mother assured me. *We didn't talk about Arden and Rory in front of the boys.* I haven't explained what's going on to Oliver and Henry. I've relied on saying vague things like *Arden's sleeping* and *She bumped her head,* and thankfully the boys haven't asked the hard questions.

Other people have sent flowers, too: the Bishop School teachers and staff, the PTA president, my father, Theo's parents, who sent twin arrangements of blush-pink roses. My parents-in-law have always been careful to treat the girls exactly the same, and so if Rory gets a cashmere sweater on her birthday in May, Arden knows to expect the same sweater when her birthday comes around in September, although maybe in a different color. They don't do this with Oliver and Henry, who actually *are* twins. If Oliver gets a set of paints, Henry will get a football. *It's important to treat them as individuals,* Sugar, my mother-in-law, has very seriously informed me. *That's her name, really?* I'd asked Theo when he'd told me that first time, thinking I could never marry a man whose mother's given name was a food additive. *It's a southern thing,* he'd tried to explain, which made me retort that D.C. was not a southern city, which made him retort, *Ha! Because the girls aren't individuals, too?* I've groused to Theo in private. I don't know why this irks me. Maybe it's because Sugar has never embraced me as an extension of her family. It's not personal, I don't think. I've noticed that she treats Gabrielle with the same polite distance, but this doesn't seem to bother Gabrielle. In fact, I think Gabrielle prefers it.

Sugar and George are in Italy for a long-anticipated trip and will head to the hospital the moment they return in six days. I have steeled myself for this. Sugar will not be dissuaded, even if we tell her the doctors have warned us the girls can't have the

155

stimulation of a lot of visitors. She and George are upset with Theo and Vince for fighting and have made their views strongly known. They don't understand that this is the way it's always been between their sons — Theo always having to rescue Vince and Vince always resenting him when he does. The last time Sugar phoned, Theo listened for a few minutes, then silently handed me the phone and strode away, leaving me to interrupt Sugar's tirade about how her sons were acting like children, how life was too short, and the importance of family. *All you boys have are each other,* Sugar was saying when I put the phone to my ear. *That's not true, Sugar,* I said. *Theo has me.* I'd caught her watching me on my wedding day as I danced first with Theo, then Vince.

"Your brothers made you a card," I tell Arden. Theo brought it back with him, an exuberantly crayoned piece of paper with their names inexpertly printed on it. "I'm not sure, but I think it's ants playing soccer." I can see my twin boys, identical heads bent and elbows bumping as they lean close, squabbling over the green crayon that is both boys' favorite color. The card will make Arden smile and I've propped it against the plastic water pitcher on her nightstand so it's the first thing she sees when she opens her eyes.

"I was thinking we could call the boys and let them talk to her," Theo says.

Hearing her brothers' voices might be a good thing for Arden. Why am I so resistant to this, though? "Maybe with my mom on the line," I hedge. Her cheerful chatter would distract the twins from noticing that Arden wasn't saying anything back. "Maybe after school."

"It's Sunday, Nat."

Right. I search back through my memory for the boys' schedule and it slowly assembles itself before me. Cub Scouts. Their den leader's big on hiking through Rock Creek, running along a trail, searching the woods for fossils. Today they're headed for the quarry. My mom will be finding chunks of quartz in their pockets for days to come. I blink back tears. "How about tomorrow, then?"

"Nat."

"You know they'll be bouncing off the walls when they get home after Scouts. Mom will have her hands full getting them to calm down enough just to eat dinner."

"We're talking about a phone call. Not running the Marine Corps Marathon."

Instead of answering, I scrape my chair over to Arden's bed and place my hand on

157

her covers. Touching, but not.

When Detective Gallagher raps lightly on the door, I startle awake. I'd fallen into an uncomfortable sleep, and somebody — Theo? — had draped a hospital blanket over my shoulders. I open my eyes to see the policeman inside the curtain and Theo beckoning to me.

"We're holding a news conference this evening," Detective Gallagher tells us as we sit in the family lounge down the hall. The door's closed and we've pushed our chairs close to him. We're going to hear secrets. We're finally going to hear the truth. I feel relief and apprehension, both. For some reason, Detective Gallagher wants to talk to us alone, without Vince and Gabrielle. "Reporters will start calling. They won't be able to get to you while you're here. The hospital staff will keep them away, but they might get hold of your cell numbers."

His glasses make him look so serious. His hands are loosely clasped in front of him. It inspires friendliness. It makes me want to lean forward, too, but I sit back. I think, *Why does the media want to talk to us?*

"It doesn't look like this was an outside job. There's no sign of forced entry and no one's seen a stranger hanging around. We don't have gang activity in this area, and there's no indication drugs were the motivation. The tox report hasn't come back yet, but we do know alcohol wasn't a factor."

I'm relieved to know this, to have my daughter's innocence confirmed.

"So you're thinking it's personal?" Theo asks the detective.

"Exactly."

Arden couldn't have inspired this kind of hatred. Neither could Rory. Is it terrible for me to wonder about Hunter? Theo's right. I don't know him or anything about him, other than my daughter had had a crush on him.

Detective Gallagher flips open his notebook and reaches for a pen. "When was the last time you talked to Arden, Mrs. Falcone?"

I've already told him this, haven't I? I've been over that last conversation a million times, played and replayed the way Arden had paused. It couldn't have been anything serious. Surely I would have picked up on it. I would have sat down instantly, turned my laptop toward me, and told her, *No, go ahead. Is there anything up?* I would have done that. I would have known. "We Skyped Wednesday afternoon. She wanted me to send her a sweater she'd left behind. Then she talked to one of her brothers."

"And how did she sound?"

"Fine. She sounded just fine, maybe a little preoccupied. I had to get to the restaurant and she had a meeting with one of her professors, so we didn't talk long."

"Preoccupied," he repeats. "That's it?"

He doesn't freight his words or throw me a questioning look but he makes it sound as though he wonders whether Arden and I ever really talked. Or maybe I'm just being defensive. "It wasn't unusual for us to have quick chats. She often called between classes or on her way to the library." Arden's always the one to initiate; she's managed this very adroitly, refusing to answer if I call or text.

"Mr. Falcone?"

Theo shifts in his seat, touches his forehead. "I guess the last time I spoke to Arden was sometime the week before. Monday, Tuesday? I came home from work. She was on the phone with Natalie."

Monday, mid-afternoon. Arden and I had talked while I cleaned out the refrigerator. *We're doing self-portraits in drawing class, right, Mom? So get this — one girl crumpled up a blank piece of paper and then spread it out. Seriously. That's what she did. A crumpled sheet of paper. The teacher loved it.* Arden had described the critique process, all the

160

students working from one piece to another and freely volunteering their opinions, good and bad. *It sounds like culinary school,* I'd joked, and Arden had laughed, pleased. Theo had come in and I'd passed my phone to him. By then I'd been on my way out the door and impatient about getting my phone back. I'd stood there as he tried to have a conversation with his daughter.

"She called me Friday afternoon," Theo says, and I glance at him in surprise. He's never said a word about this. "But I was in a parent conference and didn't pick up. She didn't leave a message."

"Did Arden call you often?"

"Not often enough," Theo says, and I squeeze his hand.

"What time was this?" Detective Gallagher asks.

"Three-thirty, three-forty-five."

Hours before the fire. "It wouldn't have made a difference," I tell Theo, but he won't look at me.

"How does she get along with the other kids in her dorm?"

"You think it was one of them?" *They're children,* I want to protest, but an eighteen-year-old is capable of splashing accelerant and lighting a match. "But you said they were all at the pep rally."

161

"So far as we know."

Meaning someone could be lying? Theo and I should have overridden Arden. We should have come for Parents' Weekend and checked things out. But how could we have known there was anything to check? "Arden gets along fine with everyone. She's pretty easygoing."

Which isn't to say she's a pushover. Arden could be stubborn. I remember a red-faced toddler lying flat on her back in the grocery store aisle, kicking her heels because I wouldn't buy her Oreos.

"Would you call your daughter an introvert?"

He's been talking to people and this is what they've told him. It saddens me to think that they hadn't gotten to know Arden, but I understand this takes time. Arden had been at EMU for only six weeks. "She's reserved," I correct. *No more hugging,* she'd sternly told me when she was four and I'd bent down to sweep her into my arms. My daughter's her own person. I've had to accept that. Arden hates attracting attention. She'll do anything to avoid the spotlight. *Try out for the newspaper,* I'll urge. *You could do layout.* Or, *That's a beautiful design. Why don't you enter it in that logo contest?* She always just sighs. *Maybe.*

162

"A loner?"

"No," I say, stung. "Not at all." This man doesn't know Arden. All he knows is the unconscious girl in the hospital bed. But he needs to understand her. He needs to fight for her. "She's just quiet. She thinks before she speaks."

"Our daughter's an artist," Theo says. "She feels things very deeply. She mulls over her feelings, examines them from all angles. She expresses herself through her painting."

Theo's never said anything like this before. I didn't know this was how he thought of our child.

"I see," Detective Gallagher says, but I'm not sure he does. "How would you say she's been adjusting to being away from home?"

"Quite well," Theo insists. "Not a trace of homesickness. Damn it." He's trying for a joke, to leaven the emotion of what he'd just said. I sigh. The two of them are so alike.

That first week or so away from home had been hard for Arden. She'd been anxious about her schedule and whether she'd find an on-campus job. We'd talked every night and I could tell she felt stressed. But once classes started and she began to make friends, things seemed better. *I'm okay,* Arden would say when I asked. *Stop worrying.*

163

I wasn't worrying, not exactly. It's more that I longed for her, wanting to know those little details about her daily life that I'd taken for granted. Was she skipping breakfast, watching TV with her arms wrapped around her bent legs, falling asleep to her music playing, the way she did at home? Was she metamorphosing into someone else, a grown-up version of the girl I loved?

"Mrs. Falcone?"

"It's true. Arden seemed happier than she had in high school." I realize how this makes things sound and I hastily add, "It's not as though she'd been depressed or anything."

"Maybe she was, a little."

I stare at Theo. "Why would you say that?"

He shrugs. "Sometimes I think her quietness is more than just temperament. Sometimes I think she really struggles."

"You do? Why didn't you say anything?"

"It's just normal teenage stuff, Nat. She'll work through it on her own."

Detective Gallagher's listening, his pen poised over his notebook. "Has she ever been treated for depression?"

"Of course not." I'm annoyed that we're talking about Arden in this way. Detective Gallagher looks at me with a non-expression. I don't like him, I realize. I know he's just doing his job, but it feels combat-

164

ive, the way he's firing questions at us. I want to push back my chair and leave, but I can't. I need to fight Arden's battle for her here, in this room. I need to steer this conversation back onto the right track. "Being away from home has been good for her. She's growing up, coming out of her shell. She's mentioned her art history professor on more than one occasion. I think she volunteered for a special project?" I look to Theo, who looks blank. I look back to Detective Gallagher. "She seems happy, challenged. She's made friends." *No, Mom,* Arden had said, when I'd asked if she was getting to know some of the other kids. *I'm living under a rock.* I'd been reassured by her flippancy. I'd laughed.

"Like who?" Detective Gallagher asks. "What friends?"

I feel my cheeks warm. I know how this will sound. "I don't really know their names, just that Arden had gotten to know some of the kids in her classes." What mother doesn't know the names of her child's friends? "D.D.," I say, remembering the pink-haired girl who'd come to see Arden and Rory, the girl Gabrielle didn't trust. "I don't know her last name. Her room was next to Arden's. You can talk to her."

"Any other names you can think of?"

Arden seemed reluctant to talk about her friends. Other than Hunter. *I have to go,* she'd say. *I'm meeting Hunter.* Once, I'd heard someone talking in the background when Arden and I were on the phone, and when I asked Arden who it was, wondering if it was the mysterious Hunter, she'd merely said, *Nobody.* "You can check Facebook," I say, and he nods. I realize he's already done this, and I feel a skewer of worry. He's talking to us, but there are things he's not saying. "Why would the media want to contact us?" I ask, but he turns a page in his notebook, frowns at what he's scribbled there.

"How have classes been going for Arden?" he asks, without looking up.

"She's always been a strong student. She's a hard worker, focused." This is a point of pride for Theo. He had been painfully careful never to show the least bit of favoritism toward her at Bishop and she had still graduated sixth in her class. "She got straight A's in high school. She could have gone anywhere to college."

She had wanted to go to USC. Even now, all these months later, I feel the scalding rush of anger.

"She went to the Bishop School, is that right?" Detective Gallagher asks.

166

I wonder why this matters. "Yes. Theo's the headmaster there." The Bishop School, educators of D.C.'s spoiled elite — piranhas, always circling, always searching for a tender bite of flesh. If it hadn't been for Rory, Arden would never have survived. Rory kept an eye on her. She included her. It pains me to admit that Rory's the leader and my daughter is the follower.

"Rory went there, too," Detective Gallagher remarks. "They were in the same class."

"Yes." Vince had made some smart investments and Gabrielle worked as a stylist for the Washington political elite. Combined, they were able to afford Bishop, where tuition was more than forty thousand dollars a year. The only way we had been able to send Arden to Bishop was because it had been free.

"And now they room together."

I'd had misgivings about that, but it seemed to have gone okay. Despite everything, Arden seemed to have been coming out of her shell, really coming into her own. Majoring in art and taking all those classes was why. Art was the one area where Arden could truly shine, where Rory couldn't go. "They're close. They've always been close. They're more like sisters than cousins."

"Sometimes sisters don't get along." His pen's poised over his notebook and he's looking at me. "Was that true for Arden and Rory? Did they argue?"

"Of course they did, but it was never anything serious." *Rory can be so selfish,* Arden would grumble. Or, *It was the Rory Show at school today.* "I can't even recall the last time there was a problem."

"We called them the Dynamic Duo at Bishop," Theo says. "They were inseparable." *Just like Vince and I had been, once upon a time.*

"Ever since they were babies." I would pick Arden up from Gabrielle's after working a double shift and find the two infants peacefully sleeping forehead to forehead, legs and arms entangled. And now they're lying in hospital beds, separated by one thin wall. I am not going to let this impassive stranger see me cry. I am not going to let him in, not one inch.

"What about boys?" Detective Gallagher asks.

"Boys have never been an issue," Theo says, firmly.

I almost wish they had been. In eighth grade, Arden had liked a boy and been ecstatic when he invited her to a dance and just as crushed when he told her at the last minute he couldn't go. No explanation — at least not one that Arden shared. Thirteen is too young to have your heart broken, but that's what had happened. After that, Arden got very tentative about boys.

"Would you say Arden had a happy childhood?"

"Yes." Why is he asking this? I need to get back to Arden. "Yes. Very happy." Scuffling toward me in my chef's clogs, her little legs like matchsticks and her hands reaching out for balance. Licking the meringue mushroom and looking up at me with awe. Juggling the twins, one in each arm, as they writhed and screamed, her expression saying *This was not the deal.*

"She ever act out?"

Now I'm getting alarmed. Arden got moody as a teenager, of course; she snapped, sometimes slammed a door. But that was it. She never stayed out late. I never got a call from another parent. Everyone told me how lucky I was, and until now, I'd smugly accepted it. "No. Never."

"Why?" Theo asks. "What does this have to do with anything?"

"Did she tell you about the fire in her room three weeks ago?"

I sit back. I have the sensation of something slipping away.

169

Theo glances to me, then to Detective Gallagher. "There was a fire in her room? And the college didn't notify us?"

"Apparently, they didn't know." Detective Gallagher studies us over the tops of his glasses. "Witnesses say it was Arden who set it. Does your daughter have a history of setting fires?" His voice is mild, but his expressionless eyes stay focused on mine.

"No! Of course not."

"What witnesses?" Theo asks.

"It's an ongoing investigation. I'm afraid I can't say."

"Bullshit," Theo snarls, and I grip his hand reflexively, astonished by this angry version of the even-tempered man I thought I knew.

"Arden wouldn't do something like that," I tell Detective Gallagher. Can't he see the truth plain on my face, hear it in my voice? I am completely open, stripped bare. "She's a good kid. She has no issues, no problems that we're hiding. She's never once given us cause to worry." It's a feeble explanation that doesn't quite ring true, but I feel the need to defend her actions until she wakes up and can explain them for herself.

"One other thing." He hasn't heard a word I've said. "The lab tests have come back. We've identified the accelerant used in

170

the fire as paint thinner."

He knows. He's accessed Arden's school records and seen that she's taking Painting 101. He's lobbed a grenade. "That doesn't mean anything, Detective Gallagher. Paint thinner's not a controlled substance. Anyone could buy it. Anyone could have it on hand."

"Look," Detective Gallagher says. "I'm a cop in a college town. I see it all the time. Kids away from home for the first time, no one watching their every move. You said it yourself, Mr. Falcone. Kids got to figure things out and sometimes they don't do so well. They make mistakes. They panic. Sometimes they end up hurting other people."

"You don't know our daughter," Theo says. "And this conversation is over."

You have to be careful, I'd warned Arden. But she hadn't been careful enough.

I hurry down the hall. I barely register the fact that the curtains are drawn inside Rory's room. I'm intent on the next door, the one that leads to Arden. I slide it open and step inside. She's right there, peacefully sleeping, all the machines working quietly around her. Theo's gone off to make phone calls and figure out if we need an attorney — with all the lawyers who have children at

171

Bishop, surely one of them will step forward to help us. Arden's shadow and stillness, a blur of white gauze and looping rubber tubes. It's been forty-four hours. *Two days is nothing,* Christine's assured me. But she's going to call Dr. Morris and talk doctor to doctor, to see if there's anything Dr. Morris hasn't confided. *I'll call you right away if I learn anything,* she's promised me. *No matter what time it is.*

Someone screams down the hall. Pain? Fear? I can't tell. Arden doesn't twitch. Her mouth is slack. The screaming goes on. Why doesn't someone help that man?

Why doesn't anybody love me? Arden had wept, when no one asked her to junior prom. I had rocked her in my arms. *They will,* I promised her. Love is such a slippery thing. It comes and goes; it leads and misleads.

"What did you want to tell me, honey?" I whisper. "Why didn't you call?"

Silence.

I sit in the chair beside my daughter's bed, reach through the railing, and find that small patch of warm, bare skin between the rigid blood-pressure cuff and the medical tape holding the IV needle in place. A narrow space all my own holding a little green-

and-purple butterfly with wings stretched open, searching. There is a lesson here, I know, and as long as I can feel my child's heartbeat, I will have hope. As long as she lies here, unable to talk and defend herself, I will do the defending for her. I had left her in that dorm room. I had left her to her own devices. I feel the pump of blood beneath her skin and release the breath I've been holding. I open one of the books Theo has brought from home. " 'Is your mama a llama?' " I begin.

ARDEN

McReidy's art supplies is in a crappy little mall in Bailey's Crossroads. You have to know it's there or you'd never turn off Route 7, steer carefully around the potholes, pull up against the dented trash can overflowing with garbage, and get out of the car. Because you might think that all that's there is the dusty-windowed Pho restaurant, the dark hardware store that's never open, the sketchy-looking tanning parlor with the green neon palm tree. But keep on walking.

McReidy's doesn't look like much from the outside, either. It's just a door between other doors, until you find the right one and step into a blaze of color — tubes of every kind of paint, soft and squishy and smelling like promise when you uncap them and pierce their foil lids; red sable watercolor brushes of every imaginable thickness; Rapidograph pens with their sturdy rectangular bottles of black ink; bright white

174

canvases so big they could fill the wall of a museum and so tiny you could balance one on your palm. Creamy pastels, kneaded erasers in smoke gray, firm tablets of colored and white papers. Buckets of colored tiles. Fountain pens and sharp-pointed colored pencils. Everything you could ever want. More.

But when I pull open the door, there's Ignacio, standing quietly beside the shopping carts. I miss him. Liz is nice, but not as nice as Ignacio. He doesn't say anything. He's waiting for me to say it and I do. *I'm sorry.* The smile on his broad face widens. I should have told my mom the truth, but I didn't. I let fear stop me.

Ignacio has two little kids. He keeps their pictures in his wallet and jokes with me in Spanish. He nods approval when I slice radishes into perfect ovals or melt the butter to the exact temperature. Maybe I will draw him a picture. I look for the stick of charcoal and a fresh sheet of paper. When I look back up, Ignacio is gone.

Early evening, the air purple and gray, the leaves maroon and burnt orange and ocher, all the dark and shadowy shades that close around a person and make them feel small. In California, it would be bright blue sky

175

and blinding yellow sun, sharp and clean. Breathable.

The cafeteria is a blast of heat and voices. Kids everywhere, laughing and talking. A few glance at me and I look away, cheeks pink. I don't know any of them. Will I ever feel like I belong? I get in line and help myself to a slice of pie, hold a crumbly-rimmed plastic glass beneath the spigot of milk and fill it up frothy white. I find an empty booth by the window at the far side of the room.

Rory's at dinner with D.D. and other kids from our floor. I know how it'll be if I go over there, so I'm here, anonymous. Rory always thought it was such a little deal. She never understood how hard I had to work, or at least she didn't want to. She just took the papers I wrote and smiled. Our little secret.

I didn't always catch my mistakes, but my teachers did. *Arden, this sounds a little familiar,* or, *You need to go deeper. You need more sources. You need to flesh out your argument better. Youneedyouneedyouneed.*

I slide into the booth. Voices rise and fall around me.

"I hate Snapchat. Every morning there are a million waiting from the night before."

"Their red eyes glowing."

Laughter.

"This morning I got one of vomit. The caption read *He missed.*"

More laughter.

I look down at my plate, the triangle of pie oozing purple-blue syrup. My mom always makes me a blueberry pie for Thanksgiving with a big scrolling *A* formed out of pastry dough on top. I drag the tines of my fork through the juice, watch the flecks of grease coalesce in runnels.

On my way out, I scrape the uneaten pie into the trash. How can I say no to Rory?

We almost never get snow in D.C. The TV weatherman can't stop grinning. *Better bundle up,* he cautions us, rubbing his hands together.

The storm rages toward us, dumping snow and ice, bringing everything to a standstill. I huddle inside and watch the lake turn white and gray and then crack with a sudden sharp bellow. A reprieve, right? But wouldn't you know it, the three D.C. snowplows do their thing and the roads are clear by late Friday night.

Rory texts me at midnight. *See u at 6,* and I know I'm screwed.

I finish my take-home history test, write an essay for Spanish, and around five-thirty, while my mom and dad and little brothers sleep, go into the hall bathroom, turn on the light, and quietly close the door. I lean forward to the mirror and carefully draw a line of black along my upper eyelids and pull back my hair into a ponytail. It takes me several tries. Rory and I both have blond hair the same exact streaked honey color and thickness. The only difference is Rory's is a few inches longer, which doesn't explain why, when she pulls her hair back, it slides smoothly. When I do, my hair fights back, throwing up ridges and bumps.

At six, I let myself out the front door, bundled in my puffy blue down coat, and slide into the passenger seat. Rory looks me over. She tugs the silver hoops from her earlobes and hands them to me, nods with satisfaction when I hook them through. "Perfect," she says. I check myself in the rearview mirror. I see a pair of unhappy eyes looking back.

We've lived in D.C. our whole lives but have never left the safe northwest part. We're nervous driving south into the ghetto where the high school stands with bars on its windows and snow lies in dirty chunks along the chain-link fence. No one we know would ever come here, which is exactly why we signed me up to take the SATs here.

Rory waits while I twist open an orange capsule, sprinkle a line of powder onto my small hand mirror, and snort it. "Good luck," she says, and pulls away from the curb, but not before I see the car door locks slide down.

The guy checking IDs at the door barely glances at me when I hand him Rory's driver's license. Still, I keep my head lowered until I'm all the way inside the gym. I've never seen graffiti on school walls or naked light bulbs hanging from the ceiling in metal cages. But once I sit down and pick up my #2 pencil, the strangeness falls away and I could be anywhere.

Rory gets me at noon, a fluffy white scarf bundled around her neck, her cheeks perfectly pink, and her lips shiny with gloss. The other kids stare at her as they troop past, and she pretends not to notice but I see her lift her chin a little, preening. "How'd it go?"

"Fine." I yank the elastic out of my hair and rub my eyes with a tissue. I'd let a few right answers go past. Rory got me to take the test for her, but she can't make me do my best. Which is what I should have figured out long ago.

Rory shoves the car into gear and we drive off, bumping across rough terrain.

■ ■ ■ ■

The sun's warm across my shoulders as I sit in The Bowl, books spread around me on the grass. "Gross." Rory wrinkles her nose at the photograph of the ancient stone fertility goddess with her jutting breasts and rolls of belly fat.

"She's not so bad," Hunter says, and she rolls her eyes.

"Pig."

He laughs.

I love the sound. I bend over my notebook.

"She needs a bra," Rory says.

"You're missing the point," I say. What is it with Rory and her obsession with this statue? It must offend her in some way. It must threaten her to think skinny isn't always perfect. "People starved back then. They didn't have Pizza Huts and 7-Elevens. They had to work to produce their food. They were at the mercy of everything. So *that*" — I wave my hand at the opened book — "was the ideal. It meant you were successful. It meant you could bear progeny and keep humankind alive. That was being a goddess to them."

"Thank you, Professor," Rory sneers.

Hunter reaches across me to flip the page.

180

His arm brushes mine, his skin warm, and then it's gone. "So don't do that one," he says. "How about these Roman soldiers?"

"Now you're talking," Rory says, and once again, Hunter laughs. Amazing how she can turn it on, leave a trail of laughter in her wake. *Boys are easy,* she told me. *Make them think you don't care and they're yours.*

Hunter's hers, even if he doesn't know it yet. He's always showing up, like now. All the thousands of EMU students and he just happens to wander past while we're out here? Rory's been going out with him at night, texting me not to come back to the room. I stay at the library until it closes at midnight, trudge back to the dorm, and sit on the floor outside my room until the door finally creaks open. *Hey,* Hunter would say, seeing me, but not really seeing me.

"You going to the Delta Delta Psi party?" Hunter asks, and Rory rolls onto her side to look at him.

"I don't think so."

"You sure? Free beer. Plus they're getting in live music."

"I'll think about it." Typical Rory, not committing until the last second, letting the guy dangle, twisting and turning. She's not planning to join a sorority. Harvard isn't big into Greek life, she told Hunter as the two of them lolled around on her bed. I'd been at my desk reading and wishing they'd go someplace else. *It doesn't make any sense to join for just one year,* she'd said, her arm lifted as she drew circles in the air with her finger. That's not the real reason, though. She can't afford the dues.

"How 'bout you, Arden?" Hunter asks.

I'm surprised he's asking. "Probably not. I've got a test Monday." Turns out frat parties aren't for me. I ran into that guy I'd made out with and he'd looked right through me. Either he'd been too drunk to remember or I'm just not that memorable.

"Just my luck," he says. "To be hanging with the only two sober chicks on campus."

My face warms, even though I know he's not really hanging with me. It's the transitive property of hanging.

"I didn't say anything about being sober," Rory says.

My first drink was peppermint schnapps that Rory stole from the bar when Ignacio wasn't looking. We hid in the office while my mom and Uncle Vince worked the Christmas rush. Happy noises filtered in, along with the smell of garlic and onions and roasted meat, as Rory and I traded the bottle back and forth. It was the worst Christmas ever. I couldn't get out of bed the next day, lying there as the room spun around and around, and pretending I had the flu. Now I don't drink stuff that pretends to be something else. I like strong bitter drinks that warn you straight up.

"You hear the drama this morning?" Rory asks. "D.D. found out Whitney hooked up with Zach."

D.D. and Whitney live next door and play music so loud it booms through the wall between us. D.D. has Barbie pink hair and a pierced tongue, and the first time she was over, told us she was bi. What do you say to something like that — *Good for you*? Rory and I talked about it later. *Can people really be bi?* I'd wondered. The room was dark, just the light from the corridor shining under our door and the moon casting shadows of leaves on the curtains. Rory's disembodied voice answered. *Maybe being bi is what you are when you haven't decided.*

"Heartbreaking," I say.

Rory makes a face. "It's the principle, Arden. D.D.'s right. You don't date your friend's ex."

D.D.'s nothing like the girls Rory hung out with at Bishop, the popular ones who stared right through you, who rolled up the waists of their skirts and spent hours straightening their hair into shining sheets.

D.D's the opposite of those girls. I want to like D.D., but I'm not sure she wants to like me. "Zach's barely an ex. How long had they been going together, three days?"

"I'd kill a friend who went out with my ex."

Hunter's texting, his head bent over his phone. That's the other thing he doesn't know: he has an expiration date. The longest Rory ever dated anyone was Blake and his Axe vapor trail, and that was only because of his family's beach place. I rotate my pencil between my fingers and draw a few quick lines. The intentness on his face emerges, the way his lips curve.

He glances over and whistles. "Hey. That's amazing."

I flush warm.

"Arden can draw anything," Rory says. Like she's in charge. Like she owns me or something.

"Let me try." Hunter reaches for Rory's pencil, which she gives up with a sly smile. He leans over and scribbles something on her notebook. She tilts her head to look at it, then giggles. Rory never giggles. My face burns.

She flips her blond hair over one shoulder, exposing the long line of her throat. "You dirty, dirty little boy."

184

■ ■ ■ ■

I stand by the window, looking down through the leafy branches to The Bowl.

You want it? Rory had asked, holding out the green-and-white-striped top. It still had the tags attached. My mom would hike an eyebrow at the price before steering me to the back of the store to the clearance racks. I finger the soft cotton knit, then take out the backless black dress Rory wore to that frat party. Her perfume still clings to it. The string of bugle beads along the neckline's loose. Rory will throw the dress away if she notices.

I tug down my jeans and pull off my T-shirt. I step into the dress and work it up over my hips. It's snug and I have to suck in my tummy. I stand on my tiptoes and eye myself in the mirror. Rory wears tall silver rhinestone heels with it, but I don't dare crouch in case I split a seam. I pile my hair into a knot on top of my head and fasten it with a clip. I try on a pair of long, dangling earrings and turn this way and that. From a distance, I look enough like Rory. But come up close and you'll see the differences: my greener eyes a fraction farther apart, my lower lip fuller, and my chin not as strong.

I'm not Rory. I can never be Rory.

I stole a bottle of wine from Double's shelves. I'd just grabbed the first thing I saw and slid it into my backpack. When Rory read the label later, her eyes widened and she grabbed my elbow. "Shit, Arden. You know how much this is worth?"

All of me, it turns out.

I wake up. My mom's talking. Her voice is cool, like a waterfall splashing down. I swim to it, spangles dancing all around.

" 'Is your mama a llama?' "

It's that story I used to love when I was little. I know all the words. I can recite them in my sleep.

Am I sleeping now? Or am I dead?

RORY

I had to tell my mom Hunter's premed. It was the only way to get her off my back. I could have told her he's a distant Kennedy, but she'd be on to me in a flash. *Which one?* she'd demand. You know how other people chart their family trees? My mom charts the Kennedys. *Four missing Kennedys,* she'd say, shaking her head. *One of life's greatest mysteries.* And, *There have been more female Kennedys than males.* She would say this disappointed.

I wasn't planning to tell her about Hunter at all, but she catches us coming back from class holding hands. I turn the corner, laughing at something Hunter said, and recognize her instantly even though she's all the way across The Bowl. My first thought is to turn around and pretend I don't see her, but she's already spotted me and is waving.

"Prepare yourself," I warn Hunter.

187

My mom eyes him as we approach, her perfect posture only making it seem as though she's completely composed, but I know she's seething inside. It's the way she lifts her chin just a fraction to look down her nose at us.

"Cherie." She reaches out with both hands to grasp my shoulders. So it's to be the kissy-kissy hello. I sigh inwardly. Too bad Hunter's in bulky cargo shorts. My mother loathes them. She says they're low-class. Sometimes I think the only reason she sent me to Bishop was because the boys at our brother school had to wear khakis and button-downs.

"Hi, Mom."

"Bonjour, Madame Falcone." Hunter holds out his hand. *"Je m'appelle Hunter Caldwell. Je suis un ami de Rory."*

I stare at him with amazement. He's got a pretty good inflection.

My mother lights up. "Ah, *bonjour."* They talk on for a little while and you might think Hunter's won her over, but she's not that easily won over. She's only reserving judgment until she gets me alone. Hunter leaves for baseball practice and she and I go up to my room. She opens the mini-refrigerator to slide in a casserole dish.

"They feed me here, you know," I say.

188

She's crouched, peering at the shelves. My lucky day. I'd just finished off the bottle of spiced rum, so if she doesn't glance into the trashcan, I'm safe. At last she straightens. "Your father made it. I told him I would drop it off."

"I thought today was Jean-Pierre." *Only the French know how to cut hair,* she insisted. Last time I'd been in, his shampoo girl had pressed her breasts hard against the side of my face and looked down at me with a smile.

My mom hikes an eyebrow, letting me know she doesn't care for my attitude. She begins looking through my closet, pulling out things and eyeing them before hanging them back up. "I have a new client in Salisbury. Her husband's looking to run for governor next year. She has to change her entire look."

It's a rope twisted tight around my wrists. Whenever my mom talks like this, it means tons and tons of hours. She's going to be here all the time. "Great."

She smiles at me. You'd never know from looking at her that she'd had to trade in her Mini Cooper or that she'd found her bag on clearance. "I have some more good news." I brace myself. "You remember Mitchell?"

"Yeah." I have the champagne glass from his restaurant right on my dresser, holding earrings. Aunt Nat used to work for him before she and Dad started Double. They have this playful competitiveness going, like who could get the best ad placement or the better Yelp reviews, though sometimes I don't think it's really so playful. "And?"

"He's been talking to your dad about buying Double."

I frown. No way is Mitchell going to take it over. I mean, I know every single tile on that floor — I've mopped them enough times. I know that the right oven runs five degrees hotter and that the early-morning light slanting in through the windows turns the entire place golden. "Dad can't sell."

"Of course he can, and he should. You had to know something like this might happen."

Maybe I did. But I'd still hoped they'd figure something out. Arden and I had brainstormed ways to save Double. Our parents could teach cooking classes; we could hold contests. We could name entrées after celebrities and get them to come for dinner, along with the media. But my mom had shot down every suggestion. "Daddy loves Double."

"I know, but it's time for him to move on. For all of us to move on."

My mother's a big one about moving on. Things change and you change with them. Bad things happen and you get over them. When good things happen you prepare yourself for the bad times that are sure to follow. She's the least sentimental person I know. It's my dad who plans special occasions, who brings home flowers, and who, when I confessed that horses terrified me, sat down on the hilltop beside me and watched the girls jump the hurdles in the ring instead. "Does Aunt Nat know?"

My mother sighs. "She'll be fine."

So she doesn't. I sink down on my bed. Things were changing. What did I expect? "Does that mean I'm going to Harvard after all?"

"Of course! That's the plan!" My mother sits down and puts her arm around me, gives me a reassuring squeeze.

This is good news, right?

"How are your classes coming along? Are they rigorous enough? Are you working hard?"

I will myself not to groan. "Yes, Mom. I'm killing myself."

"Please don't take that tone. You have to stay on top of it. Harvard won't make any allowances."

"I know."

"Okay." She pats my knee. "So, tell me about Hunter."

Her casual voice doesn't fool me. She's like this with every boy I date. But in high school who you hung out with did matter. You could rise like helium if you made the right choice or sink like lead if you didn't. Here, at Podunk U, no one cares. Except for my mother. "Nothing, Mom. He's just a guy." But even as I say it, I know it's not true. Arden's right. There's something about Hunter. I've never dated a nice guy, just ones with agendas. Hunter doesn't have an agenda. I can almost be myself with him.

"It can start that way and grow into something else before you know it."

Oh, God. Is she about to tell me that's what happened with her and Dad?

"Tell me about *just* this guy," she says.

I can't hear it, I never can, but Arden's told me my mom pronounces things differently. *Listen to her say* just. *It's not like we say it.* "He's premed. He plays baseball. What else do you want to know?"

"Where is his family from?"

"Bel Air."

Her face brightens. She's thinking California, not the suburb outside Baltimore. I know how she feels about Baltimore. I'm not going to correct her.

"Where did this come from?" Arden says later, pulling the glass dish out of our mini fridge.

"My mom brought it."

"Seriously?" She pries off the top. "Eggplant Parmesan, yum. You sharing?"

"Help yourself."

"Nice that your mom drove all the way to deliver dinner."

She knows it's just the lame kind of thing my mom would do. "I wish she'd leave me alone."

"She will."

I'm annoyed. She says it so casually. Aunt Nat never checks up on Arden. She doesn't call her a thousand times a day. I rest my chin in my hands, watching Arden move things around on top of our dresser. I swear she spends half her life looking for things. I've told her she needs to get more organized. "She met Hunter. Did you know he speaks French?"

"No kidding." Arden's got her back to me, but I know my barb stuck. It's in the way she freezes for a split second, like she's holding her breath. You don't have to be a mind reader to know my cousin has a thing for

193

Hunter. It's spelled all over her face whenever she sees him, her eyes softening and her cheeks going pink. Her voice gets weird and choked-up, like she's squeezing out the words, measuring them carefully. I've told her a million times that if she wants a guy to like her, she has to pretend she doesn't. But Hunter's mine, so I'm not going over that again.

"I told her he's going to be a plastic surgeon." *It's the best specialty,* I'd heard my mom say a million times. *Good hours and you can charge what you want.* She was probably driving home right now, dreaming about what a great couple he and I make, a plastic surgeon and whatever law specialty she's currently thinking I should go into.

"Poor Hunter."

"I saved poor Hunter's ass. She'd be so pissed if she knew he's a scholarship student."

"*We're* scholarship students."

I hate when she talks like that. We're not scholarship students, not really. Grandpa George worked out a deal where we have reduced tuition. I've told Arden to be careful not to talk like this around D.D., who is, as Aunt Nat puts it, the lead piranha. Aunt Nat says the only way not to end up as fish food is to eat the mean fish before they eat you. "My dad's thinking about selling Double."

Now she turns to look at me, her face wide with alarm. "What?"

"Mitchell wants to buy it."

"But he can't."

"You got a thing against Mitchell?"

"That's not the point and you know it. Double's our restaurant. Ours."

"I think we're going to have to face the fact that there is no *ours* anymore."

"How can you say that?" But there's no bite to her words. Arden knows how it is. "Your mom told you?"

"Yes."

"Maybe she's wrong."

I shrug. Thing is, it doesn't matter if my mom's wrong or right. *She* wants to sell the restaurant. And when my mom wants something, she has a way of making it happen.

Arden carries the casserole down the hall to the kitchen. I press my thumb against the scar on my arm, hiding it.

Later that night, lying on my bed with Hunter, the sheets twisted around our legs binding us together, I tunnel my hand through the covers to find his. *"Je t'amuse,"* I whisper.

"*Cherie* Rory," he murmurs, his lips

against my temple. The rolling *R*s sound like a kitten purring, the wind sifting through the leaves. He rolls toward me, grabs my shoulders, and presses them hard against the mattress. I open my eyes and find him staring down at me. He's not smiling. I try to wriggle free. "Cut it out."

He blinks. Just like that, he's Hunter again.

NATALIE

I sit beside Arden's bed, my legs curled beneath me, and study my phone. People have been calling, leaving messages. I should listen to them. I should check in with Liz to see how Double's doing. I set the phone down and reach for the book Theo brought me from home, the 1970s spiral-bound community recipe book I found a few months back at a yard sale. Jell-O and mayonnaise, hot dogs as protein, sangria made a dozen different ways. I switch off the flashlight and slide the book back into my bag, glance at the clock on the wall. Have the hands even moved?

I look at Arden. It's been two and a half days since she opened her eyes, sat up, smiled. Two and a half days since she did anything but lie here, motionless, helpless. I can't even tell if she's thinking.

A nurse comes in every hour, on the hour, to read the pressure gauge. If the number rises even a fraction, we have to catch it immediately. No one has spelled out why. I don't want to know. It's okay to allow myself this small cowardice. It's enough to know that Arden has to be kept calm, that nurses and doctors regularly check all her vital signs. *It's harder to come back from a brain injury,* Christine has told me gently. *You want me to cancel my operation? I can be there in a few hours.* I'd started to cry and it took all I had to tell her, *It's okay.* Those conjoined twins needed her. They really did. No one else could save them. What could my sister do for me here other than sit in the chair beside me and stare at my injured daughter?

Someone from the college had been here earlier. A man in a navy suit and a muted gray tie. He met us out in the hall, a beribboned basket of orange flowers in his hands. He set it down on the nurses' station before shaking my hand, then Theo's. *If there's anything we can do,* he'd said. *Anything at all.* His concern seems genuine. It's not fair to suspect him of ulterior motives, but I do. Theo took his card. Theo promised to stay in touch. I just waited impatiently for the man to leave so I could go back to Arden.

The door slides open. This time it's the

nurse arriving to scrape the dead flesh from Arden's body. She carries a tray of sharp instruments. I avert my gaze as she sets it down. She reaches up to tug the curtains across the glass. "Why don't you take a little walk, Mrs. Falcone? I'll be a while."

I hesitate. It's probably better if I'm not here. She can do her job without worrying about me. I'll go to the family lounge, return some phone calls. "You have my number?"

"Yes." She's already moving to the tray of instruments, her mind narrowing in on the task at hand.

Doctors in white coats cluster by the central desk. One's talking as the others listen, their expressions earnest and intent. Baby doctors, learning to fly. One of them laughs, actually laughs. I long to grab his shoulders and shake him.

I'm about to step into the family lounge when I hear my name. Turning, I see Vince headed down the hall toward me. "Fancy meeting you here." He's a different guy now that Rory's doing better. "I got you coffee, give you a break from the crap in the cafeteria." He extends a paper cup.

"Thanks." I lean against the wall.

He leans beside me. "How's Arden?"

"The nurse is with her now."

"So no change?"

I shake my head. I peel open the lid of my cup and sip: black, with a little sugar. It's delicious, a rich roast. This reminds me just how awful the coffee is here. Vince sips from his own cup I know is black. I can feel the heat radiating from his body, smell the faint spice of his cologne, which Gabrielle gives him every birthday and which he dutifully wears. He's wearing a blue shirt and I know that if I look at his eyes, they'll appear more blue than green. I take another sip. "How did it go for Rory?"

"She slept through the whole thing."

A relief. As selfish as it is, I still wish my daughter would wake up, if only for the briefest of moments, to register the nurse working over her.

"So where's Theo keeping himself? I haven't seen him all morning."

I glance to the window. Drizzle paints the glass. It must be a new storm front. It can't possibly be the same one stalled overhead. But if the weather had broken, I hadn't seen it. I haven't seen the sun in days. "He had to go in to work for a few hours."

He nods. "What do you think? Can Liz handle opening Double by herself tomorrow?"

Tomorrow's Tuesday, our slowest night.

"Sure." Liz had decided to close the restaurant Saturday night. She'd spent the day calling customers and canceling shifts and deliveries. She told me not to worry, that most of the diners had rescheduled for another night. *Most.* I try to unhook my thoughts from Arden and the hospital and the events lined up before us — hourly nurses' checks, doctors' night rounds, Foley bag emptied, IVs checked and changed out. I find I don't give a damn. I really don't give a damn.

"Wow, Natalie. I didn't think you could be so mellow about this."

If it's a dig, I don't care. "We can't afford to keep it closed."

"Maybe not, but that's not the real problem."

I glance at him and he shrugs. "Haven't you noticed? Liz hasn't been riding the line cook as much. She's not coming in as early and she's not asking as many questions."

I think about that. Vince has always been able to see what people aren't saying. I'm the one with the creative sense. We should have stayed with our strengths. "You think she's looking for another job?"

"Yep."

"Well, that's great timing." I can't help the disappointment. Liz is my friend, but

201

I'm not surprised to learn she's capable of disloyalty. The restaurant business is brutally competitive. You have to look out for yourself, especially if you're female. Ignacio had been loyal, though. All the way through. I miss him. I'd been shocked when Vince told me he'd caught him stealing from us. A single bottle of wine — expensive, true — and I'd been willing to overlook it. Surely Ignacio had had his reasons but Vince had been adamant about firing him. Vince had had to handle it. We both knew I couldn't do it. "I guess we'll work it out."

"I got a call from Mitchell the other day."

I groan. "Don't tell me Liz is going to work for him." Mitchell had been furious when I quit as his executive chef so I could open Double. He didn't speak to me for more than two years.

"Not that I know of."

"Good. I hope she knows better."

"Oh, come on, Nat. He's not so bad."

I give him a look. Vince knows better than most how soul-sucking those five years working for Mitchell had been for me. Mitchell lied. He took shortcuts. He treated people with total disdain. It's not just me. Everyone hates him. Ever since I left, Mitchell hasn't been able to keep an executive chef longer than a year. The last one left after a week. "He is that bad. He's worse."

Vince shrugs. "He seems to know how to run a business."

"It's all going to catch up to him sooner or later. It's just a matter of time."

"Well . . ."

Gabrielle comes around the corner, and Vince stops talking. She's in black today. It makes her skin look like porcelain. "There you are, Vince. I've been looking for you."

Vince immediately straightens. "Rory okay?"

"She's fine." She glances to the cups Vince and I hold, then up to Vince. "I just wondered where you were."

They walk off.

Twenty years ago, when Vince returned from Paris with Gabrielle, I found myself covertly eyeing her, trying to discern what it was that had attracted Vince so powerfully. Was it her exotic accent, her angled cheekbones, and her lovely eyes that flashed with confusion whenever we used an idiom she didn't know? The simple fact that she seemed so completely besotted with him? Or was it something more substantial, her emphatic way of doing things, her single-mindedness and focus, her intellect? A combination of it all? I had no regrets, none at all, as I planned my life with Theo, but still I found myself turning over and over what it was that Vince saw in Gabrielle that he hadn't seen in me. She was so achingly young. I knew Vince's predilection for novelty. I predicted they wouldn't last. But they had.

Which isn't to say things had been fairytale perfect. Gabrielle got silent with disapproval when Vince and I worked late into the night. He complained about having to be home at a certain time, or having to follow her rules about Rory, but there had never been anything serious. Until six months ago when Vince took all our lives, our hopes and dreams, and dashed them sharply against the rocks.

I watch the two of them now walk down the hall, a foot of space yawning between them. They're overly polite with each other. They don't make eye contact. They don't smile at each other. Of course, what has there been to smile about, especially now?

Hours later, Theo lets himself into Arden's room. His jacket's beaded with water; his hair's damp. It must still be raining. He sweeps the curtain behind him, the metal rings rattling. "How's our girl?"

I shut off the flashlight and close my book. "Holding her own."

Theo goes over to her and looks down. "Dr. Morris been by?"

"Earlier." Surrounded by a cluster of white-jacketed people who hovered around Arden's bed, discussing her accident, her admission, her current numbers. "She checked the drain to see if it's why the pressure isn't dropping, but she says it looks fine. She might try increasing the dose again. She wants to consult another colleague before she decides."

"You hear anything from Gallagher?"

"No. What do you think it means?"

"No idea. I'll call him."

Yes. That would be good. I want to hear something, even if it's that he's learned nothing further. I need to know that progress is being made somewhere. "Did you stop by the house?"

He shakes his head. "But I did stop to see the boys at school. They were out for recess." In the dimness, I can see him smile. "Henry was chasing a little girl around the playground. You know what that means."

I did indeed. "Did she have red hair?"

"I didn't notice."

It had to have been Lily. Henry's had a crush on her for months. He's very seriously requested a cell phone of his very own so he can make private calls to her; he's asked

205

me how much engagement rings cost. Oliver is still oblivious of girls, though I'd noticed them jostling to line up beside him for recess. I miss my boys with a sudden and fierce stab of pain. "I should have gone with you."

"I wish you had, but you'd never have left Arden alone."

"I miss the boys."

"We can ask your mom to drive them up for the night. They'd all love it."

We've been over this, back and forth a million times. I look to Arden. "Henry and Oliver can't see her like this. They can't."

"I don't know, Natalie. They're more resilient than you think."

"Maybe." But if I'm to be completely honest with myself, it's me who isn't resilient enough to answer the questions they'd be sure to ask. Letting the boys come now suggests things are far more serious than I can allow myself to believe.

"You've been in here for hours, haven't you?" Theo says. "Go get something to eat. Take your time. I've got this."

This — what is this? This is nothing. This is sitting in a dark room surrounded by machines, talking to myself. This is waiting for a child who might never wake up. She doesn't even smell like Arden anymore. She

206

smells like hospital, sterile and wounded.

I step out into the bright hallway. Emotion swirls around me. I press my hand against the wall.

"Mrs. Falcone?" a nurse calls over. Her face is creased with worry.

"I'm fine," I say, automatically.

In the elevator, I turn on my cell phone. My mom's called, my dad. Christine. Liz. A friend from culinary school, a couple of chefs, our neighbors, someone from the college. So much sympathy. I'll listen to their messages later. The door wheezes open to let in two men wearing white lab coats. They use terms I don't recognize. They sound pompous. They're enjoying displaying their prowess. I want to laugh. *Want to impress me? Save my daughter.*

The elevator doors open and I stop in the hall to phone my mom back.

"Hi," I say, when she answers. "Is everything okay?"

"Oh, yes. The boys are fine. We're having a grand time. I don't think they've eaten a single vegetable in days."

I miss the days when getting my twins to eat vegetables seemed my biggest challenge. "You can grate zucchini into their spaghetti sauce. They'll never know." I do it all the time, slip bits of the less discernible vegetables into their food. Bell peppers I roast to peel off the telltale skin, all sorts of squash, cooked carrots, and spinach chopped fine. "They'll eat celery if you give it to them with peanut butter." Oliver's onto my tricks. He narrows his eyes as he dips his fork into his food but he never says anything. My son and I share an unspoken pact. He doesn't mind vegetables. It's Henry who's the holdout. "How's school going?"

"Oh, fine." My mom's broad midwestern accent sprawls though, the way it does when she's unhappy or stressed. "They were thrilled to see Theo at school today. They couldn't stop talking about it."

"Theo says Henry has a little girlfriend."

"Oh, yes. But we're not supposed to know about that."

"My lips are sealed."

"So how's Arden, honey? Is the medication working?"

"Not yet. The doctor might adjust it."

"The pressure hasn't gone up, right?" This fragile straw of hope. It could be so easily snapped. "That's the important thing. It'll go down. Just give it some more time."

My mother doesn't know. None of us do.

I'm surrounded by peachy beige — the walls, the countertops, the floors — punctuated by aqua. Are these colors supposed to reassure and calm me? They do the opposite. I want lemons and cold milk, purple plums and endive. I crave colors that declare themselves and thrust themselves forward, that sweep me along with their energetic rush. These colors tell me to give up. They tell me that there are bigger things at work and that I might as well sit down on this dirty beach and press my forehead against my folded arms.

"You sound so tired, sweetheart," Mom says. "I don't know how you can sleep in that chair."

I am bone tired, but that's not it. "Theo thinks we should rent a hotel room and trade off." Currently, he and Vince are sleeping on opposite couches in the family waiting room. Gabrielle haunts the corridors; I encounter her sitting in the empty cafeteria or standing by windows looking out into the rain. She isn't sleeping, either. Her devotion has surprised me. Gabrielle's never struck me as the nurturing type. It's not that Gabrielle hasn't paid attention to Rory over the years. She has — in spades — but it always seemed to me more out of a need to do the right thing than because she really enjoyed Rory's company.

"I think that's exactly what you should do," my mother says.

"It's farther away. The hotel across the street is undergoing renovations."

"It's not D.C. Surely it wouldn't take you but a few minutes. You need your rest."

I don't want to talk about it anymore. "Mom," I begin.

"What, honey?"

Someone used paint thinner to set the fire. The police think it was Arden. Theo says she was depressed. Mom will be horrified. She will sit down hard in her chair and put her hand to her throat. She might cry. She might threaten to call my father and have him talk to the detective, which would be useless and might even make things worse. There's nothing she can say that will make me feel better. In the end, I'll be the one struggling to reassure her. "Nothing. Just . . . thanks. Thanks for taking care of the boys."

The cafeteria's largely empty, just a few pairs of people sitting at the round tables. We must be at that in-between time. The hot food and salad bar lines are closed — no doubt the cooks are having a smoke out back and putting up their feet before getting ready for the dinner rush. I select a yogurt floating in a bowl of watery ice and pay for it at the register, the cashier leaning on one elbow to ring me up. I eye the coffee urn and think regretfully of the cup I'd left

210

behind in Arden's room. Whatever was in those big metal urns at this time of day would be thick and bitter.

I find a table and peel the foil from my cup of yogurt. It's blueberry, Arden's favorite. When she was seven, she went through a period where she wouldn't eat anything unless it contained blueberries. Pancakes with blueberry syrup, cereal topped with blueberries, toast smeared with blueberry jelly. *Just like Violet Beauregarde,* I'd told her, wincing as she dropped blueberries into her bowl of minestrone, one by one by one. She'd turned her green eyes to me, wide. *Who?* she'd asked with great interest.

"Mrs. Falcone?" someone asks, and I look up. It's that pink-haired girl whose dorm room is next to Arden and Rory's. Whose dorm room *was* next to Arden and Rory's, I correct myself.

"Hi, D.D."

Just a few short hours ago, I might have assumed she and Arden were friends. Now I'm wary. Now I'm seeing monsters under the bed. *Just look one more time,* Oliver would plead, and I've learned to keep a stuffed animal under there just so I could produce it with a flourish. *It's only Mr. Teddy,* I'd say, and he'd nod, relieved.

D.D.'s wearing skinny jeans and a cropped

top hanging off one shoulder that reveals a few inches of bare midriff. A row of silver hoops dangle along the curve of one ear. Arden had grimaced when one of the servers got her belly button pierced. *Why do people do that?* Arden had muttered to me privately, but now I remember she'd been the one to get a tattoo. "How's Arden? Is she better?"

Surely this means she and Arden were friends. "She's not any worse." This is the most honest answer I've given anyone. It's the bleak fluorescent light overhead shining down on me, laying a firm hand at the base of my neck. It's this slight girl, barely five feet tall. Without her gang of friends around, she seems even smaller. "I'm sorry, D.D., but the girls still can't have visitors."

"That's okay. I had an appointment here anyway. Now I'm waiting for the bus."

She's holding a paper plate with a muffin balanced on it. "Want to join me?" I ask.

She nods, pulls out a chair. "We're holding a vigil Thursday night. Eight o'clock. Do you think you can come?"

"I'll try." So much could happen between now and then.

She glances behind me. "I wish they'd stop playing that."

I turn to see the television set mounted

212

on the wall. The news is on. The screen shows Arden's dorm, smeared with soot and gaping black holes where windows once were. I've been avoiding the TV, ignoring the newspapers abandoned in the family lounge. Now I can't look away.

A flutter of yellow caution tape droops around the perimeter; a drift of stuffed animals and candles and flowers are piled, soggy, by the entrance. I had gone through that door, arms filled with Arden's clothes. I had been focused on hiding my sadness at saying goodbye to my daughter, but she had seen it anyway. She had let me hug her, resting her head against my shoulder. *It'll be okay, Mom,* she'd told me. I'd tightened my arms around her and kissed her cheek. *The good thing about saying goodbye,* I'd whispered in her ear, *is getting to say hello.*

On the screen, Arden's window, the startling vision of a man leaning out, his face covered with a paper mask. He drops an armload of sharp and broken objects into the open-yawed dumpster below. All the pieces of my daughter's room, all the things we'd chosen together to make her transition a happy one — the pumpkin-orange comforter and matching pillow sham, the desk lamp with its reaching arm, the pink rubber shower caddy and bright yellow plastic

213

trash can. Will Arden want to come back to this place? Will she ever feel safe anywhere again?

I turn around, putting my back to the television. I don't need to see any more.

"They won't let us back in, not even to get our things." D.D. picks at her muffin, breaking off pieces of the sugared top and putting them in her mouth. "We're all doubled and tripled up while they find us someplace else to stay for the rest of the year. Our RA says it'll probably be one of those motels on Route 4. I guess that'll be okay. Maid service." She shrugs, looks at me with red-rimmed eyes. Yes, I decide. She and Arden are friends and this has deeply upset D.D. I feel Arden standing behind me, begging me not to do anything to embarrass her and I stop myself from reaching across the table and clasping D.D.'s small hand, lying just inches away. "Arden talks about you all the time, you know," she says. "You own a restaurant, right? She says you make the most amazing macaroni and cheese."

"It's always been her favorite." The first grown-up food I'd ever made for Arden. For months, it was the only thing she'd eat, patiently chasing each bit of pasta around the tray of her high chair with her fingers,

cheese sauce smearing her cheeks and clinging to her hair. If I tried to intercede and
hurry the process along by feeding her with
a fork, she'd thump her heels and howl in
protest.

"I've never eaten homemade anything.
Mrs. Stouffer does the cooking at my
house."

I smile. "I can make you mac and cheese
sometime." Sometime — that imaginary
point in time when I would make food and
bring it to Arden and her friends, stay for a
while, tease them as they dig in, encourage
them to put some vegetables on their plates,
peel back the plastic wrap to reveal the
tower of frosted brownies.

"That'd be awesome. The food here
blows." Her gray eyes are thickly lined in
bright blue; a tiny nose ring glints against
her ivory skin.

"Arden says the same thing." Theo teased
Arden when she complained. *Welcome to
the real world,* he'd told her.

"The only vegetarian thing they know how
to make is salad. They even scramble the
eggs in lard. Arden and I eat a lot of ra-
men."

"Arden's vegetarian?" The girl who loved
my roasted chicken, veal cutlets, liver pâté
smeared on rosemary crackers? Arden had

215

come home for two whole days and never said a word, not even as I pulled things from the refrigerator and set about basting and roasting and chopping. Talking the entire time to dispel the silence between us while she sat at the island and sipped tea. Disappointment about art school, I'd thought. Homesickness, I'd thought.

"She's trying it out. She's not sure she can give up tuna. I told her she could just cut out poultry and beef. That's where the real industry abuse is, anyway."

You must treat animals with respect, my instructor had scolded, looking down at the chicken I was attempting to debone. Everyone had stopped to listen and I had been mortified. After she had moved on, I'd glanced to my right and seen the pristinely sliced portions of chicken shimmering on Vince's cutting board next to mine, plump and perfect, not a vein of fat or tendon to be seen.

"Rory says there are ways around that. She says there are humane farms, but what's humane about raising animals for food?"

Sensible Rory, so very much her mother's daughter. What had Gabrielle seen in D.D. that worried her? I see nothing here but a girl my daughter's age, making choices, figuring things out.

216

D.D. pushes away her plate. "Do the police know who did it yet?"

"I don't think so, but I know they're talking to a lot of people." *Witnesses have come forward.* Maybe this girl? "Have they talked to you?"

"They talked to all of us. They had a big dorm meeting and then this dude took us each into separate rooms." She fiddles with an earring, pushing it in and out. Her features are delicate, gentle swoops, a flutter of eyelashes. Just a child, somebody's child.

"Detective Gallagher?"

"I guess. He told me his name, but . . ." She shrugs.

It hadn't mattered. She had to have been nervous, afraid to say the wrong thing. I know I shouldn't ask, but I do anyway. "What did you talk about?" I keep my voice conversational, casual. I don't let her see the anxiety rippling beneath the surface.

"I don't know. Nothing, really. Just that we're friends; we hang out together."

"That's nice. Arden's talked a lot about you, too," I lie.

She drops her hands to her lap, chews her lower lip. She's thinking.

A clatter behind us, the kitchen crew arriving for setup. I don't turn around. I'm aware only of this young woman sitting just inches away. A bird, gauging the wind for flight. "Detective Gallagher says there was a fire in the girls' room a few weeks ago. I had no idea. Arden never said anything."

She glances up with her smoke-colored eyes. "She didn't?"

"Do you know how it happened?"

A one-shoulder shrug. "I wasn't there."

Which isn't really answering the question. Who is she trying to protect? "The university didn't know anything about it, either."

"No surprise there. Our RA's pretty obtuse. All Arden and Rory had to do was cover the ceiling with scarves and leave the window open for a few days. But he still would've found out at the end of the year. I'm pretty sure you wouldn't have gotten back your security deposit."

I didn't know anything about scarves on the ceiling. When we Skyped, Arden sat with her back against her headboard. All I saw was yellowed oak, painted cinder block, and Arden's face. All I'd wanted to see was her face.

"I wasn't the one who told the police about it, if that's what you're thinking," D.D. says. "I didn't tell them about that fight Rory and Arden had, either. It must have been Whitney. She doesn't know how to keep her mouth shut."

"I know they sometimes argued," I begin, but D.D.'s shaking her head.

"I'm not talking about an argument, Mrs. Falcone. I'm sorry, but I'm not. This was a *fight.* We could hear them yelling all the way down the hall. When we got there, we had to pull Arden off Rory. She was so angry. She really hurt Rory."

"She did?" I say, stupidly.

"Rory was *bleeding.*"

It's impossible. Rain patters against the window in a sudden gust. "I don't understand. Arden's not a fighter. She'd never hurt Rory."

"I don't know what to tell you, Mrs. Falcone. I saw it for myself. I wasn't the only one."

Arden must have felt terrible. The two of them must have really been miserable about the whole thing. Was this what Arden had called to talk about? I should have seen it in her eyes, set down my car keys, shooed the boys into the other room, and pulled up a chair.

"Look, Mrs. Falcone. I know Rory can be a real bitch sometimes, but still. Arden was wrong. I'm sorry, but she was. Very definitely uncool."

"You're right. There's no excuse for hurting someone." *Does* Detective Gallagher know about this? Does he think Arden has a violent streak?

She frowns. "I'm not talking about that."

The conversation has changed direction and I've missed the cues. "Of course not," I say, but it's too late.

D.D. pushes back her chair. "I'm sorry. I shouldn't have said anything."

"No, no, it's okay." But it's not true. "What were they fighting about? Please tell me."

She picks up her plate scattered with crumbled pieces of muffin. "I have to go. I don't want to miss my bus."

My phone vibrates at my hip. I yank it from my pocket. Theo, with news? But it's my mother. "I don't want to alarm you," she says.

ARDEN

Am I awake, or is this a dream? Everything is dark around me.

Images suddenly appear in the distance and swim toward me, flashing past: Hunter's face and the way his mouth turned up the first time he really saw me. Rory staring down at her phone, the perfect line of her profile and the shining ripple of her hair, her lower lip caught between her bright white teeth. *He'll call. He won't call.* Me, sitting in the small crowded shop with my bare arm extended watching the tip of the needle dart in and out. There had been blood, quickly wiped away only to bubble up again. My mom looks horrified when she sees the result. *What did you do, Arden?*

I couldn't help myself.

Hunter's voice rises like smoke in the distance. "Hey, Arden. Hold up." I spin around and there he is, separating himself from a laughing group of guys shoving one another on the sidewalk across the street. He jogs toward me and I wait, self-conscious in my baggy rolled-up sweatpants, my decrepit nylon swim bag slung over my shoulder, my loose hair frizzy and reeking of chlorine. No makeup, my blond brows almost invisible, my lips the palest of pinks. Rory leaning close to the mirror to say, *I'm getting my eyelashes dyed.*

Hunter's been at baseball practice. He has his own gear bag over his shoulder and his curls are shower-damp, his blue eyes friendly. The scent of soap rises from him. "Headed back to your dorm?" That smile. How does Rory stand it? "Want company?"

He's only on his way to see Rory, but my voice goes squeaky. "Sure." Rory's got a special voice for when she talks to boys, her words flowing rich and sweet and slow like maple syrup. I don't know where to look, so I focus on the sidewalk squares and let them lead me along as Hunter talks.

He'd played shortstop in high school, but he'd probably have to start out at second base. His mom would be disappointed. His baseball coach was okay, though he was calling a lot of practices. This morning's pop quiz in art history had been a ringer — what the hell was that lumpy stone thing?

222

"A doorstopper," I say, and he looks at me, surprised, then grins. I duck my head, my cheeks burning. The purple sky's streaked orange, the sun gone with a soft sigh. Yellow lights are popping on everywhere. Charcoal shadows slide across the pale path and disappear into the black grass.

"My dad has a gallery in Baltimore," Hunter says. "You should check it out."

Not even a real invitation, so why is my heart pounding so hard? "What kind of art?"

"Outsider, mostly. You should see our house. My mom swears if he brings home one more thing made of barbed wire, she's making him sleep in the garage. She'd never do it, though."

"Really?" I wish I could see his house, see him walk around in it, claim his space. I've never been in a guy's bedroom. What would it look like, feel like? Rory says Blake's room was disgusting, dishes under the bed, clothes lying everywhere. She said it reeked.

"Never." He groans. "My parents actually like each other."

"I know what that's like. I can't even walk into a room without finding them all over each other." They always kiss goodbye in the morning, even when I'm in the room.

"They couldn't wait for me to leave for college. I'm surprised they didn't just make me take the bus."

"He leaves her love notes on her pillow." I'd lain down on my mom's side of the bed one night to do my homework once and heard the crackle of paper beneath my ear.

"She wears thong underwear." His voice soars high with horror. "I told her please, *please*. Don't make me do the laundry again."

I bend over, I'm laughing so hard. He's laughing, too, and I think, *This — I hadn't even known*. "I'm glad my mom has my dad," I say when I can breathe again. I didn't mean to go there. It just burst out of me. I can't leave that hanging out there sounding dorky, so I add, "She's going to lose her restaurant."

My mom smiling at me on Skype as she leans against my dad, Henry jumping up and down behind the sofa yelling *HiArden-HiArden*, Percy rigidly perched on my mom's knees with his long brown head facing away and his eyes nervously rolling back to track me. I'm laughing at him and cooing and finally he's had it and jumps down. *Aunt Gabrielle was here*, I begin, and my mother's face tightens and I chicken out. I just don't want to tell her that Uncle Vince is moving on and leaving her behind. The easy smile on her face will vanish and she'll have a million questions. *I don't know,* I'll have to tell her, because I don't. It isn't my business anyway. I'm just the one who got caught in the middle of it all. *She brought us dinner,* I ended up adding lamely.

"That blows," Hunter says.

It's stupid to feel sad. Double's just a building with doors and windows, floors covered with anti-skid mats. But it's not. How to explain the spread-open hollowness of it first thing in the morning, an emptiness that draws in on itself as the day wears on, filling with motion and sound and smell until it's a warm, tight fist at night? My mom might have another restaurant someday, but Double's the only place I'd ever seen her look up from what she was doing to smile at me with pure joy.

"Must be awesome having a mom who's a chef."

It's all I know. *What do you think?* my mom will ask, extending a fork on which is balanced a bite of filet, a flake of crab, or a spoon dipped into creamy pea purée. No one ever says what my dad does is cool. It's embarrassing to admit my dad's headmaster at an all-girls school. People kind of avoid talking about it and I can't blame them. Sometimes I'd hear his voice in the hall and duck into the stairwell. He always tries to

225

act cool when he sees me, but he never gets there. His face always changes, brightens, and I feel like a total dweeb. "What does your mom do?"

"Nothing, really. She helps my dad with the gallery. She's never really had a job or anything."

We've reached my dorm. Distant laughter, some kids crossing The Bowl, shadowy shapes. Someone yelps, more laughter. Someone's playing The Killers, too loud. Up against the night sky, the loud yellow rectangular glow of my window. Rory. He stops, staring up.

"You coming up?" I ask.

It's too dark to see his eyes. Is he smiling? He adjusts his bag over his shoulder and I feel the air charge with electricity. Does he feel it, too? He's not saying anything. No one can see us standing right outside my building, right beneath the towering trees. We are hidden from each other. A fraction of silence and then he says, "I've got an early practice tomorrow. Tell Rory I'll catch up with her later, okay?"

Something loosens inside me and floats free. "Yes," I say, knowing I won't. Things are changing. I can feel it. I've walked across campus with Hunter as the sun stretched along the horizon, setting everything on fire, and it had been enough for him, too. I stand motionless, waiting for it all to swirl around me and fly.

RORY

Chelsea Lee's wearing maroon today, a fitted leather jacket over a matching silky top. It's an outdated color. She looks right past me as she walks to the lectern at the front of the auditorium, then her gaze skitters back and holds. Hunter slides into the seat beside me and I turn to him and smile. "Miss me?" he says. He's acting cool, but I've seen him walking past my dorm and looking up at the window. He does it all the time. Is it a little creepy?

After class, I stroll down the steps to where Chelsea's gathering her slides and talking to students. I lean against a desk with my arms crossed and wait for the last student to leave, a girl with limp, ashy-brown hair that waves down to the middle of her back. Sad, really.

Chelsea knows I'm here, but she doesn't look over. She doesn't hurry the girl along, either, even though she's just rattling on about Romanesque architecture. Finally, Chelsea pats the girl on the shoulder and turns to me. "Rory?"

I unfold myself. "You said you'd think about it."

"And I have." She switches off the little lamp on the lectern. Is she going to say anything? She's just like my mom, timing her edicts. It sets my teeth on edge. It makes me want to ball my hands into fists, but living with my mom's taught me a few tricks, like faking patience when all I want to do is grab her stupid maroon leather shoulders and shake her. "Why don't you walk with me back to my office and we'll talk."

Hunter's waiting for me in The Bowl. Things have been a little weird between us lately. He'll be upset when I don't show up, though he won't say anything the next time I see him. He'll just look at me with puppy dog eyes. But I say, "Sure."

I follow her up the worn carpeted stairs to the back of the room, where she reaches for the light switch and flips off the overhead lamps one by one by one. The room falls into darkness as she holds open the door for me.

It's a pretty afternoon, the trees turning colors. Kids are everywhere, walking to class, playing Frisbee, working on their tans.

When our parents dropped us off, Aunt Nat had been excited about how nice the campus looked with all the trees and grassy lawns and brick buildings, but my mother had been silent. What she'd been looking for was harder to see.

"Explain to me why you object to writing a paper for this class." She's slid on her aviator sunglasses again, mirrored ovals that throw twin images of my frowning face back at me.

I smooth my features into my usual mask. "It wasn't listed in the class description online. I wouldn't have signed up for your class if I'd known."

"Part of attending college is learning to adjust and accommodate. And, frankly, I'm surprised it's an issue for you, Rory, given that you're a Bishop girl. Certainly you've written your share of papers in high school. I'm sure you can handle a full roster of term papers at EMU."

She's looked me up. What else has she learned? "Does that mean you haven't changed your mind?"

"It's not fair to the other students for me to make an exception for you."

"It's not fair to *me.*"

"Is there something else going on?"

"Like what?" Her eyes are covered, but

she can see right through me, I'm sure of it. I wait for her to call me on my shit, but instead she says, "You do know you could drop this class. It's not too late."

I'm majoring in math. I'd spent all spring convincing my mother it would make me stand out to law schools and she'd pored over the course descriptions, Googled each professor, talked to her friends at her tennis club. She crafted the perfect schedule for me and she'd insist on knowing why I wanted to drop this class. My father would just agree with whatever she decided. But I'm already taking freshman English, a required class I can't get out of. Eight papers strung over the course of the year, and I've calculated the number of hours I'll need to devote to each one. A midterm and a final paper for this class means I'll have to take time away from my other classes. It means a B instead of an A. "And replace it with Woodworking 101?"

She glances away, but not before I see her small smile. "I've corrected last week's pop quiz," she says, and I think, *Here we go.* "It was tough, I know. I threw in a couple of questions on material we haven't covered yet. I forced everyone to think outside the box. There was only one perfect grade. Yours." She turns her mirrored eyes back to me, and this time I see the surprise on my face I can't hide. How had that happened? I've never once gotten a perfect score on a timed test.

"Look, Chelsea," I say, and she hikes up an eyebrow.

"Professor Lee."

Whatever. "Does that mean you'll reconsider?"

"It means I won't have to. Let me know what you decide about dropping the class."

She walks away, leaving me standing on the path. She's wearing spectator pumps with a square heel. She wouldn't have lasted three seconds at Bishop.

I'm on my bed with D.D., an unlit bong teetering on the comforter rucked up between us. I play with Aunt Nat's slim silver lighter. I've gotten good at thumbing up the tiny spurt of flame. I am determined to conquer this.

D.D. has more weed in a Baggie, and I'm trying to remember how much is in there. I could have asked her, but she's talking, so I just let the picture of the plastic Baggie hover in front of my face. A teaspoon? A tablespoon? Fuck Hunter. Fuck everyone. I push the Baggie aside and stare at the crappy ceiling and wonder why there are always holes in acoustic tiles.

"Sorry," D.D.'s saying. "I mean, I know she's your cousin and all, but she's such a dweeb."

The doorknob turns and Arden comes in. D.D. immediately stops talking. I choke down laughter. We don't dare look at each other.

Arden dumps her backpack on her chair and gives me a dirty look. "You can smell that all the way down the hall." She fans her nose with her hand.

"My bad." D.D. cackles, like she's done something rude. I crack up, and then so does she. The bong topples over, splashing dirty water all over us. D.D. squeals and kind of rolls away, and we just laugh harder.

"Seriously?" Arden says. "The RA's up here all the time. You'll be in real trouble if he finds out."

"Yeah," I say. "Because we don't have enough for him."

"Oh, my God," D.D. says and gasps. "It's so true."

We're clutching our stomachs with laughter.

"You're such children." Arden kneels on her bed to shove the window sash up along its tracks.

"Happy children," D.D. says. "Happy,

happy, happy."

I put my head back weakly against the headboard. Weed isn't Arden's thing, but I hold out the bong and wiggle it. "It's good," I promise, but Arden shakes her head. "No, thanks." D.D. slides me a little glance that says *See?*

I shrug. She has a point. But I'm not giving up on my little cousin just yet. "Get this. Kyle asked D.D. out."

"Second-floor Kyle?" Arden asks. We only know one Kyle. She's just buying time to try to figure things out. D.D. confuses her. For someone who's so messy, Arden strangely likes things mentally labeled and organized. D.D. doesn't fit in a box. She's kind of a train wreck, already on her third guy and just as many girls. There's no label you can slap on D.D.

"Yep."

Arden glances to D.D. "So . . . congratulations?"

D.D. sighs. "Kyle's okay, but he's no Hunter."

"Don't talk to me about Hunter," I say. "Jerk."

"He can't help that he has practice all the time."

The only time he's not around is when he's playing baseball. Otherwise, he's always there. And even when he's not there, I'm always looking around, nervous that he's about to turn the corner and walk smiling toward me. "I wish that were the problem," I say, and Arden glances over at me. "What?" I challenge her, and she looks away.

"I thought you and Hunter were getting along."

"Doing it isn't the same as getting along," I tell her, and she blushes.

"Ooh, what's the matter?" D.D. asks me in a fake way. "Are you over him? Can I have him?"

"Sorry. But Arden has dibs."

I expect Arden to turn bright red with embarrassment, but she surprises me. "Thanks so much, but I'll pass. There won't be anything left once you're through with him."

"Guys," D.D. says. "You have to help me decide about Kyle. Should I go out with him or not? No more random hooking up. I'm getting a rep."

"Too late," I say. D.D. tosses a pillow and I duck.

Arden's opening and closing her dresser drawers loudly. She's not looking at us. It's so obvious she wants D.D. to leave. "What are you looking for?" I ask. It's her fault she can never find any of her things.

"My bathing suit."

"Your orange bikini? I think I saw it on the floor of your closet."

"My blue tank."

"Your old swim-team suit? Seriously." That horrible one-piece she'd worn way back in ninth grade that flattened her boobs and rode too high on her hips. I'd suggested she sew in bra cups and she'd retorted, *I'm swimming laps, not trying out for* America's Next Top Model. But I'd seen her finger the material thoughtfully.

"I don't care. It still fits."

I don't want to argue with her. Let her wear the stupid thing if she wants to. I'm feeling mellow. I want the world to smile with me. "How was work? Your first shift, right?"

"It was all right." Arden rocks back on her heels and scowls at the pile of clothes heaped in her closet. She's got that stiffness in her voice that tells me she'd hated every minute. Well, what did she expect? It's a crappy job and it's not like college kids tip.

She should forget her stupid suit and come sit with us, wriggle in to find a spot and tell us everything. *It sucked,* she should say. *My manager's a perv.* D.D. would have warmed right up and everything would have been cool, but Arden's weird around people she doesn't know. She doesn't know how to fake it.

"You have a job?" D.D. says. "Doing what?" Now she's being weird. It's not like she cares. She's never worked. She doesn't even know what minimum wage is.

"Making smoothies at the student union." Arden looks at me. "They still have openings, you know."

"I bet they do." Arden's worried about how I'm going to pay for books and things, but I hate being in the kitchen; I was always begging my dad to let me do things like pleat napkins into triangles or carve butter into balls of yarn. *You sure, honey?* he'd say, holding out a frying pan. *Just give it a try.* But I never did. Besides, my dad sent me money — worn tens and twenties fattening up the envelope I'd held in my hand, feeling the soft thickness and guessing what it contained.

"Smoothies, yum," D.D. says. "I'm starving."

"Hold on." I slide off my bed and kneel to pull out the bin beneath Arden's bed filled with the snacks Aunt Nat left us. My mom frowned as Aunt Nat dumped in the crackers and cookies. *Really, Natalie,* my mom had said. *Really, Gabrielle,* Aunt Nat had firmly replied. Arden and I had looked at

237

each other across the room. I root around the crumpled packages, find an opened bag of Goldfish, and shake it. A few crumbs rattle around inside. "Sorry, dude. All we have left are multivitamins and cough syrup." Even that's mostly gone.

"Tempting." D.D. pushes herself up. "But I got to go anyway. See you at the game tomorrow?"

"If Hunter ever gets around to calling."

"He will," D.D. says. "He's your love slave." She pauses by the door. "See you later, Arden?"

"Sure."

"Why do you do that?" I ask Arden, after the door closes.

"Do what?"

"Ignore her. She likes you, you know. She wants to be your friend." Not true, but possible.

"Oh, yeah. I definitely get that vibe from her."

"You know she can get you your stuff."

"I'm fine." She's lying. I've checked her stash. She has only fifteen Adderall left, barely a week's worth. "That why you hang out with her?" she asks. "Is she your supplier?"

She's pissed. Maybe something happened at work. Who knows? "D.D.'s fun," I said, though that's not it. D.D.'s dangerous. I'd recognized her the instant she looked me up and down, gauging — just another Bishop bitch. The type you either befriended or watched out for. "If you want people to like you, you have to, you know, *talk* to them."

"I don't need your help making friends. We're not in high school anymore."

"No. We're not." I lean forward to apply a slick of lip gloss, and when I lean back she's lit a candle and placed it on the windowsill. The flame's huge, a million times bigger than the tiny one of my lighter. It's curling and shivering, hungry. I look quickly away, but the aroma of honey and lavender wafts toward me. She's done it just to piss me off. I begin to sweat, but I act cool. I twist the cap onto the tube. "But that doesn't change anything." I don't look at the candle. I put it right out of my head. Instead, I watch Arden in the mirror. She has her back to me, but I see the stubborn line of her shoulders. "I heard Ignacio had to go back to Mexico." A lie. For all I know, he's in New York, making way more than he ever did at Double.

I'd been there when my dad called Ignacio into his office and closed the door. My dad never closed his office door. I sidled over, pretending to be interested in the schedules pinned to the board, but it was quiet inside. A few minutes later, Ignacio opened the door and walked over to his station. I watched him slide his knives into his case, and that was when I knew. He should have pitched a fit. He should've threatened to bring in a lawyer, demanded proof, witnesses, the whole thing, but he hadn't. When he turned around, he caught me watching him. The look in his eyes told me he thought he knew what had happened. I almost told him then.

"I'm going to tell my mom," Arden says. "It doesn't matter now anyway."

It does matter. It will always matter, in Arden World. "Sure, go ahead. Tell her all about it. Here, use my phone. I'll dial it for you."

"Don't," she says, panicked.

Behind her, I see it: the orange flame crawling up the side of the curtain. My skin pops up in a million bumps of gooseflesh. My throat closes. I can't breathe. I can't move.

"What?" Arden whirls around. "Shit!"

She grabs a towel from the floor and swings it with both hands. I don't know why she tries. The fire's going to win. It always does. The curtain billows away from the window, sending up a shower of tiny sparks.

"Rory!"

Flames are everywhere, a writhing mass of orange and yellow and furious red.

"Help me!" Arden's teetering on her bed, smacking at the wall with a notebook. An ember spirals through the air to land on her pillow and disappear from sight.

Shrieking all around us. I press my palms against my ears and put my forehead against my crossed arms. I squeeze my eyes shut, making fireworks explode.

I told you, no! My own voice, crying.

The shrieking noise stops.

I lift my head. Arden's climbing down from her desk chair. The smoke detector gapes open above her head, wires snaking out. She picks up the smoking towel from her bed and hurls it out through the open window. A shout from below. "Sorry!" she yells out. "Sorry!"

Someone's banging on our door. "We're fine," Arden calls. "It's okay." She sinks onto the floor, breathing hard, and stares up at the ceiling, at the smoke smudged there. "Shit."

I crawl over, the rug rubbing my knees, and come in close, arm to arm, thigh to thigh. She brings her foot close and examines the sole from where she stepped on an ember, twists her hand from side to side, examining it. "You okay?" I ask, a hoarse whisper.

She nods, sags against the wall. I lean against her and she puts her arm around my shoulders and draws me close. Her skin is warm, sticky with sweat. I feel my heart pounding, and hers. I can't tell which is which.

"I can't do this forever, Rory," she says, finally, and I sigh. "I mean it. What happens when you go to Harvard? Or when you get a job?"

"I know. I just need your help with this one. I promise." I rest my head against her shoulder and she presses her cheek against the top of my head.

"Okay. But no more."

I'm still holding Aunt Nat's lighter. It's cold in my grasp.

NATALIE

Janey's mother phoned all the parents. She was apologetic, telling my mother she'd had no idea Janey had chicken pox the day of her birthday party. *I thought it was just a mosquito bite. Please tell me the twins have had it.* But they haven't and I hadn't yet gotten them vaccinated against it. How would my mother manage if they get sick? *I'll be fine,* she insisted. *After all, I saw you and your sister through it.* But that had been thirty years ago. We've Skyped with the boys, balancing Theo's laptop on the coffee table in the visitors' lounge. Their wide-eyed faces, so close to the screen. I yearned to reach out to stroke their rounded cheeks and ruffle their blond hair to make it stand up. *You be good for Grandma,* Theo had told them, and they'd earnestly nodded. *We have to look for spots,* Oliver had said. *That's right,* I replied. *You tell Grandma the minute you see one.* But a sly look had slid across

Henry's face. He could be a little secretive. He was always snatching the phone when it rang and talking to whoever was on the other end, even if it was a telemarketer or an automated reminder call from the doctor's office. *Henry,* I said in a warning tone, but Theo had seen it, too. *I know we can count on you both to be the men of the house while we're gone,* he'd said. It was, of course, the right tack. Henry's very proud of being the older twin. It doesn't matter to him that it's only by four minutes.

I'd told Theo what D.D. had said about the horrible fight Arden and Rory had had, and how it had even gotten physical, and he'd been quiet for a long while. Finally, he'd asked, *What do you think, Nat? Does any of this make sense to you?* I don't know. All the things I thought I knew were slipping between my fingers. My hands are empty.

I'd planned to take this last summer before Arden left for school to do all the touristy things we never had time for: go to the National Gallery and the Hirshhorn, the Folk Art Festival, have a picnic on the Mall while fireworks showered colors overhead. But none of it happened. The bills poured in. The lawyers phoned. Customers drifted away. I did the only thing I could: I spent more and more hours at Double and let the summer go, sweeping my daughter away with it. She'd never once even casually mentioned wanting to get a tattoo. She'd become a vegetarian and I'd roasted her a chicken for her birthday dinner. Gabrielle might know whether the girls had been fighting, but she would have mentioned this, wouldn't she?

It's Monday evening. Arden's been lying in that hospital room for three nights and three days, unmoving. We're on our way back from the hotel where we've checked in to a room with a plasma TV and a dismal view of the highway. It's adjacent to the EMU campus and the girl at the front desk had cheerfully asked if we were there to visit an EMU student. I took a real shower and Theo was supposed to take a quick nap, but instead he's been on the phone the entire twenty minutes we've allotted ourselves to be away from Arden. It doesn't feel safe to leave her alone. Or right. Though of course she's never really alone. There's an intensivist, a neurosurgeon, an orthopedic surgeon, three residents, a fellow, two respiratory therapists, a pharmacist, a dozen nurses, maybe more, taking care of her. Still, it doesn't feel *enough*.

"Please tell me you've had chicken pox," I

implore when Theo finally hangs up from another phone conversation with Karen, the assistant headmistress. All hell has broken loose. Three students have been accused of plagiarism — right in the middle of college interviews and applications — and Theo's been fielding phone calls from angry parents. I've heard them squawking on the other end of the line.

He glances toward me. "You bet," he says, falsely cheerful. "I've had all the usual childhood diseases. Mumps, mono, the flu, whooping cough. I've even had my appendix removed."

Thank God. I need him here. Arden needs him, too, whether or not she's awake to know he's there, so when he tells me he might have to go to work the next day, I swivel in my seat to face him. "No!" He's already been gone one long day. A second one feels like too much.

"Just for a few hours. The board's calling a meeting and I have to be there. Tell you what. I'll take the night shift tonight and you sleep in the hotel. I'll be back before you know it."

"What if you're not here and something happens? Who cares if these kids cheated? Just have them retake the test or something."

246

"I can't do that, Nat, and you know it."

What I know is that he *could* do it if he wanted to. "Let Karen handle it. That's what assistants are for. I'm letting Liz run Double." Which was a far trickier proposition, if you asked me. Karen could put things on hold if she had to; Liz had one shot at making diners happy.

"It's better if I spearhead this thing. And while I'm there, I could run by the house to check on the boys and make sure your mother's holding up. Get you another change of clothes."

"The boys are fine. I just talked to them." I hear the relief in his voice and that's what's really bothering me. He's looking forward to getting away from the bleak hospital vigil we've been keeping, even if it's for the worst of reasons. Even if I could, I'd never leave. I'm tethered to Arden and he should be, too. He should *want* to be. "I can't believe you think someone else's child is more important than ours."

A convenience store stands on the corner, its windows garishly lit. I should ask Theo to pull over so I can run in for something while he waits. Licorice, lip balm. Cigarettes.

"I don't think that and you know it, Nat. But I can help at Bishop. Sitting around

247

here, I feel useless."

"You're not useless. You're helping *me.*" I look at his profile. He doesn't answer.

There's a nurse beside Arden's bed. Even before I enter the room, I can tell from her general build that it's Denise. I know all the nurses now. I've admired the photographs of their children and grandchildren, their dogs and their cats, heard their hopeful stories of other patients who were way worse off than Arden and are now running a business, starting a family, finishing school at the top of their classes. They've all been kind, but I'm especially glad when Denise is on duty. She smiles at Arden; she takes an extra moment to shake out and gently smooth the sheets. The other nurses do their jobs — nothing to correct or complain about — but their hearts aren't in it.

"Hi, you two." Denise reaches for the tube protruding from the bandages wrapped around my daughter's skull and clicks on her flashlight. "How was the hotel?"

I don't go anywhere without telling the nurses where I am going, even if it's to the restroom. They have my cell number, but what if I don't hear it ring? What if there's no signal? I go over to Arden, stand at the foot of the bed. Nothing has changed. We've been gone forty-seven minutes and it's as though we never left. Is this my future, staring at my daughter's slack face, holding on to her hand that doesn't hold mine back?

"The usual," Theo answers. "Though they did have an interesting selection in the mini-bar." Theo and I are still annoyed with each other. In a minute, I know, he will abruptly sit in the chair by the door and pull his briefcase toward him, dive back into work.

"Let me guess," Denise says. "Five bucks for a bag of pretzels."

"Seven, but these had cheese inside them."

"A bargain." She's still standing there, studying the gauge attached to Arden's skull. The alarm in my head starts buzzing. She should be moving over to the other monitors by now. "What's the matter?" I ask. "Is everything okay?"

"I'm not sure." She reaches into her pocket and pulls out a cell phone. "Just a minute, please," she tells us. Theo comes over to stand beside me. *This is it, just like this?* She speaks into the phone. "Dr. Morris? This is Denise. Yes, I wanted to tell you that Arden Falcone is showing an elevated pressure reading." A pause. "Twenty-four." Another pause. "Yes. Yes. Okay." She has the phone pressed between her ear and shoulder and she is brisk movement, going from machine to machine and pressing buttons. "Thank you, Doctor." She slides the phone into her pocket. She removes her latex gloves and drops them into the trash, pulls down a fresh pair from the box attached to the wall, returns to the head of Arden's bed.

"Denise," I say. "What's going on?"

"I'm draining some fluid. Don't worry. This is painless."

She's being kind. Arden can't feel anything, can she? I can't see what Denise is doing. I don't want to. I stand back with Theo. At last she straightens. She is holding a small plastic bag and I avert my eyes. I suddenly feel nauseated. Me, who once gutted a pig. "I'll be right back," she says, but I don't want her to leave. What if something happens? "I need to enter these orders into the computer system."

"Then what?"

"We should know something soon, ten minutes, maybe fifteen."

"Are you coming back?"

Denise has her hand on the curtain. "Absolutely. And Dr. Morris is on her way."

The curtain swishes shut behind her.

Theo puts his arm around me.

"We're here," I tell Arden.

"We're right here," Theo says softly.

She doesn't move. She doesn't make the slightest sound.

When Arden was two, she'd tumbled into a friend's swimming pool during a family barbecue. No one noticed until another child came running. The teenager who was supposed to be watching Arden had gotten distracted, running after a beach ball that had rolled into the neighbor's yard. I turned from where I stood with Theo and the other parents and through the metal bars of the fence surrounding the pool saw my daughter, completely submerged with just her fingertips showing.

I couldn't get around the fence quickly enough. I couldn't get to Arden. She had been the one in trouble, but I had been the one shrieking the words.

Help me.

ARDEN

Smoke crawls down my throat. *Fire!* I sit bolt upright, coughing. Then everything swims into focus. I'm in my dorm room, in my bed. I'm safe.

I fall back against my pillow and wait for my heart to stop pounding.

A rainbow of filmy scarves crisscrosses the ceiling, hiding the blackened tiles. *We should just replace them,* I'd said, worried about our damage deposit. *Oh, sure,* Rory had replied. *That'll happen. We can drive to the building supply store during lunch.* She'd yanked open a dresser drawer and pulled out a handful of bright silk — magenta, gold, turquoise, chartreuse, cornflower blue. *We'll tell the RA we're going for the Buddhist temple effect.* Yeah, if Buddhists were into Hermès. We didn't have thumbtacks so we used tape. In the middle of the night, I'd yelped when one came loose and floated down, tickling my arm. Rory hadn't even rolled over. I thought I knew her better than anyone, but living with her has revealed a few things. Like how she keeps the bookshelf above her bed empty, piling all her textbooks on the floor beneath her bed. Like how she has to sleep on her side facing the door and startles awake every time someone walks past. *At least I don't snore,* Rory retorted. But she does that, too, a little.

One second the curtains were there; the next second they were gone. It had been so scary. The shrieking of the smoke detector had made me want to run from the room. Rory had just curled up in a ball, useless. I'd been furious with her until I saw her face.

I look over at her, peacefully sleeping. Second night in a row she's stayed home. In class yesterday, Hunter had beckoned me over to sit beside him and I had slid into the seat feeling claimed while Rory sat on the other side, doodling in her notebook. *Is this how it happens?*

At the library, I pull down book after book from the shelves. Professor Lee wanted us to consult real sources, not just online stuff. I was planning to write about Giotto, but obviously I can't write two papers on him. As I reach up to slot a book back into place, smoke wafts toward me. Me, or my clothes?

I pull out a length of hair and sniff.

Lunch? Rory texts, and I bundle books into my backpack. She's saved me a seat across from her and Hunter, and beside D.D. Rory flashes me a quick smile as I set down my tray, but it's not convincing. It doesn't reach inside her.

"Hey," Hunter says. "We were just talking about you."

My face flames. I duck my head and let my hair fall forward. *Why do you even hang out with Hunter?* I'd asked Rory, because he's so not her type. Usually, she dates rich jocks with huge biceps who think beer is a food group. She'd looked thoughtful before replying. *I've never dated a baseball player before.* He's just an experiment to her. Why can't he see that?

"Tell us the truth. You're the one who aced Lee's quiz, aren't you?" Professor Lee had stood in front of the classroom, chiding us. *I don't grade on a curve, people,* she'd said. *So you'd better knuckle down.* "Come on, don't be shy."

Don't be shy, Aunt Gabrielle always tells me. *You have to look people in the eye. Otherwise, they'll think you're being rude.* I try to be as brave as Rory, who marches up to strangers and boldly extends her hand.

They always smile back.

"Wasn't me." I'd stared at the computer screen, confused. How could I have missed three questions? I thought I knew the material.

"Huh. Must be the emo girl who sits in the front row." He sits back and slings his arm around Rory's shoulders. She doesn't react, just keeps texting. "Who knows?" she says. "It's a big class. Could be anyone."

She's being so quiet. *Doing it isn't the same as getting along.* Maybe she's tired of Hunter. Maybe he's realizing they don't have as much in common as maybe he and I do.

People at the table behind us are talking loudly.

". . . need to hear this song I just found. It's a band that's performing next week."

"Bathtub Mannequins?"

"Yeah. They're so sick."

"I don't know. I think they're weird."

"That's because you're an idiot."

"Oh, okay. Glad everyone is in such a friendly mood today."

"Do you guys have tickets?"

"No, I'm going by the auditorium after lunch."

"They're probably sold out."

"Really? I don't think they're even that

255

big of a name."

"Every small, strange band is a big name here."

I sneak a peek at Hunter. He's holding his sandwich and leaning forward to make his point. He'd felt it, too, that moment walking back from the sports center — hadn't he? He catches me looking and grins. My heart beats faster.

"Hey, Arden?" D.D. says. "You going to eat those?" She points to the fries on my plate and I shake my head. She plucks a fry free and dips it in the pond of ketchup I'd squeezed onto my plate, which is gross. It feels invasive. She brings a code with her I can't decipher. She makes me feel awkward and slow. She's the college version of Mackenzie, only with bright pink hair.

Rory's right. I don't have many pills left. *Quit* is at the very top of my list. I'm not ready, though. Maybe in a month, maybe after finals. I've texted the guy I used to get my stuff from, a junior from the boys' school whose parents are plastic surgeons. *Can you mail a refill?* He'd texted right back. *Sure except it's a FELONY.* I'd stared at my phone. So this was where he drew the line? Like selling prescription meds wasn't? *It'll b ok,* I texted, but it's been four days and I still haven't heard back.

256

Rory and Hunter go one way, and D.D. and I head back to the dorm. I watch their two receding figures, trying to decide if he's leaning in to her or the other way around, then turn to D.D. Why is she spending so much time with Rory and me? Why doesn't she find someone else to hang around with? "How come I haven't seen Whitney lately?" Shouldn't D.D. be spending time with her own roommate instead of trying to steal mine?

She gives me a look that tells me she knows why I'm asking. "Ask her."

D.D. could hook me up. Rory says she can get her hands on anything, but I don't trust D.D. I don't know why, but I don't. Still, I ask, "Can you get me some Adderall?"

She doesn't even look at me, but she's smiling. "How many?"

"Thirty." Thirty will carry me to Thanksgiving break.

"Okay, sure. No problem."

"How much?"

A tick of time. "Twenty."

"Twenty *each*?" I stare at her, but she's got her profile to me. "I used to pay ten."

"Because you were fucking your dealer?"

I want to whirl around and stomp off in a different direction. I want to be anywhere but right here, walking down the sidewalk with this repulsive girl. But I stop myself. I won't let her see she's reached me. "I can't do twenty." Six hundred dollars. I don't have anywhere near that kind of money. I could work every day until Thanksgiving and I wouldn't come close to clearing that much. "Can't you cut me a break?"

"Sorry."

Which tells me we're not friends. Which tells me we'll never be friends. Not that I was hoping. "I guess Rory was wrong about you."

She glances at me now. Her gray eyes are wide-spaced. They make her look so innocent. Flames flicker at the sides of her face. Her skin is glowing. *Listen,* she says. *I need to tell you something about Hunter.*

RORY

Do not even *think* about putting candles on my birthday cake. Don't ask me to a bonfire at the beach, and you can just forget about ski lodges with their huge stone fireplaces. The two fireplaces in our house have to stay cold and empty. Sometimes, though, my parents light a fire when I'm not around. They put it out before I get back, but I can always tell. That ashy smell hits me the minute I walk in the door and makes my chest tighten so I can't breathe. It's because I got burned when I was little. Burned badly. Arden gave me her pink blanket later. A secret, because nobody knows she still slept with it; nobody knows I sleep with it now.

"Are you sure we'll have time?" Arden stuffs books into her backpack. "The bus leaves at noon tomorrow." She sounds so hopeful.

"The shop opens at ten," I tell her, and

she sighs.

She's late for art class and she hasn't brushed her hair. She hasn't said a word about the fire. In the morning, on the way to class, I saw her blue towel — at least, the charred bits of her towel — draped forlornly on the bushes beneath our window.

I toss her a hairbrush and she catches it with both hands.

"You checked this place out?" She swipes quickly at her hair and drops the brush with a clatter on the dresser.

"Yup."

She opens the door and gives me one last pleading look. "Cut it out, Arden. I want this." I've wanted this for eight years, more than I've wanted anything. Even more than Harvard. The door closes behind her and I hear her trudging footsteps in the hall slowly fade away.

"I'm glad to see you decided to stick with it," Chelsea Lee says to me after class, which pisses me off. It's not about giving up. I'm not a quitter, anyone would tell you that. Quitters don't get into size-zero jeans by spring break. Quitters don't date Blake Henderson for four months, and quitters don't get into Harvard.

"I've still got a week to decide," I retort,

260

and a corner of her mouth twitches up.

"Guess I've just been served. Come on. I'll buy you a cup of coffee, or whatever your favorite poison is."

Freshmen don't have coffee with professors. So there you go again — not a quitter.

The coffee shop's warm and dark, with lots of quirky little tables and mismatched chairs. It smells of coffee and cinnamon and warm milk. We carry our drinks to a table by the window. She stirs sugar into her cup, pours in a splash of cream that spirals around the black surface before sinking down and going invisible. I tear open a package of sweetener and she hikes an eyebrow. "That stuff's bad for you."

"Everything's bad for you." I blow on the surface of my coffee before taking a sip.

"Nice ring. Unusual."

I hold out my hand and study the engraved gold band. Same clunky style as when Bishop had been founded more than a hundred years ago, back when you sealed letters with blobs of molten wax and pressed the face of your ring down hard. All over the country there are Bishop women wearing this same exact ring. "My class ring."

"The privileges of a private school."

She makes it sound like a bad thing. "I earned this ring."

261

"I'm sure you did."

She can't know. She can't possibly know. I glance at her, but she's sipping her coffee. "You did a great job in class today." Her cheeks are pink, her eyes bright. She looks happy. I like this version of her. It's much better than the stern one who stands at the front of the classroom with her head cocked and her hands on her hips. That one reminds me too much of my mother. "You have a real eye, you know. Not many people do."

She'd put up the slide and then, out of all the students waving their hands, called on me. I'd been reaching over to scribble something in Hunter's notebook when I heard my name. She'd had to repeat the question and a few people laughed. *How do you think the painter used light to define this space?* I'd straightened in my seat, scanned the image on the screen, and then started talking. The words had just poured out. Hunter had leaned back to watch me, and some girl had turned around in her seat to stare at me. I'd hiked an eyebrow at her and she quickly turned back around, but how could I blame her, really? Girls like me don't talk in class. That's for the emo chick who sits slumped in the front row, chewing her fingernails and reeking of patchouli.

"My cousin's the artist. Arden. She's taking your class, too." Arden's the reason I'd signed up for the class in the first place. We'd been on her pontoon boat, rocking gently on the water, going through the catalog. *She'd* been going through the catalog, actually. I'd been lying on my back, trying to angle my stomach into the sun. *This one looks interesting,* she'd said, and I'd pushed myself up on one elbow to see.

"You don't have to be an artist to be able to analyze a work of art," she says.

It had felt amazing, talking so easily about the way a person's eye followed the lights and darks in the fresco. How could I understand something like that without even trying? It's not as though I've ever taken anything but the basic art classes at Bishop — jewelry-making, pottery — the ones I'd had to take in order to graduate. Still, who cares? It's not like it matters. It won't get me anywhere. It's like being able to pitch Ping-Pong balls into Flower Mart buckets, each landing with a satisfying plop. All you got for it was a lame stuffed animal. "I'm going to law school. So I doubt I'll be analyzing many works of art."

"I wouldn't have pegged you as a lawyer."

Meaning what, that I'm not smart enough? "Why not?"

"You know how many papers you have to write in law school?"

I don't need this. She can't buy me with a cup of coffee. I push back my chair and she reaches out, puts her long slim fingers on mine for a brief moment. A flash of knowing, and then her hand's gone, back to circle her cup. I can't move. "Tell me, Rory. Seriously. I want to know. Why law school? Of all the things you could pursue, why that?"

No one's ever asked me that. My saying it's my plan is usually enough to stop them.

"Is it because you want to be a champion for the downtrodden, a righter of wrongs? Or maybe you just want to rack up billable hours and put in an eternity pool?"

Snarky bitch. Law school's just two words that add up to three years on top of college. Seven years of my life planned and programmed. Seven years where I don't have to ask the hard questions, and if I try to look too far into the future, everything blurs. I wake up every morning with a panicky feeling that makes me throw back the covers and sit straight up. Then I think, *Why?* The plan isn't the problem, I know. The problem's me. "What's wrong with being a lawyer?"

"Nothing. Someone has to be one. Why not you?"

She doesn't know me. She doesn't know anything about me. "Like someone has to teach art history?"

"Exactly. And someone has to pick up the garbage, deliver the mail."

"I'd rather go to law school."

She smiles. "Just wait until you're halfway through your first year. Then we'll talk."

It feels good, making her smile. Powerful. I feel the scales lift and rock back into balance. "So how come you're teaching 101? I thought it was supposed to be someone named Llewellyn." Her name hadn't been the one listed in the catalog. Her profile isn't even on the college website.

"He had to take an unexpected leave of absence. I was hired at the last minute. Lucky for me. I'd been looking for months." She'd been teaching in Chicago, but a relationship turned bad and one of them had to split town. "I lost the coin toss." She shrugs. I can't tell if she's sad or not, but I can't believe she's talking to me like this. I can't tell how old she is. Not as old as my mom, but older than Liz, the prep cook at Double. So maybe thirty. But I bet the guy she'd been dating was older. Someone smart, funny, not necessarily good-looking. Someone who tucked in his shirt and wore bow ties and made her fondly sigh and shake her head. I wonder what had happened to make them break up. Maybe she'd gotten tired of the bow ties. Maybe he'd decided to go back to his wife.

"Guys suck," I say. They only want one thing.

"Hmm." She rotates her cup between her hands. She wears a silver ring on her thumb; her nails are all plain. "Maybe you just haven't found the right one."

"Maybe." I glance at my phone, see the time. "I have to run. Thanks for the coffee."

She nods. "See you later, Rory."

"See you later, Chelsea."

This time, she doesn't correct me.

Hunter's sitting on the low brick wall, talking with some guys on the team. I'm not sure how I feel, seeing him. Good, of course, but also a little worried. Isn't there anything else he wants to do but hang around waiting for me? He waves when he sees me, and the big smile on his face twists me up a little inside. I can't explain the spasm of guilt. "Sorry," I say when I get to him. "Chelsea wanted to talk after class."

"Hey, Rory," one of the guys says. "Hey," I say back. I've been nice to all of them, pretending to be interested in hearing about their games and the other teams and their statistics, but really, it's so tedious. We have nothing in common, but they still try; guys always do around me.

"See you," Hunter tells them, pushing himself off the wall and jumping down beside me. Today's his rare afternoon off from practice and I'd wasted part of it at a coffee shop, sipping a drink I didn't want, talking to someone I didn't know. He takes my hand. "Chelsea, huh?"

I like holding hands with Hunter, the comforting warmth of his palm against mine, the way his fingers slide around my fingers, swallowing them up. It makes me feel anchored, but in a good way. I think about that, not about how he's looking at me, even while we're walking. "That's how I roll."

"So what did Chelsea want to talk to you about?"

The other me would have rolled her eyes and told Hunter all about how pitiful it was that a professor was trying to make friends with a freshman. "She wanted to lend me a book on Giotto," I lie.

Arden's at her painting class. She knows not to come back too early. I unlock my dorm room door and push it open. Hunter stops in the doorway. "Whoa. What happened in here?"

"We decided to redecorate."

He sniffs. "You burn something?"

"Arden did. It's no big deal."

"Okay. Just, you might want to open the window."

"So open it." I walk over to my dresser to plug in my cell. He's right. That awful smoky stink is still here, lingering behind the scarves. I feel his arms wrap around me from behind and his breath warm on the nape of my neck.

"In a minute," he says. "I'm busy right now."

Hunter's a total catch. He's so hot he scorches the grass when he walks on it. There are a million girls who would jump him the minute I turn my back. I let him push me onto my bed and run his hand up my stomach to my breast. I kiss him back. He's a good kisser, his lips soft and warm.

He rolls me over on top of him. I look down at him, his beautiful blue eyes so serious. The late-afternoon sun paints shadows across his face, his bare shoulders and chest. "I'm transferring to Harvard next year," I tell him.

"Uh-huh." He slides his hand beneath my shirt and dances his fingertips along my lower back, tingling my skin.

I hold his face between my hands. "And

268

then I'm going to law school."

"You're going to make a kick-ass lawyer."

I will. I'm going to be a champion for the downtrodden, a righter of wrongs. It's been the plan for as long as I can remember. I feel completely confused.

NATALIE

Dr. Morris squirts soap into her palm and pedals a splash of water into her cupped hands. She talks to us while she does this. "How are you? Have you been outside today? Did you see the game last night?" It's clear her mind isn't really on our responses and neither are ours. She yanks latex gloves from the cardboard box, picks up the flashlight from the bedside table, and goes over to check the machines, then Arden's pupils.

"How is she?" I ask, and Theo's hand tightens on my shoulder. Dr. Morris doesn't answer. She's intent on what she's doing. I want her to say, *Don't worry. Just a false alarm.* Or, *Here's a nice surprise.* But what she does say when at last she turns and strips the gloves from her hands is "Let's talk in the hallway."

She tells us that the medication has brought the fluid buildup inside Arden's skull back down within normal parameters, but just barely. I watch her lips form these words. Her brown hair is parted neatly down the middle and tucked back over each ear. She wears small pearls in her earlobes and I wonder if she's taken the time to do this, or perhaps she inserted them weeks before and hasn't yet gotten around to removing them. She tells us that she would like to see a greater drop and she's a little concerned that it's been four days with no real improvement. Four days. It seems like forty, the water rising and our little boat rocking dangerously to try to stay afloat. Arden's not getting better. If anything, she's starting to slide in the other direction. *Stop it,* I tell myself. *Stop it.*

"You said it might take a while," Theo reminds her.

"Well, that's still true. She's young and healthy. She could surprise us, but I really was hoping to see more of an improvement by now."

"But she's within normal range," I say.

"Yes, she is."

I should acknowledge this small victory with a bottle of expensive wine poured with great ceremony into a round glass. Instead, I am eyeing the choices in the vending machine and talking on the phone with my mother while Theo naps at the hotel.

"Nothing yet," my mom tells me. She has scanned every inch of the boys for signs of itchy red spots, despite their squirming insistence that they are fine. Henry put up a struggle, which she had quelled by telling him it was the only way he was going to be able to visit his sister. But it will be ten more days before they're officially cleared. Where will we be then?

"Potato chips or chocolate?" I ask my mom, and she says without hesitation, "Chocolate," so I slot the coins into the vending machine and push the button. Mom knows about Hunter, having seen it on the news, and we've talked about the vigil that's been planned. *If you're planning to attend,* she said, *I could drive up with the boys and meet you there. They don't have to know what it's about. They'll just be happy to see you,* but I had known that Oliver would understand exactly what all the candles were for and all the weeping people. Whenever I was driving and he was in the backseat, I had to avoid passing cemeteries. He's a tombstone magnet, lurching forward in his booster seat and pointing out the window. *Can we stop, Mommy? Please?* If I could, if traffic was light and I had the fifteen minutes to spare, I'd pull over to let

272

him wander through the rows of stone tablets, past the cement angels and stiff bundles of unnaturally bright plastic flowers while Henry found something to climb onto and leap off of. But Oliver's the one who asked the questions I didn't have the answers to. *Why do people die? Will Percy go to Heaven, too?* And here I am, still avoiding having to come up with the answers. What is it about me that makes me so afraid to talk about death? I haven't always been such a coward. It's motherhood. It tears you open; it exposes you. It tells you just how vulnerable you are.

"Mom," I say. "Theo's planning to go to work tomorrow."

"I'll tell the boys."

"I'm not sure he'll have time to swing by the house. Mom, I want him to stay here."

"Oh. Well, of course you'd be worried about him on the highway, as tired as he must be."

"It's not that. It's . . ." I'm afraid. I'm feeling my walls of resolve start to crumble. *I can't lose faith. I can't. Where will Arden be if I do?*

"Natalie?" my mother asks, and I say, "Nothing, Mom. May I talk with the boys?"

They chorus over the phone, their voices echoing and scrambling over each other, hard to disentangle because my mother has turned on the speaker. It doesn't matter what they're saying so much as hearing them say it. They chatter about how Caleb wouldn't share T-ball at recess so THEY TOLD THE MONITOR who is fat but really PREGNANT, how Janey won't be in school for ONE WHOLE WEEK because she is CONTAGIOUS, they did all their HOMEWORK even the STUPID READING so can they please watch TV now? They remind me that tomorrow's their field trip to the zoo. "Don't worry," Henry tells me. "I'll keep an eye on Oliver." But it's not Oliver who has an absolute gift for sneaking away when his teacher's attention is momentarily diverted. The permission slip had come home and I had glanced at the date and thought that surely after all these long months of struggling to turn Double around every single day I could take off one morning, so I had signed up to chaperone. The three of us had been looking forward to this, our first field trip together. They don't say anything about their disappointment that I won't be going after all, and I realize with sadness that my little boys are growing up.

"Goodbye," I tell them, and they chorus, " 'Bye, MOMMY."

I'm walking past the family lounge when I

see Gabrielle and Vince inside. He's pacing and she's talking in a low voice. I'm about to continue on, to leave them to their private conversation, when Vince turns and sees me. "Natalie," he says. "Got a minute?"

His voice is clipped. He's upset about something. "Sure."

"Close the door, will you?"

Puzzled, I shut the door behind me and come into the room. It's dark outside, the window black, distant lights peppering the horizon. "What's going on? Is it Rory?"

Vince slides his hands into his pants pockets. Gabrielle moves to stand behind him and together they look at me, unsmiling. "Detective Gallagher just left," Vince says. "He told us the lab report came back. Paint thinner, Nat?"

"I know, but —"

"Hold on. He also told us about the other fire, the one in the girls' room a few weeks ago. He'd told you, too. You and Theo, but neither of you said a word to us."

"What were we supposed to say, that the police think Arden's guilty? I didn't know what to think. I didn't know what to say. I still don't."

"It just makes me wonder if there's something else you're keeping from us."

I hesitate. Do they really need to know

the girls had been fighting? No, I decide. I won't say a word. "I don't know anything more." I feel my cheeks warm. I'm a terrible liar. "I don't know what was going on with our girls."

"Maybe that's the problem," Gabrielle says. "You didn't know what was going on. Maybe if you'd paid more attention, visited your daughter just once at college, you would have seen. You might have prevented this from happening."

"Like this is all *my* fault? How? What could I have seen?" I look to Vince.

He sighs. "It's not like you and I have been talking, Nat. I wasn't going to bring it up."

Now I feel a little frantic. "Bring up *what?*"

"She was doing drugs," Gabrielle says. "I found marijuana in her dresser. There were liquor bottles under her bed."

"You went through Arden's things? You had no right!"

"I was concerned. I knew you weren't checking up on her."

"Of course I wasn't checking up on her. She's eighteen!" *Don't come for Parents' Weekend, Mom. No one does.* And, *I'm going to spend Fall Break on campus. Is that all right?*

"She's still a child. *Your* child."

"Arden has a right to her privacy. She's going to experiment." *Just like Rory,* I want to say. I look pointedly at Vince. Rory had been upset when I caught the dishwasher handing her the plastic Baggie. She'd been afraid I would tell Gabrielle. But I hadn't. And from the look on Vince's face, I guess he hadn't said anything, either.

"If I thought that drugs had anything to do with it, I would have told Detective Gallagher when he asked," Gabrielle says. "But what he didn't ask and what I didn't tell him was that something was going on with Arden. She was different. She was . . . harder."

Harder? I don't even know what that means. "Please don't try and sound like you know my daughter, because you really don't."

"I knew how she felt about Hunter. I knew he was encouraging her, leading her on. I thought it was very unhealthy. I worried."

"If that's true, why didn't you say anything?"

"I wasn't sure how you'd react. I know how you are about Arden."

"And how is that?"

She shrugs. "I tried to keep an eye on the two of them, but I couldn't be there all the time. They should never have roomed to-

277

gether. It was a mistake and I knew it, but Rory said she couldn't let Arden down. She's loyal to Arden, despite everything."

We had all loved how close our daughters were. Vince and I used to talk about it all the time. *Like sisters. Just like sisters.* He said it as often as I did. It made us both happy. Arden had told me it was Gabrielle who wanted the girls to room together, but does it matter anymore? I look to Vince. "You can't really believe Arden would try to hurt Rory."

He throws up his hands. "It's all a fucking mess, Nat. What Gabrielle's saying makes a little sense. You remember what it's like to be eighteen. Everything feels like the end of the world."

I don't want to be in here. I want to be in Arden's room. I need to be with her. "Arden knows Rory's terrified of fire."

Gabrielle folds her arms. "Exactly."

"She meant it, Theo. They both did." I'm pacing in Arden's room, three steps one way and three steps the other. I glance to my daughter and lower my voice. "Aren't things terrible enough?"

Theo stands staring at the monitor on the wall as though he can make it tell him something new. "Well, I think Arden was a

278

little jealous of Rory."

"Stop it. You're her father." He's got his back to me, a dark shape. I'm sick of swimming in shadows. I want to *see.* I want everything laid out in brightness, clearly defined.

"Honey. I'm not telling you anything you don't already know."

"Your own brother . . ."

"Vince loves Arden. You know he does."

Vince taught Arden to snorkel, fitting the mask over her little face, counting *one-two-three* before disappearing beneath the waves. I'd come down early Christmas morning to find the two of them in the kitchen, aprons tied around their waists, flour everywhere, the sweet scent of cinnamon rising in the air. "I wish you'd stop defending him. You do it all the time."

"I'm not defending him. I'm just trying to calm you down. This isn't the time to relaunch a vendetta against Vince."

"You think I'm the problem? Really?" We shouldn't be talking like this in front of Arden, but she's asleep. I correct myself. She's not asleep. She's in a coma. She's far, far away from me. It only makes me want to grab her and haul her up to the surface, wrap her tight in my arms and never let go.

"No, of course not." He sighs. "The last

time you talked to Arden . . . did she mention Hunter?" His voice is casual, but I hear the words underneath. *Is Gabrielle right?*

"What are you saying, Theo? That I *should* have kept a closer eye on Arden?"

He glances at me, his features hidden. "Of course not. I just wanted to know if she said something about him."

"Arden never talks about boys. You know that."

He nods, looks away.

I hate this, the way he edges into criticism. He doesn't come right out and tell me. He makes me work for it. I can't help myself. I say it. I spell it out. "You think I wouldn't have picked up on it?"

"You're busy. You get focused on work, the restaurant."

"You wish I'd been more like Gabrielle, always checking up on our daughter? That's what you're saying? That if I'd pushed and pried, I might have saved Arden?" I'm shaking with anger, with dread, too. Because isn't this my secret worry? That Arden had tried to tell me and I hadn't been paying attention. That I'd let everything else take priority over her. "*Now* you want me to know more about our daughter's life? *You* were the one who thought she was depressed and you never said a word."

"Did you really want to know, Natalie? Did you? You might have had to think about something other than the restaurant for a change."

Everything laid bare, stripped to the bone. I find my voice. "That's not fair. That is so not fair."

He's silent a moment, angry, too, then he sighs. "I'm sorry. All this . . . Arden. It's killing me. I just want to know what happened."

I inhale, struggle to get some control. "We should have come up for Parents' Weekend. We could have met Hunter, warned Arden away. That boy had to have been in trouble."

"Maybe, or maybe something else happened."

"What does *that* mean?"

"I'm saying we don't know. I'm saying she's our daughter and we love her, but we don't know."

"How can you say that? *I* know. *I* know."

"We don't know what was going on in any of these kids' lives." He sounds tired, defeated. "We don't, do we? Not ever. Not really."

I want to protest. I want to tell him he's wrong, absolutely wrong, but how can I? Sending a child to college is drawing that line in the sand. Your child walks over it and

281

she's not your little girl anymore. She's just not.

ARDEN

I'm at Rehoboth beach. I've got my easel propped before me in the sand. The wind whips the hair across my face and scatters sand across the wet paint. The waves smash the shore and collect themselves. They wrap around my legs, sucking and then releasing. Seagulls sweep circles above my head, squawking and beeping. Around and through these noises comes a voice. I'm not at the beach. I'm in the hospital. It's Aunt Gabrielle talking. My mom and dad were here earlier, but now they're gone.

"I don't know how much longer I can pretend," she says.

Aunt Gabrielle sounds so sad. I need to make her understand.

She comes by during my last shift at Double, which is a shock. My aunt almost never stops by the restaurant, especially not lately. At first I think she's there looking for Uncle

283

Vince, to give him more bad news, but instead she walks straight over to where I'm rinsing vegetables in the sink. She stands there watching me, which makes me nervous. Does she think I'm not getting the lettuces clean enough? Has there been a complaint? When Liz goes into the dining room, Aunt Gabrielle reaches over to switch off the faucet and I realize that that's what she's been waiting for. *You have to keep an eye on Rory,* she tells me very seriously, her eyes the shapes of almonds. *Thank God you will be with her. It is the only good thing to come out of all of this.* I'm embarrassed by her intensity. *Promise,* she says. I know what she's really asking. *Promise me,* cherie.

Promise.

I'm coming out of the bookstore when I hear a familiar voice. "Darling! Do you need some help with that?" It's Aunt Gabrielle, coming down the sidewalk toward me, the sides of her coat blowing open in the wind. She's so pretty. Rory doesn't see it, or won't. *Thank God I took after my dad,* Rory will say, but who wouldn't want red hair? *It comes in a box, little cousin,* Rory has told me. *You could have it, too.*

"It's okay." I hoist my English book more firmly under my arm. It's a rental. I've been waiting for a copy to show up for weeks. I've got the rest of my books in a heavy plastic bag, hanging from my crooked finger turning cold and stiff. Aunt Gabrielle's got another important client. She'll shake open *The Washington Post* and point out a beautiful woman wearing something lovely. *To think, the trouble I had convincing her to cut her hair.*

"Not a problem." She takes the heavy bag. "Let me buy you lunch somewhere. You are looking too thin." There is no such thing as too thin in Aunt Gabrielle's mind, and I wonder what she's really after. But I can probably guess.

"So tell me about this boy," she says when we are seated at the little sandwich shop with its rickety tables and smeared picture windows that would give my mom a heart attack. Aunt Gabrielle has ordered a cranberry Brie sandwich I know she will just nibble.

"Hunter?" I say, before I can stop myself.

She tilts her head and studies me. My cheeks flame. I should have waited for her to say his name first. Rory's so good at keeping stuff from her mom. She says the trick is to confuse Aunt Gabrielle with partial truths. It puts her antenna out of whack. But this doesn't work with my mom.

Whenever I feed her bits of truth, I always wind up telling her everything. And there are just some things my mom can never know.

"Hunter, yes. Do you know about his family, where he's from?"

"A little." I don't know many facts about Hunter, but I know him. The way he shakes back his hair from his eyes when he's pleased, the way he lets it fall forward when he's interested. He's full of restless energy, bouncing a tennis ball against the wall, walking fast so you have to scurry to keep up. He smiles at everyone, even people he doesn't know. He's happiness, through and through. But there's a serious side, too. He can look at you and you can feel seen. "His dad owns an art gallery." Is this what Aunt Gabrielle wants? "His mom works there."

"An art gallery." She raps the ring on her finger against her glass of iced tea, making stern little sounds. "Interesting. Do you know if it's successful? Never mind. I can find out for myself. Is Hunter a good student?"

"I guess." He pays attention in class. He *goes* to class, which is more than I can say for a lot of the kids here.

"So how did he end up here, at this school? Was this his only choice?"

"I don't know, Aunt Gabrielle." I'm uncomfortable. I'm stirring my iced tea, my spoon clattering around and around. She puts her hand on my hand, stopping me, and fixes me with her beautiful eyes. "Do you think Rory is serious?" she asks. What she means is *Are they having sex?*

Rory's been having sex since she was fourteen.

I'm six years old, maybe seven. I'm going to visit Mrs. Fitz next door because she has had her baby, a little girl named Morgan. My mom and I have picked out a cute pink dress at Macy's, and while she wraps it up and ties the bow I make the card. It takes me forever to write CONGRATULATIONS. It is the longest word I have ever written. My mom spells it out for me, letter by letter. Mrs. Fitz comes to the door carrying the baby wrapped in a blanket, just the round bald top of her head peeping out, her tiny face. Mrs. Fitz isn't walking funny anymore and her stomach is a lot smaller. I look at her and then at baby Morgan. I can't figure it out. I wait until we get home and then I ask my mom: *How does a baby get inside a mommy's tummy?* She's sitting with a cookbook opened in her lap and she looks at me. *Well, when a mommy and a daddy love each other . . .* I know where this is going. I have

287

heard this silly stuff before. I shake my head, stopping her. *No. I want to know how the baby* actually *gets in a mommy's tummy.*

Rory had sex before me, but I knew about sex first. I hold this in my hand, a prize.

We lie on the pontoon boat, staring up at the sky. Clouds drift past in listless stretched-out shapes that don't resemble anything. I hold up my hands to try to frame them into interesting shapes. I will do a series of cloud paintings, see if I can make them look both hard and soft, white and filled with color. *We could have been sisters,* Rory says. This is because my mom knew Uncle Vince before she met my dad. It's not a secret, but no one talks about it. Did they date? Did they have sex? It's gross to think about, but Rory is obsessed. *Your mom could have been mine.*

Which means Uncle Vince could have been my dad. I point this out and Rory squints at the sky. *You're right,* she says. *This is a stupid game.*

Who said it was a game? I was there when the back grill caught on fire. I saw Uncle Vince pull my mom back. I saw the way he held her.

What's that weird shushing sound? It's all

around me. I try to open my eyes. I try to swallow.

Uncle Vince says, "Let's just wait for the tox results."

"Why?" Aunt Gabrielle says.

"It could explain why the girls didn't get out."

"Every time I think about it . . ."

"I know, Gabby."

He's the only one who calls her that. His voice is serious, serious as a heart attack. He's a good listener and he keeps secrets, even when you don't actually tell him, when he just figures it out on his own. Not that he ever says that he knows. You can just tell. He'd sent me a birthday cake that Rory ate while I was gone — eight thin layers, each a different flavor and color, all frosted white so that when you sliced into it, it looked like a rainbow. I love Uncle Vince, but not like a dad.

Uncle Vince finds us crouched in the basement storage room, hiding from Aunt Gabrielle. Rory and I have been playing with her mom's makeup, turning up all her lipsticks into soft shimmering tubes of pinks and reds that we touched with tentative fingertips, squealing at the stickiness. We opened the creamy bottles of foundation and sprayed perfume in waves across the room, and, sneezing, dropped one on the floor to shatter. He looked down at us with a smile I knew he was trying to hide. *You should see yourselves.* Crouching, he holds his arms wide.

I miss him. I was so angry at him, but now I get it. He just made a mistake. Don't we all do that? I want to tell him this. I want to let him put his arms around me and hold me, rocking me from side to side the way he always does.

"Hunter was crazy about Rory," Aunt Gabrielle says. "Who knows how far it went."

My eyes burn with tears. Hunter loves her so much. There is only one small space for me and I squeeze into it and try to stretch it to fit.

"You had no warning signs?" Uncle Vince says.

"Not really. He seemed so nice, but he posted so many pictures of her on Facebook. There was almost nothing about this baseball team he's on. Don't you think that's odd? There were only two of Arden, and Rory was in one of them. It was all Rory."

It was. It was.

"Don't beat yourself up about it, Gabby."

"I just can't believe . . . Arden?"

Arden, *what*? They're both looking at me. I want to run and hide. Something is holding me down. Something is in my throat, gagging me with a huge fist.

"What's that?" Uncle Vince says.

"What's what?"

"That. Did you hear that?" Uncle Vince's right beside me. If I could open my eyes I would see him. He would understand. *Why can't I open my eyes?* "Sweetheart?"

"What is it? Is she awake?" Aunt Gabrielle says.

"I'm not sure."

I want my mom. I want this thing out of me. My words crowd uselessly inside my brain. I have a terrible headache. It's slicing my head into pieces.

"Get the nurse, Gabrielle."

No. I don't need the nurse. I need my mom. I want my mom. I clutch the sheet, but it stays smooth beneath my fingers. It won't bunch up. It won't fight back.

The pressure around me changes. Someone else is bending over me. "Are you in pain, honey?"

Everything's on fire. It blazes through me, eats me up. This thing in my throat. I try to claw at it, but my hand won't move. I want to cry. I imagine the big paintbrush, dip and swirl. Dip and swirl.

"She was like this when we first brought her in. I just need to adjust the drip."

Make her stop talking. Listen to me.
". . . a good sign?"
"We need to keep her calm."
I try to thump my heels against the mattress, but my legs are too heavy. My heartbeat booms slower and slower. The last thing I hear is Uncle Vince's quiet voice in my ear, his breath a warm puff against my cheek. "Hang in there, Rory."

Wait. He can't be talking to me. He can't. Because I'm not Rory.

292

RORY

Back when I was ten years old and trapped at Arden's house for the day — admittedly better than being trapped in my own house — I decided how we were going to celebrate our eighteenth birthdays. It was a rainy day and Grandpa George was supposed to be watching us, which meant he was in the living room watching a ball game and we were in the den watching the kind of crap TV my mom would never let me watch, not in a million years. The show we were watching had a bunch of people living together who were constantly fighting and then cuddling under blankets. One of them, a girl named Marcie, was my favorite. She had long black hair poufed on top, which I was obsessed with for some reason, and thick eyeliner that made her eyes look catlike. She wore a lot of tight clothes that zipped down the front, and her arms and neck were covered with colorful vines and flowers that looked like

293

someone had been drawing on her with permanent markers because they never rubbed off. It was on this particular afternoon that it suddenly dawned on me that they were tattoos. Dumb, I know, but in my defense I was only ten. Plus, up until then, I'd never met anyone with a tattoo.

So it was in the spirit of discovery and daring that I rolled over and said to Arden, *Let's get matching tattoos when we're eighteen.*

She frowned a little and didn't take her gaze off the screen. *What?*

I could tell she was reluctant. Arden could be a real wimp. I wheedled, *It'll be like we're sisters.* That's how I used to think. Arden stared at me, and inspired, I added the clincher: *you draw it.* Because even back then Arden knew she was going to be an artist. So she pushed herself up and went to get her colored pencils. When my mom came in and found the TV playing, she switched it right off, but we didn't mind. *What are you girls doing?* she asked. I smiled right up at her, big and bright. *Nothing,* I told her. Even then I knew this was something she could never find out.

My birthday comes four months before Arden's, so her eighteenth birthday's the one that mattered, but mine was when the real countdown began. It was a quiet enough day. I raked in presents, which, if you ask me, is the only reason to celebrate birthdays. But we didn't go out to dinner and we definitely didn't have cake with candles. *Are you sure?* my dad asked, looking disappointed. *Very,* I told him, and meant it. It's not that I hated the thought of getting older. Frankly, getting older was the one thing I was looking forward to. That night, I texted Arden. *113 days to go!*

But I could tell Arden was starting to have second thoughts. She kept dropping hints. *I hear it's really painful,* she'd say. Or, *What if it gets infected?* I tried not to be impatient. *Don't worry,* I'd say. *It's going to be amazing.* And she'd give me a nervous smile.

I begin researching tattoo parlors Monday afternoon. It's not as easy as you might think. The one with a good Yelp rating looks totally sketchy in the photographs. The one that looks like a day spa was called StInk. I try to involve Arden in the process, turning my laptop so she can see for herself. The Kitchen Ink. The Ink Empire. She frowns her Arden frown and says, "Maybe we should hold off."

As if. I've forgotten the name of the TV show we'd been watching, and Marcie probably died of some drug overdose long ago, but I want this tattoo. I want to honor that ten-year-old I'd been, that girl who really believed that just maybe life would be okay.

Turns out D.D.'s friend has a friend and on Saturday morning, I walk down the sidewalk past a coffee shop and a used bookstore, a hardware store, a gas station, and a consignment store that Arden tried to get me to go to once, but hello? When we pass it, the door's wide open like a big hug and I know Arden's slowed down to take a quick look, but I just walk faster. The shuffle of steps behind me as she tries to keep up. "We could go shopping for shoes," she says, sort of breathless. I have to give her credit; this is something that would normally work.

I stop, and she bumps into me. She wears a blue sundress that floats on her. Has she lost weight? "I don't want to go shopping. I want to do this."

"I know, but . . ."

"You promised."

"We were *ten*." Her eyes are shiny. She's going to cry. I'm immune to her crying. She does it all the time. But today *is* her birthday.

"Fine. Be a pussy. I'll go by myself."

She chews her lower lip. "No. You're right. I did promise."

"Okay, then."

I turn and push open the door. It's a long, narrow space with pictures all over the walls and a glass display case filled with jewelry. It doesn't look that clean in here. The linoleum floor's crappy and some of the pictures taped to the walls look a million years old. But D.D.'s friend's friend had said this was one of the best places in town, and I know that if we leave now, Arden will never go through with it.

The guy behind the counter kind of stands up, staying a little hunched as though he's not that sure he wants to be vertical. "Help you, girls?"

He's bald with a long straggly red beard that hangs way past his belly. Not the most reassuring look. His arms are covered with ink that runs up beneath his T-shirt and around his throat, black and red and green dragons all fighting one another with their mouths wide open, showing their fangs. I try not to stare. Gold hoops dangle from both eyebrows and solid ivory gauges the size of quarters fill his earlobes. It takes years to get them to that size.

I reach into my jeans pocket and pull out a piece of paper folded into a square. "We want this." I spread out the paper on the glass counter. It doesn't lie perfectly flat: the creases are eight years old and it's been traveling in the tight pocket of my jeans for the past twenty minutes. But the image in the corner is clear: a little purple butterfly with green stripes, our favorite colors back then. *Cool,* I'd told Arden, and I'd meant it.

She leans in close. "Wow, you still have it?"

Now I know she's in.

The guy says, "That's a nice one. That's going to turn out real good."

"How much?" I ask.

"I'll give you the student discount. Say, seventy."

Seventy's good, and I'm about to nod when Arden speaks up. "Could you do sixty?"

I settle myself into the chair and stretch out my right arm. *Do I want to watch?* In the end, I do, wincing and biting my lip as the butterfly spreads its wings on my forearm, angry skin, ink, and blood.

Arden's going to surprise her parents by showing up for the weekend. I bet that's not all she's going to do, but it's in my best interest not to say anything, so I don't. When we get back to the room, she starts scooping up clothes and shoving them into her bag. She's not even folding them. It makes me want to elbow her out of the way and do it myself. I see the tank top I'd tried to give her lying crumpled on her bed. She hasn't even taken off the tags. I fight the urge to grab it back and hang it up properly in my closet. I mean, I'd paid full price for that thing.

"You could come with me, you know." She's grinning, her eyes bright. She's relieved it's over. It didn't even hurt that much and now it only itches.

"Sounds like a blast, but no." I undo my jeans. The waistband's been digging into me all morning. It's a freaking relief to yank them off.

"Mackenzie will be there."

I hold up my Free People jeans and examine them. These are the ones I usually wear when I'm PMS-y and huge. "Like I want to hear all about how fabulous Princeton is and how she's dating some movie star. No, thank you." My jeans slide on, soft and easy. I stand up on my chair to examine myself in the mirror over the dresser. They look okay. I climb down and go to my closet.

"You don't even have to tell your parents. You can stay with me."

I slide the hangers. Nothing preppy, nothing that makes it look like I'm trying. I pull out a backless yellow blouse with long sleeves. *Perfect.* "What's the deal, Arden?

Are you afraid to take the bus alone?"

"No."

She is. I can tell. "You'll be fine." I pull off my T-shirt and slide the silky yellow shirt on, flip my hair over one shoulder, and pick up my brush.

She sits on her bag and zips it shut. "What are you going to do all weekend?"

"It's not even all weekend. It's twenty-four hours. I think I can find something to do." I'm brushing my hair with slow, even strokes. It's getting long. I might need a trim next week. Do I trust the salon in town?

She stands and looks around. "I hope I'm not forgetting anything."

"You've got half the room in that bag." I shake my hair back and think about earrings. Silver hoops. They always work.

She slings her bag over her shoulder. "Rory?" she says, and I glance over at her. "It was a good idea."

I surprise myself again. I close my jewelry box and go over to hug her. Her hair is soft and slippery against my cheek and smells of coconut. We use the same shampoo. "Better hurry or you'll miss your bus."

Why don't you come by for dinner tonight? Chelsea had said. I'll make my famous risotto. She doesn't know risotto's what my dad makes when he's uninspired and just throwing something together. Kids had been filing out of the classroom. A few glanced over at us. I'd told Hunter I had to return Chelsea's book to her. I'd told him not to wait for me after class. *Dude,* I said to Chelsea, trying not to let my surprise show. *You have got to get a life.* She'd laughed. *Does that mean yes?*

My mother's trained me. *You never arrive at someone's house empty-handed,* she's said, sliding a bottle of wine into a gift bag or wrapping up a box of scented soaps. I'd glanced around my dorm room, which looked even worse after Arden had thrown everything around during her packing spree, and picked up one of the two white bakery boxes perched on her nightstand.

There's no doorbell, so I knock instead. Chelsea swings open the door. "Ooh," she says, eyeing the box. "What's this?"

"Cake." Birthday cake, and I hope it doesn't have Arden's name scrolled across the top in icing. I should have checked, but now it's too late.

"I can always start my diet tomorrow. What can I get you, red or white?"

So that's how it's going to be. Cool. "You have any champagne?"

She hikes a dark winged eyebrow. "On my

301

salary? You're lucky I've got both red and white."

"Okay. White sounds good."

"Be right back. Make yourself at home."

I wonder why she asked me over. I wonder why I said yes. I walk around the living room, looking at the art on the paneled walls, the shiny pieces of gray pottery arranged on a credenza. The furniture is white and overstuffed, the rug a faded Oriental with tangled fringe. Everything is pale and washed out. I'm disappointed, somehow. This isn't how I'd imagined it. I run my finger along the spines of the books on the shelves and pull one out. The cover shows a bald man in an orange monk's robe with his palms pressed together. I try to read the title. "*The Dog in All of Us*?" I say it out loud.

Chelsea says behind me, "You know I'm subletting this place, right? None of this stuff is mine. It belongs to a religion professor on sabbatical in Tibet."

I slot the book back onto the shelf. "So you don't collect crappy paper fans?" I turn to face her and see she's holding glasses and a bottle of wine.

"Hey, don't knock it. They're a thing of beauty when a storm takes out the electricity and it's a hundred degrees in here." She hands me a glass.

302

The wine is chilled and delicious. It slides down easily. "At least they have good taste in wineglasses." Riedel. *Not bad.*

"Nope. They're mine. I'm from Portland, where we take our wine very seriously."

Which Portland, I wonder, East Coast or West? Do I really care? "I thought you were from Chicago." I'd visited Chicago on a college trip with my mom and the wind blew at me sideways, making my skirt fly up and my hair dance around my head. The sun shone down, turning the sidewalk to glitter, and tall buildings rose all around. Everything felt trapped, penned in. *I could never live here,* I'd decided, and crossed Northwestern off my list.

She's studying a framed poster on the wall, one of those lame Matisse pictures you find in beach rentals. She's wearing Levi's, but not vintage, and a shirred, red tube top that shows off her tanned shoulders. Her dark hair is loose and flowing. No earrings, which is a mistake. Big silver hoops would be perfect. I should take mine off and hand them to her. "That's just where I was teaching last. Before that, I was in Phoenix, and before that Nashville. But I grew up in Portland."

"Nashville must have been dope." All those country stars. I pick up a glazed ceramic ashtray that looks like some kid made it, all lumpy and uneven. *Is this supposed to be art?*

"It was fun. You ever been?"

"I've never lived anywhere but D.C." I've never even been out of the country. Except for junior year, when I went to Puerto Rico with Mackenzie and her family for spring break, but all I saw was the hotel room. I spent the whole time puking in the bathroom.

"You make it sound like torture. A lot of people would love to live in D.C."

"Not their whole lives." *Who wants to live anywhere their whole life?* Boston would have been a change. Boston would have been a start. I'd loved Boston the minute I stepped onto its crazy sidewalks going everywhere and saw all the ivy creeping up the sides of the buildings. This no-name town in Maryland doesn't count as anything. It's just like all the other no-name towns near the ocean that my family's vacationed at here and there, like a pebble skipping across the water.

"I'm surprised, actually. I thought you were one of those girls."

I lower my glass. "One of *what* girls?"

"Relax. I meant it as a compliment." She reaches down to switch on a table lamp,

304

springing the room into light and shadow. "I thought you were the kind of girl who takes ski trips to the Alps, spends the summer in Milan. The lucky girl."

I look like that kind of girl. I've spent my whole life trying to look like that kind of girl. "I wish." I hold out my glass. She smiles and lifts the bottle. The wine gurgles into first my glass, then hers. "I'd love to go to Europe. I have family there. My mother's French." *Later,* my mother would say when I would ask about my grandparents and if I had any cousins. *Another day.* Arden and I snooped around when we were kids, looking for old family albums or clues to my mom's life before she came to America, but there was nothing. Not even a passport. My dad's never met them and Aunt Nat said she wasn't sure my mom really had a family overseas, but I think I have grandparents somewhere and that they're wondering about me, too. *Maybe they didn't want your mom to marry your dad,* Arden would say. Arden the romantic. I hate to think what the real reason might be.

"And you've never been."

"My dad's always too busy to take time off and my mother . . ." My mother doesn't like traveling. My father had had to beg her to go away for their anniversary last year

305

and even then they'd come home a day early. I'd almost died when I saw their car pull up out front, and I'd barely gotten everyone out in time and cleared the countertop of all the liquor bottles before the front door swept open. I shrug and glance at Chelsea.

She's studying me. "Hungry?"

We sit in the dining room, a creepy space painted dark brown and filled with heavy mahogany furniture. The paintings are hideous landscapes in ornate gold frames, nothing like the modern stuff in the living room. "This place has a split personality." I pull out my chair. The thin rug catches beneath the legs.

"I know. I'm kind of obsessed with trying to figure it out. My guess is they inherited some of these things and picked up other pieces when they lived in other cities. Or maybe this is a second marriage for both of them and they combined their households. Or maybe they just have really terrible taste."

I look around the room, trying to picture the people it belongs to. It would be horrible to inherit stuff you hated. I'd give it away, I decide. "Where's your stuff?"

"I have no stuff. I don't want anything weighing me down."

"Nothing?"

"Nothing that can't be packed in a few boxes. Clothes, a few books. These wineglasses. You know, the important things." She watches me take a tentative bite.

"Good, right?"

I chew. It's not anywhere as good as my dad's. "It's okay. Maybe cooked a minute too long."

"Yeah, well, that's the minute I took to answer the door."

I smile.

When she undoes the bakery box, I see a slice has been cut out. She looks at me. "I guess Arden got to it first." At least it doesn't have candles and balloons frosted all over it. The cake is delicious. We each eat two pieces and sag back in our chairs. "I'm definitely going on a diet tomorrow." She stands to clear the dishes. "Coffee? Cognac?"

I'm supposed to meet Hunter at a party. I'm already late. Dinner's taken way longer than I'd expected. We've been through a bottle of wine and talked about our favorite movies. I love horror flicks with a dead guy chasing people with a chain saw, but she's all about weird indie films that make no sense. *Give me a good tangled subplot any-time,* she'd said. Turns out she's a reality-TV junkie like me. *I'm a sucker for those cooking shows,* she'd told me. I didn't tell her my whole life's been a cooking show.

Clattering noises come from the kitchen. Chelsea's loading the dishwasher. "Have you decided?" she calls to me. A distant rumble of thunder. It's going to rain, soon.

This is a huge house for just one person. She must go crazy, being here all alone. "Cognac sounds good," I call. Before she comes back into the room, I slide the pottery ashtray into my bag and snap it shut.

We're in the living room, sitting side by side on the couch. I'm not a fan of cognac, but this stuff is okay. One sip heats me through and through. I've got a nice buzz that insulates me. I don't care that my jeans are too tight or that I'm stuck at some crappy college where the biggest thing to do is go to football games and get loaded at my professor's house. I don't care that I might get into a second-rate law school as a result and never amount to anything. Most of all, I don't care that my mom looks at me with disapproval and my dad barely looks at me at all. Chelsea's got her legs curled beneath her and her glass cupped in one palm. She reaches into the bookshelf behind us, red and blue and smooth tanned skin, and hands me the book I'd pulled out earlier, the one with a picture of a praying Buddhist on the cover. "What does this say again?"

Her face is so close to mine. I could reach out and touch it.

NATALIE

There's been an accident on the highway. It takes Theo four hours instead of two and a half to get back. I pace outside Arden's room and then he rounds the corner. His face is lined with fatigue. He carries his briefcase heavy in one hand.

We sit on the couch in the family lounge and Detective Gallagher takes his usual chair. I don't want to talk to this man. I don't even want to see his long face, his dark hair waving back from a high forehead, but I have to know what he's thinking, what people are telling him about Arden.

He explains that the lab's matched the brand of paint thinner to the same one used by EMU's studio art department, which buys its supplies in bulk. A student working alone in the printmaking studio Friday evening saw Arden leaving with a five-gallon jug of paint thinner.

"Arden's taking a painting class," Theo

says. "She must have needed it for an assignment. Didn't she say something to you about that, Nat?"

"They were doing self-portraits. Arden wasn't happy with hers. It's a large part of her grade, so she was planning to work on it over the weekend." *See?* I'm saying. *A completely innocent explanation.*

"Her professor didn't seem to know anything about that," Detective Gallagher says. "He says he's strict about keeping supplies in the studio."

"So she broke the rules," I say. "Students must help themselves to art supplies all the time."

He gives me a look. "Let's talk about her relationship with Hunter."

It's a quick change of subject. "Yes, okay," I say, uneasy, not meaning it. "But she didn't really talk about him. They were friends, that's all." Answering questions he's not even asking — it just makes me sound guilty. It makes *Arden* sound guilty.

"What *did* she tell you about him?"

I don't look at Theo. "Nothing, really. She liked him. They were taking a class together."

"Is that all she said?"

"I know how it looks. I know how it sounds, but that doesn't mean she was hid-

311

ing something. It just means that she didn't think there was anything to tell us."

"We've told you," Theo says. "Boys have never been an issue."

"Are you sure?" Detective Gallagher says.

Meaning what? I frown, rub my hands together.

"We don't monitor her every move," Theo says. "We don't interrogate her. We respect her need for privacy. I work with teenagers. I see it all the time. The parents who are the most controlling end up pushing their kids the furthest away. Those are the kids who will do anything to assert their independence."

"Arden talked to us," I say. "We have a healthy relationship. We know the important things."

"Did you know she was having sex with Hunter?"

He says it so baldly. Trying to startle me into an unguarded response? I hadn't known. I'd had no idea. But I'm not going to admit this. I'm not going to help him blame my daughter for anything, so I don't reply. I just sit there. My hands are tightly twisted together and I unclench them.

"Sex doesn't mean the same thing it did when we were teenagers." Theo's using his headmaster's voice: formal, with a slight choked quality. It tells me he's hating this. "It means, in fact, almost nothing. I'm sorry to say it, but it's true."

But I know it would have meant something to Arden.

"How did Rory feel about it?" Detective Gallagher asks, and I suddenly understand why Arden and Rory had been fighting.

"I don't know," I say in a perfectly neutral voice. I can't even remember the last time I talked to Rory. Would she have confided in me? She would talk to me in her Rory way of dropping a single clue and letting me ask the question that would lead to the next clue. Together we would assemble the whole. She is my niece by marriage only but I had always felt a kinship with her. I had always felt I understood her. I'd gone from Arden's hospital room to Rory's, to read to her the way I'd just read to Arden, as I had when they were little — both of them together, separated by a thin wall.

"What about Arden? Did she mention anything about how she and Rory were getting along?"

Theo folds his arms. "What are you getting at?"

"Look. You're a father. You work in a high school. Are you telling me you didn't pick up on any signs that something was going

313

on between the girls?"

"Is this some sort of indictment over our parenting style?"

"It's just my experience that parents always know more than they're willing to reveal. They mistakenly believe they're protecting their kids when all they're doing is making things worse."

"I don't know what kind of parents you've been dealing with, but that's not the case here. We want you to find out who did this."

"Even if it proves to be your own daughter?"

"Yes." Theo says it unhesitatingly, with conviction.

Detective Gallagher studies him, then glances to me. "Another thing." *How can there be anything more?* "Did you know Arden was being brought before the committee for student misconduct?"

This can't be true. The school would have informed us. Then I think, *No, they wouldn't.* Arden's eighteen. In their eyes, she's an adult.

Theo covers my hand with his. "How is this relevant?"

"It goes toward state of mind."

"You don't know our daughter's state of mind," I say. "You don't know her at all."

"Look, Detective Gallagher," Theo says,

ever reasonable, ever calm. "Maybe Arden did have a romantic relationship with this boy. Maybe she and Rory argued about it. I can buy that. But girls don't set fires just because they're jealous."

"Unfortunately, Mr. Falcone, that's exactly what they do."

I swish the curtain closed behind me, metal rings rattling. Theo's somewhere nearby. Down the corridor, outside the hospital building, I don't know. He's on the phone with the university, trying to track down a dean so we can find out exactly what misconduct Arden is being accused of. It's early evening and he probably won't reach anyone until tomorrow, but we can't just sit here and do nothing.

But that's exactly what I'm doing, sitting here doing nothing. Arden wouldn't set a fire to frighten or hurt Rory. She just wouldn't.

I can't see Arden's face. I can't read her features. *Wake up. Wake up, Arden. Tell us what really happened. I can't help you unless I know.*

Arden wanted to be a mermaid when she was little. The sight of blood makes her queasy but she'd stared entranced at the X-ray of her broken wrist. In ninth grade,

315

she came home from school every day smelling of darkroom chemicals, and in tenth grade, the knuckle of her right index finger was permanently stained black with India ink. She gets cold easily and has a slight overbite that three years of braces couldn't quite correct. She props a book in front of her cereal bowl, and curls one foot around the other as she reads. She ducks when Theo kisses her soundly on the top of her head, making her giggle. I do know this girl. I'm not going to listen to what people are saying about her.

A nurse comes in to check the monitors. She doesn't cheerfully say hello when I greet her, which alarms me. "Is Arden okay?" I ask, and she nods tightly. "No change." But she doesn't linger by Arden's bed the way she had the afternoon before. Maybe she's had a fight with her husband, maybe her back is hurting her, but I can't help but wonder if somehow she's heard the suspicions circling my daughter.

I pull my phone from my bag and press the buttons. The phone rings, but my mother doesn't answer. She must be driving the boys somewhere. Or maybe they're at the park. My mother's a big one for fresh air. Maybe she thinks this will stave off the chicken pox. I had Skyped with them that morning, before school. The boys had been all motion, eager to show me their homework, a scrape on Henry's knee, a cardinal perched on the bird feeder they had given Theo for Father's Day. But they're not there now. I leave a message. "Hi, Mom. Just wanted to know if you've heard how Christine's operation went." Two little girls with dark curly hair, attached chest to chest, their arms wrapped around each other. A complicated surgery, Christine said, but not as complicated as some. I wonder how the girls will feel when they're no longer connected. "Call when you have a chance."

The door slides open. It's Theo. "Any luck?" I whisper, and he shakes his head. "My mom's on the line." He comes into the room. "She wants to say hello. That okay?"

I hesitate. Sugar can be overbearing. But Theo's already extending the phone and I slide my own phone into my pocket and speak into his.

"Hi, Sugar." I let myself out of Arden's room.

"Now, listen. I'm going to tell you what I told Theo. You kids need a good lawyer."

Her voice is strong, purposeful. She's used to getting her way, being heard and listened to. George may be the successful businessman but Sugar's the one really in charge.

Vince had been the one to introduce me to his parents. Sugar had held both my hands in hers and studied my face before hugging me hello. I've always wondered what she'd been thinking.

"I know. We're on it." I walk down the hallway to the family lounge. Someone's been in here, leaving behind a paper cup on the table and a crumpled blanket tossed across the back of the couch.

"No, not someone through the Bishop School. You don't want everyone knowing your business. You need to be able to speak your mind."

We need to be able to afford it. "Speak our mind about what?"

"You don't know what a police investigation could turn up."

"Arden didn't do it, Sugar."

"Well, of course she didn't!" she exclaims, sounding surprised. I'm relieved at this support from an unexpected source. "But you don't want everything bared for public consumption. She called us, you know."

I stop walking. "Arden? When?"

"Oh, just before we left on our trip. She wanted to thank us for her birthday present. It was all right to send the girls money this year, wasn't it? That's all they asked for."

318

An oblique reference to the fact that we had so little of it. "It's fine. Of course it's fine. Thank you."

"George and I will send them more for Christmas, too. They're in college now; they have expenses."

Will Arden be home for Christmas? I'll have to come up with a vegetarian substitute for turkey, something special that she'll love. I rest my forehead against the cold glass, look down onto the rain-soaked parking lot below. People hasten to and from their cars, umbrellas whipped by wind, folded newspapers gripped between two hands to form a waterproof shelf. They seem so far away. Arden had fallen even farther. "What did she say?"

"What did who say?"

"Arden. What did she tell you? How did she sound?" Sugar's a talker. She probably didn't let Arden get in a word edgewise. Still, I need to know. Had Arden sounded happy? Had she sounded okay? I need to know I hadn't overlooked something that would explain how *this* happened.

"Let me see. I asked her how classes were going and she said fine. I asked if there were any boys on the horizon and she told me no one special. I hope you're not worried about that, Natalie. Some girls are just late bloomers."

But there had been a boy. Had Arden fallen in love with Hunter? Would she really have pursued her best friend's boyfriend? Arden's always been a private person, even as a child. It's a quality I've always understood and respected. But maybe I should have pushed a little. Maybe she'd been waiting for me to ask.

"It was a quick conversation. She had to get to class. I was packing to get ready for our trip. But, Natalie, she sounded fine. She really did."

I very much want to believe this.

"George and I will be home in a few days. We'll head directly to the hospital. Call me if you need anything in the meantime. I'll keep my phone by my bed."

"Thank you."

"I do wish we were there, Natalie. I truly do. It's such a terrible time for all of you. This split between you and Vince isn't helping things. Don't you think it's time you forgave him?"

Again. "I'm not thinking about Vince right now."

"It's not just him I'm worried about, honey."

"Vince thinks Arden set the fire. He thinks

she tried to kill Rory."

I'm glad I've said this, put the shocking words out there. Let Sugar see who her son really is. Even Theo has doubts. I'm the only one holding fast. The scene below me blurs, tiny headlights flaring on, and a car slowly pulling away.

"He's just upset, Natalie. He doesn't know what he's saying."

It's exactly what Theo said. "We're all upset. Stop making excuses for him." I have never spoken to my mother-in-law so sharply. I've crossed a line, slammed a door shut I can never reopen. My mother would be horrified.

There's silence. Sugar's sorting her words. "All I'm saying is you need to pull together," she says, at last. "You need to be prepared. You don't know what's coming."

It's the middle of the night. I sit beside Arden's bed. The machines blink. Christine's reassured me over and over. *There's no timetable. Every case is different. We should know something in the next day or so.* Through the curtain, I see the shadowy shape of someone walking past. It looks like Vince. Probably going out to sneak a cigarette.

I've tried everything I can to save my

restaurant — firing people who'd worked hard and were my friends, begging suppliers for credit extensions and loan officers for a break, coming in early and staying late, all in a desperate attempt to keep the slippery sliding mud from pushing past me and taking my restaurant with it. But the mud had come, knocking me to my knees.

I had been so focused. I had let things go unremarked. When I didn't hear from Arden, I should have called her. I should have asked her how things were going, but I thought we could talk later. I always thought there would be a later.

The nurse comes in to take another reading. A short woman with gray curls. I close my cookbook and set it aside. "How is it?"

It's a moment before she answers, a split second that stretches to eternity. "Twenty-two."

That damned number. It's concrete. It's lead. Arden's not as resolute as Rory. She sometimes takes the path of least resistance. "Could we get her a fresh sheet?" I ask. "And maybe some new socks?"

I lift the end of the sheet to reveal my daughter's legs, bulky compression boots around her calves, and gently tug a sock free. The nurse's flashlight sweeps past and my daughter's pale foot is revealed to me, each toe swollen, and the gentle sheen of silver polish. A sophisticated shade. Not like the bright colors Arden loved before she went off to college.

The flashlight moves on and we are left once again in darkness.

ARDEN

"Who's Chelsea Lee?"

I wake with a gasp. It's Uncle Vince talking. He sounds close. *Why do you think I'm Rory, Uncle Vince?* Maybe there's something wrong with my face. I try to touch my cheek. But my arm lies stiff, throbbing.

"I think she's one of Rory's professors," Aunt Gabrielle answers.

"Nice of her to send flowers," Uncle Vince says.

People send flowers for funerals. But I'm not dead. I'm burning alive, smoke rising up.

"I saw that pink-haired girl again," Aunt Gabrielle says. "She was standing by the elevator. I think she was looking for Rory's room. I don't know why. I told her the girls can't have visitors."

D.D. leans close and whispers, *You fucking bitch.*

"She's young. She doesn't understand."

324

Uncle Vince says it in the way that means he doesn't want to be having this conversation but doesn't know how to stop it from happening. It's like that all the time between him and Rory. *Daddy,* she'll say when she wants something, and he'll pretend he's listening. *Hmm?* He'll smile at her, but not really. It never deters her. She just goes right around to face him. *Daddy, Daddy, Daddy. I have a question.*

But if I say *Daddy?* to my dad, he immediately stops to look at me. I'm careful what I let him see. When all that crap was going on in eighth grade, he knew. I caught him standing in his office doorway and watching. *I'm fine,* I told him whenever he asked. Because here's the thing: I couldn't stand to see the sadness collect in his eyes.

"Gabby? I called you Friday night, but you never answered. Where were you?"

"Did you? I suppose I didn't hear my phone."

"You heard it when the hospital called."

"Yes, thank God."

My leg is on *fire.* I can't catch my breath. I need to stay awake, but the pain rolls in.

I'm in my bed at home. Something fierce lies curled in my belly, trying to claw its way out. The overhead light snaps on.

Arden? My mom bends over me. I moan,

325

roll around, clutching my stomach. I stumble to the bathroom while she calls the doctor, her voice low and clear. She's scared, too. When I see the blood, I'm embarrassed. *Mom. It's okay.*

Someone's screaming. *Is it me?*

Henry howls from the basement. The animal cry makes the hair on the back of my neck stand straight up. Dad rushes him to the hospital while I watch Oliver, the two of us pretending to play Crazy Eights. I'm tucking him into bed when he whispers, *I didn't mean to.* His mouth crumples like he's going to cry. *Mean to what?* I whisper back. But he turns his face to the wall.

Where is Rory? Why isn't she telling everyone who I am? Is it Rory screaming?

But Rory doesn't scream. Rory doesn't even cry. She's never broken her arm and she's never had her period. It's her thinness that keeps it away. When I found that out, I tried starving myself, too, but I couldn't make it one day before sneaking down to the pantry in the dark to eat handfuls of crackers straight from the box. Still, Rory knows pain, too. It's just a different kind.

The man next to me on the Metro keeps trying to look down the top of my dress. He reeks of B.O. I turn my shoulder to him and watch cement walls zoom past. I'm dragging by the time I get to Zorba's and my arm's itching like it's on fire. The things you think are cool when you're little are not the things that really are cool when you're grown-up. I'm surprised Rory never changed her mind about getting a tattoo, but I'm glad I went through with it. I'm glad I made her happy.

The screen door bangs shut behind me, stirring up dust motes that spin around in the weak sunshine. The wooden table and chairs are battered, and the place reeks of mildew and stale grease. How did I ever think this place was so sick?

Toby's by the soda dispenser. The place is empty except for him. "Hey." He presses his paper cup against the lever. Dark soda fizzes in. He's got his black messenger bag slung across his chest and he's broken out in angry zits across his forehead and chin.

"Hey. How's school going?"

"College apps suck, man. How many stupid essays do I got to write?"

"Can't your coach help you?"

Toby's parents own a spa clinic in Alexandria. He gets good grades but doesn't play a sport, so he's screwed. He's been working with a college prep coach since eighth grade. "She says I have to do it on

327

my own." He sucks on his straw, shrugs. "I might buy some essays online."

"They'll find out."

"There are sites."

I should tell Rory that. I pull out my wallet and he frowns, jerks his chin to a booth. I'm dismayed. I don't want to sit. I want to get this over with. He slides onto the bench. I sit down opposite, wincing at the sticky surface beneath my bare thighs. He nods and I glance to see Ed's gone into the kitchen. Ed has to know what's going on. He'd be an idiot to think people would want to hang with Toby for any other reason. I push across a folded sheaf of bills and Toby quickly thumbs through them. "You sure this is all you want? Won't last you long, the way you're burning through them."

Like it's any of his business. The sixty bucks I'd paid the tattoo artist meant six pills I couldn't buy. "I'm sure."

He flops open the flap on his messenger bag. "Look, I hate to give away business, but coke's a lot cheaper, you know. Or, hey. Go to the doctor. Tell him you can't concentrate. You know what to say."

Coke's for addicts and my family doctor will just raise his thick white eyebrows at me and tell me the only way he'll give me a prescription is if I go to therapy, too. But really, I'm afraid. I'm terrified of all the ways things could go wrong. This is what I know, meeting Toby for a soda at a crappy pizza place. This is safe. "It's illegal," I say, lamely.

"Dude." He tosses me the small white bottle. "Calm down."

The house is lit up when I get home, all the windows glowing. I unlock the door and step into the front hall. It smells just the same as always, of wood and leather and lemons and rosemary and melting butter. It almost looks the same, too, the tumble of small blue sneakers by the front door and clogs and loafers, the glass lamp filled with seashells turned on in the living room, shining a big circle across the pale green carpet. There's something missing. I can't figure out what. I drop my bag on the floor.

Everyone's in the family room, talking while the television's playing. "Can we go out for Chinese food?" I call out, a joke between my dad and me. I'm always asking to go out to eat and he always answers, *Do you know any good places?* Percy lets out a volley of barks, then he and Oliver skid into the hall. "For real?" he says, as Percy bounds toward me, his long ears flopping. "You're here for real?" Henry is right behind him. "It's a miracle!" he shouts.

My mom's car crunches into the driveway and I push back my kitchen chair. Oliver and Henry jump up and down. "Guess what? Guess what?"

Her measured voice in the hall, happy the way she always is when she's talking to the boys, the clatter of her keys in the bowl. "You won your game?"

"Hi, Mom."

She stops in the doorway, her fingers pressed against her mouth, her eyes shiny with tears. She doesn't move, not even after Dad grabs her shoulders and squeezes. "Look who's here, sweetheart!" I go over to my mom because she's not moving and she drops her hands and opens her arms. We hug for a long time, but nothing about it feels the same. She feels smaller, somehow. "You came home for your birthday. Thank you, darling."

She had wanted to drive up with Dad and Oliver and Henry and take me out, but I had told her no. She had sent a cake instead, chocolate fudge with mocha buttercream and my name carefully scrolled on top in purple icing, packed in dry ice. It had probably taken her a long time. She's not a pastry chef like Uncle Vince. He sent me a cake, too, but I don't tell her that.

My bedroom doesn't look anything like I left it. My bed's made, my clothes hung neatly in my closet and folded in my drawers. The dirty dishes under my bed have disappeared, my trash can's been emptied, and the carpeting shows vacuum cleaner tracks. It smells clean and fresh. I lie down and stare at the ceiling. I know every stucco whorl, the five-fingered crack around my ceiling fan, the wiggly brown stain above the window where the roof leaked. I hold up my arm and look at the white gauze covering a little purple butterfly. Now Rory and I are as close to twins as we'll ever be. My brothers are twins and so are Grandpa Howard and Great-uncle Melvin. I look at them all old and wrinkly and try to picture my little brothers grown up like that. My aunt Christine separates twins who are born connected, which grosses Rory out. Whenever I talk to her about it — two babies sharing a heart or a brain or three legs — she makes a face and covers her ears. *Shut up, will you?* she'll say. But I want to know. Where do you draw the dividing line?

My arm's itching. *Give it a week,* the guy had said. *Don't peel it. Let it flake away by itself.* I pick at the corner of the gauze to sneak a look.

A knock on my door and my mom's there.

"I've brought you some towels." She stops and frowns with concern. "Did you hurt yourself, honey? Let me see."

I slap my hand over my arm. "It's nothing."

"It's not nothing. I can see that it's not nothing."

"You have to promise not to be mad."

"Why would I be mad? Oh, Arden. What have you done?"

I'm in the front hall, crouching beside my bag, stuffing in my gloves and scarf for the cold mornings that are right around the corner. My mom's upstairs, getting my laundry out of the dryer, and my dad's in the boys' room, supervising as they make their beds. "Like this, Daddy?" Oliver says. "I got it," Henry says.

There's still something missing. I look around, searching. I see my brothers' shoes, my dad's briefcase leaning against the table in the hall, Percy's leash hanging from the hook. A toy airplane, my mom's gardening gloves. Now I see it, what's missing. It's me.

RORY

The streets shine with rain. The trees drip, a sudden cool splash on my head, the back of my neck. Music thrums, growing louder as I turn the corner. The house on the corner's filled with light that sprays out, dusting the lawn. Shadows of people moving inside print themselves against the windows. I walk up the steps and through the front door. The first person I really see is Hunter, in the middle of a bunch of people, the way he always is. He sees me and comes over. "Hey, babe." His smile is tight. "You get lost?" He holds out a plastic cup of beer and I shake my hair, wipe moisture from my bare arms. "Let's go." I grab his hand to pull him through the mob of people. "Whoa," he says, following along, laughing.

When we get up to his room, I slam the door and twist the latch. It's quieter in here. A person can think. "What's going on?" he says. "You okay?" I turn into his arms and pull his T-shirt over his head. "I'm fine. I just missed you." I kiss the warm skin of his neck, feeling his steady pulse beneath my lips. I breathe in his clean-boy smell. "Got a problem with that?"

He kisses me back. He doesn't answer.

When I get back to my room Sunday, I hear voices coming from inside. Arden's back and someone's with her. *D.D.?* I unlock the door and swing it open. "Hello, bitches." Too late, I see it's my mother. I'm not even wearing long sleeves.

"Oh, Rory. You know how I feel about that language." The things on my desk are out of order, the papers moved from one side to the other, the drawer left open half an inch. She's been looking through my stuff again, probably while Arden had her back turned. My mom can be very quick about this sort of thing. Had I left anything out — the Baggie of weed, the strip of condoms? My mom would freak if she saw that. She still thinks I'm a virgin. I used to leave her traps, like the fake diary under my mattress. Arden and I would giggle as I wrote sappy entries just for my mom's sake. *I can't believe he likes me! But I won't even let him kiss me. I'm saving myself.* She believed every word. I

334

know she did. She tells me all the time. *I want you to grow up to be a strong woman. I don't want you to settle. I don't want you to rely on a man to make you happy.* Which tells me a lot more about my parents than I ever wanted to know.

I pull down a hoodie from my closet and tug it on.

She comes toward me, her expression smooth and not yielding clues, which doesn't mean I'm in the clear. As we hug, I throw Arden a dark look. She makes a face back. "You should have come home, too," my mother says. "We could have gotten you in to see Jean-Pierre. Ah, well. Thanksgiving will be here soon enough. I'll make you an appointment. Come on, I want to take you both shopping. I owe Arden a birthday present."

"No, you don't," Arden says, and I quickly add, "Hunter's coming over."

"Yes, I do, Arden, and that's perfect, Rory. He can come, too."

Which is the entire point of her coming here, isn't it? "Hunter doesn't want to go shopping, Mom."

"Well, of course not. He can join us afterward. We can go back to that little place I took you to, Arden."

This is the first time I've heard anything

about *that*. "We were planning to study," I say. Arden rolls her eyes. I ignore her. "We have a big test tomorrow."

"Just a quick bite, then. Boys are always hungry. Hunter's an athlete. He can do that carbo-loading."

I want to die. "Please don't say that around him, Mom."

"That's not the right expression?"

"Don't you want to beat the traffic?"

"Oh, *cherie.* You make me feel like you don't want me here."

Sunday afternoon's a terrible time to go shopping. Most of the shops are closed, so we end up at the university bookstore, going through all the lame EMU stuff. Maroon and gold are just two colors that don't belong together.

Arden keeps pulling stuff on and my mom keeps shaking her head. "I'm not sure that does anything for your figure." And, "That's just not special enough." Finally, she decides on a cashmere scarf that Arden insists is too expensive, to which my mom replies, "Don't you think you're worth it, darling?"

Finally, we go to the coffee shop around the corner. I look around, but she's not there.

"We'll be right back." I give Arden a look. She rises from her chair with a noisy sigh and pushes into the bathroom behind me. Only one stall, and we crowd in front of the mirror.

"Don't be pissed," Arden says. "It's not my fault. She found out I was home and offered to drive me. She said she was coming to see you anyway. I texted you."

I'd seen her text come through but ignored it. "Whatever. Did you tell her?"

"No, but my mom knows. She totally lost it."

That surprises me. I'd have guessed Aunt Nat would've been cool with it. "Too bad."

Arden crosses her arms. "You want to tell me what happened to my birthday cake?"

We take a booth in the corner, and when Hunter comes in, I wave him over.

He's wearing a button-down shirt and cologne. My mom will notice he's making an effort. I'm not sure whether this is good or bad. I'm annoyed with myself for even caring. "Hello," he says politely. I slide over to make room.

"I'm so glad you could join us," Mom says.

After we order, my mom leans forward, her hands clasped. "I've been to your family's website," she says to Hunter. "It looks like they have quite a lovely shop."

337

This is her way of telling me she's on to me, that she knows exactly where he's from and it's not an exclusive area in California. She's been with me for more than an hour and has kept this information tucked inside her. She's very good about timing revelations so they'll have the greatest impact. She went through my college essays — the ones Arden helped me write — moving things around so that they read more like short stories. "Are they artists themselves?"

"Not really. My dad took a few classes in community college, but that's it. My mom quilts."

Great. My mother's biggest threat while I was growing up: *You don't want to end up at community college, do you?* I can't even look at her face. I know it's gone rigid with politeness. I want to throw up. I want Hunter to stop talking. Doesn't he realize how this sounds?

"They must be so pleased to know you're going into medicine."

I press my knee against Hunter's and he says in a slightly startled way, "They are."

"Do you know where you'll be applying?"

"Uh." He looks to me.

"Mom, seriously. It's too early to be thinking about that."

"I wish that were true, but you remember

338

what your guidance counselor said. College is just a stepping-stone. We have to think of the big picture." My mother, reading glasses perched on her nose, leaning over and nodding as my guidance counselor pushed papers across for her to examine while I sat there, bored out of my mind and texting beneath the table. "I'm not talking about you, Hunter. How you figure these things out is of course your own business. But Rory knows." She fixes me with a meaningful look. "In order to get into the best schools, you need to start planning now. Speaking of which, have you started on those summer internship applications? You'll need two letters of recommendation. Congressman Simmons says he'll write one. Do you have a professor you can ask?"

My mother's emailed me a list of links, with her helpful comments. *TOP priority! Not sure they take out-of-state applicants. Two essays, but maybe you can use the ones you wrote for your college apps. We might know someone in this firm.* I've clicked the links, the tiny print swimming before my eyes. Mr. Simmons is the congressman who lives next door. I can just picture my mom banging on the door and smiling when he finally answered. "I don't know. Maybe."

"You'd better think about it. Internships

at the best law firms go fast. You don't want to end up at some little general law firm in the suburbs. You might as well work scooping ice cream for the summer."

I feel Hunter shift uneasily beside me. "Mom, I've got four years."

"Four years is nothing. It will fly by, I promise you. You need to think of the big picture."

"Why? I have you to do that for me."

Her mouth tightens and she sits back. "Tell me, Hunter. Do you talk to your mother this way?"

The waitress arrives and sets down our cappuccinos. "I'll be right back with your pie."

As I pluck a packet of sugar from the bowl, my mom says, "Careful, darling."

Careful, Rory. Don't touch.

She raises an eyebrow as she sips her coffee, her way of telling me that she's noticed how I'm wearing my blouse long to cover the undone top snap of my jeans. My cheeks burn and I drop my hand to my lap. Arden's got her head lowered with embarrassment for me. Hunter looks puzzled, like he knows he's missed something but he's not sure what. My mother's talking to Hunter, badgering him about his family. Now Arden's shooting me sympathetic looks that

340

bounce off, harmless rubber balls. My mother's voice swims. I listen carefully to all the syllables flowing together but still can't hear her accent.

"Isn't that right, Rory?" I don't know what my mother's talking about now, but I nod anyway. Of course I do.

The house is dark.

The wooden steps creak. I stand on the rough, bristled mat, the carved wood of the door lost in shadow. An owl hoots. It makes me think of Lake Barcroft, the birds rustling in the trees as Arden and I drift on her boat. It feels very far away. A dog barks. Another one barks back. A car drives slowly past, the sucking sound of tires kissing pavement. I knock. I pull my hoodie around me. I'm shivering though it's a warm night, and still.

I knock again, louder this time.

The porch light flashes on. Someone's peering at me through the tiny circle of glass. The light flashes off, draping me in darkness. The rattle of the latch and she's there, standing in the doorway, her robe tied around her waist. Her hair is loose and shining. She's smiling. "Hey."

I step forward.

NATALIE

My cell phone buzzes. It's Liz, texting to say she needs to talk. "There's a problem at the restaurant," I tell Theo, standing. "I'll be right back." I let myself out of Arden's room and walk down the hall.

Liz answers immediately. I cut her off before we can go into the whole conversation about how Arden's doing. I don't want to talk about Arden. "What do you mean the linen order's been canceled?"

"I know it's not the kind of thing I should be bothering you about, but I sat on it for two days."

"That's okay. I'm glad you did. Can you give me the linen company's phone number? I'll call and straighten this out."

"Sure, but, Natalie, he won't budge. We haven't paid him in two months."

"Wait. That's not right." I scramble back through the days. "Saturday. Just this past Saturday. I had the payment queued up."

"I know, but the florist bill came due at the same time. You know we had that VIP party coming in and the florist threatened to cancel the delivery. I couldn't reach you, so I asked Vince. I'm really sorry. I know I'm not supposed to, but I didn't want to make the decision on my own."

"Vince told you to pay the florist bill instead of the linen bill?" I can't believe it. Flowers are a nice touch, but napkins and tablecloths and aprons are essential. Vince knows that. "What the hell was he thinking?"

"He said he had a good relationship with the linen company and he'd sweet-talk them. But I guess . . . you know."

I know. I really do know.

"We can make do tonight," Liz says. "But it's going to be tough tomorrow."

"All right. Give me the contact info and I'll deal with it."

"I'm sorry."

"Me, too." I slide open the door to Arden's room. "Your genius brother did it again."

Theo looks up from his laptop. "What happened?"

I drop my phone into my bag and twist the elastic from my ponytail. "We don't have linens for tomorrow. Vince thought flowers

343

were more important." I yank my hair back tighter, thinking hard. Would Mitchell lend us linens to last us a few days until I sort things through?

"I'm sure Liz can figure something out."

"She can't. That's why she texted me."

"Well, I'm sure it was an honest mistake."

"The deal is, *I* handle the finances. Not him."

"Are you ever going to let it go, Nat? Are you ever going to just drop it? It's just Vince being Vince. You of all people should know how he is. You knew what he was like and you still went into business with him."

"You were happy when we decided to open a restaurant together!"

"What was I going to tell you, that it was a mistake? You were miserable working for Mitchell."

"If you thought it was a bad idea, you should have warned me."

"You wouldn't have listened."

"It kind of sounds like you think this is all my fault."

"Well, why didn't you keep a closer eye on things?"

I'm utterly astonished. Theo has never once hinted that he felt this way. "Are you serious? How could I have possibly predicted he'd buy that stock? There's no way.

I don't want to talk about Vince anymore."

"Frankly, that would be a relief."

"Have you talked to your father?" my mom asks.

"A little while ago." Mary Beth, Dad's second wife, has been online and found terrible stories of women setting their lovers on fire or burning the houses where the other women lived. It seems to be a female crime, she's told him, a message he's passed on to me. I don't tell Mom I'd stood there, listening in disbelief and understanding that the distance I'd always felt was not my doing. I don't tell her I'd hung up without saying goodbye. I don't tell her that Theo and I are fighting, that I'm out here in the hall making phone call after phone call, just to avoid him. "He's going to help with the legal fees."

Because now we have a lawyer, a woman named Hannah Murphy. She's young and energetic. She's going to call Detective Gallagher to find out whether they plan to arrest Arden. *Will they post an armed guard outside Arden's room?* I'd asked Theo. *In case she plans to escape?*

"Good," my mother replies. "It's the least he can do."

I caught Christine earlier, on her way

between hospital and home. The surgery had gone well and the little girls were in recovery. The next twenty-four to forty-eight hours were critical. *Dad can be such a bastard,* Christine had told me with feeling. *Don't let him in your head.* She's always seen things so clearly. *Don't talk to the police anymore. You need to focus on Arden.*

"I took the boys for haircuts. They got the same style, long on top and short on the sides and back. They look adorable."

I try not to get the boys matching anything. I want them to choose, and the way it always goes is Henry picks first and Oliver hurries to follow. Henry likes Oliver following his lead. He never tries to dissuade him. So what I end up with are two little blond-haired boys who look exactly alike, right down to their little sneakers. *They'll outgrow it,* Theo says, although he can't know.

"Henry was a little champ. He climbed right into that chair and sat as still as a soldier. Oliver got a little teary. I had to hold his hand and give him a lollipop, which made sort of a mess, I'm sorry to say. It got covered with hair."

Yes, Oliver hates change. He's my sensitive one, my little chef. He studies the food on his plate, takes tasting bites, offering his

346

opinions and asking questions in his piping little-boy voice. Henry's my sturdy politician, who's more interested in why people do the things they do and whether they say what they mean. He's the one who will break up arguments among his classmates, who will reason with my mom when she babysits. He's a walking, talking lie detector who never really bought into Santa or the Easter Bunny and the Tooth Fairy. Henry's the one who looks long and hard at me when I tell him I love him, gauging, and then, satisfied, nods.

The elevator arrives with a muted ding. I don't even remember having pressed the button. "Poor Oliver. Poor you."

"Oh, we're fine here. The boys miss you and Theo, of course, but we're staying busy. Don't you worry about us." She sounds content, despite everything. I had wanted Mom to be closer so I could watch over her. I never once considered the possibility that she would end up watching over me.

"I have to go, Mom. I have another call coming in." The nurse, with news? Theo, calling to apologize? I disconnect and glance at the display. It's a phone number I don't recognize. "Hello?"

"Natalie Falcone?" A man, confident.

347

"This is Chris Rogers from Fox News. Do you —"

Horrified, I press the end button. He'd sounded so smug. What did he want? How did he get my number?

The elevator shudders to a stop. The lobby's deserted. The floor gleams. Muted lights hang from the ceiling. I step forward and the doors whoosh open with a hiss. The air is cool, the purple sky streaked pink and orange. The glitter of first stars, and in the distance, the murky line of trees. The Chesapeake Bay is out there somewhere, a mere twenty miles away. My bag is slung over my shoulder; inside it are my car keys.

The road's a stretch of ribbon winding into darkness. I follow another car, its red brake lights a distant comfort. The road dips. When I reach the summit, the car is gone, having turned off onto one of the narrow roads crisscrossing the fields. I roll down the windows and salty air fills the car. Arden loves the beach. As a toddler, she'd crouch in the sand, sunhat tied around her chin, and dig little trenches decorated with broken bits of shells. She could play like that for hours. I'd lie nearby on my blanket and watch her, and feel so lucky. I'd never understood how pure love could be. There's just the ocean rolling in and out, seagulls squawking overhead. Joy stretching in all directions.

The road ends. I turn left, toward the glow of lights.

Streetlights appear, sidewalks, storefronts. I'd been surprised, and relieved, at how pretty the campus turned out to be — lots of trees and grass, brick buildings, a water fountain in the middle of the traffic circle. Early September, the leaves had been just turning colors.

Look, I'd pointed. *They've got a nice gym.* I'd hoped Arden would take swimming up again now that she didn't feel the pressure to compete on a team. She'd merely sighed and looked away. I'd known she was thinking of USC. *Am I going there next year?* she'd asked while we were up late packing the night before, just the two of us, and all I could think was that everything I was doing at that moment to help her get ready to leave was the very last thing I wanted to be doing. It was one of those times as her mother that I did what I had to do and tried not to think about it. *I hope so,* I'd begun hesitantly, and she'd said, *Which means no.* Her face shuttered closed.

Which means, daughter of my heart, that where you go to college is important, but not as important as our being able to pay the mortgage. But I didn't say that.

I had shaken my head at the piles of her belongings in the entry hall waiting to be loaded into the car. *If you need anything,* I'd told her, trying to figure out how we were going to fit them, and us, into the car, *we can always bring it to you.* Theo had put his hand on my arm. *It's all right, Natalie. We'll make it work.*

I'm going slow this evening, looking for that convenience store Theo and I had passed, when a student steps off the curb in front of me. I brake sharply to let her run across the road. My headlights catch on her jeans, her swinging arm, the backpack strapped to her shoulders. She steps onto the far curb and disappears beneath the spreading branches.

It's called The Bowl, I had told Arden as we carried armloads of bedding across the parking lot. She had been quiet for much of the three-hour trip. *Here it is,* I'd chirped. The twins had come running. They'd been the only ones fooled into thinking we were having fun. I'd been a relentless tour guide that day. *They have an arboretum. There are bike trails leading down to the Bay.* I wince, thinking of how artificial my cheerfulness had been. Arden had borne it all stoically,

350

saying little as she hauled her stuff up three narrow flights of stairs. We'd left her and Rory putting away their things as the sun eased itself below the horizon, softening everything in its path as we drove away, the boys' chatter in the backseat the only sounds that accompanied us on the long drive home.

I stare through the windshield. In the distance, hundreds of tiny lights flicker. The vigil for Hunter. I'd forgotten.

It's a silent crowd gathered in front of the dark brick building. Between people's shifting shoulders, I glimpse the marble steps piled with stuffed animals and cellophane-wrapped cones of flowers, cards and posters, and the occasional flickering candle, which seems unkind. The air is damp with all the recent rain, the ground smelling rich. This is the last place I want to be, but here I am.

Someone hands me a votive candle in a paper cup. A young woman, about Arden's age. Her face glows in the candlelight. "Thank you," I whisper, and she nods.

Hunter's parents are up on the front steps, Phil's arm around Janet's shoulders. They can't see me where I'm standing, well back and in the shadows. I recognize the man

351

beside them, the school official who'd been by right after the fire to offer his help. He's been by a second time and Theo had been the one to talk to him, to tell him we were fine, we'd let him know if we needed anything. What we needed was to be left alone. What we needed was a miracle.

"Did you know Hunter?" the girl asks me, and I shake my head. "No, but . . ."

No, but my daughter did. No, but my niece did.

I look up through the branches to the gaping black hole that was my daughter's dorm window. Was it only six days ago that she woke up and stretched, rummaged through her clothes, laughed with friends? I see her sitting cross-legged in her plaid bathrobe, her hair messily tied back and her lower lip caught between her teeth as she stares at an open textbook. I don't see her splashing paint thinner across her room, striking a match, and stepping back. I stare at that window ledge she'd crouched on, the wooden sides she gripped before letting go and falling forward.

Arden had surprised me by coming home for her birthday. I had been speechless with emotion. I had thought, *She's here.* I had meant it in every sense of the word. My daughter had come home and everything would be the way it once had been. But that's not what happened. Arden had changed; she was more subdued, with a tattoo she'd gotten only just that morning. Arden had come home, but that was it. She hadn't really been there.

". . . his whole life ahead of him," Phil is saying. "He wasn't sure what he wanted to do, but we knew he'd figure it out. That's the way he was with baseball, too. He'd tried a couple sports, but nothing clicked until he picked up a bat. And then nothing could keep him back. That's just the way he was. When he set his mind to something, he wouldn't let go until he got there."

Like Rory? What has Detective Gallagher learned about Hunter? What terrible things has he been firing at the man and woman standing bravely in front of all of us, working to say goodbye to their son?

"Hunter was a good boy. He was a sensitive boy." Janet sobs and turns into her husband's arms. Another man steps forward and clears his throat. "I was Hunter's coach. From the very first practice, I knew . . ."

After a while, the swaying crowd moves and breaks apart, and people start to disperse. An invisible signal's been given. Hunter's parents are talking to some of the kids, a few adults.

"It rained so hard that night," someone says beside me. "It was like the skies were crying." A woman in her thirties, exotically beautiful, with dark winged eyebrows, creamy skin, and a cascade of black curls that gleam beneath the streetlight. "Did you know Hunter?"

"He was my daughter's friend."

She nods. "He was one of my students, but I didn't really know him, either. It's a large class and early in the semester." She wears a white blouse with neatly folded cuffs and a dark narrow skirt. She smells of some light floral fragrance. I am aware of how grubby I am, how for days I've done little more than brush my hair. "How's your daughter doing?"

It startles me, and then I realize of course she doesn't know who my daughter is. "I'm Natalie Falcone. Arden's mother," I say, extending my hand, the one not holding the candle. Her expression immediately softens and she takes my hand in both of hers. "Oh, Mrs. Falcone. How is she doing? How's Rory?"

"The same." I'm so tired of this question. "Please call me Natalie."

"Natalie, of course. I'm Chelsea Lee. Arden's in my Intro class. So was Rory. They all were." She looks away, then back to me.

"I stopped by the hospital, but they told me the girls couldn't have visitors."

I don't know who's come to visit, who's called or stopped by. I've been trapped inside my daughter's room, a fly buzzing from wall to wall. "Arden loves your class." *I'm thinking I might double major in art and art history,* Arden had said. She'd sounded happy and I had thought, *Maybe EMU's a blessing after all.*

"She's a bright girl, a hard worker. She's really into Giotto, which is amazing, truthfully. Not many beginning art history students are able to grasp just how important his contribution was, but she just lights up talking about him." She smiles. "I told her to wait until we got to Vermeer."

I doubt Arden will be back in school this semester, and this realization floods me with sadness. Chelsea Lee is regarding me. "It must be so hard," she says. "It must be impossible."

This teacher, who smiles when talking about my daughter, who had inspired Arden. "Everything's just so wrong," I blurt out. "Arden's been accused of cheating." I take in a breath, ready to unfurl the entire story, when Chelsea Lee says simply, "Yes," and I am stopped. This bald acceptance of what can't be true. I look at her. "You know?"

"Yes, I do. I'm sorry."

Does the whole faculty know? Everyone's talking about Arden, rummaging through her life. "You don't understand. Arden's a good student. She's always been a good student. She's not a cheater."

"I do understand." She hesitates, choosing her words carefully. "Arden's very smart. It's a shame what happened."

"How do you know about it?" And then I understand. "You?"

"I shouldn't have said anything. I really can't talk about it."

"You have to talk about it. You have to tell me."

"I'm so sorry."

I'm crying, to my horror. Arden's not here to defend herself and I need to set things straight. I need to make things right for her. Gabrielle's accusations beat hard in my ears. Chelsea looks at me with such sympathy. I need her to stop. I don't want any kindness from this woman. I don't know her. She hurt Arden. She threw Arden into the worst possible light. "You have no right. You should be ashamed of yourself." I need a tissue. I know I have one in my pocket because the boys are always needing one,

356

and for some reason that only makes me cry harder. "You've made a mistake," I sob.

"I like Arden, Mrs. Falcone. I really do. I can't explain why she'd feel the need to steal someone else's work, but it's a difficult class. I expect a lot from my students. She must have felt overwhelmed."

"You've got to be kidding! It's art history. Not molecular biology."

She sucks in a breath and steps back. At least she's dropped her arms. A firmness has settled on her features. This I can deal with. I know this. I've dealt with a thousand people, a hundred thousand people demanding something from me. It's better when we get it all out in front of us and I can see what needs to be done. I need this woman on my side. I need her on Arden's side. "I'm sorry, I shouldn't have said that. But we can't have these accusations hanging over her. The police are thinking terrible things. You have to tell them it's not true."

"But it is true, Mrs. Falcone. I'm so sorry. I truly am." She looks up at the dark and empty building. "She must have felt so desperate."

I stand there, holding on to a tiny flame in a paper cup. I want to fling it at this beautiful woman and wipe that knowing expression off her face. For the first time, I

357

understand how something like this could happen.

ARDEN

A muffled creak, the feel of air moving across my lips. "There you are," Uncle Vince says. "I brought you something to eat."

Can I eat? When was the last time I ate anything? I don't feel hungry. I'm dulled and thick. Everything hurts. I can't move my arms or legs.

You were in a fire. Do you remember?

"I'm not hungry," Aunt Gabrielle says.

"It's here if you want it," he says.

I smell roasted meat. It makes me gag. I haven't had meat in ages. When D.D. had asked why I wasn't eating, I snatched at the first answer: *I'm thinking about going vegetarian.* It was the right thing to say. Her face relaxed immediately. But now I'm stuck. I can't even sneak fruit snacks. D.D. says they have gelatin in them, and she's got her spies.

Uncle Vince clears his throat. "I ran into Detective Gallagher on the way back just now."

359

Detective, like the police?

"Does he have news?"

"Not that I know of. We talked about you, as a matter of fact."

"Me? How odd."

"He asked me what you were doing on campus Friday night. He wanted to know why you hadn't mentioned it to anyone."

Aunt Gabrielle's always on campus. Rory says she should just get her own damn dorm room and move in.

"Gabby?"

"I should have mentioned it, I know. But I wasn't thinking. I was worried about Rory."

"You should have said something."

"Why are you talking to me like this? What are you implying?"

All of a sudden, I can see. My eyes are open, just a tiny bit, but enough to see the darkness everywhere and the faint whiteness of the sheet covering me. I try to move my head, signal with my fingers.

"I'm not implying anything. I'm telling you. He had a lot of questions. Some of them I couldn't answer."

Look at me look at me look at me

"I'll talk to him, then. I'll answer his questions. I'll explain. I was with a client."

"At nine o'clock at night?"

360

A knock on the door. "May I come in?" A cheerful voice. A nurse.

A knock on the door makes me look up.

It's Hunter, backpack slung over his shoulder. I put my hands up to smooth my hair, and stop myself. *Stupid, stupid.* "Hey," he says. "Know where Rory is? She's not answering her texts."

"Sorry." Rory's gone into one of her solitary phases. It usually happens after Aunt Gabrielle's done something to upset her. I can't blame her. It had been horrible in the coffee shop. For once, I was glad not to be Rory.

"She was going to help me with calculus." Hunter leans against the doorframe. "I guess she forgot."

The only times Rory forgets about plans she's made with a guy are the times she's trying to make a point. I surprise myself. I say, "I could help you."

I have three favorite photographs of Rory. The oldest one's from when we were babies propped side by side on the sofa, cushions supporting us. Rory looked like a fat-cheeked caterpillar next to little me, but by the time we started third grade, Rory was taller and much skinnier. By the time we were in seventh grade, we were both the same height, but she was the one everyone wanted to be friends with. I've slid that photograph out of the album and stuck it in my mirror at home. I like to know there was a time when I was the prettier one.

The second photograph is from when Rory was five and I was four and a half — when you're that little, four months count. I don't remember when this one was taken, either. I've tried to pull this memory out of my brain, but if there's anything there, it stays firmly lodged behind something else, like when a boy named Mark ate two glue sticks and threw up in the kindergarten sandbox, or when I won the second-grade reading competition and got to take home a big trophy with my name on it. The story is that Rory had burned herself, just a little burn, but it hurt, and Rory had to go to the ER and get it looked at. So no big deal, other than the ugly scar it left on Rory's arm, but Rory was upset and so she ended up staying at our house for a few days. That's what my mom told me when I asked about it later, when I was going through the photo albums, looking for a picture of me to take in for my sixth-grade Get to Know Me poster, and came across one of me and Rory standing in front of a metal fence. In the background, I could see playground equipment, a wooden bridge suspended between two purple towers. I remembered that thing. I was so scared of it, the way it swayed beneath me when I tried to walk across it. I was so proud the day I was able to cross it without holding on to the rope. *Wait,* I'd asked, *Rory went to Mount Hebron, too?* How could I not remember that? *Just for a week or so,* my mom answered. She was busy studying recipes and her voice was totally casual. I asked Rory about it the next day after school and I could hear her shrug on the phone. *No offense, Arden,* she'd said. *But that was a pretty lame school.* She just didn't want to admit that there was a time when she needed me more than I needed her.

But I definitely remember when the third picture was taken. This one's on my phone, locked in and bolted. It's the selfie from when Rory and I sat on the swings and talked, trying to figure it out, until Rory finally said she didn't want to talk about it anymore.

"What's up with her?" Hunter says. We're walking back from the library, where I was supposed to be reading *King Lear* and writing a French essay, but I'd spent the whole time drawing caricatures of the people sitting around us and giggling as Hunter wrote the captions. *Help! I'm being held prisoner by the fashion police!* for the guy with dreadlocks and an orange beanie. *Are you talking to me?* for the girl who kept looking up to throw us annoyed looks. *Let's dance* for the guy listening to his iPod and tapping his pencil.

After the librarian came by for the second time to tell us to be quiet, he closed his textbook. *Let's get out of here,* he'd said, and so we had. It's after ten, everything muted by darkness — the music coming through an opened window, the scent of damp earth and leaves, the whir of bicycle wheels as someone pedals past and whizzes around the corner. It's like we're alone, but of course we're not. Rory's here, even when she's not.

"Look," I say. "She gets this way sometimes. She just needs to be alone."

"Where? Where is she being alone?" He throws his arms wide. "It's like she's disappeared. Or maybe she's with someone else. You'd tell me, wouldn't you?"

"Sure." Though I'm not sure I would. I'm not sure I could.

"Man, I know I'm being played. Just when I give up and think it's all over, she shows up like nothing's the matter. I can't figure her out."

"Rory's complicated." Like I haven't heard this a million times before. Blake had been this way, too, back when Rory got pissed at him for talking to some chick at a party and gave him the cold shoulder right before prom. Right before she was supposed to put out.

"I've never met anybody like her."

I'm silent. I'm so done talking about Rory and how amazing she is, how she can make the whole world light up and just as dramatically turn it all black again.

"Sorry. I don't mean to keep talking about her. It's just that you're so easy to talk to. I feel like I can tell you anything."

"I feel the same way." All my shy words unstumble themselves and spill out. *I was kind of a geek in high school. I love my mom, but . . .*

Hunter puts his arm around me and squeezes. It feels so right, so perfect. He's just tall enough so that my shoulders fit into his embrace. He nods. He answers. He says all the right things. One by one, all the hurdles topple over. "You're a good friend, you know that?"

Take risks. Before I can stop myself, I say, "I wish I were more." My words fall into a little shocked pool of silence. All I hear is the slap of our shoes on the pavement. Is he going to say anything? Now it's all out there. Now there's nowhere for me to hide.

He drops his arm, which says it all. "Dude."

My cheeks flame. I can't look at him. "Whatever."

"No, wait." He reaches out and grabs my arm, pulls me back to him. The branches throw his face into shadow. I can't see his eyes.

"I shouldn't have said anything. Let's pretend I never did."

"I can't do that."

No, of course he can't. My words are skyscrapers, too tall to climb over.

He looks away and shakes his head. "I wish I'd met you first."

"What does that even mean? Like you're her prisoner? Rory doesn't own you, you know. You're not hers." I put my palms against his chest and give him a little push. He doesn't answer. He just looks down at me. I feel the warmth of his skin beneath the cotton of his shirt. I feel his heart pounding just as hard as mine. I clutch his shirt, wrap my fingers in the cloth, and pull him close. I'm tingling all over. I'm on fire. His face is thrown in shadow. I can't read

366

his expression. I don't know what he's thinking.

I rise on my toes and bring my lips to his. Soft, soft, soft. He doesn't stop me.

Doesn't he know? I'm not Rory.

". . . seeing a better oxygen rate by now," a woman says. Her voice is clear and confident, in charge. I've heard it before. It's the doctor. I feel her leaning over me. A brief flash of light.

"What does that mean? Vince?" Aunt Gabrielle's voice sounds high, frightened.

"There's a treatment I'd like to try called ECMO, extracorporeal membrane oxygenation, which is essentially an artificial lung." The doctor moves away. "It'll take over oxygenating her blood until her lungs can do it themselves. It's shown great results in otherwise healthy patients and I'm hopeful it will work for Rory."

She's talking about me. She thinks I'm Rory. I'm Arden! Someone tell her. Someone look at me and *see*.

"How risky is it?" Uncle Vince asks.

"Well, of course there are risks with any procedure. There's a slight possibility of perforation during cannulation, and any time you have open sites to the body, you run into the possibility of infection. But the thing we need to be most concerned about is bleeding. We'll be closely monitoring her platelet counts."

"Okay," Uncle Vince says.

"There's a small chance she could develop a thromboembolism."

"What is that?" Aunt Gabrielle says. "I don't understand any of this."

"Of course, Mrs. Falcone. I realize I'm throwing a lot at you. A thromboembolism is a blood clot."

"A blood clot? Is that dangerous?"

"Depending on size and location . . ."

"What you're saying is it could kill her."

Panic rears up and clamps down hard. I don't want to die. Not like this. Not now. I want my mom. I want my dad. I want them in here, talking to the doctor and taking care of me.

"We'll have her on heparin as a preventative measure. And thromboembolisms really are rarer in the form of ECMO that we'll be putting her on."

"We haven't decided to go ahead with this," Aunt Gabrielle says.

"I understand. I can give you some literature . . ."

"I'd like a second opinion."

"I can arrange for that. But I do urge you to decide quickly. It's your decision, of course, but I do believe the benefits greatly outweigh the risks."

"Thank you, Dr. Morris," Uncle Vince says.

"I'll have my nurse get you some literature, and I'll set up a consultation for you with another doctor."

She's leaving. *Please don't go!* She looked right at me. Right at me and through me. I want her to look again, to tell Uncle Vince to look, too. *Get my mom and dad.* I don't want Aunt Gabrielle making any decisions for me.

Quiet gathers around me. I don't know where anyone is. Am I alone? Then I hear muffled weeping, and Uncle Vince saying, "It's all right, sweetheart."

"I don't know what we should do."

"I think we should go ahead with it. This procedure sounds like it might work."

"They already tried to kill her once. Do we really trust them?"

"I don't think we have a choice."

"We do. Of course we do. Maybe we're trying too hard. Maybe we should accept the facts."

"The facts are this procedure may save her."

"But you heard her. Rory's lungs aren't working."

My lungs. It's my lungs that aren't working. Right? I want to put my hand on my chest and feel its reassuring rise and fall. I'm breathing, aren't I?

"We can't just give up. We can't do that." His voice is soft cotton, wrapping around.

"What kind of life is it to live attached to a machine?"

"It's only temporary."

"Until what? She's *scarred,* inside and out." Aunt Gabrielle's crying. "Tell me you believe me. Tell me you understand. I couldn't help it. I couldn't."

"You couldn't help what, sweetheart?"

"Nothing. I'm just tired. I need to sleep."

Yes.

RORY

Chelsea just won't let it go. "What does this say?"

The first time was when she handed me that book with the monk on the cover. Of course I'd figured it out by then. I didn't even have to look. *The God in All of Us,* I'd told her, so casual. I thought she'd back off, but now it's a thing. Every so often, she hands me something to read. I humor her. Sometimes words fit themselves together and sometimes they don't. The more time I have, the better. So I pretend to be distracted by the long corkscrew of hair hanging over her bare shoulder, twisting it around my finger. "Stop it," she says, lightly slapping my hand. She points to the page. "Right there."

"The twin spires of Notre Dame . . ."

She tilts her head and looks at me. I nailed it, I know. Usually, this is enough, but she just turns a few pages. "How about this?"

Too many words and not enough white space. I'm tired. We've been up all night. She'd traced the tattoo on my forearm, making me shiver. "What — are you testing me?" I ask now.

"Yes, I am. What does this say?"

My kindergarten teacher looking at me with impatience. "I'm not five, you know."

"Is that when you first noticed it?"

I don't ask her what *it* is. I just gather my clothes from the chair and tug them on, keeping my back to her. I feel her gaze burning a line down my spine as I fumble with the clasp on my bra. I don't say good-bye.

When I get back to the room, Arden's there, on her bed with her laptop propped in front of her. She looks up at me and, I swear, the disapproval on her face makes her look just like my mom. "Where were you last night?" she demands.

"Out." I drop my bag on my bed and reach for the towel hanging up in my closet. I sniff it, then fling it over my shoulder.

"You're seriously not going to tell me?"

"I'm seriously not going to tell you." I don't know what I'm thinking. I don't know how I'm feeling and I'm not going to talk about it with Arden. I'm not going to talk about it with anyone.

"Suit yourself." She looks back to her laptop. "Hunter was looking for you."

"Tell me something I don't know." He's texted me a thousand times, the last one at two a.m. *U ok?* I'd propped myself up on one elbow to read it. If it had been me being stood up, my last text at two a.m. would have been more like *Fuck you asshat.* Hunter's too nice. I don't deserve him.

"Well? Aren't you going to call him back?"

"How is that any of your business?"

"Hunter's my friend, too, you know."

"Uh-huh. Saying it doesn't make it true."

"What's *that* supposed to mean?"

"It means, little cousin, back off. Anyone can see you've got a thing for him."

"I don't have a thing for him." Red rises up her throat and stains her cheeks. "He's just my friend. Believe it or not. We're just friends."

She's so predictable. Why can't she just stop? Bash the walls of the box she's hiding inside and step out? I feel sorry for her. I really do. "You can't be friends with guys, Arden. They only want one thing."

"Hunter's not like that!"

I want to laugh, but I can't change it up. She needs to know that nothing's happened. So I give her a stern look. "Don't tell me what my boyfriend's like."

373

"The way you treat him, I bet he won't be your boyfriend much longer."

I fold my arms and look at her. She tries to look defiant, but it only comes out looking worried. "He'll be my boyfriend as long as I want him to be."

"What about what he wants?"

I laugh. "I know what he wants. I already told you." I pick up my shower caddy and head for the bathroom. In the stall, I let hot water drum the backs of my shoulders. Steam rises. *The lucky girl,* Chelsea had called me. I draw a four-leaf clover with my fingertip on the tiles.

I end up sitting beside a player's mom. Not my choice. She's the one who walked down the long, empty bleacher and set her big knitting bag beside my feet. "Hi," she said with a smile, like we knew each other. She sat, pulling out a fat bundle of yarn and a pair of pink aluminum needles. They reminded me of the ones Grandma Sugar tried to teach Arden and me how to use. We'd both sucked.

"You know, they only put in Michael because his dad's the coach at College Park," she confides, because it's been half an hour and we're now best buds. I don't have a clue who Michael is. I'd had to stare long and hard to figure out which of the guys on the field was Hunter, only to realize he was the one coming up to bat. He'd glanced over in my direction and paused before going on.

Not Michael's Mom clutches my arm. "How did number twenty-three make it to second? I totally wasn't paying attention!"

"I missed it, too." Like I even know what that means. *What do I do about Chelsea? What am I doing with her?* Not Michael's Mom buys me a hot dog and I take a big bite. I don't even like hot dogs.

"That was a ball! That was a ball! How can they call it a strike? Blind as hell."

"For sure." I wrap my arms around my bent knees. It's lame how few people are here watching, even though these games don't count. It's nothing like football games, where the stadium is packed with thousands of people. If I were a guy, that's the sport I'd play. Not this one, where no one's there to watch you shine. Unless that's the point.

After the two teams line up and slap one another's hands, I climb down. Hunter glances over, claps some guy on the shoulder, and laughs. I stand there, feeling stupid. I deserve the silent treatment. I deserve to be ignored. But honestly? It's never happened. Sure enough, Hunter turns and slowly walks over. "Hey," he says.

"Great game." I know where this is going, even if Hunter doesn't. This is familiar terrain for me. I can walk it with my eyes closed. "Even though that was so definitely a strike."

"You know what you're talking about?"

"Umpire's blind as hell."

The corner of his mouth twitches. He takes off his cap and runs his fingers through his hair. "So, what is this, Rory? You want to tell me what's going on?"

"I wish I knew."

"What kind of answer is that?"

I shrug. "The truth."

He looks away.

"I was thinking," I begin, and when he glances back to me, I know. Nothing's changed.

We end up going back to my room. His roommate's got a study group and Arden's at the art studio, working on her self-portrait. *I don't know what to call it,* she'd said, propping the canvas on the classroom easel — a girl walking away and looking over her shoulder. Arden had smeared blossoms of red paint around the face and the girl's eyes glittered like emeralds. Arden stood beside me, nervously wiping her brushes with a stinking rag that made my eyes burn. *It's great,* I told her, meaning it. Only thing was, it was like looking in a mirror.

Arden's left the door unlocked, with a note scrawled on the dry-erase board. *Back at 8.* I swipe two fingers across it and close the door behind us. "I should join a sorority next year. Get my own room."

"I thought they didn't have sororities at Harvard."

"Figure of speech." I kick Arden's clothes out of the way and sink down on my bed. "Let's get high."

"Can't. Not during the preseason."

"You're no fun."

"I can be fun."

"Show me."

This is what I know. This is easy.

Later, he reaches up to push my hair back from my face. "Hey," he says softly.

"Hey yourself." I am mellow, lying on my back, staring up at the scarves stretched across the ceiling. Arden and I had tacked them up in a hurry before someone caught us, but the randomness turned out to be so pretty. There's my navy-and-green Hermès print, my fuchsia Kate Spade, my black-and-white-and-tan Chanel, my tangerine Tory Burch. It's not fair they're my scarves and not Arden's, but she didn't have scarves.

377

All she had was dirty laundry. The RA had come by and not noticed a thing. I turn onto my side and smile at Hunter. "Everything better now?"

"Look at me."

"I am looking at you."

"No, you're not. Where are you, Rory? Where are you, really?"

I'm annoyed, my pop of happy glow punctured and deflating. "I'm right here."

"You sure?" He gives me a long searching look, as if he's trying to see inside me. Doesn't he know? There's nothing there to see. I push him away and sit up. "I'm starving. Let's grab something to eat."

It's weird. I look everywhere, but I can't find my key card.

NATALIE

A noise startles me awake. I've fallen asleep in the chair beside Arden's bed. I sit up, my neck stiff and sore, and glance around for the source of the noise. Is it one of the monitors? Alarmed, I straighten and look to the machines lining the walls of the room. No, it's just Theo snoring in the chair by the door, his arms limp by his sides. He's exhausted. He's working hard to keep everything going. I look at Arden, lying peacefully in the bed beside me. I'd lowered the railing earlier in the night — it wasn't serving a purpose, anyway — and now I reach for her hand, lying beneath the sheet. I'd had a nightmare: Arden had been arrested and given a life sentence. I'd talked to her through the bars of her prison cell, assured her that I would get her free. But she'd just looked at me and said she'd got what she deserved. What is my subconscious telling me? I rub my neck and push myself up.

Out at the round reception desk, two nurses sit entering information into computers. Denise looks up with a smile. "Hey. I'm glad you finally got some sleep."

"I'm going to get some coffee. Can I get you anything?"

"Oh, no. I'm good."

I'm in line balancing two cups and a plate when I see Arden's face smiling down from the TV in the corner. It stops my heart with longing. It's not a picture I've seen before and I wonder who took it and how this TV station got hold of it. Then, in quick succession, images of Rory and Hunter, followed by words in lurid yellow: DEADLY LOVE TRIANGLE? I pay for the coffee and pastry with trembling fingers.

Up in Arden's room, I grasp Theo's shoulder and he's awake instantly. "What is it?" He comes to his feet, glances toward Arden's bed.

"No, no."

We talk in the family lounge and then he's calling Hannah. How good a lawyer can she be, that she takes our calls so quickly? But she comes highly recommended by my father-in-law's golf buddy, who says she was at the top of her class at Georgetown. That's what impresses Theo, but I'm more comforted by her confidence, the way she drills down to the marrow: "I'll call the station. Which one was it; do you know?" She's a take-no-prisoners girl. She'll demand the story be pulled; she'll try to find out where they got the information. She doesn't want us talking to reporters. Any media contact should be handled with *No comment* or, better yet, not answered at all. "Has she heard from Detective Gallagher?" I want to know. Theo shakes his head. "It's only been a day," he reminds me.

He's been getting emails from Karen. Parents have been calling, wanting information. *Is it true Arden Falcone was about to be expelled? Is there a cover-up going on at Bishop?*

Terrible things, defeating things. I want to protest. I want to insist it's all a lie. Arden's a smart girl. She earned her grades. But aren't parents always the last to know?

"I'd better go in," Theo says, and I nod. But as he stands, I stop him. "Theo? Do you think we pushed her too hard?"

"Maybe Bishop wasn't the best place to send her."

We'd been so delighted when Theo got the job as headmaster. It meant we could send Arden to the best school. She'd be set for life. We'd been talking about figuring out a way to send the boys to Bishop's brother school, but now I wonder.

After Theo leaves, I call my mother. She's seen the news, too, and she's been waiting for my call. "It makes me furious," she says. "How can they do this? How can they get away with saying all those terrible things?" Her voice is shaking. "Do you think I should keep the boys home from school? I don't want them overhearing anything."

I think about it. Their teacher wouldn't say anything and neither would another parent, not about something like this, not to six-year-olds. "I think school's okay, and soccer practice. But maybe no playdates." I picture them in their sleepers, Oliver curled under his covers like a comma, Henry sprawled out like a starfish.

"Okay."

"And, Mom? Don't answer the home phone."

"Oh. Okay, I won't."

I look down the hall. Dr. Morris stands outside Rory's room, talking with a man in a long, white lab coat. She's nodding, arms crossed, as he talks. "Something's going on with Rory," I tell my mom in a low voice. Rory's in a medical coma and has been drifting in and out of consciousness for days. They've been fighting to keep her sedated and calm.

"Like what?"

"I don't know. But if it's serious, Gabrielle and Vince would tell us." But it ends up being Denise the nurse who tells me Rory's going to be put on an artificial lung.

"Permanently?" I ask, in horror.

"No, no. It's a temporary measure." She shines a flashlight to check Arden's IV.

"Her breathing's no better?"

Denise shakes her head.

I peek into Rory's room, but Gabrielle and Vince aren't there. Maybe they're talking to the doctors. Maybe they've gone to the hotel. I dial my sister's number.

Christine answers the phone immediately. Her voice echoes. She's got me on speaker in her car. "How's Arden?"

"The same. Can you talk?"

"Of course."

"It's Rory. They're going to put her on an artificial lung. Do you know what that means?"

"ECMO?"

"I don't know."

"That's probably what it is. It just means that her lungs still haven't started working and they want to be more aggressive about giving them a chance to heal. Try not to worry, Nat. It's a fairly safe procedure. It's been around a long time."

I sense what she's not saying. "But?"

A pause. "But I wonder why they didn't put her on it earlier."

I glance toward Rory's closed door. "Does this mean it won't work?"

"No, no," Christine says.

I call Theo next, and when he doesn't answer, I leave a long message on his phone.

That afternoon, they wheel Rory out of her room. I hear the rattle of gurney wheels outside in the hall, the voices going past. Gabrielle says, ". . . in here?" as she passes by.

It's a simple surgery, Christine has explained, and sure enough, within the hour, Rory's wheeled back into her room. I crane to hear something, anything, but all is mysteriously silent. I've been online so I know there's a seventy percent chance this procedure will help. I can't help but think of the thirty percent no one is talking about. I text Vince. *How's Rory?* I'm still holding my phone, waiting for a response, when the nurse comes in to empty Arden's Foley bag.

I stand. "I'll be out in the hall," I tell the nurse, and she nods.

Gabrielle's alone in the room with Rory. She stands with her back to me, and doesn't turn around as I approach. She's intent on something, and as I come closer, I see she's fiddling with Rory's breathing tube. We've been told not to touch our daughters' breathing tubes. We can't adjust the monitoring equipment; we shouldn't touch the bandages covering our girls' burns. If we notice something awry, we are to summon immediately for help. "Do you need me to get the nurse?" I whisper.

She spins to face me. "Natalie! What are you doing creeping up on me like that?"

"I'm sorry. I thought you heard me coming in. I wanted to see how Rory's doing. Vince isn't answering his phone."

Her hand is at her throat, her charm bracelet dangling from a narrow wrist. Every charm was given to her by Vince, mementos from their trips across the country. She's never left America, not once in twenty years. *There's so much to see here,* she once told me in a chirpy sort of way, but I know Vince always has a hard time convincing her to leave home. She inhales, turns back to Rory. "She's doing as well as can be expected, I suppose."

Rory's features assemble before me in the darkness, her swollen cheeks squeezing her eyes to slits, the rise of her throat, the triangle of skin where her gown gapes open. Her pale hair spills over the pillow. Arden's hair had to be shaved for surgery. All we've seen of it is that single wisp protruding from the bandages wrapped around her head.

"They've taken off her helmet. That's good news."

"Yes."

"Do you think she's awake?" Is she listening to us now? I try not to envy Gabrielle this.

"No, she's asleep."

A new tube has been taped to Rory's neck. It's filled with dark fluid — blood. It travels across her pillow and over to the small white machine on the table against the wall. That small white machine is doing the work that Rory's lungs can't. "Maybe she won't have to be on that long."

"Maybe." Gabrielle's voice is carefully neutral. She's upset and trying not to show it. She lifts up the sheet. It floats above Rory and slowly settles.

"I guess you've seen the news," I say.

"It's everywhere. How could I not?"

"It's horrible. I don't know how people can live with themselves." A deadly love triangle. Gabrielle thinks it's true. She said so herself. "You haven't been talking to the press, have you?"

She glances at me, frowning. "Of course not. I don't want anything to do with them.

This is private."

Her words have the ring of truth. Gabrielle values privacy, I know. Still, where had the television station gotten that photograph of Arden? What am I suspecting Gabrielle of, exactly — asking questions? Having doubts? I'm guilty of the same. I tell her, "Our lawyer's going to have them take the story down."

"It's good that you have a lawyer."

I glance to her, sharply. Is she threatening me? She's tidying the things on the small nightstand. Then she adds, "I think we'll get one, too."

The glass door slides open and Theo ducks around the curtain, slings his jacket onto the chair by the door, and holds up a plastic bag. "Mama Joe's special fish taco, extra avocado." By unspoken consent, we're avoiding the cafeteria. We keep our heads down in the corridor. Within hours, we have become recognizable — the parents of the burned girl in the ICU, the desperate girl facing expulsion who might have set her roommate on fire. "Thanks," I say, though I'm not hungry. We're both tiptoeing around each other, afraid of saying too much, afraid of unburying another truth.

He waggles the bag. "Chips and salsa, too."

Arden loves salsa: the spicier, the better. She sprinkles red pepper flakes over everything; she bites into a jalapeño and winks at her brothers watching her with awe. He goes over to Arden. "Reinforcements have arrived," he tells her. The soft wheeze of the blood-pressure cuff fitted around her forearm is the only response.

"How did it go?"

"I met with parents all day. Some of them just needed to talk it through. Some of them had already made up their minds."

I guess it's not surprising. Many Bishop parents are more concerned with status and reputation than academics. "Let them. You have a waiting list of girls wanting to get in."

"It's hard after the school year starts." He adjusts the sheet around Arden's shoulders. "Any news about Rory?"

"It sounds like the procedure went okay. They took off the helmet."

"That's great."

"You haven't talked to Vince, then? He isn't answering my texts."

"No."

"He hasn't been by to check on Arden. He's avoiding me. I guess I shouldn't be

388

surprised." Theo's just standing there, looking down at Arden. "What is it?" I say, worried, getting up to look.

"Is there something else going on?" he says in a low voice.

"What are you talking about?"

"You and Vince. It's like you're taking his betrayal personally."

"I am. Of course I am." Why are we suddenly talking about this?

"Do you still have feelings for him? Is that why you get so angry with him?"

He can't know. I've never breathed a word to anyone about that night. It's dark in here, but he's standing so close. Can he see the guilt plain on my face? Can he see the story unravel in my eyes? A snowstorm had blown through, trapping Vince and me at Double. The power had gone out and we were huddled in the dark, laughing over the customers we'd had that evening, intrepid tourists who didn't speak English, and Vince had gone out to pantomime the dishes. *Do the chicken one again,* I'd said, laughing so hard I was crying, and he obligingly got up and did the chicken dance. I looked at him, with his bent elbows and knees, jerking his head back and forth, and thought to myself, *Did I make a mistake?*

When he collapsed on the floor beside me,

I put my hand on his thigh. I only meant to clasp it, but he shifted and I turned and his mouth found mine. He moved to unbutton my shirt and I put my hand on his, stopping him. *No,* I said. *We can't.*

Eventually, snowplows had come through and I'd slowly, carefully driven home. The light had been on in Arden's bedroom, shining around the door, and I'd almost knocked before deciding not to waken her in case she'd fallen asleep. I'd climbed into bed beside Theo, who'd sleepily turned toward me to sling his arm around me. *I'm glad you're home,* he'd murmured and I'd lain stiffly until dawn, staring up at the ceiling.

"I get angry with you, too," I say, now. "Whenever you leave your dirty socks on the floor of the closet. You know it drives me crazy." I lean against him, slide my hand beneath the collar of his shirt and feel the warmth of his skin. I close my eyes and smell the lingering trace of cologne he'd dashed on hours before. "I love you, Theo. With all my heart."

It had just been the one time.

ARDEN

I'm Venus, pastel and pure, rising from the sea. Silvery bubbles dance past me on their way up to the surface. I've been down here too long and it's time to leave. I try to suck in a deep breath, but something stops me. Something's covering my nose and lips. A hand? It presses against the thing in my mouth, drives it deeper into my throat. I see fire-engine red and black and twinkling stars.

"Natalie! What are you doing creeping up on me like that?" Aunt Gabrielle's using her angry voice. *Put that down, Arden. Could you girls be a little quieter?*

"I'm sorry. I thought you heard me coming in. . . ."

My mom's smooth voice twines around Aunt Gabrielle's prickly one. They make a thick and thorny vine. *Your mothers are oil and vinegar,* Grandma Sugar told Rory and me once. *They are as unalike as two people can be.* Rory and I know who is the floating oil and who is the bitter vinegar.

I love my mom, but she doesn't get it. She thinks Rory's perfect. She won't listen when I try to tell her. *You girls are too close,* she'll say. *You need to give her some room.* She doesn't know about Rory's drinking, or sleeping with half the guys in high school, or that she's the one who sneaked a fish into our guidance counselor's car where it sat in the bright sun all afternoon. She doesn't know I wrote all of Rory's college essays and most of her school papers. No way does she know I took the SATs for her.

The one time I did tell my mom a secret about Rory was back in eighth grade, when I told her Rory had been making herself throw up. My mom freaked and told Aunt Gabrielle and Uncle Vince, which ended up being a nightmare. Rory had to meet with a therapist and keep a food diary and weigh herself in front of her parents every night. She wasn't allowed to be on the swim team or do any sports at all until her weight went up. Worst of all was the fighting between Aunt Gabrielle, who said that everyone was overreacting and that Rory looked fine, and Uncle Vince, who said Aunt Gabrielle had a skewed idea of what fine was. Rory still hasn't forgiven me. So of course I'm not going to tell my mom what I think's going on with Rory. I'm not sure myself.

You were in a fire. Do you remember?

I remember holding the heavy can against my chest, liquid sloshing around inside. I remember twisting off the metal cap. It smells terrible, but I don't stop.

"Stop hanging out with my boyfriend," Rory says, and I look over at her with alarm. She can't know. She sits cross-legged on her bed, hunched over and painting her toenails silver. She's not even looking at me.

"We're just studying together. You should try it sometime." Maybe that's all we are, study partners. I came back from the art studio last night to hear Hunter's low murmur on the other side of the door and Rory's answering giggle. I backed away, confused and horrified. I've been so stupid. When have I ever won over Rory?

She looks at me with her green, green eyes. "You do know that Hunter's not interested in you."

"You can be such a bitch."

"Just trying to keep you from humiliating yourself."

"Why? Because you think Hunter and I might actually have something in common?"

393

"Oh, Arden." She gives me that pitying look I know so well, the one that smacks me down. It's the only time ever that she looks just like her mom. "You can't possibly understand. You've never even had sex."

Hunter and I kiss forever, his hands sliding up beneath my shirt and pushing up my bra. I am going to melt right into the tree he's pressing me against. My legs are shaking. I want to run; I want to lie down. I can't get enough of him, his mouth, his hands, his warm skin. I work my hands around his waist, under the waistband of his jeans. I want to pull his whole body inside me and melt us into one person. A long, searing wolf whistle from a group of kids walking past makes us stop, panting.

"We can't," Hunter says. His mouth is at my temple.

"No, we can't," I murmur against his throat. But we do.

"Remember," Chelsea Lee calls from the front of the classroom. "You need to get me your essays by next Thursday."

The bell's rung and we're gathering up our iPads and tablets. I've got an idea I want to explore with her, and I take the steps down to where she's standing, talking to a bunch of kids. When it's my turn, I say, "Professor Lee?"

She's busy pushing a folder into her briefcase and she stops and looks at me. She's so pretty, even prettier up close. She's wearing black today, a long-sleeved dress cut short. Her legs are long and tanned. "Arden, right?"

I nod, smiling. Somehow she knows me. I haven't even spoken up in class. Maybe my quizzes haven't sucked that bad. "I wanted to talk to you about our term paper. I was thinking about doing Giotto."

She tilts her head. "Far be it from me to discourage you, but are you sure? There won't be much source material on him. How do you plan to get around that?" Her gaze moves to a point behind me, and I turn to see Rory slipping out through the classroom door.

What is that blinding light? Pressure on my eyelid, then it's gone.

". . . going to try her back on the ventilator," Dr. Morris says, close to my ear.

"Do you think it's safe?" Uncle Vince asks. They're talking about me and I'm afraid. Where is Aunt Gabrielle? I feel her nearby. I hear the rustle of her silk clothing.

"We can put her right back on if we need to."

A snake slides across my throat, tightening. I panic, try to scrabble at it with my fingers.

"Is she awake?" Uncle Vince says. "Rory? Honey?"

I'm not Rory!

"She may be in some discomfort," Dr. Morris says. "Some patients can't tolerate being on the ventilator. We can't have her agitated."

She's going to give me more drugs. *I can't fall back asleep. I can't.* I think about swirling the tip of my paintbrush into azure blue. Sky, sea. But . . . everything's already getting woozy in my head.

"Is it working?" Aunt Gabrielle's voice is whip-hard against my skin. When she tells you to do something, you do it. You don't ever want to piss her off.

Rory's always been afraid of her mom. She was drunk when she told me why.

RORY

I get a new key card at Student Services. The old lady behind the desk glares at me, like it's going to kill her to stand up and walk over to the little machine on the table behind her. "Are you sure it's not somewhere in your room?" she says in her pissed-off old-lady voice.

I don't waste my smile on her. I know who it will work on and who it won't. "Look. My roommate's a pig. I'm lucky I can even find my own bed in that mess."

The only thing Arden is really careful with is her stash of Adderall, which she keeps in her bathrobe pocket, in the small leather change purse our grandma gave each of us for Christmas one year. I check it every so often, to see how she's doing. Arden doesn't think I know, but I know everything about her. Even the stuff not worth knowing, like how she scoops back the right side of her hair first and then the left when she's making a ponytail, or how she taps her teeth with her pen when she's thinking hard. How she eats Sour Patch Kids in this order — red, yellow, orange — and how she never eats the green ones. How she pretends to get along with D.D. when everyone can tell she can't stand her.

I'm in D.D. and Whitney's room, watching a show on Whitney's laptop, when Arden stops in the doorway. "Your mom's car is in the parking lot."

I sit straight up — I'd forgotten to check in earlier. I've knocked over Whitney's can of soda. "Shit." She swipes her hand across her pillow.

"Sorry." I slide off her bed and grab my bag. "Gotta go."

"Where?" D.D. says with interest. Which is how all four of us end up running down the stairs and out the side door. We're laughing as we're going, thinking about how we left everything just lying out in D.D.'s room, like a crime scene. Arden's in her pajama bottoms and a T-shirt and carrying her toothbrush, and Whitney's barefoot. *Ouch,* she keeps saying, as we run across The Bowl. *Ouch, ouch, ouch.* Which only makes us crack up harder.

We end up roaming through neighborhoods, creeping through alleys and across people's backyards. We have the vague idea of heading to Fraternity Row, which Arden's trying to get us not to do. "I look like crap," she protests, and D.D. hooks her arm through hers. "No way. You look cute." I'd told her Arden had gotten her stuff from her old connection and now D.D.'s trying to suck up — which is totally hilarious.

We turn a corner and I realize I've been on this street before, the way the trees on both sides of the street arch their long branches to touch in the middle like the ceiling of a church. This is Chelsea's street, and there, four houses down on the corner, is her place, with its narrow porch and heavy oak door. "This way." I try to lead everyone in the opposite direction, but Whitney grabs my elbow, stopping me. "Hold on." She bends and lifts her foot. We stand in a clump on the sidewalk. "I think I'm bleeding."

"Want us to call nine-one-one?" D.D. jokes.

"Seriously. I think there's glass in it. Someone, turn on your cell-phone flashlight so I can see." My cell phone's in my room, plugged into the charger. Good thing, too, because I know it's hopping all over the place with the thousand texts and phone calls my mom's probably sending me right this second. Arden had been on her way to the bathroom to wash up, so it's D.D. who shines her cell phone across the bottom of Whitney's foot. Sure enough, there's a bright red smear of blood.

"Oh, yuck," D.D. says.

"I'm going to be sick," Arden says.

"Will you hold that steady?" Whitney says.

"Yes, ma'am," D.D. says.

The porch light's on at Chelsea's house and there's a car parked in the driveway, some sort of sedan. The rest of the house is dark, except for one glowing window upstairs.

"Just pull it out," D.D. is saying to Whitney, who snaps back, "I'm trying."

Arden's standing beside me. She's looking up at the bright window, too.

I thought I was in the mood. I mean, texting Hunter at three a.m. and getting him to let me in and kick out his roommate is about one thing and one thing only. But I keep seeing that glowing oblong of light that I know came from Chelsea's bedroom. I keep seeing the unfamiliar car in her driveway. I hadn't been close enough to see the plates. There was nothing at all about it I would recognize in broad daylight, not even if it came roaring down the street toward me, its

400

license plate getting bigger and bigger until it was the last thing I saw. Hunter finally leans back to look at me. "You there?"

I reach up to brush his hair from his forehead. "Sorry. I've just got a thing going on with my mom."

"Oh. Your mom. Right."

"What does *that* mean — 'Oh. Your mom'?"

"Nothing. But you got to know how she is."

"Tell me. How is my mom?" I sit up and swing my feet to the floor, reaching for my dress lying in a crumpled heap at the foot of the bed.

"Oh, come on, Rory. Don't be like that." He grabs my arm. I shake him off. "So what if she's a little protective?" I demand.

He doesn't even answer me. Doesn't that say it all?

It's still dark when I let myself into my room. Arden's there, asleep in the mound of clothes she calls her bed. I can see her hair shining in the moonlight from the bare window. "Arden?" I whisper, but she doesn't answer. I curl up in my bed, slide my hand beneath my pillow to finger the soft square of pink blanket — all that's left of Arden's baby blanket she gave me when we were little — and listen to her breathe.

401

"How are classes going?" my dad asks the next morning. I press my cell phone to my ear as I search through Arden's bathrobe pocket for the change purse. I click it open and pour the tablets onto my palm. "Fine." I know he's asking only because my mom told him to call me and Make Sure I'm All Right. Only thirty-eight Adderall left. Which means Arden's upping her dose.

I'd borrowed D.D.'s cell phone to call my mom last night, pretending I was at some study group. *Sorry,* I'd told her. *I forgot to call earlier.* A pause. She was trying to decide how far to push it. At last she'd said, *I worry when you don't check in.* Nothing about how she'd gotten in the car and driven all the way to campus to hunt me down; nothing about how she was probably standing outside my dorm room right that second.

"How's Double?" I know this will derail Dad. He hasn't wanted to talk about work in months. He's shrunken up like popcorn you've spilled soda on. It's still recognizable, but shriveled and sad-looking. The stuff you throw away.

"Same old same old."

Does he even hear himself? "Mom drove up here again last night." Silence tells me he didn't know. "You have to stop her. It's embarrassing."

"Your leaving's been hard on her, honey."

"She has to get over it."

"She will, Rory. Just give her time."

"Why do you do that? Why do you pretend she just needs time?" Where have you been all these years, Dad? "What are you going to do after you sell Double? Where will you go?" Where will I go? Where will I be? If he gets rid of the only thing I've known, does that mean he can so easily get rid of me?

"What do you mean, sell Double?" he says carefully.

"Oh, my God." I snap the change purse closed and drop it into the pocket. "You didn't think Mom would tell me? She tells me everything." Way more than I ever want to know.

"I'll talk to her," he says in that distant voice that means nothing.

"Whatever, Dad. Just forget about it." By the time we hang up, I know he already has.

Chelsea doesn't say sweetheart, or honey, or darling. She's clear. She's direct. There's no guessing with Chelsea.

"I texted you," I say.

She grabs her long hair and pulls it over a shoulder. "I was up late getting ready for class."

"Did you need help with that?"

She looks at me over her reading glasses, taps the papers in her lap. "What's this about?"

"You weren't alone. You had someone over."

She sits back in her chair and looks at me. "Let's get something straight. I don't do jealousy."

"You think this is jealousy? Oh, I promise you. You'll know jealousy when you see it." It's not jealousy. It's fear, the unpleasant sloshing in my stomach. I bend to pick up her cat, winding around my ankles. I press my face against her head, the soft fur tickling my nose. I want to believe her. I have to. "No one knows about us."

"I didn't think we had to talk about why." So many reasons. She reaches across the table and takes my hand in hers, interlacing our fingers together. Her cat meows and jumps down. "Look, it was just my mom. She was on her way to Maine and I gave her my bedroom. Okay?"

It's weird to think of Chelsea having a mom. I wonder how they get along. Arden understands more than anyone, but Arden's not there anymore, not like she used to be. Something's changing between us, so who's left?

"I hate this place." I take her hand and turn it palm up and trace her heart line with my finger.

"There's nothing wrong with this place. There's nothing wrong with you. It's just that you two don't belong together."

"I don't think I belong at Harvard, either." I can't believe I've said this out loud. I don't dare look at her.

"Maybe not."

I let out my breath and look up. Her eyes are molten brown, not even a speck of gold. "So where do I belong?"

Chelsea tilts her head and looks at me. She doesn't say it. She doesn't have to. I know what she's thinking. *With me.* I pull my class ring off and push it into her palm. "You can borrow this if you want."

NATALIE

Detective Gallagher wants a few minutes of our time. He's alone in the family lounge, sitting in the chair facing the door. What does he do, chase everyone else out when he wants to use this space as an interrogation room?

"How's Arden?" he asks as Theo and I come into the room. It's a pleasantry, something to say. I don't think the man cares, not in a genuine way. I don't bother to answer, but Theo says, "We're worried. There should have been improvement by now."

I don't want Theo to share this and expose our vulnerable fear to this man who only wants to hurt us. But that's Theo. He always thinks the best of people. He lets them trip over their feet. He reaches out a hand to help them up. I stand by the window, with my arms crossed. "Have you spoken with our attorney? She doesn't want us talking to you without her being here."

"It's all right." Theo throws me a warning glance. "What is it? What do you need to know?"

"When was the last time Arden was home?" Detective Gallagher says.

We've been over this before. I don't answer. Theo says, "Two weeks ago, for her birthday. She surprised us."

He nods. "What about since then?"

"Nothing. Why?"

"She ever say she was afraid of Hunter?"

I turn toward the man in surprise. "No." I look to Theo, who shakes his head. "Never. We'd have told you if she had."

"She never told you he texted her Wednesday: *I know where you live?*"

I come over, sit in the chair opposite him. "No."

"Have you ever talked to Hunter?"

I find Theo's hand. "We've never even met him."

"So you've never talked to him."

"No," Theo says.

"What about last Thursday afternoon when he called your house?"

"What?" I look to Theo. He looks back blankly.

"We didn't talk to him," Theo says.

"Someone did. For five minutes and

twelve seconds."

But that's impossible. I scroll past through the days, the hours. "Thursday afternoon? I was at the restaurant."

"I would have been home with the boys after school," Theo says. "What time did he call?"

"Four-thirty-eight."

Theo sighs. "It was Henry. I caught him on the kitchen phone. He hung up as I came in the room. I thought it was a telemarketer." He looks to Detective Gallagher. "He knows he's not allowed to answer the phone, but he does it anyway."

What could Hunter have talked to Henry about? "What does this mean?" I let hope dance past. "Do you think it was Hunter who started the fire?" But Detective Gallagher just flips his notebook closed. "Thank you for your time," he says.

My mother calls that afternoon. "Oliver wet the bed," she says in a low voice. "I found his pajamas in the laundry room, buried under the towels."

Poor Oliver. "He hasn't done that in years." Of the twins, he was the first to get out of diapers.

"I think you need to talk to him."

I take Theo's laptop into the family lounge

and prop it open on the small table. I put a big smile on my face and tap the video call button. It rings, connects. I hear the chatter of voices, then see my little boys, jostling for space on the couch, their round faces and neatly combed hair. The image tilts this way and that, and then my mother's voice. "Here, let me put it right here. Okay? Then you both can see."

"Hey, guys," I say.

"Hi, Mom."

They sit close together, their shoulders touching. They're wearing their favorite red-striped polo shirts. The collars aren't curling up the way they usually do, so I'm guessing my mom went to the trouble to iron them. "I like your haircuts," I say.

Henry beams. "It's way cooler than Caleb's. So, haha."

"Haha, indeed. Do you like your haircut, Oliver?"

His eyes are so blue. I never before noticed how much the boys look like my sister. In the week that we've been apart, they've grown, their cheeks hollowed a tiny bit, the blue of their eyes deepened. Or maybe it's just a trick of the computer screen.

"I have an owie." Henry crooks his elbow. He frowns at the image of himself in the corner, works to angle his arm so the

Superman Band-Aid is front and center.

"Yikes. How did that happen?"

"Caleb pushed Lily, so I pushed him back."

"Henry has a girlfriend," Oliver informs me.

"I do not."

"Yes, you do."

They squirm.

"Boys," my mom chides, her voice coming from somewhere.

"Mom, it's okay," I say, and there's a pause and then she says, "I'm going to go check on the bird feeder. The squirrels have been feasting. You two behave for your mama, got that?"

Oliver's eyes track her departure and then he says, "Grandma gives us ice cream for breakfast."

I smile. "That's okay, honey. I told her she could."

"With chocolate syrup," Oliver whispers.

Henry's nodding. "And mini-marshmallows."

"Well, you two better live it up, because when I get home, it's going to be zucchini and brussels sprouts twenty-four/seven."

Henry giggles. "You're so funny, Mommy."

"Yep. I'm a real card."

"What does that mean?"

I think about it. "I don't know. It's just something your grandpa used to say."

"Grandpa George? I never heard him say that."

No, my own father. Somehow, he's crept into this conversation. It's the way Oliver's looking so steadily at me. I blink. "So listen. I wanted to talk to you two about Arden."

"Okay," Henry says. "Is she better? Can she Skype?"

"No, not right now. She's sleeping."

He pouts. "Every time she's sleeping."

"I know."

"Sleeping's another word for dead," Oliver says.

"Oh, honey," I say, dismayed. "No, it's not."

"Yes, it is. On Captain Fantastic it is."

"You know that's a cartoon. In real life, sleeping isn't being dead."

"What about *Sleeping Beauty?*"

"That's just a fairy tale. It's pretend, too."

"But *why* is she sleeping?" Henry asks.

"Well, you know how when you're not feeling well, you just want to lie down and rest?" Solemn nods. "Well, Arden's not feeling well, either. She's resting so her body can get strong again."

411

"It's taking a long time. It's taking *forever.*"

"I know. It feels that way to me, too."

"Sometimes when I'm resting I just pretend to be asleep," Henry says. "Maybe Arden's doing that, too, pretending."

"No way. She can't wait to Skype with you guys. She'll want to hear all about Lily."

"Lily *isn't* my girlfriend," Henry says.

"Right," I agree. Oliver's got his head down. I can see the track of comb teeth and his crown where the hair springs up. "What's the matter, Oliver?"

He shrugs.

Henry says, "Oliver doesn't think Arden's going to get better."

"Is that true, Oliver?" The rise and fall of one small shoulder. "What makes you think that, honey?"

Henry says, "That's what Caleb said. He says his mom said that when people bump their heads like Arden they don't wake up ever."

"Does Caleb's mom know Arden?"

"No," Oliver says. He's still got his head down.

"Has she been here to see all the doctors and nurses working to help Arden get better?"

"No."

412

"Does she know they're giving her special medicine?"

Oliver looks up. He's a big believer in medicine. "No."

"Okay, then."

Oliver shrugs.

"I'll tell you what. Maybe Grandma can bring you up for a visit soon. But you'll have to promise to be super-quiet so you don't wake Arden up." I wish they would. I wish they'd charge into the room and bump into things and laugh and climb all over her and find all her ticklish spots.

"Okay, Mommy," Henry says. "Can I go now? I want to help Grandma with the bird feeder."

"Hold on just a second. You remember the rules about answering the phone?"

Henry's eyes slide away from mine. "Maybe."

"It's like opening the front door. You know how you're not allowed to do that unless Daddy or I are there. Right?"

"Yesss."

"But you answered the phone the other day and talked to a stranger, didn't you?"

"He wasn't a stranger," Henry protests. "His name's Hunter. He's Arden's boyfriend."

"Arden's boyfriend?" I try to keep my

voice light, but this knowledge shimmers. "What did he want?"

Henry shrugs. "Just to talk to Arden. Can I go now?"

"You talked to him for a long time. What about?"

"I don't know."

It makes me uneasy but Henry's face is guileless. "You realize it's a safety rule?"

"Sorry."

"When you're older, you can answer the phone anytime you want."

"Okay."

"You can go now."

"Finally!" Henry reaches for the laptop and puts it in Oliver's lap.

Oliver's face is centered on the screen. "He didn't mean to be bad."

"I know he didn't. It's okay." Is it? We might never know.

He nods. He looks so serious. I put my face close to the screen. "I see you," I whisper.

"I see you, too," he whispers back.

"I love you."

"I love you most, Mommy."

Toward dawn, I wander down the deserted stairs and step out into the dim lobby. No one's at the reception desk at this hour. The big glass doors beckon, and as I walk toward them, they glide open to gray pavement and velvety purple sky.

"Storm's coming." It's Vince, sitting on the low brick wall encircling the flower beds, smoking.

I go over and look down. "Done avoiding me?"

He shrugs. "I have some practice being on the receiving end of that." He taps a cigarette from the pack and extends it. I put it between my lips and lean down as he thumbs the lighter. The punch to my senses is dizzyingly familiar. I've missed this. Another broken promise. I sit down. "How's Rory?" Vince had never texted me back; he hasn't stopped by Arden's room. Vince being Vince.

"You hear about the artificial lung?"

"Christine says she might not have to be on it long."

"To know your kid can't even inflate her own lungs . . . makes me wonder about all the other things going on inside her we don't even know about. How's Arden?"

I look off into the distance, to the smudged fringe of trees on the clouded horizon. "Nothing's working, Vince. Nothing."

"They can't get the fluid down?"

"It keeps building back up. It's relentless.

415

And then I think, *What if they do get it back to normal levels but it's already too late? All that fluid pressing on her brain . . ."* Saying this out loud breaks the glass. It allows me to pick my way through the pieces. "What if Arden's already gone?"

"Do you remember when you brought the boys home and she showed up at our house with her little pink suitcase?"

I can't get any sleep over there, Vince had told me she'd pronounced when he swung open the door. "I still don't know how she got all the way to your house. I have this horrible suspicion she hitchhiked."

"I bet Rory had something to do with it."

"I bet she did. When did Arden ever do something that Rory wasn't in on? Or, more often, take the lead on?"

"I think it was Rory who wanted to room with Arden, not the other way around."

I glance at him in surprise. His profile's to me, the clean line of his forehead and nose, the shadow of his cheek. I remember when he tried growing a beard, how mercilessly I'd teased him about it. I'd called him a Brad Pitt wannabe and he just puffed out his chest. "You do?"

"Rory needs Arden. Hard to be a leader when you don't have a follower."

"Arden's not just a follower."

"Of course not. Arden's secure enough in her own self to let Rory boss her around. She doesn't have as much to prove as Rory does."

This is the closest Vince's ever come to admitting Gabrielle's been hard on their daughter. "What do you know about Hunter? Did you ever meet him?"

"No, though Gabrielle spent some time with him when she visited campus. She said he seemed like a nice boy, but not good enough for Rory."

"I doubt she'd think anybody would be."

"True."

"He called our house last week, looking for Arden."

"She was home?"

"No. That's what's so strange. Why would he think she would have been?" I exhale a stream of smoke. "What if the police don't find out who did this? What if we never know?" A boy was dead. Will suspicion hang over Arden the rest of her life?

He taps the end of his cigarette against the edge of the curb. "Maybe it'd be better that way."

"How? How can that possibly be better?" I frown. "You're the one who said we had to know."

"I've been thinking. Do we really want to

417

know who did this? What if knowing makes everything worse?"

"How can it be any worse than it already is?"

"I'm just saying. Maybe it's better to let things go. Focus on the girls recovering, like you said."

"I don't know if I can."

"Good old Natalie."

It's started raining, a quiet drizzle that leaves a sheen on the pavement. A car drives past, headlights a distant glimmer. Vince shakes his head. "Why didn't you wait for me, Nat? I called you from Paris. You never called me back."

Surprised, I look at his profile. This is the first time he's ever mentioned it. I wasn't even sure he remembered proposing. *Come to Paris,* Vince had said. What if I had gone? I wouldn't be who I am today. There wouldn't be Arden, or Henry, or Oliver. There wouldn't be a small dachshund with floppy ears, a house on a lake with a ramshackle party barge, and a sun that eases itself up over the pines to flood my kitchen with light. There wouldn't be Rory. "You've always been about the chase, Vince. I knew that once you were done chasing me, we wouldn't have anything left. I decided it was better to be your friend than just another conquest." And that, I understand suddenly, is why he fell in love with Gabrielle. She keeps a part of herself closed off. She keeps him guessing. He must feel like he never knows who's going to be there when he gets home.

"It would have been different with you."

"No. It wouldn't have."

He doesn't answer. Silence stretches out, heavy. Then he says, "Liz got a job offer."

He's changed the subject abruptly. I know we'll never talk about it again. "She never said anything." She'd been texting me all day. *I'm sorry to bother you but should I get the dishwasher repaired/hire that busboy/keep our seafood order as is? Want me to call the bank/landlord/customers coming in for a birthday/anniversary/business meeting?*

"She didn't want to upset you. I told her to go ahead and take it."

I'm annoyed. "Why would you do that? We'll never find someone else as good." It had taken us months to find her, after we'd had to fire Ignacio. I can't even bear to think of taking up a new search, espccially now.

"I need to tell you something," Vince says. "Before you find out another way."

I look at him. Haven't I had enough revelations?

"Mitchell wants to buy Double. He'll keep

us on, but he'll own the restaurant."

"No, he won't. I won't sell to him."

"He's the only one who's made an offer. It's a crappy offer, but it's the only one in play."

"It's not in play. I won't accept it."

"Why not? This way, we can just cook. We can make fucking raspberry torte if we want to. We can just do what we've always wanted to do."

"For how long? You really think Mitchell will keep us on? He's just going to train his team and then we're out."

"You don't know that's true. We'll have money in the bank. Let someone else have the headache of running the business."

"How have you been dealing with it? You've been coming in late, leaving early. It's like you're not even trying, and you're the one who got us into this to begin with."

"Because I can't stand it anymore. I walk into Double and you look at me with such disappointment."

"I know you, Vince. I know you think it's going to be easier working for Mitchell, but I've worked for him. I know what it's like. You'll hate it, too."

"Damn it, Natalie. I'm over it, all right? Let's sell the fucking restaurant. Let's just move on."

"Where's this really coming from, Vince? Is it Gabrielle?"

"It's time we accepted the truth. Double isn't ours anymore."

"We can turn it around. We just need a little more time."

He tosses his cigarette onto the sidewalk, where it smolders in the spitting rain. "We did everything we could. Now we're just wasting our lives."

I sit back. Eight years of my life, gone just like that? "You're giving up."

He pushes himself up. "Don't you think it's time you did, too, Nat?"

I sit there and finish my cigarette. Raindrops tap the pavement. Puddles glisten beneath the bright hospital sign. All these years I'd been so focused on what Vince saw in Gabrielle. I never thought about what I saw in Vince. He was fun. He was charming. But that's not enough to build on. And it's not enough to build a friendship on, either. And just like that, in one night, I'd lost both.

ARDEN

"Something's wrong," Aunt Gabrielle says. "Get the nurse, Vincent."

I don't want Uncle Vince to leave. I don't want to be alone with my aunt.

"I followed Rory after class," I tell Hunter. We're lying on his bed, facing each other. He's circling his thumb around my tattoo. He loves it. He says it's sexy and it makes me kind of a badass. He says he never knew I had that side to me. I tell him he doesn't know me and he tells me he plans to change that. But we're not just talking anymore. We're way past talking.

"Okay, crazy," he says.

"I'm serious. I think there's something weird going on."

He swirls his fingertips along my arm, my skin lighting up at each soft pass. Does he touch Rory this way? Does he tell her she's kind of a badass, because she's the one who really is? I'm just the one who can't say no. Not even to myself.

He's not listening. "Dude," I say. "Pay attention. Don't you want to know?"

"Sure, sure. Tell me."

"She went off campus, like way off campus. She knocked on someone's door and went inside." The same house she'd been staring at the other night. "I saw who answered."

"Hmm."

"Professor Lee." Our essay's due in a of couple of days and I haven't even started. I should be in my room right this second, writing. Instead I'm here. What is *wrong* with me?

His fingers don't even stop moving. "So? Maybe she's tutoring her."

"I don't know why we're even talking about her."

"You're the one talking about her."

It's true. I'm the one who can't push Rory out of my mind. I put my head back on the pillow. "What am I doing here? Why are we doing this? I feel horrible."

"I can fix that."

"You know what I mean."

Hunter's thin cotton T-shirt stretches across his shoulders, the hem curling up over the low waistband of his jeans and I catch a glimpse of tanned skin. "You're tan all over," I tell him, sounding almost accusing, which I guess I am. I don't like the idea of him lying naked on some beach. I don't like the idea of who he's been lying naked with. He laughs and pulls me to lie on top of him, our legs all tangled together, and I can feel him rising beneath me. "Say it."

"It doesn't matter."

It does matter, and I can't understand why he doesn't get that. Sometimes I wonder if he gets off on Rory and me being cousins. "It matters to me." This is a risk. He can always roll to his feet and gather his things. We are still new. But his fingers don't stop tracing across my shoulder blades and down my spine, like he's drawing words on my skin, as though he has all the time in the world, dancing his fingertips around and down and between. My legs slide apart, I can't stop them, and I hear my breath moving in my throat.

"It shouldn't."

But it does. "Say it," I say through my teeth. "Say you like me more than Rory." I'm not as sexy as Rory, but I want to be. I'm not as fun or confident, but he can talk to me. That has to mean something. I can learn to be sexy. I can.

"I'm with you now, Arden. Isn't that

enough?"

"What about later? What about tonight?"

He nips my earlobe, draws it between his teeth, his breath warm and stirring the hairs on the nape of my neck, his fingers still moving, teasing.

"Say it." I'm panting. I hold on to the part of me I know so well — the part that needs to know — but the part that doesn't care, that traitorous stranger self, is growing larger and taking over. "Do you *love* me more?"

His touch so light, so certain. The world spins, delicious and within reach. Everything I want is right here, all around me.

"You ready?" he murmurs in my ear. "Ready?" Wanting me to say it. Wanting me to admit it, but I won't. He's not in charge. He's not. But when he takes his hand away, I moan.

He rolls me over and pins me to the mattress, one swift fierce motion, his warm body solid and heavy, his beautiful face just above mine. "Tell me, California Boy," I whisper. Which is a joke on what Rory told her mom about Hunter. Even now, Rory is here, with us. "Say it." Almost a whimper.

I thought I knew about sex, but I was wrong.

■ ■ ■ ■

Who's touching me? I try to lift my hand. I try to open my eyes. Firm pressure on my chest, then cool air and the softness of cloth fluttering onto my body, sealing me. "I was hoping to see some improvement by now," Dr. Morris says. "Rory's lungs aren't taking over oxygenating her blood. She's relying completely on the ECMO machine."

Not Rory. Me. They're talking about me. I'm the one relying on a machine.

"Maybe she just needs more time," Uncle Vince says.

"Unfortunately, that's not the case. I was hoping that putting her on ECMO would allow her lungs to rejuvenate, but the damage is too extensive."

My lungs. I try to feel them.

"So now what?" Uncle Vince says, and the panic in his voice scares me. "What do we do?"

"I'm going to put her on the lung-transplant list. With her age and health, she should be near the top."

Am I dreaming this?

"What if she isn't?"

"What if we never leave?" Rory says. "Let's

426

stay here forever."

We're swaying on the swings by my old apartment, the hems of our long dresses dragging in the dirt, the splintery wooden seats beneath us bumping into each other. It's after midnight, just a few stars shining above, and we have the place to ourselves. Maybe that's what she means, because this place is kind of a dump. It used to be so magical when we were little. It used to feel like Disneyland.

Or maybe it's the vodka talking.

Rory tips the bottle to her mouth. It's a big bottle and takes two hands — she's dumped out half the cranberry juice and poured in vodka. She's right. It's good that way. So things are starting to look perfect to me, too.

Prom had been a bust. Rory's date had passed out and she'd ended up driving him home and leaving his car in front of his parents' house. And then she'd texted me the address. My date had damp palms and a nervous habit of licking his lips, so I was okay dumping him at the after-party and borrowing my dad's car to drive to Bethesda. We were in the area so we drove around. Past Booeymonger, Red Door, Zorba's. We'd ended up here.

"People think I don't remember, but I

do," Rory says.

"Remember what?"

"When I got burned." Her face is all shadows.

"I don't remember." I have the story in my mind, the one my mom told me a long time ago, when I asked about Rory's burn. "And I was there."

"You were there *after,* Arden."

"There will be some scarring," Aunt Gabrielle says. She's talking low and quiet, and she's been talking for a while. Is she talking about me? "But we can keep it covered up. Maybe some plastic surgery down the road. So don't worry, Rory."

I am not Rory.

Something soft brushes my cheek — a sleeve. Aunt Gabrielle's reaching for something above me. The light flares on, making me squint. Through a haze of pain, then wonderment, I open my eyes. I see the charm bracelet dangling from her wrist, the pale curve of her palm. I look up, past her hand, and see the shadowy planes of her face bisected by her arm, one rounded cheek, half her mouth painted red, and one beautiful almond-shaped eye. She's staring down at me.

RORY

Chelsea opens the door, revealing the burnt-orange hallway behind her, the distant bright yellow of the kitchen walls. It's like the whole house is smiling hello. "Hey," she says. "Hey," I say back.

I glance behind me before I step inside. Two kids Rollerblading, swaying in gentle motion, talking to each other. They don't even see me. The guy next door's collecting his mail from the box at the curb, his head bent as he shuffles through his envelopes; across the street, a woman's walking her pug and texting. Way down at the opposite corner, I see a flash of motion. I pause.

"You in or out?" Chelsea asks.

The motion doesn't repeat itself. I step over the threshold and she closes the door behind me.

It's almost two o'clock in the morning when Arden lets herself into the room. The door-

429

knob turns and then the hallway light angles in. She comes in and slowly closes the door behind her. She stands there in the dark, waiting for her eyes to adjust, I know.

"Were you following me?"

She lets out a muffled shriek. A thud. "Damn it!"

I reach for the lamp on my nightstand and turn it on. She's standing there in her bright yellow jacket, arms filled with books. One's fallen. "Were you?"

"Why would I do that?" She drops the books on her desk, where they go sliding. "What are you doing here, anyway?"

Like deflection's going to work. I'm the queen of deflection. "What do you think you saw?"

"Nothing." Pink creeps up her cheeks. She's realized her mistake.

I push myself up onto my elbow. She saw me go into someone's house. Does she know whose house it was? She's busy plugging in her laptop, fiddling with her phone charger. She's nervous. "Where've you been, Arden?"

"At the library. Our art history essays are due Thursday, remember?"

Actually, I'd forgotten. I could probably get Chelsea to let me off the hook for the paper, but it would really mean letting Arden off the hook, and I'm not sure I want to do that. "Did you change your clothes there?"

She glances at me. The guilt on her face is obvious. *Interesting.* "What?"

"Your shirt's on inside out." She looks down at herself. "You had it on the right way this afternoon."

"Oh." She tugs it off, drops it on the floor. She kicks through the pile of clothes there and unearths her pink nightgown.

There's only one reason you'd take off your shirt and then put it back on inside out. "What's his name?"

Her cheeks flame. "Who?"

So it *is* a guy. This is getting more interesting. I throw back my sheet and swing my feet to the floor. It's stuffy in our room at night, but little air comes through the open window. "That guy at the frat party our first week?"

She's trying to pull on her bathrobe, but the sleeve's twisted and her arm's getting jammed. "What about him?" She sounds a little relieved. So it's not him, which is good, because he's a real player. *Hmm.* Maybe it's some dork she's embarrassed to admit she likes. "Your manager at the snack bar?" Which would be gross because he's a pig

431

and no wonder she wouldn't want to tell me.

"Oh, right. Because he's so hot. Why are you being weird?"

"I'm not being weird. You're being weird." I narrow my eyes at her. "Are you going to tell me who it is or am I going to have to find out on my own?"

"Go ahead. There's nothing to find out." She's got her towel slung over her shoulder and she's pushing aside clothes to reach her shower caddy hanging in her closet. Which, if you want to know, I hung up for her. I was sick of worrying about her shampoo toppling over and spilling across the floor where I might step in it. Better it spilled across the floor of her closet.

"You are so the worst liar in the world."

"I'm not lying!"

There's nothing convincing about the way she says this.

Arden tells me everything, even the stuff I don't want to know and couldn't possibly care less about. I have a sick feeling. I have a really sick feeling. "Is it Hunter?" I say, testing. Because it would be ridiculous. Because it would be impossible. She tries to push past me and I grab her arm. She shakes her head, but I know. My whole head empties out. It's like complete white space.

"Oh, my God," I whisper. "You're fucking Hunter?"

"It's not like that," she says, but it is. I can tell it is.

Everything's buzzing in my brain. I give her a shake and her towel slides off. She tries to pull away, but I grip her arm harder. She flinches. "Are you fucking kidding me?" I hiss.

"You treat him like shit." Her chin's up and her eyes are bright green, brighter than I've ever seen them.

My heart's yawning wide open. D.D. could have fucked Hunter. Chelsea could have and it wouldn't have hurt half as much as finding out Arden had. "Today?" I demanded. "Was today the first time?"

She looks away from me.

So more than once. I'm seeing red. I'm seeing black. "How long?"

"A week." She says it defiantly, like it's something to be proud of.

A week. Who knows how many times they've screwed in a week. Once I could get over. Once is an accident, a collision, being in the wrong place at the wrong time. But more than that is intentional. More than that is practically a relationship. I drop my hand and she rubs her arm. "Oh, little cousin," I say in a sickeningly sweet voice.

"You think he loves you, don't you?"

She blinks. I laugh, an icy laugh that spurts right up from the center of me. "You really do. How stupid can you be? He's fucking you and me, and you think that means he loves you? You're pathetic."

"You just don't get it."

"Oh, I get it. I really do. Hunter's pretty good. Better than most guys. At least he cares if you finish."

"Stop it!"

Her cheeks are flaming. She's so easily embarrassed. It barely makes it any fun. "He likes to be on top first, right? Then he flips you over." She tries to step around me, but I block her. "He's such a good kisser. But he could work on his timing."

Tears are spilling down her cheeks. "You don't know. You don't know."

"Let's call him and ask. Make him choose. What do you think he'll say?" Her pulse is beating rapidly in her throat. Her eyes are wet. She's not pretty when she cries. "Guys always like to break in virgins, but there's nothing special about you now. Nothing at all."

"You're so mean. You're the meanest person I've ever known."

"It's not mean to tell you the truth. I'm doing you a favor."

434

"You've never once done me a favor. It's always been about you. I'm the one always doing you a favor, helping you. All the things I gave up because of you. AP classes. Swim team."

"Oh, please. Like you were that great?"

"I wasn't that bad, either."

She's actually crying, full on. I feel the tiniest twist of remorse. "So that's what this is about? Payback? Don't you get tired of playing the victim?" I make my voice sing-songy. "I don't know how to make friends. I don't know how to fit in. All I know is how to stuff my face. No wonder you don't have any friends. You're pitiful."

"You're the one who's pitiful. My mom may have fucked your dad, but she'll *never* be your mom."

A rush of heat. I slap her, hard, my palm stinging.

Arden just stands there, stunned. Then she launches herself at me, fingers spread into claws. I grab her wrists and we wrestle around the room, grunting. Things topple. All I see are her buggy eyes and open mouth. I want to hurt her, slam her into a corner and break something. "I hate you," I hiss, panting. "I fucking hate you."

"What the hell, guys?" It's D.D., standing in the doorway. "We can hear you all the

435

way down the hall."

I jerk myself free and we stand there panting, glaring at each other. "Yeah, Arden. What the hell." My arms are throbbing and I look down to see angry red gouges from her nails.

"Sorry," Arden says. "It's nothing. Go back to sleep."

"It's not nothing." D.D. comes into the room. "Look at your knee, Rory." I look down. I've banged my knee, blood trickling down my shin. I don't even feel it. "Seriously, guys. Are you going to tell me what's going on?"

"Ask Arden," I say.

"It's none of your business," Arden snaps.

"No, really, Arden," I say. "Tell her. Tell D.D. how you fucked my boyfriend."

D.D. whirls to look at Arden. "What? No way!"

"He never even *looked* at you, did he?" Arden shoves past D.D. and out the door.

On the floor lie the broken pieces of Chelsea's pottery ashtray.

I end up at Chelsea's. It takes her a long time to answer the door, and when she finally does, I fall across the threshold and into her arms. I was on my way to Hunter's, to have it out with him in person, but halfway there I veered right and kept going. Chelsea's driveway was empty, all the lights in her house off, but still it felt right to run up the steps of her porch and pound on her door.

"Oh, baby. What's the matter? What happened?"

She pulls me into the safe darkness of her house and closes the door behind me. The firm rasp of the bolt sliding home is a relief. I haven't cried since I was four years old. I won't cry now, but my words come in jerky, breathless gasps. We're sitting close on the couch in her living room, our knees touching and my hands in hers, when she looks down. "You're hurt. Hold on."

She rises, and when she returns she's holding a bowl and a plastic box with a handle. Sitting back down, she swirls a washcloth in the basin of sudsy water and lifts it, dripping, to be firmly squeezed and pressed gently against first my right arm and then my left. "They look worse than they are," she tells me. It's warm and comforting. I relax. "How did you leave things?" She lifts my leg and props my foot in her lap. She's wearing long pajama bottoms and a tank top. I watch her dab away the dried red streaks of blood, the muscles in her arm flexing and unflexing.

"We didn't. She just left, and then I did, too."

D.D. had stayed behind while I got dressed, wanting to know the details — what and when and how I'd found out. But D.D. wasn't the person I wanted to talk to, and then, as it turns out, neither was Hunter. I wince as Chelsea pats my knee dry. I see the cut now, a small slice across the bone. She bends forward to study it, lamplight gleaming on her slippery black hair. "No stitches, I don't think."

"You a doctor?"

"I've had my share of scrapes and bruises." She glances up and quirks her dark, angled eyebrow. "I went to college on a lacrosse scholarship."

"I'm dating a jock." As soon as the words are out, I want to reel them back in. We're not dating. I don't know what we're doing, but I know that word doesn't fit. But her expression doesn't change. She leans forward to set the bowl of water on the table.

"I tore my rotator cuff and that was that." She snaps open the plastic box. "How does Arden look? Is she okay?"

I bristle. Arden's the one who broke the rules. She's the liar and the cheat. She's the one who should be cut and bleeding. "Why don't I call her and ask?"

She pats my leg. "Okay, okay. I get it. Just asking."

"She only wanted him because he was mine."

"She's not the only one at blame here, Rory."

"You mean Hunter?"

"I mean Hunter." She folds a piece of gauze into a square and covers my knee. "Here, hold this."

I put my fingers against the gauze as she yanks a piece of tape from the roll.

"Have you talked to him?"

"No. I'll kill him if I do."

"You know you need to have it out with him. You can't just hold Arden responsible."

What would he say? How could he defend himself — would he even try? Then I have a horrifying thought. *What if he and Arden are together right now, talking about me?* I curl my hands into fists. I should have gone to Hunter first, cleared the path so there was nothing left standing for Arden.

"Maybe have it out with yourself, too."

"What the hell does that mean? I didn't tell them to screw around."

"These things don't happen in a vacuum, Rory. You're close to Arden, right?" She presses lengths of tape around the gauze, sealing it in place.

Arden's my best friend, my blood sister. Too many things. I can't say them because I know she's none of them anymore. "She's my cousin." If I could, I would make that disappear, too.

"And Hunter must be a nice guy. You wouldn't date a jerk."

Hunter's not a jerk, but he's not just a regular guy, either. He's always there, which is nice but kind of not nice, too. He's *always* there. I don't know how I feel about him. But one thing is for sure: I'm not going to let Arden have him. She needs to *know*. "I've dated plenty of jerks, trust me."

She smiles at me. "There you go." She has her hand wrapped around my ankle, warm and strong. "All better."

Chelsea's a present I keep unwrapping. She's a mirror I hold up to myself.

NATALIE

They're going to cut out a section of Arden's skull. Nothing else is working to lower the fluid seeping into her brain — not siphoning it off, not pumping medications into her veins or oxygen into her lungs, not elevating her bed to let gravity have a say. This is a last-ditch effort, but Dr. Morris is confident. "This procedure is well established," she assures us. "We've seen situations turn around completely." This is more or less the same pep talk she's been giving us from the beginning, but this time she's unusually brisk. More alarmingly, she's not stepping out into the hall to have this conversation out of Arden's hearing.

I put my hand on her arm as she's tapping on her tablet and she raises her head. I see the faint gleam of her eyes in the light from her screen. "Thank you. Thank you for taking care of Arden."

A neurosurgeon is on his way to perform

the emergency procedure, which is called a decompressive craniectomy. I Google this on my phone, guessing at the spelling, getting it wrong over and over and over. At last I find it and learn that this is a controversial operation that's been around since prehistoric times and the medical community is divided as to whether it does any good. Dr. Morris says they will try to preserve the section of bone they cut out, to be reattached later. I don't know where they will keep this piece of my daughter. I don't know what they will do if they can't reattach it, and I don't want to know if there's a possibility they may never even try. I think of Dr. Morris's steady brown eyes. We don't have time for a second opinion.

I'm phoning Christine while Theo's talking to my mother. He hangs up and says, "She's on her way. She'll pick up the boys from school and be here before it's over."

Brain surgery. It will take hours. My mother and my boys are going to stay in the room Theo and I have booked, and just knowing that they'll be here soon loosens the knots inside me. I picture them jumping on the beds, squabbling over the television remote, and begging to watch Nickelodeon. They will throw their arms around me when my mother brings them to meet us in the cafeteria downstairs and I will kiss their cheeks and inhale their little-boy smell of soap and strawberry jam and dirt. For those few brief moments, the center of my world will hold.

Arden lies in her bed as the nurse works around her. The beam of the flashlight passes over her still face, a glimpse of chin and lower lip. She's completely removed from the tension swirling around her. Arden has found a peaceful place. I am fighting this battle for her. I am going to win. This is not beyond me. The hospital nurse on the other end of the phone puts me through to Christine, and my sister's confident voice soothes me. "I'll find someone to cover my shift. I'll be there as soon as I can."

"Christine's coming," I tell Theo, and he nods. He's squinting at the tiny screen on his own phone. He's been trying to reach his parents, who are out of cell range, but they haven't been answering his emails. "It was just a stupid cruise," I say. "We should have told them to come home right away."

He doesn't look at me as his thumbs move over the tiny keypad. "They'll be here soon. Don't worry."

"Are we doing the right thing?"

He rubs his forehead tiredly. "I don't think we have a choice."

We've gotten to this place so quickly. Yesterday had passed in the same exact way as the day before and the day before that. Nurses coming on and going off duty; Dr. Morris appearing first in the morning and last thing in the evening; meals and phone calls and quiet conversations. There'd been no warning we were climbing steep terrain. Maybe the signs had been posted all along the path and I just missed them in my steadfast refusal to see anything but the distant horizon when we could take Arden home.

The orderly comes and pulls up the railing, releases the brakes, hooks the IV pole onto the bed, and removes and places the monitor on the sheet between her legs, coils of tubing across her chest. The nurse helps him steer it out of the room, and together they push Arden out the door. Bright light slides up her body to her face. She doesn't flinch; her lips don't tighten. Her gently curved fingers don't grasp for purchase. There is nothing about her that resembles a person other than the general shape beneath the gauze. Theo and I walk with her as far as we can, down the hall and into the elevator. We stop outside the surgical suite as the automatic doors whoosh open to admit Arden and leave us behind. "We'll be right

444

here, honey," I tell my daughter, because surely, surely, despite what the doctors say, she can still hear me.

The doors close, and she's gone from sight.

"Remember when you had to pick her up from daycare because she wouldn't eat?" Theo says, softly. "What was she, nine months old?"

I don't want to play this game. I turn and begin walking.

Theo falls into step beside me. "You dropped everything to rush her to the doctor. We thought she was sick, but it turned out she was just sick of baby food."

It had happened overnight. Arden was done with mashed-up prunes and peas. She clamped her tiny mouth shut and turned her face when I held up the spoon. She screeched and kicked when I pushed the cart down the baby-food aisle. I found myself pleading with her: *Mommy just has to get diapers. Look, here we go. See? We're all done.* She was ready for the good stuff, whatever Theo and I were eating. She'd watch closely as I diced zucchini lasagna, salmon, potatoes au gratin into bits, and when I placed the plastic dish on her high-chair tray, she'd look over to see if it matched the food on our plates before contentedly tucking in.

"What about when we took her to Williamsburg?" he says. "All she wanted to do was collect acorns. It was like she'd never seen an oak tree before."

Our first family vacation and Arden had spent the entire weekend crouched on the ground, filling her pockets with broken pieces of shell. When we got home, she insisted on lining all our windowsills with them. Theo and I had watched wonderingly. *Do you think it's some kind of ancient ritual?* he'd asked me.

Theo slides his arm around my shoulders. "What about that time she won that poster contest? She didn't even tell us she'd entered the thing. We didn't even know she could draw."

The citywide anti-smoking campaign the D.C. mayor had held. Arden had been the youngest child onstage, and she'd looked so small shaking the mayor's hand. I think guiltily of the cigarette I'd smoked with Vince. I vow that it was my last.

"Look how she wore you down about getting a dog." I hear the smile in his voice.

I'll walk it, Arden had promised. *I'll feed it and clean up after it. You won't even know it's here.* But I'd refused. I knew my limits. Then one afternoon when I went to pick her up from her volunteer job at the local humane society, she'd persuaded me to come inside. There was Percy curled up in his crate, his long tail tucked around his body. As I walked in, he clambered to his feet and looked at me with brown eyes.

We've reached Arden's room. After a week of darkness, the overhead light is on, casting the space in bleak yellow light. It looks so barren. It looks hopeless. I don't want to be here. I don't know what to do, where to go.

Theo's right beside me. "What about when she learned to drive and ran over our mailbox?"

I whirl to face him, hands fisted. He hasn't shaved; his collar's rumpled. "Stop it, Theo. I can't do this." I won't be cheered up and encouraged. Words are just words.

"Arden's strong. She gets that from you."

"You don't know. You don't know anything."

"I know you never planned to get married, not to me, not to Vince. I know you never wanted kids."

I've never told him this. I've never even whispered it. "I love our kids." It sounds lame. It sounds pitiful.

"Of course you do, and they love you. But here we are, Natalie, in another place you

447

never expected to be. You need to figure this out."

"That's it? That's all you've got for me — *figure it out*?" I turn away, and he grabs my arms.

"You can do this, Natalie."

His green eyes so like Arden's. His face blurs. "I can't."

"You can. I'm right here, sweetheart. I'm not going anywhere." He kisses my forehead, my cheeks. "I'm never going anywhere." He presses his lips against mine. I taste the coffee on his breath, the salt of my tears. I put my arms around his neck and pull him toward me. This man, the father of my children. My best friend, my lover.

The first time you hold your baby and see she's all right, you breathe a sigh of relief. You think you've crossed the finish line. You don't realize that the race has just begun.

My mother phones me from the hotel. I get up from Arden's bedside and go out into the hall, almost running to answer her before she hangs up. It's a three-hour trip from D.C. and it's been more than five since she called to tell me she was about to leave. A million things could have happened en route, but I didn't dare phone her while she was driving. "We're here, honey. How's Arden? Is she out of surgery?"

"She got out a couple of hours ago." The intracranial pressure has already decreased, which is a very good thing. Now all we can do is wait and hope that it drops even lower. She's still heavily sedated. There's no way to know how she's doing. There's no way to predict if she'll start to move, open her eyes, smile. I have spent the past forty-eight minutes watching the machines pump oxygen and drip IV fluid and a complex cocktail of medication into my daughter. Watching, but not really seeing.

We've heard from Denise the nurse that Rory's been put on the lung transplant list. Theo is in Rory's room, talking to Vince and Gabrielle. Everything feels precarious. Fear and loss loom tall in every corner.

"Could you please tell the girl at the front desk to let us into the room?" my mom asks.

I hear squealing in the background and guess that Henry's torturing Oliver or vice versa. I glance at the clock over the door as I talk to the girl. *Yes, she has my permission. Yes, please bring in a rollout. You can charge it to our credit card.*

"How was your trip?" I ask my mom when she gets back on the phone, meaning, *What took so long?* She sighs. "It's raining."

Still? I glance to the gray window streaked

and smeared. Arden loves rainstorms. She huddles outside beneath the porch overhang to watch the thrashing trees and bright bursts of lightning. The boys sit with her, Oliver leaning in to the curve of her arm, while Henry darts forward to capture a handful of water gushing from the down-spout. The three of them swimming in the same gene pool and yet each so different.

"Do you need help settling in?" I ask my mom. There are two nurses in the room. They are watching Arden very closely. Theo could run over to the hotel, or maybe I could. I am craving my sons. Now that they are so near, it feels unbearable.

"No, no. We'll be fine. Give us a few minutes and then we'll be right over."

They're already seated at a far table by the time Theo and I get down to the cafeteria. My mom's focused on cutting Henry's sandwich into triangles while Oliver carefully peels the foil from a cup of yogurt. Henry's hair's been combed, the cowlick at his crown lying flat. My mother's doing. Henry will never sit still long enough for me. Oliver's got on his favorite Pokémon jacket, a size too small. The sleeves ride up his wrists and the zipper barely closes. I'd put it in the donation pile, but Oliver must have persuaded my mom to take it out.

450

They look so ordinary and extraordinary, both. Henry spots us first and shoves back his chair. "Mommy! Daddy!" Oliver looks up and then both of them are running toward me.

I crouch and they crash into me. I wrap my arms around them and hold on tight. They feel exactly the same, smell exactly the same. I can't get enough of them. When I stand, I hug my mom. She's wearing the gardenia perfume Theo and I gave her for Mother's Day and this gesture touches me. Theo tousles first Henry's hair, then Oliver's, and we all sit down. Oliver clambers onto my lap while Henry leans against me, a thrill. He doesn't like to be confined. Even as an infant, he'd raise his head away from my shoulder to see what was happening around him. He's always the last to fall asleep, the first to wake up. "I've missed you guys so much," I say, nudging Henry's plate toward him, handing Oliver a spoon.

"We've been looking for the chicken spots," Oliver tells me quite seriously between bites. "But we don't have any."

"That's terrific." I cuddle him. The curve of his head is hard and whole beneath my cheek. I've seen photographs online of somber-faced people with sunken depressions above their temples that look as though someone took a bite out of each side, leaving behind a narrow isthmus of face. Theo had noticed what I was doing and closed the laptop. *You don't need to see that,* he told me. *You don't need to prepare yourself for that.* Arden's head is contained in a helmet of gauze. I don't know what I need to prepare myself for.

"How's Rory?" my mother wants to know, and Theo says, "She's on the transplant list, but they're worried . . . ."

"She's so young. Shouldn't she be at the top?"

"Lot of people on the list, Mom." Theo has always called my mother this, and it pleases her when he does. It draws the circle closer.

Henry's telling me about the hospital gift shop Grandma had walked him past. It has Cool LEGO Sets in the window, and stuffed animals that Look Real. "Want to check it out?" I look to Theo, who nods. "You go on. I'll get us both something to eat. What can I get you?" he says to my mom.

I take the boys by their small warm hands and they pull me across the cafeteria. It's late afternoon, but the storm outside the windows makes it look like midnight. The cafeteria's blessedly empty of gawkers and whisperers. No one jerks a chin toward us;

no one turns away abruptly as we approach. There's just an elderly couple holding hands at a small table, a woman sitting back in her chair and texting. A cafeteria worker is mopping the floor. No one's paying any of us the slightest attention. The boys are my good-luck charms. They always have been.

I buy Oliver a stuffed tiger and Henry a plastic dinosaur with beady yellow eyes. The boys practice roaring as we make our way back to the cafeteria. They're arguing over which beast makes the scariest noise, and I'm enjoined into volunteering an opinion. I'm keenly aware of the time ticking past. Arden's been alone now for twenty minutes.

"Look, Grandma." Henry elbows Oliver out of the way and jumps his dinosaur toward her.

"Oh, my. That's a scary one."

"Not as scary as THIS." Oliver smacks at Henry's dinosaur with his tiger.

This is an interesting development — Oliver's never the instigator. Theo and I exchange looks. We are always urging Oliver to stand up for himself. "There are lots of dangerous animals around in the forest," my mom says to the boys. "Your dinosaur and tiger would be better off working together to defeat them."

"Good idea," I say.

"Yeah," Oliver says. "One of them can be the lookout."

"They need a secret password," Henry says. "In case the aliens abduct them."

Theo's gotten me a salad. "Thanks." I pick up my fork. I haven't eaten anything since nibbling the burrito he brought me — was it today? Yesterday? I'm suddenly ravenous. It's an ordinary salad, but the lettuce is green enough and the tomato not too mushy. I take a bite and chew. I think about a light poppy-seed dressing and seared bay scallops. Fresh bread smeared with goat cheese and sun-dried tomato. A tablespoon of good olive oil.

I catch Theo looking at me. "What?" I reach to brush something from my chin, my cheek. "Where is it?"

He smiles. "No. You're fine."

"Your phone's ringing, Mommy," Oliver says, wrapping the long striped tail of his tiger around his finger.

ARDEN

Aunt Gabrielle lowers her arm. Now I can see her whole face, the round swells of her cheekbones and the dark hollows beneath them, her almond-shaped eyes and high plucked eyebrows pushed together in a frown. She glances over her shoulder, then brings her face closer. "Rory?" I feel her breath light against my lips.

Not Rory. I look into her eyes. She's the only one looking at me, and so I have to trust her. I have to reach past. I don't know what I'm afraid of, just that I'm afraid.

Look at me. See who I am. Tell me — am I awake or am I asleep? I try to move my hand to grab her arm, but I'm frozen. I'm stuck to this bed. *Am I paralyzed?* My eyes go hot with tears.

"Gabby," Uncle Vince says.

She suddenly straightens, turns away. *"Qu'est-ce que c'est?"*

No no no. Come back.

455

"It's Arden." His voice is choked.

Uncle Vince sees me. He's missed me, too! But no. Now they're both gone and I'm alone.

After our fight, I curl up on one of the grungy sofas in the lounge and listen hard for any noises down the hall that can tell me what's going on. Stupid me, I stormed out of the room in my nightgown and without my phone. Sad little me, I don't have anywhere else to go. So I wrap my arms around my bent legs and rest my cheek on my knee and try not to cry. *You can be such a baby,* Rory's scolded me. *You really have to get a grip, little cousin.* Will she ever call me that again? Will she ever *talk* to me again?

All my fault. All of it.

I hear D.D. go down the hall, and a little while later the door to our room closes. When I peek out, I see Rory going around the corner. I have to wake the RA to get him to let me in my room. *Sorry,* I keep saying. *Sorry, sorry.*

I find my cell at the bottom of my backpack and fish it out. Hunter answers it, laughing. "Hey," he says. He's with people. I can hear noises in the background, but as I talk, the noises go away. Hunter's gone into a room by himself. "Shit." His voice is dull.

"What do we do?" I wail.

"I'm such an asshole."

We both are. "Rory's on her way over there. She should be there any minute."

"She hasn't called or texted."

"She probably knows I'm giving you a heads-up." I stay on the phone with Hunter, pacing in the darkness and kicking piles of clothes out of my way, but Rory never shows up. I don't know where she is.

Rory's already there by the time I get to class the next afternoon. I stand in the doorway and scan the room and there she is, over in a middle row. I'm stopped by indecision. Where do I go? What do I do? I wait for Hunter, but he never shows. He's upset with me, too. I've ruined everything for everyone.

Professor Lee walks into the room and goes to the lectern. "Lights, please," she tells her assistant, and as the room goes dark, I slink into a seat at the back of the auditorium. Rory never once turns around. Fifty-five minutes spin past, slide after slide popping up on the screen and then disappearing. When the lights flare on again, I look down at my notebook. I haven't written down a single thing.

Rory's standing up. Turning, she sees me across the room and her face goes blank. She looks exactly like her mom. Our whole lives, I've never seen her face look so still and cold. It's as though I'm not even there. I gather my things and rush to meet her at the top of the stairs. "Rory, we need to talk."

"You said plenty last night." She won't even look at me. She just keeps on walking. I hurry to keep pace.

"I screwed up, okay? It's over. I'm sorry." I told Hunter this last night on the phone. *I don't get it,* he'd said. *Isn't this what you wanted?* To have him all to myself? Yes, desperately, but not this way. He hung up without saying goodbye. I don't even remember falling asleep, but when I woke up, I felt hollowed out. Empty. I'd blinked at the early-morning sunlight slanting through the open window and glanced toward Rory's bed, which lay smooth and untouched.

"You think apologizing can make everything better?" She'd gone back to the room at some point, showered and changed, applied her makeup. She smells bright with flowers; she's been especially careful to blend her eye shadow so you can't tell where it starts or ends. I imagine her doing this, humming as she leans close to the mirror with her little brush, happy with self-righteousness and a clean conscience. Yes, she's upset and hurt and betrayed, but this time she stands on the good side.

People are pushing past us, trying to get through the door.

"What can I say? What can I do?"

"Nothing. You're nothing to me. I can't stand to look at you."

Her voice is rising and I'm embarrassed. "Please, Rory. Can't we go somewhere?"

She puts her face close to mine. "You want to go somewhere? I know where you can go."

She turns and steps into the stream of students, and just like that, she's gone.

Aunt Gabrielle's in my room when I drag myself back. Hunter's texted me twice and I'm looking down at my phone trying to decide whether to text him back when I hear her talking on the other side of my door. I'm confused. She can't be in there with Rory. I'd just left her, going in the other direction. When I open the door, she's by Rory's bed. The nightstand drawer is open and she's reaching inside, turning things over. "Can we move it to tomorrow?" she's saying, and I realize she's got her cell phone pressed to her ear.

I let the door bang against the wall and she turns and sees me.

"Hi, Aunt Gabrielle."

She holds up a finger to signal me to wait. She doesn't even look guilty about going through Rory's things.

"Yes, that will be fine. Thank you." She turns off her phone and slides it into her lime-green bag. Aunt Gabrielle has a million purses, all colors and sizes. My mom has one slouchy black bag that's worn on the bottom from being dropped to the floor a million times.

"*Bonjour,* Arden. How are you?"

"Fine." I'm a bird, small and nervous.

She looks around the room. "You girls need to spend some time tidying up in here." Aunt Gabrielle's house is so clean I'm afraid to get a glass of water even on the hottest days. She keeps a black plastic tray on the floor by the front door for people to place their shoes. I'm always nervous walking across her gleaming floors in my socks.

"My parents want me to focus on my studies." A total joke. The last thing I've been doing is studying. I can't even cut it at this place, where partying's practically a major. I've got a Spanish test in the morning, a million math problems due, my self-portrait that still isn't finished because Rory's right — it looks just like her — and that freaking art history essay. What about Rory's paper? I could still do it for her. It might be a way to bring her back. At the mention of my parents, Aunt Gabrielle's lips tighten. She's wearing her usual orange-red lipstick. It makes her eyes glow umber. Like a tiger's, I think.

"Yes, well. Do you know where Rory is? I've been calling and calling."

"We just got out of class. I don't know where she is now." I drop my backpack on the floor. "How did you get in here?"

"The girl who lives next door let me in. She saw me waiting in the hall and took pity on me."

"D.D.? Whitney?"

"The girl with the pink hair. As if that's at all original." She's shaking out a short pleated skirt of Rory's and re-clipping it to the hanger. "You know, she's been lying to you."

Aunt Gabrielle's been going through Rory's things. She must have found her stash. Does she know D.D. supplies her? "Who, D.D.?"

"She doesn't come from money. Her mother's a nurse at the hospital and she doesn't even have a father."

461

Typical Aunt Gabrielle. She is scary good at finding out stuff about people.

I wonder if Rory knows this about D.D. I want to talk to her, see what she thinks. Will we ever have a conversation again? Will we sit on the swings and talk, or are all those days over? I don't want Aunt Gabrielle to see me cry. She will only ask why. She won't give up until I tell her. The only one who can lie to Aunt Gabrielle is Rory. "D.D. doesn't have a key to our room."

"Well, apparently, she does." Aunt Gabrielle stares at me coolly, daring me to decide which one of them is the liar.

Are my eyes open? I blink. *Yes, yes!*

A woman's talking in a muffled voice. ". . . you get that?"

A curtain covers the wall. Someone's moving down by my feet. Everything else is shifting shades of gray.

"Got it," another woman says. She's closer to me, up by my head. A nurse? Two of them, talking around me like I'm not even there. I want to yell, *Look at me! Talk to me! Tell me where everyone is.* "Such a pity."

"A real tragedy. You must get down on your knees every night to thank the good Lord for sparing your girl."

"When I think that she could have been

caught in this . . . She moved back home, did you know that? Went straight into her old room. I hear her crying every night. The clinic had to give her something so she can sleep. Daphne was a good friend with all three of them."

Dizzy Doolittle. Daffy Dishes. *Daphne.*

"She blames herself. She saw Arden carrying that can of paint thinner down the hall. She said she should have suspected something was wrong."

There's no way. D.D. — Daphne — is lying. She was at the pep rally with everyone else. She never saw me carrying anything.

"You tell her it's not her fault. Who would have ever thought a girl with everything going for her would do something so terrible?"

They think I set this fire. They know I did. Did Rory and Hunter tell them? The nurse is standing close beside me. I see the front of her green top, the bottom of her chin. If I could, I'd reach out and touch her. If she reached down and put her hand to my heart, she would feel it leaping out of my chest.

"It's this generation. They're spoiled. They never had to work a day in their lives. Everything gets handed to them. And when things don't go their way . . . Too bad they learned their lesson too late. None of them will grow up to see that time heals all."

"You don't think so?"

I close my eyes. I lie perfectly still. I feel my chest rise and fall, air pushed in and air sucked out, by the machine beside me. Where is Rory? Why hasn't she been in here once to see me?

I Skype my mom Wednesday. I am going to tell her everything. I am just waiting for the right time. I am going to make her stop and listen. I talk about blue sweaters and then Oliver takes the laptop and we talk about ant farms. I want my mom to take the laptop back so I can tell her, *Mom, I'm so scared.*

I call my dad Friday. Things are even worse, and I'm holding my cell against my ear and pacing back and forth. I've bitten off all my nails. My jeans hang loose. But my dad doesn't answer and I don't leave a message. What could I say? I've already done it; I can't undo it. I hang up. I turn to my self-portrait, propped on the easel by my bed. I run a finger around the oval of my face. I look into my painted eyes.

I am Alice in Wonderland. I have fallen down the hole.

RORY

I spend Thursday night with Chelsea, curled up in her massive bed with its heavy comforters that we push to the floor. She's working beside me, her laptop on her lap, frowning at the screen. I'm doing math problems, or pretending to. "Have you ever been to France?"

"No, can you believe it? I've never been to Italy, either. There should be some sort of law that says people who teach art history have to actually see the stuff in person. It's ridiculous."

I think of this, the two of us walking along the streets in Paris, going into shops and talking to the salespeople. I'd have to translate everything for her and she'd be so amazed. *I had no idea,* she would say. We would eat at sidewalk cafés, lingering over bottles of wine or cappuccinos. I'd use sugar, not sweetener, and she would smile at me.

"You know, your essay was due today," she says.

"Right. I meant to turn that in." I don't even try to make it sound like the truth. She should know that I've had other things on my mind.

She lifts one of her eyebrows, a swift in flight. "You can't just not turn in work."

Like I'm a child? I'm pissed. I rub the eraser hard across the paper. "I know."

"Is this the way you treat your other professors?"

I look at her and raise my eyebrow. "Oh, so that's what you are?" She's got her hair pulled back into a messy ponytail and she's wearing a man's shirt with the sleeves rolled up. I wonder where she got it from, but I haven't dared to ask. She sighs and shakes her head. "What?" Are we about to fight? I feel on the edge, tense and jittery. I can't deal with her heavy sighs and superior way of looking at me.

"Have you ever been diagnosed?"

I frown. She can't be talking about my trial run with anorexia. "Is this the reading thing again? Are we going to play a fun little game? You know how much I enjoy that."

"Were you tested in school?"

"Of course not." I go back to my math

problems. She's looking at me, but I ignore her.

"There's nothing to be ashamed about, Rory." Her voice is velvet, smooth and soft. "Lots of people have dyslexia. It's just the way your brain is wired. There are things you can do. There are tricks you can learn."

"I don't have dyslexia." My brain is fine. My brain is perfect.

"Rory. I care about you." This makes happiness bloom inside me, a warm circle that pushes the dark shadows all away. She sits up in front of me and cups my face between her hands. "How on earth did you manage all this time without help?"

I did have help. I had Arden.

Hunter's been texting, which is so lame. He should know by now that I'm not going to answer. If I'd run into him, I'd have had it out with him, loud and dramatic and sure to humiliate him in front of everyone. But I haven't seen him and I guess that's because he knows exactly how it'd play out. What a coward. I delete our text conversations, all the emoticons and exclamation points gone with the press of a red button. *Buh-bye.*

My mom's been texting, too. *YOU NEED TO CHECK IN.* She uses all caps when she's really upset. Then she moves on to exclamation points, and finally she just gets in the car. While Chelsea's in the shower, I think about what to text back. My mom won't want to hear apologies. I've already used the study group excuse. In the end, I don't answer her, either. Let her get in the car. "You're going to have to go back to your room sometime," Chelsea says as she's toweling off. A flurry of alarm. "You getting sick of me?" I pull on my jeans and she smiles at me. "Of course not. But you do need to work things out with Arden."

"There's nothing to work out."

"You can't just cut people out of your life like that."

"My mother did."

She gives me a look. "That's the source of all of this, your mother? You know, you're a grown woman, Rory. You need to stand on your own two feet."

Is that the way she sees me? "My mother's the source of nothing, and I'm pretty sure I didn't ask for your opinion."

She laughs. "Fair enough. Just think about it, okay? I'm going to be working late tonight." She pushes papers into her worn leather briefcase. It's not Coach, but it still looks ruggedly cool. "I have to get through these essays."

"On a Friday?" So she won't be at the pep

rally tonight. I'm disappointed, although I don't know what I expected. It's not like we could sit together and hold hands. Not yet, at least.

"On a Friday." She comes up close. Her arms are bare, the collar of her blouse open to show the tan skin of her neck, the hollow of her throat. We are the same height, eye to eye. She is beautiful, warm and distant at the same time. "Let's go to Paris," I say.

"Sounds like a dream." She kisses me, the lightest pressure against my lips, teasing. I've kissed a girl before, but that was high school. That was pretend, just being silly. This is different. This isn't silly at all. Is this who I really am? I feel my legs quiver, but she moves away. "Talk to Arden. I'll see you tomorrow, okay? We can go to the shore or something. Get out of this town."

"Your name is like poetry."

"You can't really think that's my name." She shoos me out the front door, then turns and locks it securely behind us.

NATALIE

Dr. Morris stands beside Arden while a short, stout woman with a cap of brown hair and red oblong glasses fiddles with the dials on the machine. She's the respiratory therapist. She doesn't smile as she watches the monitor. She and Dr. Morris are talking to each other briefly and in code. I can't access any of it. I don't know what's going on.

Turning, Dr. Morris spies us in the doorway and comes over. "Arden's pupils aren't dilating. I sent her for a CT scan. Unfortunately, it looks like the edema is worsening."

Unfortunately. Unfortunately. A mouthful of syllables. I can't hear them. I can't assemble them into sense. I look past her to Arden, but too many people stand between us. "I thought the surgery was supposed to fix that," I hear Theo say.

"We hoped it would. It did alleviate some of the pressure, but not all. Fluid is still

470

building up."

She's talking so slowly, in such measured tones. Her brown eyes are clear, her face smooth. She is complete and whole, and I am cracking into pieces. I want to shake her. "Can't you drain it off?"

"We're trying to. What you need to understand is that there are some things we are helpless to control."

"She just came out of surgery. Everything looked fine." A last-ditch measure and Arden had sailed through. Things had looked stable. I had left my daughter's bedside and gone down to hold my sons. I had gone shopping with them and smiled at their chattering. I had put food in my mouth and chewed.

"I know. These things can happen very suddenly."

"What things?" Theo says.

"The scan also showed signs of herniation."

This is a new word, another assault against which I am defenseless. I glance to Theo and he's frowning with confusion. "We don't know what that means." My voice is high and querulous.

"Arden's brain stem is expanding outside her skull into her spine."

There's a buzzing in my ears. I feel Theo's

arm go around my shoulders.

"I'm sorry, Mrs. Falcone, Mr. Falcone, but Arden's prognosis is not good. We're going to continue sedation and continue draining fluids from the catheter. We'll give her an increased hypertonic saline through her IV in case . . ."

". . . then what?" Theo's voice is far away.

I push my way to Arden. She lies propped against the pillow with her eyes closed. A plastic tube is taped between her lips, forcing oxygen into her lungs. I want to unwrap the gauze from around her head. I want to peel the bandages from her arms and torso. I want to crawl onto her bed and pull her into my arms, let my heart do the beating for hers, let my lungs breathe for hers. "Arden?" I whisper.

I had glimpsed reprieve. I had cupped hope in my palms.

Arden was five years old when I miscarried my second pregnancy. It happened very quickly. I woke up cramping, saw the blood, and rushed to the hospital. By dinnertime, I was back home again, woozy with grief. I had been far enough along that we had made the announcement to our families and so the announcement had to be unmade. I was careful not to let Arden see me cry. I was careful to be cheerful, but still, one day a few months later, Arden started sobbing in the backseat while we were out running errands. *If Baby can die, doesn't that mean you can, too? And Daddy?*

She was inconsolable. I searched for something for her to hold on to, a conviction, a way of seeing the world that made sense, but I'd never been religious and neither had Theo. We were out of our depth. It was Gabrielle who suggested we take Arden to talk to the pastor at Gabrielle's church. So one spring afternoon Arden and I wandered through the church gardens with a slim, pleasant-faced woman who told us to call her by her first name. I can't recall what her name was, not anymore, but I remember her taking Arden's hand and traipsing along the stone path between pink and yellow flowers as I trailed behind, letting them talk. She explained to Arden that our bodies are like caterpillars. We are tangible and very real, but when we die, we transform into something else, something just as real. We become butterflies.

At seven-thirty, the medical team arrives for morning rounds. Theo and I stand there, stiff with fear. Christine has arrived and is beside me, listening and watching. Nurses

473

have been in and out of Arden's room all night. Nothing's changed. Nothing.

The resident gives the summary in a quiet voice. I strain to parse out a few phrases. "Patient has fixed pupils and no gag reflex . . ."

"How do you know that?" Theo interrupts to ask, and the resident nods. Together they go over to Arden and the resident wiggles the tube in Arden's mouth. Christine squeezes my hand. She has talked to Dr. Morris. She has gone over Arden's records. She hasn't smiled once.

". . . riding the vent."

The resident turns the dial on the ventilator and everyone turns to watch my daughter.

I am holding my own breath. *Breathe, Arden. Breathe.*

But she doesn't. The red line on the screen flattens.

". . . recommend discontinuing sedation."

I look to Christine. She has her lips pressed together. She glances to me and shakes her head. I am standing bolstered between my sister and my husband, and it is not enough. I have my arms wrapped around myself, trying to stay upright. I can't seem to get enough air.

The room empties and Dr. Morris comes

over to us. "We've discontinued sedation."

"What does that mean? Have you given up?" Theo asks.

"Not at all. We're going to see what happens over the next twenty-four hours. If nothing changes, we'll do an electroencephalogram to check for brain activity."

"So there's still hope?" I ask.

Dr. Morris puts her hand on my arm. "There's always hope."

"There's always hope," Christine repeats later, after everyone's out of the room and it's just us, Arden, Vince, and Gabrielle. Vince and Theo have been talking quietly by the ventilator while Gabrielle stands at the foot of our daughter's bed. The nurses are debriding Rory's burns. The ventilator is still working. The room is still shrouded in darkness. The only thing that's changed is the IV is no longer dripping medication into Arden's bloodstream.

"But," I say dully.

"I'm sorry, sweetheart. I'm so sorry."

Christine's explained that tomorrow morning the doctors will conduct an apnea test. It will take about thirty minutes and Theo and I will have to leave the room. I can't bear to think what will happen during that time, and why we can't be there to witness it. The point of the test is to determine, once and for all, brain death. There will be no more hope after that. "Dr. Morris is going to come in and talk to you," she says. We're sitting side by side and she's got my hand clasped in hers. "About organ donation."

I yank my hand free. "I don't want to talk about that."

"I know." Christine has pale blue eyes. They stay steady on mine. "I know you don't."

"Not now. Not . . ." I glance to Arden's bedside. What if she's listening?

"She can't hear you. I'm sorry, Nat, but she can't."

"We don't know that."

"Take your time. You don't have to decide anything now. But I wanted you to be prepared."

"Arden's an organ donor," Theo says. Vince stands beside him. I am looking up at their faces, both carefully holding the same expression, and I realize they have already talked about this, maybe in the hall, maybe in the cafeteria getting coffee. "I took her for her driver's license. I know."

"She's eighteen. She's still a minor."

"She's an adult," Theo says.

Christine looks to him, then to me. "Nat, Theo and I've been talking. If we can't get

Arden back . . ."

Why are they all looking at me like this?
Even Gabrielle's come up to join the circle.
"We *can.*"

"Maybe." Christine nods. "But if we
can't . . ."

"I think we should save Rory." Theo
crouches in front of me, puts his palms on
my knees. "Honey, think about it. We could
save Rory."

My cheeks are wet. "You can't give up on
Arden!"

"No one's giving up on her."

I'm gasping for air, shuddering. I push his
hands off my knees and stand. I go to Arden's bedside and grab on to the railing. I
look down at my trusting child.

*Banky, mimi, 'ghetti, Dada, Mama, 'nana,
rainbow, juice.*

Her small world, the things she loves, safe.

"I'm not giving up. I'm not," I promise
her. "You keep on fighting."

Hours later, in the hall, I stand stiffly beside
Theo, not touching, and tell Vince and Gabrielle that I will agree to donate Arden's
lungs to Rory if the apnea test confirms
brain death. Gabrielle leans against Vince,
her hands to her face, sobbing. "Thank you,
Natalie. Thank you." My sister's given me a

pill to swallow. I've taken it without question, spilling the water in my haste to get the pill down.

I want to see my boys. They're with my mother in the family waiting room down the hall. Theo and I are trying to decide if we should let them in to see Arden one last time. *I think it's a good idea,* Christine's told us. My mother had turned Arden's bandaged hand over and over in hers, as though pressing life back into it, her face collapsed and uncertain. She looked old and frail, not the sturdy woman who's been running after six-year-old twins for a week. Theo's parents are on their way. Their plane should be landing at D.C. National within hours, and they are renting a car and driving up.

These are all the people who were there to welcome Arden into the world, and they will all be there to see her leave it.

ARDEN

"You wanted to see me?"

Professor Lee looks up from her desk. The window blinds are slanted half open to show the bright green grass and blue sky behind her. "Yes. Come in, please, Arden, and close the door." She doesn't smile. "Have a seat."

I sit in a creaky wooden chair, set my backpack on the floor at my feet.

"I've been looking over your essay." She's got her laptop open and she turns it around so I can see the screen. "This is yours, right?"

I look to see if it's got my name on it, not Rory's. "Yes."

Professor Lee leans back. Her long, curly black hair is pulled into a ponytail and the sleeves of her blouse are folded to her elbows. She looks so competent, so certain. "Some of it looks familiar."

I'd been in a hurry. "What can you say about Giotto that hasn't already been said a million times?"

"That's not what I'm talking about, Arden, and you know it."

"Well, then I guess I don't know what you're talking about." But I do. I do know.

Professor Lee tilts the screen of her laptop toward her and begins to read. *"Giotto's use of light is transcendently the first example of what filtered to Vermeer and then, hundreds of years later, became the Impressionist movement."* She looks at me. "Did you write that?"

I rub my palms against my jeans.

"And not . . ." She looked at her laptop again, then up at me. "Guy de Passari? Because that quote is famously attributed to him."

I open my mouth, but nothing comes out. All the words are gone. I'm empty, helpless.

"I've gone carefully through your entire essay. You've copied from several sources. Is any of this your work?"

My dealer, Toby, had sent me the link. *Foolproof,* he'd texted. *2 obscure to be discovered.* I can't even answer. I've never once done anything like this. I've never even come close. I called my dad to tell him what I'd done so that he could try to help me fix it, but he didn't pick up. I didn't leave a message. I guess I knew what he would tell

480

me to do. "Could you give me another chance? Please? I can redo it. I can fix it."

"I wish I could. I do. But this is a serious breach of ethics that I'm bound by just as much as you are. You plagiarized, Arden. I have no choice."

"You do have a choice. I'll rewrite it. You can fail me if you want. But please, *please*. Don't report me." I know what happens to girls who get reported for cheating. They get kicked out of school. No one ever hears from them again.

"It's too late. I'm sorry. I've already emailed the chair of the committee on academic misconduct." She presses the lid of her laptop closed and that's when I see it, the gold ring on her finger. "Someone will be contacting you to set up a hearing."

I look down at the chunky signet ring on my own hand. It's identical to the one Professor Lee is wearing — that thick band and flattened domed top. I had gotten silver because it was cheaper. Rory had gotten gold. When was the last time I saw Rory wearing her ring?

"Arden," she says, patiently. "Is there anything else?"

I'm thinking, hard. "Could you email them to say you changed your mind?"

"Absolutely not. You thought you could

481

take a shortcut. You thought I wouldn't find out."

"I'll tell," I blurt out.

She tips her head to the side and regards me. She looks genuinely curious. "Tell what? That you didn't know what you'd done? Arden, this is practically a word-for-word transcription."

My heart beats fast with daring. I've never been so brave. "I'll tell them about you and Rory."

Her face goes still. So it's true. Rory's been spending all her time with Chelsea — Professor Lee, our professor, who's so pretty, with her dark eyebrows and wide mouth. Does Rory love her? Does she love Rory? She's looking right back at me, trying to see inside to what I know and what I'm guessing.

"Do not threaten me." She rises. She looks so tall, all her features arranged in a mask.

"I just want another chance," I whisper.

"We have a second chance." Is that Aunt Gabrielle, standing over me? I smell her rose perfume. I hear the soft jingle of the charms on her bracelet. I keep my eyes shut. I try not to clench them. I try not to peek to see if she's staring down at me.

"I know, I know," Uncle Vince says.

"Thank God." His voice is thick, choked. I wonder what they're talking about. "But Arden," he says. "Arden."

"Maybe it's fair, Vince."

"I can't think like that. How can you be so hard?"

"My heart is broken, Vince. I just don't put it on display for everyone to see."

I'm in the art studio trying to fit together the pieces of the frame. I don't know why I'm even trying. The painting's due Monday. The building's empty, everyone getting ready for the pep rally, striping their faces with paint and filling flasks with mandarin vodka or Jameson. I was supposed to go, too. Rah.

I hear Hunter's voice in the hall and my heart beats butterfly fast. He'll listen and tell me what to do. He'll help me figure out a plan. I can't be kicked out of college. I can't. And then I remember. "Where's the painting studio?" he's asking someone.

"First door on your right."

"Thanks."

Hunter comes into the room, but I keep my head down. My face is swollen with crying. The framing nails are tiny and headless. They go everywhere but where I want them to. I tap the end of one and it splinters the wood. I tug it out with thick fumbling fingers and try again.

He comes up behind me. I feel him looking over my shoulder at my painting but I don't turn around. "That's pretty good. It looks just like her."

"It's a self-portrait," I say, between my teeth.

"Oh. Sorry." He tries again. "I've been calling you. I thought you'd gone home or something. I even talked to your little brother."

He's trying to make me smile. I shrug.

"That's it? Seriously? You're both going to pretend I'm dead?"

I clear my throat. "Sorry," I say, in a most ordinary voice. "I guess we use the same playbook."

"Yeah. I guess so."

I'm lining up the narrow lengths of wood to meet and make the corners. If I get the outside right, maybe I can fix the middle. The middle's all broken. Somehow, everything has fallen apart in my hands. Hot tears prick my eyes. I blink them hard away.

"Arden, are you ever going to look at me?"

I take a breath and raise my head. He looks terrible, like he's been sleeping in his clothes. His eyes are red and his hair's a worse mess than usual. His mouth is loose, like he's forgotten how to use it. "So. You're not okay, either."

He does care about me. I've broken his heart. I feel a swell of regret and hope. Maybe . . . maybe it doesn't have to be over. I put down the hammer. "Can we talk? Can we talk about this?"

He gives me a watery smile. "We can. More than anything, I want to talk. I've missed talking to you."

"Me, too."

"I'm so fucked, Arden. It's killing me. Rory's not answering my texts. She won't talk to me at all."

I let this sink deep into me. I absorb this. I'm not the one he's broken up about. I want to laugh at myself. It's better than crying. I've been doing enough of that. "Well, you could have gone to class. Rory was there."

"I was too wasted."

"Good move, Sherlock."

"I missed practice, too. The coach is going to suspend me for sure."

"I don't want to hear it. We screwed up, okay? End of story. Time to move on."

"You're angry. I get it. But, Arden, I need to explain."

"No, you don't. Just go away."

"I like you, Arden. I really like you. But

Rory . . ." He sighs and shrugs.

D.D. was right. *I need to tell you something about Hunter.* She'd leaned close and hissed. *You are nothing to him. Nothing.* It's always been Rory. It will always be Rory. As long as I'm in the same room with her, as long as I'm at the same school, I will never be good enough. No one will ever look at me with heartbreak in his eyes. The pieces of wood fall apart in my hands, leaving just the face of the girl looking out at me. I stare back. I got my answer.

I'm suddenly awake. I can feel cloth beneath my fingers. My leg is throbbing. I'm afraid to try to move it.

"It's hard to answer something like that." It's Dr. Morris. "I've never handled a directed donation."

I slit my eyes open the tiniest fraction and glimpse movement off to my right. The doctor's standing nearby, but not right up beside me. Not close enough to see.

I've been practicing. Not only can I open my eyes, but I can move my right thumb back and forth. Either they're giving me less medication or I'm getting used to it. I have to be careful not to let them know. I don't want them to dial up the meds again and knock me into that distant, helpless place, but maybe Dr. Morris will pay attention long enough for me to signal her. It's her name that gave me the idea to use Morse code. Not the real one because I don't know it, but purposeful blinks might work instead. They might stop her. I scratch the sheet, try to dig in hard enough to make it rasp.

Look at me!

"But it's possible, isn't it?" Aunt Gabrielle says.

I close my eyes and lift my thumb.

RORY

It's beautiful outside, one of those nights when you could drink the air, it's so delicious. People are crossing The Bowl, laughing and talking, everyone headed to the stadium. I feel a part of something bigger. I don't care what Chelsea says. I'm not talking to Arden. I go through the whole day without seeing her, or Hunter for that matter. If they're hanging out together, then they deserve each other. I've texted D.D., and she and Whitney are going to let me sleep on their floor. The three of us are coming back from dinner when I see a car approach, its two headlights perfect circles, sickeningly familiar. I stop.

"What?" D.D says, looking toward the dorm, trying to peer between the heavy branches to my fourth-floor window. "Is it Arden?"

"You still have to get your things," Whitney reminds me. "Come on, we'll go with you." She's the one who got the tickets, a block of four, back when Arden was part of the block. She gave the ticket to Kyle, D.D.'s on-again, off-again boyfriend. *Guess he's on again,* D.D. had said, sighing.

"It's all right." My mom's car pulls to the curb and the headlights flash off. "You go on to the pep rally. I'll meet you as soon as I put some of my stuff in your room."

"You sure you don't want help?" D.D. asks.

"I'm sure."

"Hurry," D.D. says. "You don't want to miss the mascot relay race."

Football must've been big at her high school, but sometimes I wonder about D.D. She's a little off. Like the time she described this girl with an overbite as being able to eat corn on the cob through a picket fence. That's just not how people talk.

The car door opens, a shaft of light falling out. My mother's legs swing to the pavement. "Rory!"

I stand on the sidewalk. "What?"

My mother slams the door and crosses over to me, heels clicking sharply on the pavement. "I was *this* close to calling the police."

"Come on, Mom. Nothing's going on. I don't need to call you every day."

"You think you know everything. You think you are so smart."

You have the ability, Rory. You just have to focus. "You're the one who doesn't think I'm smart."

"No, that's not true. You're just lazy. That's always been your problem."

"I'm not lazy. I have dyslexia."

"Oh, everyone has something these days. When I was growing up we had nothing but hard work."

We're on the sidewalk, my building beside me. Arden's in my room. Where do I go? I just stand there. Shadows of people hurry past. Laughter filters over. Everyone's excited about the rally. No one's paying us any attention. "You have to stop coming here. It's embarrassing."

"I'm worried about you. You're spending time with the wrong people."

"They're my friends, Mom."

"You need to make better choices."

"How about this one? How about I quit school?"

"Don't be absurd."

"Harvard was never my dream. It was yours. You and your stupid Kennedy obsession."

"Why are you acting this way? What happened?"

490

"Nothing, Mom. I'm just over it. I'm done. I don't want to pretend anymore."

She crosses her arms and looks impatient. "What do you think you're going to do?"

"I'm going to travel, meet my relatives in France." As soon as I say this, I know it's true. I am flooded with freedom. Chelsea will join me. She'll charm everyone and ease the way.

She laughs. "Do they know about this plan of yours?"

She's so confident. She knows everything, everything. My whole life, all she's done is push me into corners. I want to step out of the darkness. "Do you really love me, Mom?" I'm determined not to cry. "Do you really want me to be happy? Or is it all about you?"

"How can you say that? I've sacrificed everything for you."

I hear her accent now. *Go ask your father. Don't touch that! Behave yourself. Stand up straight. That neckline's too low. That skirt's too tight.* It's the way she presses down on her consonants. It's the way the syllables rush together, a river. *That's the wrong fork. You don't want people to talk. I think you can do better.*

"Like what, Mom? What have you ever done for me that hasn't been about what's important to you? I'm just a walking, talking doll to you. My feelings don't matter. They never have."

The streetlight shines down. Her eyes are dark, unreadable. "You ungrateful little brat. I can't tell you how much I wish you'd never been born."

I hear the truth plain in her voice. She took birth control pills to make sure a mistake like me never happened again. I take a few steps back. She moves toward me, but I turn and run. I hear the clacking of her heels behind me.

"Rory!"

The sidewalk veers in front of me, popping from circles of light to darkness beneath the streetlights.

"Rory, stop! Come back!"

I kick off my flip-flops and run faster. Until I don't hear her at all.

I limp down the sidewalk. Gravel and sharp sticks bite into the soles of my feet. It makes me think of Whitney the other night, the four of us running across campus, laughing and clutching one another. Three days ago. I don't even know that girl I'd been, happy, reckless, brave. I'm small now, and fearful. Is this the real me, revealed in the space of finishing a sentence?

I wish you'd never been born.

I need my passport. How to get it from my desk at home? Aunt Natalie will do it for me. She'll face down my mom and push past my dad. She's the mother I should have had. *She'll never be your mom,* Arden had yelled, but she doesn't know.

I'm closer to the stadium now. Off to my left, the sky's lit up like a Stephen King movie. A sudden roar tells me the mascots must be on the field now. Tons of parties tonight, but I won't be at any of them, because I'm headed home, too — to the big house on the corner of the next block.

I stop to brush the grit from the bottom of my feet. Will Chelsea be there by now? If she isn't, I'll go to the art history building. I'll find her in her office and tell her what happened. I'll tell her I'm ready to leave now and that she's right. I need to stand on my own two feet.

She can meet me in Paris or Rome when the semester's over. I'll get a job waitressing at some little café. One evening, I'll turn around with a tray of drinks and see her coming through the door toward me, her long curls bouncing and a big smile on her face. I'll barely manage to set the tray down before she throws her arms around me.

I turn the corner. The trees arch up and

over, holding hands across the middle of the street. Fallen leaves clump the curbs and lie in thick drifts on the broad lawns. Chelsea's porch light is on and light blazes from all the windows. It's as if she knows I'm coming. I start to run, big long strides that carry me over the cracked and torn-up squares of pavement. I am free.

I veer onto the front path and up the sagging wooden porch steps. The covered furniture there, the dusty cobwebs in the corners, all of it seems infinitely embracing. Home isn't perfect. Home is messy. Home takes you the way you arrive, barefoot and snotty, incoherent and empty-handed. I pound the door with my fist. *Let me in!*

Chelsea's muffled voice on the other side of the door. "Let me get that," she says. "I'll be right back." She sounds happy. Has she seen me coming?

The door swings open. Chelsea's there with a glass tumbler in her hand. Her hair's pulled loosely back in a style I've never seen her wear before, baring her tanned shoulders. She's wearing a tight black tube-top dress and long dangling earrings. Her smile fades as she sees me. "Rory?"

Behind her is a man, some guy I've seen around the halls of the Art History Department. He's got on worn jeans and a white shirt open at the neck. He's holding a glass, too, and as I stand there, he comes up and slides his other hand around Chelsea's waist. I glance to my right and see the same sedan in the driveway that Chelsea told me belonged to her mother.

You let yourself open, like a flower with soft, soft petals, but you should know better, because everyone lies. Didn't I tell you?

NATALIE

Theo's beside me on the sofa, his face buried in his hands. We've been banished to the family lounge while the doctors are in Arden's room. *I'll come find you the minute the test is over,* Dr. Morris promised. Christine's pill is wearing off. Soon I will ask her for another. I will keep asking, as long as I need to.

On the other side of Theo, Vince clears his throat. But he doesn't say anything. Gabrielle stands by the window, looking out. Henry and Oliver are bent over the small table, kneeling on the padded chairs. They are making window stickers from the craft set that Christine has miraculously known to bring for them. My sister's handing them bottles of colored glue that they drip onto acetone sheets. They are making one for Arden and one for Rory, and they are making a mess. They are in a race to see who finishes first.

My in-laws have arrived, orange-tanned and loudly optimistic. Theo and Vince have Sugar's green eyes rather than George's pale blue ones, but they have inherited his broad shoulders and easy laughter. Sugar and George sit on the other sofa with my mother, one on each side of her. My mother's cardigan is misbuttoned; there's a gap in the fabric near her throat. Sugar has my mother's hands in hers, patting them, while George holds a foam coffee cup. He keeps saying things like *Thanks for holding down the fort, Lorraine,* and *Maybe you'd like to stay with us for a few days.* They know she is losing her only granddaughter while they will still have one. I can see the guilt in their eyes. And the relief.

I stare at the clock on the wall. It's just like the one in Arden's room. The hospital must buy them in bulk and hang one in every room. So we can monitor time. So we don't let go of it. This clock tells me nine minutes have passed since we came in here. It tells me I have twenty more minutes before the apnea test will be over. But I already know the result. I saw it in Dr. Morris's brown eyes.

I push myself up.

In the bathroom, I hold my hands beneath the faucet. Water collects in my palms and I bring it cool and dripping to my face. I look at myself in the mirror — my eyes, my nose, my mouth. Somehow the outside of me is holding together. I blot my cheeks dry with rough brown paper towels and let myself out into the hall.

Arden's door is still closed. I stare at the curtained glass as if I can see through it to the other side. I imagine the two women and lone man moving around, testing, jotting things down. Are their faces grim? Are they talking? There's only silence.

Rory's door isn't shut all the way. I slide it open.

The room is deep in shadow. I go over to the bed and sit in the chair there. I put my hand over hers, my thumb on hers, my fingertips resting on her fingertips protruding from the lumpy cast. "Hello, my darling."

Rory's thumb is long, the nail slightly square and clipped short. It's achingly familiar. It could be Arden's. These two girls are like sisters. How many times had I glanced out the window at them splashing in the pool, and for the briefest moment had difficulty determining which was which? How many times had I heard one of them calling out in laughter and couldn't tell if it was my daughter or Rory? *Mommy,* Rory sometimes called me when she was little. I never corrected her.

I'm glad Arden had Rory. I'm glad they had each other.

"I've decided not to put chestnuts in the stuffing this year," I tell my niece. "And no raisins, either. Promise."

Do I imagine it or does Rory's thumb twitch beneath mine? I look down. Is it some small automatic gesture or intentional? No, I'm certain there are movements. I stand and reach for the remote control lying on the nightstand and turn on the lights. The bulbs beneath the bed light up. An indirect glow, but enough for me to see that her thumb is moving, back and forth, small movements, but movements.

Rory's eyes are open. She's looking straight ahead, at the curtains across the room. The simple thing of seeing my niece like this, alert and awake, fills me with dizzy gratitude. Yes, we will save Rory. We will save this precious girl.

"Hey, sweetheart," I say, softly.

Her eyes flick toward me and widen. There's a bruise on her cheek, mottled purple. Her lips are chapped.

"We've missed you." I smile and bend closer. "It's so good to see you awake."

She blinks.

499

"Are you having any pain? Let me get your mom."

Her brow puckers. She looks confused.

"Honey. You were in an accident. But you're okay. You're going to be okay."

She shakes her head and starts to cough. Has the ventilator tube become dislodged? I scrabble for the remote, hit the button again. The light above the bed goes bright. The plastic tube is still taped in place between her lips. But she's clearly in distress. "I'll get the nurse, sweetheart. Just hold on." I look at her as I start to turn, and freeze. Slowly, I sink back into my seat. My heart's booming. I put my hand on hers and lean forward. "Rory?"

She shakes her head again, this time frantically.

I whisper it. "Arden?"

Her fingers clutch mine. A tear pools in her right eye and spills.

Disbelief propels me to my feet. "Oh, my God." *How can this be? I'm wrong. I must be wrong.* I smooth back her hair and see the freckle high on her left temple.

"Oh, my God. Oh, sweetheart. I'm so sorry I didn't know you. Of course it's you. Of course it's you." Tears are dripping down my chin. "Darling! My darling girl!" I'm laughing and crying, both.

500

Her eyes are already drifting closed.

Dazzling light surrounds me. I thought I knew joy. I've never known joy. Everything I've ever felt — my marriage, having Arden, having my boys. Nothing comes close. *This.* Champagne bubbles in my veins. I'm floating. This is what drug addicts chase. This feeling can't be natural. Normal people don't get to feel this. I'm the luckiest person in the world.

The curtain behind me swishes open. The nurse is coming in, blue-gowned, carrying a plastic-wrapped bundle. "I'm sorry, Mrs. Falcone. I need to change Rory's dressing."

I love this nurse. This nurse is taking care of my daughter. "Thank you." I clutch her arm. "Thank you."

Her eyebrows wrinkle together above her paper mask. She nods.

I have to tell Theo. I have to get the doctors.

I push open the door to the family lounge. Everyone's there, my boys still at the table, heads bent as they work. I sweep them into my arms and squeeze them close. Their soft hair tickles my cheeks. "You're such good boys. I love you so much." I'm crying, hiccuping. I can't stop kissing them. "You're such good boys."

"Mommy, stop. Don't. I got the glue."

My mother says, "Natalie?"

I rock back on my heels, look to her. "Where's Theo?"

"Getting something from the car."

I kiss the boys one last time, made giddy by their puzzled faces, and straighten. As I go out the door, my mother calls, "The doctors are looking for you, honey."

I punch the elevator button, pace. I stand back, look up at the lights over the closed doors, give up, and take the stairs.

It's a radiant day after so much rain, sunlight gilding the parked cars. I lift a hand to shield my eyes and see Theo standing fifty feet away by the opened sliding door of our minivan. His hand rests on the roof of the car and his head is bowed.

I run to him and put my hand on his back. "Theo?"

He turns to me. I see how terribly this week has aged him. I place my hands on his shoulders. I can't stop grinning. I want to jump up and down. He listens as I talk and shakes his head. "Honey, this doesn't make any sense."

"I know. I know it sounds crazy. But listen. Arden's eyes aren't the same green as Rory's and they slant more."

"Natalie —"

"Theo, her freckle. We never pulled her hair up to see it. We never saw." I laugh. "Her freckle!"

"A freckle."

"She was always putting concealer on it. She hated it. Theo, it's Arden. She looked right at me. She knew me." I slide my hands to his biceps. "Come. Come see for yourself." I start to pull. "You'll know her, too. It's Arden!"

But he won't move. "Honey." His voice is raspy. "The tattoo. We both saw it."

"The tattoo." I laugh again. "Of course, they both got one! Why wouldn't we know that? They did everything together. Arden would *never* have gotten a tattoo unless Rory talked her into it. She *hates* needles."

"The hospital wouldn't make a mistake like this."

"Hospitals make mistakes all the time." And this is the best mistake in the world.

"But they did blood work for the transplant."

I hear the doubt in his voice. "They were just trying to match for the transplant. And we weren't looking. We weren't trying to figure out who was who."

He's starting to believe me. I see it on his face.

I grip his arms. "It explains the nail polish. The silver polish that Arden would never have worn." My stomach suddenly dips. That girl lying alone in that dark room.

He's shaking his head. He still doesn't believe me. He doesn't dare to.

"Oh, Theo, darling, I'm right. I can prove it to you. Let me show you."

Theo clings to me, helplessly weeping, this strong, resolute man I love. "I just don't . . . I can't."

I press my cheek against the warm cotton of his shirt, my arms tight around him. Our hearts beat together. Our breath. "My darling. My darling." We will see our daughter grow up. We will watch her stroke a brush across a canvas again; we will hear her laughter as she teases her brothers. Our home will be full, and happy. And someday we will watch her come down the aisle in radiant white. I clutch at him; I press him close.

Behind me, I hear the curtains swish open. "Oh, honey," Gabrielle says. "Oh, Natalie. Theo. I'm so sorry." She squeezes my forearm where it rests on Theo's arm.

I pull away from Theo's embrace. I look at Gabrielle. I feel my joy ebb for the first time. Our miracle is going to kill this woman. I don't know how to tell her. How

504

could I have forgotten Rory? *Rory,* lying in the bed beside us? That beautiful, beautiful girl so full of life. Theo and I have been embracing like lovers, delirious with happiness. When had we lost her? Had she heard me reading to her, talking to her in the long hours of the night? Had she longed for her own mother's voice? Had she been soothed by my love for her, even as I thought she was mine?

Vince stands behind Gabrielle. Around us in this stuffy room, the monitors blink, wheezing and whirring. The overhead light's on — revealing Theo's briefcase slumped on the floor, my sweater half off the back of a chair, the untouched coffee cup, the bed with its crisp sheet spread across the girl lying there. It's so bright in here. Eight days of darkness and rain and now this.

Theo clears his throat, rubs his face. "There isn't any way to say this, Vince. I need to show you."

"Show me what?"

Theo reaches for his brother's hand. Carefully, he lowers Vince's fingers to Rory's forearm — the girl who we'd believed all week was Arden — and onto the image of the butterfly, green and purple, wings outstretched. He runs Vince's forefinger back and forth. "Feel it?"

"No, what am I feeling?" Vince flicks a worried glance toward me.

"Right there," I say, softly. "Can you feel it?"

Vince strokes a fingertip back and forth across the tattoo. He looks at Rory's face. "But . . . that's impossible."

Gabrielle pushes her way to Rory's bedside. "What? What's impossible?"

Vince takes her hand in his, and as he lowers her fingertips to Rory's arm, I see it again — the shiny twist of scar tissue beneath the butterfly's body, hidden by black ink and visible now beneath the slant of light.

Gabrielle snatches back her hand.

Vince grabs it back.

"No," Gabrielle says. "No."

"Honey." Vince grabs her.

That long-ago burn, the one that Rory was so self-conscious about. Gabrielle had phoned me, panicked, and I'd rushed over to find her standing at the kitchen sink with five-year-old Rory, holding her daughter's arm beneath the splashing water as Rory sobbed.

"No! No!" Gabrielle pushes at him. "No! I would know my own daughter!" She's screaming, looking to Vince and back to the

506

girl in the bed. "Rory doesn't have a tattoo!"

Tears are streaming down Vince's face. He's trying to hold her, and Gabrielle is smacking at his arms. "She probably got it and didn't tell us," he says. "She probably hid it."

"She hid a lot of things," I say.

Gabrielle whips around to face me. "*You.* It's always you. Every bad part of my life has you in it."

"Honey," Vince says, reaching for her, but she yanks free. Her eyes burn into mine. "This is *you. Your* little scheme. Everyone listens to you. Even my husband thinks you walk on water. Well, you're not taking my daughter, too. So just shut up!"

The curtain opens. A short woman with dark hair steps into the room. "I'm so sorry to bother you," she says, in her soft, gentle voice. She puts her hand on my shoulder, and holds out a clipboard. "There's just one more spot to sign."

The transplant! How could I have lost sight of that? I nod, take the clipboard from the coordinator. My heart is pounding.

"There's been a mistake," Vince tells her.

Gabrielle snatches the clipboard from my grasp, and I gasp, surprised. She holds the clipboard against her chest. "*This* is not happening. You can't have it. You can't have everything."

"Gabrielle, you can't be serious," I say.

"I know this is hard," Theo says to Vince.

"Are you kidding me?" Vince says. "How do you expect us to deal with this? You need to back off. You just need to back off."

"You poisoned my marriage from the very beginning," Gabrielle hisses at me. "You think I *liked* our daughters growing up together? I hated it. I hated every minute, the way Arden followed Rory around, imitating her every move. I hated how you looked down on me. You think you're so much smarter than me. You think you can have your way."

I'm stunned, utterly stunned by this. Panic begins to swirl inside me.

"I'm sorry," the coordinator says. "Is there a problem?"

Gabrielle whirls to face her. "This is *my* daughter and I don't want the transplant."

"Stop, Gabrielle," I tell her. "We don't have time for this. We don't have time for tantrums."

"You think this is a tantrum? You've not seen a tantrum."

Furious, I shake off Theo's hand. "You would really let my daughter die because of *spite*? You may not have cared for your daughter when she was alive, but do the right thing now."

Gabrielle turns white.

Vince says quietly in a hard voice, "You both need to leave. Now." He slides his arm around Gabrielle's shoulders, pulls her to him.

As the door closes behind us, Theo says, "Why couldn't you have given them a little time? Why do you always have to *push*?"

"But we don't *have* time, Theo!"

"They gave it to you."

"I know, but the transplant . . ." I search his eyes, wanting him to see, to understand.

"May not happen now. We may have just lost our daughter."

"No!"

"You heard Gabrielle. You know how she is."

He's right. The venom in Gabrielle's voice, the things she'd said. I'd had no idea she felt that way. Vince won't stand up to her. He never has. I turn back to the door and Theo grabs my arm.

"Don't you dare go in there. You have to let this go."

"I can't." It's a wail.

"You don't have a choice, Nat." He releases my arm and lets himself into Arden's room.

Voices echo down the hall. An orderly sweeps a mop across the floor, head down, black earbud cords swimming from his ears and down into the pocket of his navy jumpsuit. A nurse comes out of the room across the hall, sees my face, and steps forward to ask me if I'm okay. I don't answer. I look past her to the open door, into another patient's room.

Someone new has moved into that room. What happened to the previous patient? Had it been a man, a woman? Someone's child? I can't remember. All these stories around me. Some of them have to have happy endings — don't they?

ARDEN

The world is alien, the sky a weird navy color, almost green. The trees are stiff and angry. They hold their branches low and crackle them in the wind. Clouds push past the moon, obscuring it. A storm is coming.

People walk past, talking and laughing, going in the opposite direction. No one looks at me. A low rumble in the distance sounds like a spaceship has crashed into the ground, but it's just cheering from the stadium. Everyone's already drunk, for sure.

I'm awkwardly carrying my painting and a huge tin of paint thinner that I stole from the studio supply cabinet. It sloshes coldly in the curve of my arm and I have to stop and switch it to the other arm every few blocks. The scary emptiness of the art building had crawled around me on insect legs and is chasing me back to my dorm. I see it ahead of me now through the trees, and I realize I'm just going from one empty build-

511

ing to another.

The wind's picked up, scuttling leaves across the pavement and whipping my hair across my eyes. I let myself into the building and climb up the stairs, panting when I reach the fourth floor. The tin is so heavy, but what was I going to do, pour it into a plastic cup and carry it half a mile? I'd throw up from the fumes.

I unlock my door to darkness and reach for the light switch. The overhead bulb flares on, dusting everything pale yellow. The room is empty, the way I knew it would be. Still, I'd hoped. I set my painting on the easel and look at it. Even I can see it doesn't look like me.

I need something to decant the paint thinner into. I glance around as the door bangs open. *Rory?* But no. It's Aunt Gabrielle. *Again.* I grit my teeth.

"Oh," she says. She's disappointed to see I'm not Rory. Isn't everybody? "Do you know where Rory is?" she asks, coming in and closing the door.

"Probably at Chelsea's." I pick up a bottle of hairspray and tug the plastic cap free. It's the right size. I need it to hold only a few tablespoons of paint thinner, enough to swish my brush around in. "That's where she's been spending the night these days."

"Who's Chelsea?" She's acting strange, picking things up only to put them down again without really looking at them. She doesn't seem to notice the empty vodka bottle on Rory's nightstand, the twisted lacy thong lying in plain view.

I'm brave with treachery. I say it right out loud. "Our art history professor." I hold the hairspray cap and look at it, hesitating. Does paint thinner dissolve plastic? *Better play it safe.* I put it down and reach instead for the happy-face glass ashtray D.D. gave Rory as a joke.

"Why would she spend the night at her professor's house?"

"I don't know." I unscrew the cap on the paint thinner and set it on my easel. "Ask her."

"What has gotten into you girls? You think going to college means you can behave like this?"

I shouldn't even be at this stupid school. I should be in California, where no one knows Rory. Emotion rises within me and I blurt out, "Going to college means getting away from you. Rory counted the days."

I can't believe my daring. I stare down at my shaking hands.

"Look at me," she says, but I won't. I don't have to listen to her. I won't. I pick up the tin of paint thinner and hold it over the small glass ashtray. If I pretend she's not there, she'll go away.

She comes closer, bumping my elbow. "Look at me," she says again, and this time I do. Her pupils are black circles floating in amber. Her mouth is precisely shaded with apricot lipstick. "You think you are so special?"

Her perfume swims around us, sweet and cloying.

"You're nothing without Rory. Nothing. The way you follow Rory around like a lost puppy. You know what her friends called you in high school? Oompa-Loompa. They called you other names, too, but I won't repeat them."

"I don't care." But I do.

"Oh, Arden." She sighs, her mouth crimping. "You keep hoping that someone, someday, will love you. I blame your mother. She made you believe you could be loved. But what does she know about love? That *whore.*"

I flinch, shocked. But she doesn't stop. She pushes her face close to mine. "Always throwing herself at my husband. She doesn't think I know, but I do. All those late nights, just the two of them. I was glad the restaurant folded. Something had to come between them."

This is all a lie. I know it is. But I remember the way Uncle Vince had held my mom the day the grill caught on fire. I clutch the paint thinner to my chest. I try to swallow.

"Your father didn't like it, either. But what could he do?"

"Stop."

"I won't stop. It's time you know the truth."

"I already know the truth." I've known since I was sixteen. Rory and I had leaned forward, staring at the words of the news story marching across the screen of her laptop. Rory has family in France, but she's afraid to visit them. "You were mean to your little brother. You hurt him." I would never hit Henry or Oliver. Never.

She draws back. If she's surprised, she doesn't show it. She is so strong. She is so powerful. She's thinking, hard. "He wouldn't do his chores. He wouldn't listen."

I don't believe her. I don't believe her at all. "Just like Rory wouldn't listen?"

Time stretches out, a rubber band. She stands utterly still. It makes my skin prickle, but I have gotten to her. At last, I've said something that digs into her and twists.

"What are you talking about?" she finally says, a warning clear in her voice, but I push on. She thinks she can talk like that about my mom?

"Rory remembers, you know. She remembers everything." I'd cried when Rory told me. She'd gotten up and walked away from the swings. "It wasn't an accident. You told everyone it was, but that was a lie. *You* pushed her arm over that gas stove. *You* held it there. You did it on purpose." I have nowhere to look but right at her. She stands so close, her sleeve touching my arm. The ivory column of her throat, the gold necklace with its tiny cross. I have never known her to go to church.

"Of course you only heard her side of it. Did she tell you she kept playing with the dials, even after I told her to stop? I was trying to teach her a lesson."

"She was *four.*" I hold the heavy tin against my chest, armor. My heart is thumping, hard. "I'm going to tell. I'm going to tell *everyone.*"

"No one will believe you."

"My parents will. And so will Uncle *Vince.*" Rory will be angry, but Rory is already angry.

Aunt Gabrielle's face slides into stillness, and I know I've won. But I'm scared. Her face is a mask. She doesn't even look like herself. She glances around and stops at the painting propped on the easel. "What is *that* supposed to be? *You?*" She goes up close. "My goodness."

She doesn't know. She doesn't know anything about art.

She puts her finger on my painted eyebrow and presses hard. The canvas bends beneath her fingertip. "You should have given yourself better eyebrows. You could have at least pretended they were even." She scrapes her fingernail down my painted nose and halts. I put my hand to my nose, to the small bump there. "Honestly, I don't think this can be fixed. You can just say it gives you character when people comment. I'm sure they already have."

My face is hot.

She jabs her finger at my painted mouth. The paint crackles. "Those braces never really did the trick, did they? Such a pity. I know how much your parents spent."

The orthodontist had tried to fix my overbite. She had spent hours leaning over me in the chair, an intent expression on her face.

"And your chin. I know you've lost some weight recently, but . . ." She shakes her head and crosses her arms. "You'll always have a fat little face."

Rage bubbles up, hot and spreading. *Calm*

517

down, my mom warns me. But I see it, the lost look in my eyes, the hopeless droop of my lips. Aunt Gabrielle is right. It's pathetic. *I'm* pathetic. I swing my arm and hurl a great looping stream of paint thinner at the canvas.

Aunt Gabrielle gasps and jumps back, brushing at herself. "What the devil are you doing? Stop that!"

I heave another dripping, stinking stream of liquid. Colors smear. My painted eyes run, my painted mouth turns down. It feels good. It feels excellent.

"Arden! For God's sake!"

I whirl around, faster and faster, holding out the heavy tin, paint thinner spraying everywhere. On the walls, on the floor, all over us. The room is alive with ghosts, all the times Aunt Gabrielle mocked me, Kent Stegnor dumped me, Hunter looked at me with empty eyes. I'm a butterfly. I don't even see Aunt Gabrielle leave.

Why can't I feel my lungs swelling and shrinking with air? Does this mean I'm dead? The machine against the wall beeps faster and faster. I want people to hurry into the room. I want someone to save me. Then I think, *Why?*

■ ■ ■ ■

"What the hell happened in here?"

It's Rory and she's talking to me. I drop the empty tin and look at her. I'm panting hard. Fumes rise up. I need to open the window. "Your mother happened." Her face is puffy. Her eyes are red. She's not high. I peer at her. "Have you been *crying*?"

"I just came to get my things."

"Get them. I don't care."

"You sure you don't want them? You take everything else of mine."

I don't want anything of yours. The words are right there, ready to spill out, but they suddenly dissolve. "What's going on? What happened?"

She shakes her head. She sinks onto her bed and cradles her face in her hands. Slowly, I sink down beside her. She's actually crying, her shoulders shaking. I put my arm around her. "Let's not fight anymore, okay?"

"We're fine. We've always been fine. It's everything else. I'm a total fuckup."

"No, you're not. You're the most wonderful person. I wish I were like you." I squeeze her close and press my cheek to her shoulder.

"You've got to stop that. You don't want to be like me, trust me." Her voice is muffled, her face pressed against her palms. "I thought she loved me. What am I going to do?"

I'm not sure who she's talking about. "Let's go to the pep rally. That'll cheer you up."

She raises her face to mine. Mascara's smeared beneath her eyes and her cheeks are blotchy. She looks like a little girl. "Don't you get it? All of this is over." She swings out an arm. "All of it. I'm leaving. I'm quitting."

At first my heart lurches with fear. I bite it back. "Where will you go?"

"I told you. Where I should have gone to begin with. France. I'll go to France."

It comes to me all of a sudden, in a great burst. "I'll go with you."

"Be serious, Arden."

"I am. I'll go with you." We'll find her French relatives together. We'll work it all out.

"What will we do for money?"

"We'll open a restaurant." I'm being crazy. I'm trying to make her laugh, and it works.

A smile tilts a corner of her mouth. "Yeah. Let's do that." She pushes herself to her feet. "We'll open our own restaurant. What will we call it? The Big Fuck-You?"

"Perfect." She picks up the bong from her dresser and pulls something from her pocket. I see the silver gleam of my mother's lighter and Hunter standing in the doorway. "Rory?" he says.

"Wait!" I yell, lurching to my feet.

But Rory's already turning. A flicker of flame in her cupped hand and then it flares. A hot whoosh. The door's on fire, the posters curling on the walls. Hunter's gone, just parts of him visible through the plumes of yellow and orange. His mouth's wide open. He's screaming, a terrible sound. I yank my comforter from the bed and try to throw it over him. He's stumbling around. I can save him. I can. But the comforter's soaked and it goes up, too. The floor's leaping with flames.

"Help!" I gabble. "Help us!"

I grab Rory's arm. Other things are catching on fire now. Gray smoke writhes up. I'm screaming at her. "Hurry!" She turns a dazed face to mine. I pull her onto my bed. I struggle with the window. The metal handles are scorching. The window won't slide up.

"Move!" Rory yells at me, and I jump back as she swings my desk chair at the glass. It cracks. She swings again and this time, it shatters. We kick out the broken pieces with our heels.

I'm gasping, every breath sharp. My lungs are filled with pointed gouging things. We climb onto the window ledge. It's cooler here. The ground yawns below us, a million miles away. Rory and I look at each other. I see panic carved in shadows on her face.

My mom says, "I love you, sweetheart. It's going to be okay."

But I am not a little girl anymore and I know better.

NATALIE

The last I see of Rory, she is being wheeled down the hall toward the operating room where my daughter waits. The bag of clear IV fluid sways from its pole, the ventilator rides along with her, on the stretcher between her legs covered by the sheet. Vince holds Rory's left hand, and I hold her right. Theo walks beside me. Gabrielle has left the hospital. She won't answer Vince's calls. In the end, it was Theo who sat down across from Vince, their knees touching. Vince's head was bowed as Theo softly talked to him, and when I saw Vince nod, I knew.

The orderly presses the square metal button on the wall and the automatic doors swish open. Vince bends to kiss Rory's cheek. The bandages have been removed from her face so we can see her to say goodbye. Theo kisses her, and I do, weeping. This girl, the precious child we have loved. We straighten and the orderly pushes the stretcher away from us. The doors close and we turn to the waiting room. We will wait together, for Arden.

ARDEN

When I wake up, the room is bright. *Heaven?* Then I open my eyes and see Oliver leaning close. He's gotten a haircut, his blond hair standing up a little in the front and short along the sides. His cheeks are red and he stares very seriously at me. My dad's holding him, and I see his face behind my brother's. My mom's on the other side, holding Henry. "No kisses," Oliver instructs. "Because they're gross."

I smile and go back to sleep.

The next time I wake up, my mom's there, reading in a chair beside me. As I turn my head, she sets down her book. "Arden?" Her face is filled with worry. It's been so long. I've missed her so much. I've felt so lost and here I am, found. Tears drip down my cheeks. "You're all right," Mom murmurs. "You're going to be all right."

This time I believe her.

It's spring break and Oliver and Henry are racing around the pool with Percy trotting along behind them, barking at nothing. It's too cool to open the pool, so the pavement's not wet, but still. "Be careful," I tell them as I set up my easel under the shade of my favorite dogwood.

My mom and Uncle Vince sold Double and the first time we all drove by, just to take a quick look, it was a hurt as painful as a burn. But I've been by it several times since and it no longer hurts the same way. My mom's in the kitchen now, cooking. She'll take a photograph of whatever she's making after it's done and give it to me. It's for the cookbook she's writing. I'm painting the illustrations. We hope to have it done by the time I start school in the fall. I won't go back to EMU. I'm starting school here, in northern Virginia, where I can be close to my family. I'm not ready to leave them yet, but I know that time will come. There's no rush.

My mom's got the windows open and delicious smells are drifting out. Every so often, Percy stops and lifts his head to take a sniff. I have to do that, too — take sniffs on a regular basis.

The self-portrait I was working on was destroyed in the fire, of course, along with everything else. It's just as well. It wasn't right, and no matter how many times I went over the eyes and cheeks and mouth, I would never get there. I'm working in pastel now. I'm seeing myself emerge, the way I really am and not who I thought I wanted to be.

The back gate bangs open. "Uncle Vince!" Henry yells, and the twins scramble up the stone steps. "Hey," Uncle Vince says, laughing. "Take this in to your mom, okay?" He hands a plastic cake carrier to Oliver, who takes it in his arms and very carefully turns toward the house, Henry pelting ahead to slide open the glass door. Percy's given up on them both and is nosing around the bushes leading down to the dock.

Uncle Vince's writing the pastry section of the cookbook, and though he and Mom are working together again, they don't talk much to each other. Not in the easy way they used to. We're all being very careful.

"Hey, Arden." Uncle Vince heads down the steps toward me. "How are you feeling today?"

"I'm okay."

I was in the hospital for weeks. I had to

527

learn how to breathe again, blowing hard into this plastic tube called a spirometer, which measures how much air my lungs can hold and how much air I can breathe out. I have to cough regularly and take a bunch of pills every day. I have to be careful to eat plenty of fruits and vegetables, and I'll have to see a doctor for the rest of my life. But he says I might be able to start swimming again, so that's okay.

When Uncle Vince came to see me in the hospital, he just sat beside me and held my hand. The third time he came, he asked me what had happened. I'd told my parents. I'd told the police. But what he wanted to know was if Rory had been okay, in the end. I tell him she was brave. I don't tell him she'd been brave her whole life. I haven't seen Aunt Gabrielle once, but Dad told me she and Uncle Vince are getting a divorce. I haven't figured out how I feel about that yet. I decided not to tell anyone the truth about Rory's scar, the one she got when she was little. That's the way Rory would have wanted it.

I have scars. Small round ones where the catheters were placed, long red ones scissoring my chest. They'll fade with time, the doctor tells me, but it's okay. They remind me that I'm not alone. I never will be again.

Rory's with me, always.

We had sat on that narrow window ledge, the ground far beneath us. Heat from the flames behind us burned our backs and shoulders. She had grabbed my hand and looked me right in the eyes, orange light playing across her beautiful face smudged with ash and tears. *I love you, Arden,* she'd said. I said it right back. *I love you, Rory.*

I'm glad those were the last words she ever heard.

Really. It was a good goodbye.

ACKNOWLEDGMENTS

I am deeply grateful to my brilliant editor and friend, Kate Miciak, and to everyone at Penguin Random House — dream makers and magicians all — who breathed life into this story: Marietta Anastassatos, Gina Centrello, Kelly Chian, Susan Corcoran, Toby Louisa Ernst, Jennifer Hershey, Kim Hovey, Libby McGuire, Julia Maguire, Cindy Murray, and Allyson Pearl. I am so very lucky to be working with each and every one of you.

Thanks to my amazing literary agent, Dorian Karchmar, and to the rest of my extraordinary team at William Morris Endeavor: Alicia Gordon, Tracy Fisher, and Cathryn Summerhayes.

Thanks, also, to:

Alan Siqueiros, MD, Pulmonary and Critical Care Fellow at UNC–Chapel Hill, who gave generously of his time and energy to help me build the complex medical world my characters entered. Any errors are mine and mine alone.

Kim Floresca, co-executive chef of the beautiful, fabulous [One] Restaurant in Chapel Hill, who gave me a glimpse beyond the glitter into the real working life of a chef.

Marghi Fauss, aunt of my heart, who taught me how to make bread from air, and Bryan Nelson, who helped me brainstorm scary business crises.

My gifted sister, Liese Schwarz, for profound insight when I needed it most. I'm so glad you put yourself within driving distance, always answer the phone no matter what, and remember what Barbie doll hair smells like.

My "sister" in Canada, Chevy Stevens, who lives too far away but is always there when I need her, despite distance and time difference. Someday, we *are* going to live on the same side of the world, even if I have to kidnap you.

My dear friend Jenny Milchman for so generously sharing your book tour, your wonderful family, and your wisdom with me.

My husband and soulmate, Tim, for being the center that holds, and to Jillian, Jonathon, and Jocelyn, who light up all the dark corners.

ABOUT THE AUTHOR

Carla Buckley was born in Washington, D.C. She has worked as an assistant press secretary for a U.S. senator, an analyst with the Smithsonian Institution, and a technical writer for a defense contractor. She lives in Chapel Hill, North Carolina, with her husband, an environmental scientist, and their three children. She is the internationally bestselling author of *The Good Goodbye, The Deepest Secret, Invisible,* and *The Things That Keep Us Here,* which was nominated for the Ohioana Book Award for fiction and a Thriller Award as best first novel. She is currently at work on her next novel, *The Reluctant Mother.*

carlabuckley.com
Find Carla Buckley on Facebook
@carlabuckley